KILLOBYTE

PIERS ANTHONY

ACE BOOKS, NEW YORK

This Ace Book contains the complete text of the original hardcover edition. It has been completely reset in a typeface designed for easy reading, and was printed from new film.

KILLOBYTE

An Ace Book / published by arrangement with
the author

PRINTING HISTORY
Ace / Putnam hardcover edition published 1993
Ace paperback edition / January 1994

All rights reserved.
Copyright © 1993 by Piers Anthony.
Cover art by Den Beauvais.
This book may not be reproduced in whole or in part,
by mimeograph or any other means, without permission.
For information address:
The Berkley Publishing Group,
200 Madison Avenue, New York, NY 10016

ISBN: 0-441-44425-3

ACE®
Ace Books are published by the Berkley Publishing Group,
200 Madison Avenue, New York, NY 10016.
Ace and the "A" design are trademarks
belonging to Charter Communications, Inc.

PRINTED IN THE UNITED STATES OF AMERICA

10 9 8 7 6 5 4 3 2 1

THE ASTONISHING WORLDS OF PIERS ANTHONY

THE MODE SERIES

His newest adventures—in which five friends from alternate worlds face love and danger across time and space.

"Fresh, imaginative!" —*Publishers Weekly*

THE APPRENTICE ADEPT SERIES

The incredible story of one world inhabited by two spheres—the technology of Proton and the magic of Phaze.

"It's fun-and-games time again with the Gamemaster himself, Piers Anthony!"

—*Rave Reviews*

HARD SELL

Who'd be stupid enough to buy real estate on Mars? Meet Mr. Fisk Centers. Hero or sucker? You be the judge.

BIO OF AN OGRE

Piers Anthony's enthralling life story.

"Incredibly honest ... entertaining ... fascinating!" —*OtherRealms*

MERCYCLE

The ingredients include one boy, one underwater bicycle, and a mermaid or two—instant adventure, just add water!

"Piers Anthony [is] always entertaining!"

—*Rave Reviews*

THE BOOKS OF TAROT

On the planet Tarot, dreams can come true—as well as nightmares.

"Anthony is as facile as he is prolific."

—*Cincinnati Post*

CONTENTS

one

NOVICE

"Draw, tenderfoot, or I'll plug you where you stand!" Walter Toland blinked. There before him stood a gunslinger straight out of false western American history: broad cowboy hat, leg chaps, low-slung holster and all. The man's right hand hovered near his six-shooter. Could he be serious?

"Look, mister," Walter started. "I don't know what you think you're—"

The man's hand dived for his weapon. He *was* serious! Walter threw himself to the side, behind a barrel of nails.

The gun fired. Glass shattered behind Walter. He scrambled on hands and knees, trying to get away from the vicinity without exposing himself.

"You lily-livered coward!" the gunslinger shouted. "I'll rout you out and lay you away! Stand up and fight like a man!" The gun boomed again, and there was the thunk of a bullet hitting the barrel.

Walter cowered behind the barrels. But there were only three of them, and nothing beyond. They hid him, but he was trapped. What could he do?

"So you want it in the ass!" the gunslinger said, his

voice rich with contempt. There was the sound of his footsteps crunching the dirt as he approached the barrels.

And that was just about where he'd get it, too, Walter realized, because the man was coming toward his rear. Frantically he cast about.

Then he discovered that he too was in cowboy dress—and there was a gun at his hip!

"All right, you sniveling snake!" the gunslinger said as his shadow fell beside the barrels. "You're done for."

Walter yanked his gun out of his holster and pointed it at the shadow. Then the body of the man appeared.

Walter pulled the trigger. The gun fired. It bucked in his hand, and smoke puffed from its muzzle.

The gunslinger stiffened. Daylight showed through a hole in his belly. He fell forward.

Walter scrambled out of the way, so as not to be pinned under the man. He didn't quite make it; the gunslinger's head struck his foot. It was curiously light.

In fact it wasn't a head at all. It was cardboard, flat and blank on back. The whole man was cardboard!

A sign appeared in the air about six feet away. Walter stared at it, for the moment not comprehending its nature or message.

```
PLAYER: Walter Toland

LEVEL:  Novice

SCORE: 1   OPTIONS
```

Then it registered. He was a player in a game! A computer game. He had finally gotten the equipment to enter the most sophisticated class of games, the ones that put the whole person in, in effect. The helmet, the gloves, the special connections—it had happened so suddenly and completely and compellingly that for the moment he had forgotten the reality and just lived the scene.

And what a scene it had been! It had seemed completely real, as if he had been physically dumped in this little western set and made to fend for himself. Sink or swim.

What would have happened if the gunslinger had plugged him? Then he would have been out of the scene, with a score of 0. A real humiliation for one who had once been pretty sharp on the primitive computer games, the kind where things danced on the screen and had to be shot down before they got too close. Or where things had to be collected to use to penetrate to the finish. But that had been before the accident.

He shut that out and studied the sign. It identified him as the player. Fine. His level was Novice. Okay, fair enough; this was a new game to him, and he was just starting. And his score was 1. That must be one kill. But what were the options? How did he invoke them?

Then the sign faded out, leaving only the scene. Walter got up, dusted himself off, holstered his gun, then lifted the cardboard. It was a mock figure, painted on the front with the clothing, gun, and menacing face. There was a hole in the right side of its abdomen, where his bullet had torn through.

Walter shook his head. How could he have been fooled by that? A cardboard cutout! Yet it had spoken to him, challenged him, and advanced on him. It had shot at him, too! There was the broken glass of the store window, and there was the slug in the side of the keg of nails. Those had been real bullets, not cardboard ones.

That reminded him of his own weapon. The gunslinger's gun was now cardboard, but his own was not. He drew it again and looked at it. It was a solid six-shooter, probably of authentic design; he knew modern guns, but was no expert in ancient ones. Whoever had crafted this game could readily have done the necessary research. So this much, at least, was probably real. Within the framework of the game.

Something else bothered him. Since when did a bullet in the gut kill instantly? If that man had been alive, he would not have died; he would have staggered back in agony. So this was a game thing too: any score on the torso was fatal, by definition. It didn't have to be through the heart. Novice-level marksmanship.

He reholstered the gun, set the cardboard figure down, and walked across the street. The far side turned out to be a painted backdrop: tavern, horse hitches, and scenery. Even the sun: a bright yellow disk against the blue background. He touched it, and it was room temperature. Absolutely unreal.

Then what had cast the shadow, when the gunslinger had approached the barrels?

He walked back to where he had started. Behind the broken window was a dark wall; there was no chamber there. Now he saw that directly behind his original location was a door. The store was a façade of wood and glass, but the door was real. It was in a sturdy frame, and it had a brass knob. He must have stepped through it to enter this scene, though he didn't remember doing it.

So was this also the way to leave the scene? In which case, would he be out of the game with a low score? He wasn't ready to quit, yet. It was obvious that he had a lot to learn about this game, and already he was feeling the fascination of it. It was a lot more intriguing than his outside reality.

So if he didn't use the door, how should he move on? There had to be a way to encounter new challenges and rack up higher scores. But he couldn't do it against cardboard figures.

He walked down the street to the left of his original stance. It ended twenty feet along, in another painted backdrop: a picture of a street continuing through the town.

He tried the other direction, which he thought of as south. This ended similarly, twenty feet away, in a painting of a few more houses and then the open country beyond town.

He was in a chamber about forty feet long and twenty feet across. He was unable to touch the top, but ten feet seemed reasonable. Wait, he could check it. He took a nail from the keg and threw it up into the sky. It struck almost immediately, scratching the paint of a white cloud. Ten feet had been a good guess.

So it seemed that there was nothing more to do here. Unless he wanted to smash down the scenery, he would have to use the door. He had made his score, and this scene was done.

Still, he did not quite trust that door. It might be a decoy, or the exit for a quitter. Like the escape key on a computer keyboard: hit it when you're in over your head and just want to get out. The challenge was to figure out how to control his destiny within the game. How to get into the next scene.

He walked across the street again and put his hands on the painting of the tavern. He tried to shove it to one side or the other, but it didn't give.

He went to the kegs of nails and tried to lift one. It was either too heavy to budge, or bolted to the ground. He tried to twist it, as if it were a big knob, but that didn't work either. So he started taking out the nails, in case there could be something useful hiding among them. But the nails turned out to be only an inch deep; they were another kind of façade. Below was just a panel, painted with more nails.

This was curious. Why hadn't the kegs become cardboard too? Since this was all a game set, it should have been easy to do that. The nails must have been left in their "real" state deliberately. So that a novice like him could use them to throw at the ceiling and scratch the cloud? That didn't seem sufficient.

What else offered? There had to be something. Some devious key to the next step. If he could only find it. He cursed himself for being rusty on games. It was probably obvious; he just didn't have the right mind-set. He didn't see the simple way out of the locked chamber.

Then he heard something. The ground was shuddering. He looked around—and there in the distance, where the street left the town and wandered into the prairie, were shapes. Big ones. Many of them.

In fact those were cattle—and they were stampeding. Already they were funneling into the town and thundering down the street, directly toward him. A cloud of dust was roiling up behind them. He had to get out of the way or he would be trampled in seconds.

Trampled? By animals in a picture?

But the gunslinger had fired real bullets at him.

Those cattle looked excruciatingly real. So did the setting, at the moment. In fact the cutout of the gunslinger now looked like a body—and there was a pool of blood beside it. He heard music from the tavern across the street.

He took another nail and threw it at the sky. It flew high, arcing well below the cloud, and landed in the street. The bright sun cast shadows.

The set had come alive again.

The first steer outdistanced his companions and bore down on Walter. The thing looked dangerously real. The hide was flecked with dust and foam, and gouts of dust leaped from the striking hooves.

Walter drew his gun and aimed at the animal. But he hesitated.

That was merely the first of dozens of steers, and he had only five bullets left. Or so he hoped; he hadn't checked the remaining chambers of his six-gun. Even if any hit on the body instantly felled the animal, five was all he could take out before he got trampled. The gun could not save him, this time.

Meanwhile the creature was looming frighteningly close and large. It was a juggernaut. A picture? No way! This was real.

Walter dived for the door. He felt the wind stirred by the first animal as he grabbed the knob and turned. He yanked; the door opened; he threw himself through.

As he left the scene, he thought of something, too late. He could have taken those loose nails and scattered them across the street. Or maybe driven them through boards and set them out with their points projecting upward. That well might have stopped the stampede. Maybe such a ploy wouldn't work well in real life, but he suspected that by game rules it would. It explained why the nails had been left solid in an otherwise painted scene: to allow the player to prepare for the next challenge.

He was in the next scene. It was a jungle. Literally. The air was dark and steamy, and the trunks of tall trees were shrouded by clinging vines.

There was a growl. Walter looked—and there was a tiger crouching as it oriented on him.

He whirled, lurching back through the doorway. But there was no doorway there. Only a solid tree. Once he had used the door, he had committed himself irrevocably, it seemed. Unless he had thought to do something like jamming a nail into the crack to stop the door from closing behind him.

The tiger pounced. Walter hurled himself to the side, as he had before when attacked by the gunman. The tiger landed where he had been, snarled, and turned, reorienting. The thing was massive, and certainly capable of killing him.

Walter grabbed for his six-shooter. But now it was a snub-nosed rifle. He wrenched up the muzzle as the tiger sprang again, and fired.

The tiger screamed with pain and dropped to the ground. The landing was light: it was a paper tiger, literally. With a hole through one shoulder.

The sign appeared:

```
PLAYER: Walter Toland

LEVEL: Novice

SCORE: 2   OPTIONS
```

No big surprise there; he had scored again. He was still a novice, and still didn't know how to invoke the options. He had ascertained that the door did not lead out of the game, but to the next setting. And that the scene turned unreal when the action was done. And real again when more action came. He had had about ten minutes between actions, so wasn't unduly rushed, but when an action did start, he had to act within seconds. The rules were coming clear. It seemed like a well-designed game.

He got up and inspected the new setting. The trees turned out to be cardboard mockups, the vines painted on them. The tree behind him was painted on a wall—and there was now a door in it. Yet all of it had seemed real before the kill. Surely it had been real, in the context of the game. For the game could do that. It could animate its settings and creatures, making them almost as tangible as reality. That was the appeal of this class of game. Its realism. What was known as virtual reality.

Walter's living body was sitting in a wheelchair, with a sophisticated helmet on its head. Goggles and earphones connected to it, providing three-dimensional sight and sound, and wires were attached to skin patches at strategic locations. There was even limited odor emitted from a noseplug. Gloves and boots picked up the attempted motions of the extremities, so that his game body moved as he willed it to. It was, literally, like stepping into another world.

It had taken him a long time to arrange this, because this class of equipment was expensive. In the interim whole new classes of computer games had evolved, prospered, and faded back into relative oblivion. It didn't matter; they remained the most popular genre available. Because they represented vicarious experience which was so close to direct experience that the distinction blurred. He had heard that there were sex programs that some claimed were better than the real thing.

But sex was not his object, here. Sex was gone from his life. He wanted diversion. So his first game was a hard-hitting adventure. He hadn't even bothered to read the instruction manual; those things were always way too big and obscure to make much sense. It was more fun just to wade in and learn by doing.

So he had ten minutes before another challenge came for him, in this jungle setting. He intended to use it, because he didn't want to take the easy route, door to door. He wanted to discover the more devious aspects of the program. Because this was the one game he had for rental, this week, and he wanted to make the most of it.

He lifted the paper tiger and used it to prod the ceiling. Still ten feet. He felt the walls on all sides. Still a twenty-by-forty-foot chamber, though the painted walls made it look larger. It would have been nice to check it while the full animation was on, to see whether then he could really travel miles through it. It seemed impossible, yet this was not reality, but an emulation that approximated a chosen situation. So the game could make a jungle seem to extend for miles, if it was programmed to—and perhaps it was. He wanted to find out how to explore the parts of the jungle that the makers of the game didn't intend players to reach. Maybe he could do that, if he could just find the way to extend the setting while it was in its "real" phase.

He found a number of sticks on the ground, and realized that these must have been fallen branches when it was animate. Was there a reason for them to be here? Just as those loose nails in the top of the keg, in the western scene, might have been used to stop the stampeding cattle? Maybe these sticks had something to do with the next challenge.

He picked one up and hefted it. It was actually a fairly solid length, possibly serviceable as an aid to hiking, about six feet long. Others were shorter, but thicker. He also saw several lengths of cord strewn across the mock trees; probably those were vines during animation. Not much use at the moment, though.

Something changed. The trees became real, and the cord did indeed become vine. The set was coming alive again! Sooner than the other one had, unless his perception of time was distorted.

There was a rustle. He looked, and saw a snake. A big one. A python, slithering toward him. No doubt of it: the next challenge was starting.

He backed away from the creature—only to realize that one of the cords had become a serpent in a tree, now lifting its head to strike at him. He ducked, avoiding it, but more were appearing on the ground. He recognized rattlesnakes, water moccasins, and what were probably exotic pit vipers. If any of them bit him, he would be dead, and out of the game.

Walter still held the stick, which was now a black staff. He used it to fend off an advancing cobra.

He had to get out of here. But he had foolishly allowed himself to be caught away from the door. The space between him and it was filling almost solidly with a river of snakes. All of them surely poisonous.

A tiny snake tried to score on his toe. Walter knocked it on the head, and it hissed and fell back. What had it been, during the null period? A piece of string? If he had gathered up that string and tied it in a knot, could he have stopped the snakes before they got started? He had foolishly frittered away his time, and now was in trouble.

Three more snakes slithered purposefully toward him. He knocked them back with the staff. But there were too many; soon they would overwhelm him. He was sure that just one bite would wipe him out, by the rules of the game. But how could he reach the door without stepping on the myriads of snakes which now blocked the way?

There was rustling behind him, and to the sides. Then Walter got a notion. He pointed the staff ahead, took two running steps, and jammed the staff into the ground, heedless of what it might land on. He heaved himself up in a crude pole vault, passing over the massed snakes. He crashed into the door, scrambled to wrench it open, and fell through to whatever lay beyond.

He found himself in a car, speeding at about a hundred miles an hour. He had no idea where it was going.

Then a brick wall loomed ahead. He was on a dead-end drive. He stepped on the brakes—and his foot plunged to the floor. The brakes were gone!

But the wall did not extend beyond the pavement. He could veer off the road, crash through the wooden barriers, and roll to a stop. He turned the wheel.

The wheel spun in his hand. The steering was also out. This car had really been pied.

But Walter had been in trouble before on the highway, and his reflexes were fast. He used the clutch and jammed the gearshift into low. Thank God racing cars didn't use automatic shift! The low gear made the motor drag on the wheels, and the car slowed. But not enough; he would still hit the wall. So he grabbed for the handbrake, and that slowed the vehicle further. He did reach the wall, but only nudged it.

The seat collapsed under him. The cardboard could not sustain his weight. Then the sign appeared: SCORE: 3. He had gotten through another challenge.

He pushed aside the cardboard side of the car as the sign faded, and climbed to his feet outside. The wall was the only solid part of this set, and now he saw the door in it: his entry to the next scene. But again he didn't take it; he wanted to explore while he could, to see what other avenues offered.

He was in another chamber, of course, with the scenery all around painted on, including the blue sky above. There was no way out except the door. Maybe this was a straight-line game, with no real choices along the way. If so, it wasn't much. The effects were marvelous, and he loved having the full use of his body, instead of being confined to his wheelchair. But largely mindless adventure would not entertain him long. He remembered the three or four types of conflict, from a long-ago class on literature: man against nature, man against man, man against society. And maybe man against himself. This was really man against nature, even when it was against a man, because the gunslinger had been programmed for attack, not interaction. The car had been much the same as a beast; riding a tiger would have been similar. So this was pretty simple stuff, and pretty readily handled. The right reflexes were all that was required.

So what would the next challenge be here? Not a speeding car, because the only way it could threaten him was to try to squish him against the wall, and it would smash itself in the process. Even if it tried, he could simply step off the road to the side, avoiding it. In any event, he still had several minutes to prepare.

He checked the painted chamber, but it was tight. If there were secret buttons to push, he didn't find them. He went through the cardboard car, but there was nothing special there either. That was an interesting device, turning things to cardboard once the challenge was done. But the novelty of it was already wearing thin. The computer could do whatever it wanted, and realism was as easy to program as artificiality, with the equipment available. Which suggested indifferent programming. He hoped that this wasn't the limit of what the game had to offer.

Because Walter was looking for high-powered diversion. He had what amounted to no life at all, in the real world. His legs had dwindled to ugly sticks; he kept them constantly covered not for warmth but for shame. Once he had been athletic. Now he couldn't walk at all, and even sitting up would have been a pain except for his intricate harness. The doctor, with an attempt at humor that hadn't been effective, had informed him that they had patched up the lower half of his body so that it worked, but not to put any weight on it. So a game like this was the only place he could move normally. He could walk, here, because the boots picked up the feeble efforts of his legs to move, and translated them to directions for the game-figure legs. Obviously his game figure didn't have to do much balancing, because it remained erect without his effort. That was nice.

But what was the point of poking around a closed painted chamber? As virtual reality went, this was a virtual prison.

There was a honk in the distance. Walter looked, and saw that his own car was now alive again: metal instead of cardboard. The next threat was coming already! It had hardly been five minutes.

In the distance a shape loomed, growing rapidly larger. It was a semitrailer truck. It was so massive, and coming with such velocity, that it was evident it would not be able to stop if it wanted to. It would smash him and his car and the wall, and hurtle on through regardless. So much for his notion of safety.

He ran to the side, and banged into the painted wall. He had forgotten that the scenery wasn't real. He couldn't step off the road—and now he saw that the truck filled the entire space. He could not avoid it. The damned set was coming only partly alive: the part that would kill him.

He dived for the door. As he wrenched it open, he realized that he had missed a bet: he could have thrown himself to the pavement in the center, and let the truck pass over him. There had to be enough clearance, in a vehicle that size. He could have bested it.

But he was already passing through the door. He saw the grille of the truck looming close.

Then he was in a square roped enclosure. He was wearing sneakers and white shorts. Big soft padded gloves were on his hands. Boxing gloves.

Uh-oh. He caught his balance and peered ahead. Just in time to see the other boxer closing in on him. The one in black shorts.

The other threw a roundhouse-right punch. Walter wanted to duck, but didn't have the time. He wanted to draw back, but his inertia was wrong. So he did the only thing he could: he threw himself forward, into the other boxer. A clinch was the first refuge of the incompetent. He wrapped his arms around the man and hung on.

"Get off me, jerk!" the man sputtered. "Stand up and fight like a man."

But Walter knew that if he did that, he would get knocked down or out. Because he had discovered in the course of his job training that he was not cut out to be a boxer. He had learned how to duck a punch, and that was his most effective ploy. What he didn't know about this sport would fill an encyclopedia.

"One. Two. Three. Four." There was no visible referee, but Walter heard the count, and knew that he had better stop clinching in a hurry, or be penalized. So he broke and staggered back, holding his arms up to try to protect his head and upper torso.

It wasn't much good. The other boxer was boring in, battering his shoulders and sides. Walter didn't feel pain, exactly, but he did feel the impacts, and knew he couldn't protect himself long. Each time the other scored on his arm, the arm dropped a bit lower, and Walter couldn't bring it up again. It seemed that the game had ways of forcing the issue. His face would soon be open to attack.

So defense was no proper ploy. He had to take the offense. Even if he wasn't any good at it.

He aimed a right at the other man's face. But the man simply moved aside, then caught him on the ribs with a solid counter-punch. Walter realized that he had laid himself open, and it had been an elementary matter to capitalize on it.

But maybe he could use his brain. The other man was a figment of the game program. He would probably react the same way to the same situation.

So Walter set himself and aimed the same punch again. But

this time he was planning on counterpunching the counterpunch. He swung, the other countered and scored on the ribs again—and Walter let fly at the man's face with all the power his left fist could muster.

He scored. His white glove flattened the man's nose and rocked his head back. The man fell—and it was a cardboard cutout that landed on the floor. In life a single punch would have been unlikely to end the fight, but this was the game.

The sign appeared. SCORE: 4. OPTIONS.

Suddenly Walter got a notion. He poked a finger at the sign, the cardboard glove sloughing off. He touched OPTIONS.

The sign changed. Now it read:

```
NOVICE OPTIONS:

    HELP

    FORMAT

    REPLAY

    QUIT
```

Walter feared that the sign would disappear in five seconds, as before, so he quickly touched the FORMAT option.

The screen changed again. Now it offered him three of what it considered to be formatting options: VELOCITY, SUB-STANCE, and BOX. What did those mean? Again, he was afraid to wait, so he touched BOX.

New words appeared: SIZE LOCATION DURATION ITEMS.

Aha! It was referring to the information box. Since he wanted time to consider, he touched DURATION.

The new words were what he wanted. DURATION: SEC-ONDS 0–60 MINUTES 1–10 PERMANENT DEFAULT 5 SECONDS.

So he had noted. He touched PERMANENT.

The prior information appeared. This time he touched SIZE.

This enabled him to make the box smaller, so it wouldn't obscure his view of the action. LOCATION let him move it to a corner of the chamber. ITEMS let him specify what he wanted it to cover, of the choices he had already seen. He decided to leave that alone for the time being.

But now the next challenge was upon him, only about two minutes after the boxer. The game was squeezing him harder, and it seemed that postponement was not one of his options. Unless VELOCITY covered it. But right now he had to focus on the threat.

This turned out to be a martial artist in a white jacket and trousers, tied with a black belt. Karate, probably. Walter knew just enough about it to know that black was the master level. He didn't want to mess with this man!

The man faced him and made a little bow with his head, not taking his eyes off Walter. Walter turned around and found the door he knew would be there. He turned the handle and stepped through.

He was high up on a chilly mountain. He was in mountain-climbing gear with spiked boots and heavy gloves. A rope was anchored to a heavy harness around his body, the other end connected to a piton just above him. His fingers were clinging to a tiny ledge. Below him the mountain sloped steeply, until it converted into a vertical drop-off. He was evidently making his laborious way across one of the bad spots, inching toward a larger ledge that would allow him to walk, carefully.

A stiff gust of wind tugged at his body. The fingerhold ledge gave way, and that jogged his boots loose. Walter slid abruptly down the face of the mountain, his horror making the slide seem slower than it was.

Then the safety rope went taut. He hung there, just above the drop-off, scrambling for purchase. His heart was thudding in his ears. This was almost too much realism!

He felt a vibration in the rope. He looked up—and saw that the anchor piton was starting to give way. It wasn't quite tight, and was nudging down. In a moment his weight would pull it out of the rock, and that would be all.

Walter looked wildly around. There was no other person near. The rock within reach was a flat face, offering no purchase at all. All he could do was watch the piton slowly change position.

Maybe he could hammer in another piton! He felt around his

body, but found only a hammer. If he had any other pitons, he couldn't find them in the few seconds he had.

Then he had a better notion. He braced his feet against the steeply slanting rock, closed his gloved hands about the rope, and walked himself up the face. The effort was easier than it would have been in life, as the game responded to the muscular twitches of his real body. In a moment he was up within reach of the piton.

He drew his hammer, set himself, and pounded the piton back into the rock. In a moment it was firm again, and he was in no danger of falling. Now he had only to find new handholds, so that he could complete his traverse and put his feet on the ledge ahead.

But there turned out to be no need. The mountain became cardboard, and the box in the corner said SCORE: 5.

It now appeared that the drop-off was only the painted floor. It had certainly looked realistic a moment ago! And where had that wind come from?

Walter made his way to the ledge and sat on it. He couldn't follow it on around the mountain, because that too was a painted scene. So he reached for the score box and touched OPTIONS. He might as well make use of his time to learn anything that might improve his chances in the next challenge.

He didn't want to quit yet, and he certainly didn't want to re-play that wild swing above the abyss. That left HELP and FOR-MAT. He didn't want to ask for help yet either; that seemed too much like cheating. So he touched FORMAT, and then VELOC-ITY.

It turned out that he could indeed adjust the time between challenges. He could make the second challenge in a setting come immediately, or he could delay it the maximum: ten minutes. The default was ten minutes for the first challenge, eight for the second, and so on down to two for the fifth. So he hadn't been imagining the shortened time!

Then the mountain shuddered. The abyss below took on the semblance of reality. The second threat was upon him.

Walter looked up. Something was stirring up there. An avalanche was starting! Already the first small stones were plunging past, bouncing off the slope and disappearing beyond the drop-off.

He didn't hesitate. He grabbed for the door in the mountain

and wedged himself through before the main part of the avalanche passed.

This time he was in a comfortable waiting room. He looked nervously around, alert for the next threat, but saw none. Instead the opposite wall became a screen.

CONGRATULATIONS, NOVICE! YOU HAVE COMPLETED THE CHALLENGES AND ARE NOW A JOURNEYMAN PLAYER. YOUR NAME HAS BEEN ADDED TO THE ROSTER OF PLAYERS ELIGIBLE FOR THIS LEVEL.

A list of names appeared. There was a considerable number, filling several columns of the screen.

Walter hadn't anticipated this. He had thought this was a stand-alone game, but evidently it was multiple-player, with each computer serving as a separate input. He should have realized that before, because it required a modem: a phone connection to the central game authority. Well, that was all right, though it did seem to make for some crowding.

He looked at the list. He recognized none of the names. His was the last. The next to last was BAAL CURRAN. Funny name! Walter wondered what the man looked like. Not that it mattered, since the player would probably appear in the game in the image the computer dictated, rather than the real one.

WHEN YOU ARE READY TO PLAY, TOUCH YOUR NAME.

Good enough. Walter touched his name.

two

BAAL Baal Curran stood in the Journeyman anteroom, reflecting on the experience she had just had. By all accounts, Killobyte was a fantastic game, but her experience made her doubtful. So it had threats coming at her thick and fast; so what? All computer games did that, unless they were the dull intellectual kind. So that was nothing new. Still, that scene with the shark coming at her in the water had really frightened her, and as for the jump from the airplane when the parachute didn't open . . .

It also had good realism. But it was just one of a class of games a person could play with the helmet and wrappings. Virtual reality, they called it: making you feel you were right there in the scene. That aspect was pretty good—only then it turned everything to cardboard, so you *knew* it wasn't real and never had been. Of course you could turn off the cardboard with the OPTION FORMAT SUBSTANCE, making it into sponge rubber or gray blankets or something. But what was the point? It was still dreadfully unreal.

However, it was supposed to get better as it went. Of course they had the Novice stage simple and pretty obvious, so that new players like her could learn the ropes without getting killed. The Journeyman stage was supposed to be a considerable step up in sophistication. So maybe that would give her a better taste of what she really wanted: death.

Well, not death, exactly, but the experience of dying. Death didn't seem so bad, but she was afraid of dying, so she wanted to know more about it. Not the pain of it, because she had a just-about painless way, but the larger experience of it. The feeling, the finality, the wholeness—she needed to get a better glimpse of that, before making the commitment.

She wasn't suicidal, really. It was just that death just sort of seemed like maybe the best alternative, now. Oh, she knew her folks wouldn't agree, and maybe they were right. Here she was, eighteen, a high school graduate with good grades and a good record, maybe bound for college in a year or so if she decided to, with supportive parents who were still married to each other. She was an only child, even, so hadn't had to fight with siblings. Half the kids of the world would be satisfied to trade places with her, except for one thing.

But what a thing that was. It had ruined her life. She had thought she had it under control, emotionally as well as physically. She had thought she had a life ahead. Until it fell apart.

But it was pointless to let herself be diverted by that right now. She had a game to play, and with luck it would distract her from what she couldn't change.

Baal gazed at the array of basic characters. They were naked and uniformly gray, as if carved from nondescript stone. There was True Blue, who was the all-around good guy, and Doodoo, the all-around nothing. In between was Joe Blow, who was, appropriately, in between. There were also three female types, similarly spread: Royal Lady, Lone Woman, and Bad Girl.

Obviously subtlety wasn't the strong point of this level. Well, she still appreciated having some choice of character, since there had been none in the Novice level. She would take the top male character. Maybe the time would come when she could settle for an in-between, but right now she needed the top of the line. And she didn't like being female right now, and it was all right to take the other sex. That kept her anonymous, pretty much, even in the context of the game. Anonymity was what she needed. Because she was ashamed of what she was in real life.

She selected True Blue. He was a little statue, and when she touched him, a screen appeared behind him. The first choice was

COLOR. She touched that, and a color palette appeared, ranging from white through shades of yellow and brown to black. She considered, then touched it at light brown. In real life she couldn't choose her color; this could be interesting.

The statue turned brown. That did make it more intriguing.

The next choice was HAIR. She touched it, and a more limited palette appeared. She extended her hand to make her choice—and a bell rang.

For a moment she was disoriented. Then she recognized it. The doorbell! Way back in real life. She was alone in the house, so she would have to exit and attend to it.

She reached to OPTIONS on her regular screen, and when the subscreen appeared she touched QUIT, and then SAVE. She would return to this at the same place as soon as she could.

The scene went dark. It took her a few seconds to reorient. It wasn't just that she was now out of the game and back in the real world, it was that the helmet and gloves and boots locked into place during the game, effectively anchoring the player, so he couldn't react to things in the game and wave his limbs wildly, hurting himself. The game paused while processing a player out, getting the setting saved.

Then the fastenings released, and she was able to draw her hands out of the gloves. She reached up and lifted the helmet from her head. The earphones and goggles and chin cup retracted as she did, letting the sound and light of reality in. She still wore the huge boots and attachments to her body, but those could remain. Now she wished she had decided to play the game while her folks were home, so that one of them could have answered the door. But she had been so eager to start that she hadn't waited. Anyway, this was a rental system, so she had to use it while she could. She could never have afforded to buy anything like this!

She touched the door intercom. "Yes?" she inquired.

"Delivery for B. Curran."

"Delivery? I didn't order anything."

"From Carto Enterprises. The order date is six weeks ago."

Now she remembered. She had ordered something over a month ago, to be delivered on this date. She had never thought to cancel it.

There was no help for it. She hauled her feet out of the boots, stood, grabbed a voluminous bathrobe to cover her leggings, armings (well, what *did* you call them?), and torso wrap, and strode to the door. She accepted the box and brought it in to the table. She didn't open it. She knew what it was. An ornate brass relief map of the state of Pennsylvania.

It had been intended as her gift for Ty, on his twentieth birthday. Ty: Tyson Blunt, her boyfriend. She had paid for it in advance, though it had taken a hefty chunk of her meager savings. She hadn't known then that they were going to break up shortly after she placed the order.

Baal suffered a surge of grief that threatened to darken her whole life into oblivion. She sat on her bed, trying to fight her way through it. She wanted to get back into the game, but she sort of had to settle with herself first, or she'd be unable to concentrate, and just get herself killed off right away.

Well, one thing the Killobyte game had done was give her some fleeting objectivity about this dreary alternate realm that was reality. For the moment, she could review her situation, maybe without breaking up into emotional goo. So now was the time to get it straight. Maybe it would give her a more specific notion what she really wanted in the game, or out of it. What was the point in dying, if she didn't know exactly why she was dying, and how it felt in that mood? Wouldn't it be ironic if she died when she really didn't want to, all things considered? Or if she lived when she shouldn't? She had to know what was right before she did it, either way.

It had started, really, about six months before. When Ty had come into her life. It had been great, until . . .

She had been in the throes of her senior year, working hard, active on committees for this and that, maintaining herself at a halfway-frenetic level mainly to prove she could do it. And to keep her mind off her social life, which sucked, and her curse, which was part of the reason. The main reason her grades were good was that she didn't have anything better to do than study.

The fact was that Baal had never been part of any "in" group, and social popularity had always been at the opposite pole. She had been shy as a child, and it had gotten worse as she grew. The rest of the world just seemed to grow faster. In ninth grade she had gone on a school-arranged date with a male classmate, to a school program; it was an introductory deal, trying to get students to mix in socially acceptable ways. The boy had been polite, and treated her exactly as the guidebook recommended.

Which was to say, he had ignored her. She had been nervous about all sorts of things, but when she saw how some of the other girls had to fend off their dates' encroachments, she realized that she had assembled the wrong basket of fears. The boys wanted to steal kisses, because their dates had kissable lips. Baal wasn't even allowed to wear lipstick. The boys tried to stroke their dates' nice curling tresses, as if pacifying them for greater intimacies. Baal's hair was straight and boyishly short. The boys put their arms around their dates, which was permissible, and tried to get their hands in between their dates' arms and their torsos, which wasn't. Because in that region, fingers could touch the side of a breast. Baal would have had to pad her bra to have enough to touch. The boys tried to let their hands slide down to the hip and thigh region, where the school proctors couldn't see if they stroked some of the flesh a girl sat on. Baal had narrow hips. The boys tried to whisper naughty nothings in their dates' ears, to make them blush becomingly. Baal hadn't learned how to force a blush. The boys murmured their dates' names, making them seem suggestively sexy. But no amount of suggestion could give the name "Baal" sex appeal. It derived from the Hebrew word for "master," or "mistress," and was the name of an ancient god who might once have been held in high regard among the Phoenicians, but whose reputation had suffered elsewhere. In fact he was said to have consumed innocent babies. How it had ever become a female name, and how her parents had ever happened on it for her, she could not imagine. When (ha-ha) friends teased her about it, she pretended it was like "bale" as in a bale of sweet clover, or "bail" as in getting bailed out of jail. So her date behaved. She was humiliated.

After that, dates were voluntary, and by the boy's choice. No one asked Baal. She went to school dances, and danced with other shy girls, hoping a boy would cut in. It never happened. After a time she got the message and became even more withdrawn, as far as dating went.

Her body started to catch up with things, and when her family moved to Chicago and she transferred to a new school in tenth grade she had hopes. It had occurred to her that part of the reason for her neglect might be her malady, so she was careful to not let it be known here. Unfortunately the teachers had to know, and some teachers with the best intentions were nevertheless blabbermouths, not realizing the importance of the matter, and so the word leaked out and got around. But even at the beginning when other students didn't know, there was nothing. So she knew that it was fundamental: she was just an unattractive girl. Sweet sixteen was a mockery in her case.

Then when Baal was seventeen, it happened. Her friend, Marsha, who was no raving beauty but who had personality, somehow got herself into a blind-date situation with a college freshman. She was nervous about going alone, so she talked him into double-dating with her friend. She meant a different friend, one who was adept at handling unknown quantities. But that friend canceled out, having unexpectedly made up with an estranged boyfriend. Such sea changes were not unusual in the teen years. So it was desperation mode, and Baal just had to fill in at the last minute, as a matter of life and death, according to Marsha.

"But I don't know anything about—" she protested.

"There's nothing *to* know," Marsha assured her. "It's a double date. Moral support. Anyway, we'll stay close to home, just in case."

That wasn't earthshakingly reassuring. "And my—if they know, they won't want to—"

"Oh, shut up, Baal! Who's going to tell them?"

That too was not exactly ideal. But a friendship was on the line, and who knew, it might work. Until the guy got a good look at her face. Then the politeness would set in, and he would suffer through the chore, and she would never see him again after that evening.

Still, foolish hope was better than despair. Marsha helped her pick out a suitable outfit, that made her look demure. Some girls dressed to show a lot of flesh, but that was because they had the flesh to show. Baal did better leaving more to the imagination, which might be kinder than reality.

"Oh come *on!*" Marsha exclaimed. "There's nothing wrong with your body. It's within the suitable range."

"And my face?"

"It's time you got into makeup. I'll handle it."

She did. She applied lipstick and foundation creme and powder with considerable finesse, then went to work on the hair. In due course she showed Baal a mirror.

The change was amazing. The face in the mirror was ordinary

instead of homely, and the hair framed it to suggest that with the right break it might even be acceptable.

"But suppose all that paint starts flaking off?" Baal asked.

"It'd have to be some pretty heavy necking to do that."

"But I don't even know how to kiss," Baal protested.

"Time you learned, girl. If he comes at you, just hold your head still and purse your lips."

Of course there was really no danger of getting kissed. So it should be all right.

The boys came in a car to Marsha's house to pick them up. One was short and jolly, with freckles and acne. He turned out to be Marsha's date. It was his car, which went far to redeem him. His name was Donald.

The other was tall and handsome, evidently co-opted in much the way Baal had been. He seemed reluctant to come forward, but Donald hauled him along.

Introductions were hasty and clumsy. "This is Baal Curran," Marsha said.

"This is Tyson Blunt," Donald said.

Ty extended his hand, somewhat awkwardly, and Baal shook it, just as awkwardly. So much for beginnings.

Donald and Marsha rode in front, because he was driving. Ty and Baal sat in back. Neither spoke, or even looked at the other. The continuing awkwardness was almost tangible.

They stopped at a cheap cafeteria for a token meal before going on to the movie theater. Donald and Marsha had been talking at a great rate from the start, and continued now. Baal and Ty just sat there.

After somewhere short of an eternity they returned to the car. Finally Ty made an effort and said something. "You from around here?"

"Not exactly. We moved here from Pennsylvania two years ago."

He brightened. "You did? So did I. My folks are still in Reading. I had to come here for a college summer session, to get some missing credits. Where were you?"

"West Chester," she said, foolishly gratified.

"Why, that's not far! Maybe forty miles. We're neighbors."

She had to laugh. Just like that, it started to work. They talked about how their folks bemoaned the loss of the old-fashioned Horn and Hardarts in Philadelphia, where you put nickels into slots and opened little doors to take out the food. And how far it was from one part of the airport to the other, because the incoming and outgoing flights were always as far apart as possible. It turned out that their schools had once encountered each other in an athletic or intellectual event, but neither could remember which event.

By the time they got to the movie, they felt like old acquaintances. When they took their seats, Ty also took her hand and squeezed her fingers gently. "Don't get me wrong," he whispered. "But I don't feel so homesick anymore."

By the time the movie was done, his arm was around her shoulders. She thrilled to his touch. She kept thinking about how it was going to end soon, but meanwhile it was wonderful.

On the way back, he popped the Question: "May I see you again, Baal?"

She could hardly believe it. "Yes," she said, and gave him her number.

She was afraid he wouldn't call, but he did, the following night. They talked briefly, and she was astonished to discover when she hung up that forty minutes had passed.

It continued from there. Ty did see her again. He did not have a lot of money, he explained apologetically, and he wouldn't take hers, but if it was okay to walk in the park or something? His folks were going to give him a car for his twentieth birthday if he kept his grades up, and he knew he would, so then he'd have wheels. But right now he was afoot, if that was all right with her, and the park could be really nice. She was glad to oblige, and it was just great. They sat on a bench and held hands and talked.

Afterwards, she realized that she had been so distracted by the prospect that she had never thought to get Marsha to paint her with makeup. She had been her garden-variety self. Had she lost him?

On the third date she threw caution to the winds and asked him: "Ty, I know I'm nothing special. What do you see in me?"

"You're a nice girl," he said.

"Nice girls aren't very interesting."

"You're from home. I feel comfortable with you. And you're not bad looking, you know."

"Yes I am," she said, hating herself for saying it.

He got serious. "You figure a girl has to look like a movie starlet? I'll tell you something. I was dating a really beautiful girl. I—well, the truth is, I'm sort of on the rebound now. She found someone she liked better, and I guess she never was serious about me. It really hurt. So I knew it didn't pay to date someone too popular, you know? Your face didn't bowl me over, but when I learned where you were from, well, when I look at you I see Pennsylvania, and I really like Pennsylvania."

She stared at him, stunned. Could it be true?

"I guess maybe you don't believe me," he said.

How she wanted to! She had never dreamed that anyone could see her that way.

"Is it okay if I kiss you?" he asked.

After a moment her mouth worked. "If you want to," she whispered.

Slowly he brought his face to hers, and slowly he kissed her. For a brief eternity she hardly dared believe it. Then for another she allowed herself to believe it. Then she lost control, and flung her arms around him, pulling him closer.

"I guess you feel that way too," he said when they finally disengaged.

"I guess I do," she agreed, her heart burning with joy.

Donald and Marsha never dated again, but Ty and Baal were serious. He came to the school dances to dance with her, and Baal couldn't help being gratified by the astonishment others showed. Not only did she have a date, he was a handsome college man! She had come out of her shell like a rocket.

But there was a strengthening undercurrent of worry and guilt, because she had never told him about her major liability. She knew she should, but she didn't dare. What would she do if she lost him?

It continued. It was evident that Ty really liked her, and she liked him. They did not speak of marriage, but they were starting to maneuver around the subject, obviously aware of its proximity. She mentioned that she was about to pass her eighteenth birthday, making her of age, and he mentioned that there was a good job he might take instead of going back to college. They spoke of traveling to Pennsylvania to meet his folks. They came, obliquely, to certain tacit understandings.

Baal's grades suffered, but she was oblivious. She was in love. She coasted to graduation and attended the final prom with Ty. It was glorious.

That night they got really serious. They left the prom early

and went to her house. Her folks had another event to attend, and
didn't expect her back for hours, so the house was empty. She
took him to her room, and they made love. It wasn't perfect, but
they had already agreed that they didn't expect it to be. The first
time never was. Everyone knew that. Still, after due allowances
were made, they agreed that it had been the most exciting experience of their lives.

But Ty had one question, after. "I saw you had some marks on
your stomach. Did you get hurt, or something?"

Suddenly she knew it was time. "Ty, I should have told you
before. But I just couldn't. I'm not a druggie, or anything. I'm
diabetic. Those are needle scars."

He stared at her. "Oh, God! My grandma died of that."

"It's under control," she said quickly. "I have to give myself
a shot of insulin morning and evening, and prick my finger to
test my blood four times a day. It's routine. I can handle it."

"I'm not sure I can," he said. "God, Baal, I wish you'd told
me before. When I think how Grandma—"

She saw the pain in his face. She realized with a terrible sinking feeling that he was as serious about this as he had been about
his love of Pennsylvania. He had looked at her and seen his beloved homeland. Now he was looking at her and seeing a relative
die horribly. That same emotional connection that had brought
him to her was now driving him away from her. She had become
something tainted.

So it was that they broke up. It was an amicable separation,
for all the pain of it. He apologized again and again for "taking
advantage" of her before he knew, and she apologized for not
telling him. They were equally guilty.

Now they were apart. She knew that he was hurting, as she
was. But she also knew that the way his mind worked, their romance was done for. He had been ready to marry Pennsylvania.
He was not about to marry his grandmother's wasted body.

Yet she understood that if she had not concealed her illness
from him, their romance would never have happened. And she
knew that if she had it to do over again, she would do it the
same way. Because those had been the greatest months of her
life. They had gone all the way from first word to full sex, a lifetime's experience crammed into five months, and probably the
only such experience she would ever have. Even as she plowed
through her suicidal depression, she took joy in that illicit ro-

mance. For a time she had lived and loved like a complete human being.

So it was the diabetes that had torpedoed her prospects, as it had throughout her life, from the time it had been diagnosed when she was ten. From the time she had lost friends, who didn't want to catch *it* from her, never mind that it wasn't contagious. Children were prone to snap judgments. She had been caught the same way, this time: Ty was hostage to the way he saw things, and he couldn't look at her and see a human being with a liability under control. All he saw was the liability. She couldn't blame him; she was after all used to this kind of thing.

So now she was flirting not with a man, but with the notion of death. Because was there really any promise of anything better in her future?

Killobyte was supposed to be as close as you could get to dying without doing it for real. Not just because the scenes had a lot of realism. Because when you died in the game, it gave you a jolt of something that made you *feel* it. The pain and disorientation, and maybe a glimpse of Heaven or Hell, depending on your religion. Certainly there was time in the coffin. So players deliberately let themselves be killed in the game, to get that experience.

Not her. She didn't want some game programmer's notion of dying. She wanted to know how she, personally, felt about it as she fell out of a plane to her doom, or got chomped by a shark, or whatever. She was so constituted that she couldn't deliberately die; she had to be caught by death. But if she concluded from the game that she could handle death, then she might indeed take the step in real life. Maybe.

Well, she was wasting time. She had to get back into the game, which had the promise of getting interesting now.

She got up, checked her blood, and resumed her seat in what she called the electric chair. She had never removed the wrappings around arms, legs, and torso, so a little adjustment was all they needed. They were for feeling, while the gloves and boots were for control. When she tried to move her fingers or hands in the gloves, they picked up the pressure and translated it into the appropriate motions of her game figure. The boots did the same for her feet, so she could walk or jump or kick or squat. When she spoke, the helmet picked up her words and fed them into the game scene. When her eyes moved, the goggles tracked them and showed the appropriate game scenes. But the wrappings were as important in their way, because they fed several basic sensations to her body. They could turn warm or cool, or they could vibrate, or deliver a slight electric tingle. It was amazing how realistic these things were in the game. If her arm rested against a wall, she felt the heat or coolth of it. If she sat in the game, her legs felt the fabric of the couch. Indeed, her body felt the fabric of her game clothing, and the tiny touch of a breeze on her bare limbs. All from that little tingle, or maybe a combination of sensations. It was easy to forget that they were limited and artificial, and just go with the flow. Her whole body seemed to be in the scene.

She paused, remembering something else. One of the torso wrappings resembled what she called cast-iron panties. She suspected that they could apply the same sensations that the others did, but they had not done so in the Novice-level exercises. Well, yes they had; she remembered now: when she sat in that roller-coaster seat, the sun-heated plastic had pressed against her bottom. Then when she had hung on the safety rope on the mountain, the harness had pulled tight about her crotch and chest. It had seemed so real at the time that she hadn't even thought about the specific effects. So the iron pants were operative.

According to the manual, certain special effects were possible. Baal had heard that "special" could mean sexual. The manual didn't say it outright, because the game proprietor didn't want to get the bluenoses down on the game. It was said that some players were into it not for the killing but for the other experiences they could get. Vicarious sex? Baal had not had much more than idle curiosity about sex, until her association with Ty, and was not now looking for it elsewhere. But the idea of absolutely safe sex, with no chance at all for pregnancy or venereal disease or heavy emotional commitment, was intriguing. If she ever wanted to experiment, the game was the place to do it. Could the game actually make it seem real?

The more she considered that, the more curious she became. Of course she would never say that to another person. But if the opportunity arose, she just might pursue it, so as to compare it to the real thing. It seemed impossible that it could feel all-the-way real, but perhaps with imagination it could get most of the way there.

But it was pointless to sit here thinking naughty thoughts! What would she want with fake sex? Having it with a man who wasn't really there? Who would disappear into the labyrinth of the game after it was done, and maybe never be seen again? She had already had enough of that sort of experience with Ty!

So on with it. She inserted her feet into the boots, donned the gloves, adjusted the wrappings so that they were exactly where they belonged, and brought the helmet down over her head. When everything was secure, she laid gloved hands down on the armrests and used her fingers inside them to turn on the system so that she could re-enter the game. "True Blue, here I come!" she murmured as she felt things clamp into place. And of course the helmet picked it up, and she embarrassed herself by saying the words in the Journeyman-character annex.

three

PRISONER

Warrer found himself in a hall with six little statues. Three were male, three female. The background screen advised him of their general qualities. True Blue was honest and straightforward and popular. Joe Blow was strictly average. Doodoo was sneaky and dishonest. The three women had a similar range of characters. They were Royal Lady, Lone Woman, and Bad Girl.

The obvious choice was True Blue. What male player would settle for one of the other men? What female player would choose less than the most attractive woman? So what were the choices, really?

He looked at the three female figures. They were nude, and in truth were similar, physically. Each was slender, with nice breasts and a bald head. Only their names distinguished them, and their listed characters. There seemed to be an element of sexism there, because the names of the women were directly descriptive, while the names of the men were merely suggestive.

He reconsidered even as he looked. Perhaps no woman wanted to be indifferent, but Bad Girl might have a certain appeal. She might be free to ignore the normal constraints on women. That could be fun, in the game.

He reached out and patted Bad Girl on the head. "You may have your points," he remarked.

A separate screen appeared behind the statue. It listed several choices:

APPEARANCE: COLOR, HAIR, STATURE
MENTAL: INTELLIGENCE, CREATIVITY, DISCIPLINE
SITUATION: CLASS, LUCK, PERSUASIVENESS
PHYSICAL: STRENGTH, REFLEXES, ENDURANCE

Oops! He had forgotten that touching something invoked it, in the game. He had just chosen Bad Girl as his game character. Well, it *was* only a game, so why not? It might add another point of interest. He had read and enjoyed novels with the female viewpoint, and this shouldn't be much different in principle.

He touched COLOR, and a palette appeared. It seemed that he could determine her race this way. He touched the white section, and the statue turned white.

He touched HAIR, and gave her brown hair. When he did that, her eyes also turned brown; apparently they weren't worth a separate listing.

And STATURE: he could make her tall or short, slim or buxom, pretty or plain. So he made her average in all ranges, on the theory that she might be more anonymous that way. After all, he wasn't going to date her, he was going to *be* her. He wanted to score in the game, not with an illusory female.

That made him pause for another thought. Would he encounter other males who were interested in "scoring" with females they encountered, including this one? He noted his own mental use of quotes for that word, now that he was viewing it from the female's perspective. Could it be that a man scored, while a woman was "scored" on? He had never thought of himself as a sexist, but this made him wonder whether the subtler aspects of it did after all taint him. Already the game had taught him something, or at least made him think. He was becoming more intrigued with the notion of being a woman, despite the accidental nature of his choice.

He touched INTELLIGENCE, but nothing happened; he was unable to affect it. The same was true for the others; they were listed, but apparently he was stuck with set qualities the game program determined. Cosmetic changes were all he could make.

However, he had now seen enough of this game to suspect that at such time as he made it through the Journeyman level, the other options would develop, and he would be able to have a smart, strong, or lucky character. He had that to look forward to.

"Okay, I guess that's it," he said. "I'm ready to play."

Nothing happened. So he looked around—and saw the door at the end of the hall. It must have appeared while he was adjusting his character. So he walked to it and opened it.

He saw a dingy chamber, with several women in dull gray blouses, skirts, and shoes, sitting on the floor, leaning against a wall. A prison? This might not be much fun. But he didn't seem to have a choice. He stepped through.

The first thing he noticed was the change in his own body. He was now a woman, exactly as he had chosen. Her skin was white, her hair (and doubtless her eyes) brown, and her size, figure, and general appearance average. She had breasts, and presumably the other attributes of the female gender. One hand started down in spot-questing before he realized.

But this was not the moment for introspection or self-exploration, which was not the same thing. He was now with others, and it would probably be best to merge with the group and get his bearings. To keep his skirt on, as it were. For he was dressed exactly as the others were.

Was he the new one here? Or was the episode now starting, and the others were all game constructs who would pay no attention to the past? It made a difference. If he was new, he would have to get acquainted. If they were all equal, or if the others had no separate identities, then he should just pretend he had always been here.

He decided that the episode had come into existence with his entry. So he sought no introductions. He just stood where he was, as if bored with his captivity. He needed to learn more about his situation before trying to act.

How was he to do that? The others merely remained where they were, not volunteering anything. Evidently they were set to react, not to act. They did not seem to be any immediate threat to him.

But there had to be a threat, and probably not a subtle one. He was going to get killed, if he didn't find a way to stop it, and it wouldn't be as easy as dodging a six-gun shot or hammering in a piton. He would probably have to prepare for it.

He gazed around the cell. He went and tried the solid-wood door. It was locked. So he couldn't just run and hide.

What kind of threat was it likely to be? Well, this looked like a crude prison cell, so it could be execution.

How was he to avoid it, if he didn't escape the cell?

Then there was the sound of someone approaching. Already? Walter considered trying to ambush the guard who opened the door, but he just couldn't believe that the game would let it be that easy. So he sat down against the wall with the other women, and pretended to be one of them.

A key clicked in the lock. Then the door creaked open. There stood a matron, with a massive armed male guard behind her. Walter was glad he hadn't tried to ambush them; he would have been clobbered, and might have lost his game life right there.

"Pee time," the matron said with a thick foreign accent. "Form into line and follow."

That was right: there were no sanitary facilities here. This might be the game, but for the sake of realism the needs of the prisoners had to be acknowledged. This also could be an opening for an escape, if Walter played it right. Or for immediate death, if he played it wrong.

The women got up and formed the line. They were of all different appearances, but there was nevertheless a sameness about them. Then, as he took his place in the middle of the line, Walter placed it: they were all aspects of the three women available as characters. That is, Royal Lady, Lone Woman, and Bad Girl. Their hair colors differed, and their sizes and figures, and their races, but all were about the same age and quality. It was as if they were all sisters. They had similar bones, perhaps. There were two of each type, himself included.

There turned out to be two male guards, who fitted no type Walter could fathom. Both were armed with what looked like foreign-made assault weapons. They kept their distance, and remained apart from each other. It was evident that they could and would gun down anyone who tried to make a break, and even if one could be overcome by some trick, the other would still be effective. No hope there.

Unless they could take the matron hostage, and force the

guards to let them out. But probably the guards would simply gun down the matron along with the prisoners.

Well, they were male guards, and these were female prisoners. Could the guards be vamped? Walter dismissed that as soon as he thought of it; he would not be able to stomach such an effort anyway.

They marched down the hall, past other cells. Some of them had metal bars instead of solid-wood doors, so they could see the prisoners within. All of them were male, along the pattern of the choices for male characters.

They turned a corner, passing a window. Now Walter could see that they were on the third or fourth floor of the building. Beyond it was a high barbed fence, and beyond that was deep jungle leading up to a volcano. The game wasn't stinting on the scenery!

But that meant that this was not in America as he knew it. America had no jungle volcanoes that he knew of. It could be anywhere in the world where there were tropics and volcanoes together.

There was another guard at the entrance to the lavatory. He was reading a newspaper. The print was in a language Walter could not read. The banner at the top said OBSCURIA. Was that the name of the newspaper, the city, or the nation? Maybe it didn't matter. It confirmed that this was a foreign country. So escape from this prison building might be only the beginning; there might be a thousand miles of volcanic jungle to slog through.

The facility was cramped and filthy. By the smell, it had had heavy use. Probably it was the only one for the floor, and there seemed to be about ten cells here. That could mean sixty prisoners, if the others had the same number his own did. There were just two toilets, so they had to take turns. Walter did some quick thinking while he waited. Could he afford to try actually to use the toilet, here in the game? How did it connect to reality? He remembered childhood dreams of using a urinal, and waking to discover that he had wet the bed. Better not to risk it. So when his turn came, he faked it. He lifted his skirt and sat on the toilet, but did nothing except verify that his body certainly seemed to be female in every respect.

When they emerged from the lavatory, he saw that there was a stair or fire escape beyond. But the matron hustled them back up the way they had come. No chance to explore.

Walter did not want to be locked in the cell again, but saw no alternative. This setting certainly didn't seem to be offering many chances for individual action!

But at the cell, the matron addressed them. "Your people not believe we serious," she said. "We prove we are. Choose one you be executed in four hours. If no choose, all be killed." Then she shut the door on them and twisted the key.

Walter turned an appalled gaze on his companions. Now the screws were being tightened!

None of the other women spoke. Walter realized that he was the only player. It was up to him. He suddenly saw that this was his chance to learn what he needed to know. If he played it right.

"We must find a fair way to choose," he said. "Let's do a spot survey. Are any of us ill, perhaps dying anyway, so it wouldn't be too great a sacrifice—?"

No one answered. Either they didn't understand him, or they were sponges. He had to make them talk, because they surely knew more of the game background than he did.

"You," he said, pointing to the other Bad Girl. "Are you sick?"

"No," the girl replied. She was sitting against the wall with her knees up so that her thighs showed under her skirt, in the manner of one to whom decorum was a nuisance. Walter realized with a small start that his masculine interest had diminished; he saw her pose as an indication of character rather than sexually appealing. In fact she had been sitting that way all along, and he hadn't noticed until now. Had he been a game man, instead of a game woman, that would have been the first thing he saw. He was becoming a woman, to a degree.

But what of her answer? It could be a lie, since she was not the honorable type. However, she did look supremely healthy. In any event she had answered Walter's real question: did she speak his own language? Actually this had seemed likely, since the women had evidently understood the matron's directives.

He asked the others in turn, and all denied being sick, in the process confirming the language. So he could talk with them. They might not volunteer anything, but they would answer when spoken to.

"Then let's review our situation," he said. "There may be some aspect I have overlooked, that offers some hope for escape, before the end."

He saw the other Bad Girl turn her head, as if making a mental note of something. That gave him an idea: maybe she was a spy planted by the captors! It might be her job to watch out for any planned escape, and tell the captors, so they could foil it. She was after all dishonest; this role fit her.

And maybe he could take advantage of that.

He pointed to a Royal Lady, who stood decorously near a corner. Her garb was the same as that of the others, but somehow it seemed more elegant. "Please summarize how we got here, as you see it."

"Of course," she said graciously, and he realized that he had been wasting time; he should have done this at the outset. "We are tourists from America, on a three-week package tour to exotic primitive regions. Some of us came to appreciate nature; others came to appreciate the native bare-breasted dancing girls." Her gaze flicked to the side, where the cells of the male prisoners were. "Consequently our party consists of men and women in roughly equal number but of different types. However, our stay at a local hotel happened to coincide with local unrest. We were not informed that there is an ongoing rebellion against the local government, or that the rebels have become unusually active recently. During the night they took over the town, and we woke to discover ourselves the prisoners of rough men who with few exceptions do not speak our language. But because they were unable to hold the town, they evacuated us to this ancient castle in the jungle, where we remain hostage. They took all our possessions including our clothing, requiring us to don prison apparel. I believe they hope to ransom us for a large sum of money."

There was the game setting, sure enough: the rationale for the prison. But it wasn't complete. "I noticed that there were mostly men here. How would you explain that, to someone who had just come upon this scene, such as a representative of our government?"

Royal Lady made an aristocratic frown. "The distribution of the sexes in our party was approximately even. But our captors were in a hurry, so they took only what they deemed to be the best hostages. These consisted of the wealthiest men and the most attractive women. Thus we six were selected, instead of older women or children, alone among those available."

"And what do you think happened to the others?" Walter asked, realizing just too late that this could be an awkward question. But of course if these were merely game figures, they had no feelings.

"We hope they were left unharmed, and are now on their way home," she said. "But we fear they were killed. Some of us are married, and we are concerned for our families."

"Maybe some of your husbands are among the men here," he suggested.

"No. We have looked, as we walked the hall, and they are not."

Walter looked at the others. "Do any of you have anything to add to that?"

Mistake. They did not respond to a general query, only to a specific one. So he tried again. He faced one of the Lone Women. "Do you have anything to add?"

"No."

He tried again. "Are you one of the married ones?"

"No."

Because then she wouldn't be a Lone Woman. "Do you believe your family will pay a ransom for you?"

"No."

Was she programmed always to answer no? "Would you like to escape this captivity?"

"Yes."

Well, he had succeeded in eliciting a positive response. But he needed a lot more than that. He had to formulate an escape plan, and he couldn't get advice from any of these women on that.

Well, maybe he could, if he played it right. "One or all of us faces execution in four hours. Is there anyone here who does not want to escape?" He looked at each in turn, making the query personal.

No one answered. That was a tacit agreement. "I think the chances are that the ransom will not be paid." Because the game wouldn't let him off the hook. "So choosing one of us to be executed is only a postponement; they will execute another later, and another, until all of us are dead." Actually the game would end when Walter died, and he would surely be the first chosen to die. But the assumption was that all of them were at risk, and they all had to try to escape. Except the spy, who had to try to mess up their escape plan.

Walter saw no likely way to escape alone. The challenges of the Novice level had been individual; this level might require him to work with another person or the group as a whole to succeed. Probably the others would cooperate with any plan he suggested. But the spy would see that it failed.

He had to be rid of that spy! But he couldn't; they were locked in together. So he had to nullify her some other way. Could he arrange it so that she was the one chosen to be executed? No, because the game wouldn't let that happen, and if it did, the captors would simply replace her with another spy. Exposing the spy wouldn't work either; the execution would proceed regardless.

Was there any way to reverse the ploy? To use the spy to help him escape, though the spy thought she was doing the opposite? Maybe there was. After all, why have a spy at all, if there was no way to escape? There had to be a way, but not a simple one. At any rate, not as simple as the escapes had been at the Novice level.

Suppose others were plotting to escape? The captors would want to identify and get rid of all of them, so that there was no further danger. So the spy was charged with the task of identifying as many as possible of the plotters.

Which meant that the spy would not blow the whistle on Walter, if he claimed to be in touch with any other plotters. And he could make such a claim, though it was untrue, because he was a Bad Girl: one who could lie, or seduce men, or betray a companion, or do any of the other things society frowned on.

It was coming together. He would have to work with the other Bad Girl, for two reasons: she was the only other captive who could do a dishonest thing, such as trying to sneak out, and she was probably the one he had to neutralize. Well, no, all of them would try to escape, because that was the duty of a stalwart citizen who had been illicitly captured. But Royal Lady would not lie to a guard to do it, while Bad Girl would.

Also, the spy should know how to get out of this cell, in case she needed to make a secret report.

So how would he organize this? He saw only a few ways to get out of this cell. One was to get hold of a key. But there was no keyhole on the inside; the lock could only be worked from the outside. So he'd have to get outside before he could use a key, and then he wouldn't need it.

Another was to find a loose stone in the wall that gave access to a secret passage. But if they found such a stone, the spy would summon the guards. Unless she thought they would be linking with other conspirators.

Could they tie up and gag the spy, while they made their escape? Maybe. But Walter preferred to try a more subtle approach first. He had just thought of a way to use a key, if he could get it.

"We'll have to draw lots to select the one who gets executed," he said. "Does anybody have pencil and paper?"

Bad Girl did. It figured. This was in the game plan. They tore six little squares, and marked one with a bold X. One woman made a cup with her two hands, and another balled the bits of paper, shuffled them, and put them in. They took turns drawing them out again.

Walter got the X, of course. Could he have changed the outcome by suggesting that the X eliminate the first one from execution, so that they would then draw again among five, and four, and so on, until one woman had never drawn the X, and she would be the one to be executed? No, they wouldn't have agreed, and if they *had* agreed, Walter would have been the one selected.

But he had allowed for this. "So I am the one to be executed," he said. "Naturally I want to save myself if I can. So I will try to escape. What can they do to me if I fail? Execute me?" He paused, but none of them smiled. They weren't programmed for humor. Not that it mattered; he had said it so that it would be clear that he was trying to escape, alerting the spy.

"Now I am going to see how I may escape," he said. "If I find a way, the rest of you will be welcome to use it too. Does anyone want to help me escape?"

There was a pause. Then Bad Girl spoke. "Yes, I want to escape too. I will help you."

Ha! That confirmed his diagnosis. He would have been disappointed if he had guessed wrong.

"Then we shall see if there are any loose stones," Walter said. "This is an old castle, and it probably has double walls. If we can get inside them, we may be able to get out without alerting the guards."

He and Bad Girl felt the stones of the floor and wall. Soon Walter found one that wiggled. He pulled on it, and it slid out, leaving an irregular hole. "Got it!" he whispered.

They gathered around. They pulled other stones out, making a hole large enough for a person to crawl through. There did seem to be an avenue there, leading somewhere.

"I want to tell the other escape conspirators," Walter said. "So they can use this too. But I can't just yell out the news; the guards would hear. I wish there were a way to get a key."

Bad Girl was paying close attention, but she didn't volunteer any information. The game constructs never did. He had to think of all the ideas himself.

"Let's see if I can vamp a guard," he said. "Maybe I can get him to take me out of the cell, and then I can get his key." Then he paused, as if suffering an afterthought. "But I need to go tell my contacts. Someone else has to distract the guard." He looked at Bad Girl. "Will you do that?"

"Yes." But she did not move.

Still no initiative. Walter sighed inwardly. "Then do this," he said, opening his blouse to show his bra and breasts. "Lean forward and beckon silently to him."

She opened her blouse, leaned forward, and beckoned. But she was standing in the back of the cell, by the hole. Walter saw that these literal-minded game figures couldn't be trusted to do anything right. He would have to do it himself, after all, or at least get it started.

He took a deep breath, nerving himself for the effort. This might be a game, and his present body was just a game mockup, but it did seem real. As a man, he would love to have a shapely woman vamp him. But he was now a woman, and one who was deliberately average in description. He abhorred the idea of trying to lure a man himself, as if it were a homosexual encounter. And how was he to do it, with modest endowments? The other Bad Girl had more of what was necessary.

Still, he himself, in his real body, would be glad to settle for a woman like him in his game body. If she wasn't phenomenal, neither was she repulsive. She was neutral. And it wasn't just what a woman had, it was how she displayed it that counted. How she moved it about. So maybe he could manage.

"You four stand in front of the hole, so it can't be seen," Walter said to the others. "You come here beside me, and smile at the guard when he comes." Because he was pretty sure the guard would come now; he was on the game track.

Bad Girl joined him by the little window in the wood door. Walter put his face down to peer out. There was a guard lounging across the hall. Now, what was it that loose women were supposed to say? "Hey, honey!" Walter whispered. "Do you want a good time?"

The guard heard this whisper and looked toward the door. Walter straightened up and flashed his bosom in the window. Afraid it wasn't enough, he put his hands at the sides and pushed in and up, trying to make his breasts bulge. He wished he'd had more experience at this, but there just hadn't been any opportunity, unsurprisingly.

He heard the guard walk closer. The man said something in the unintelligible language. Walter realized that it didn't matter what he said, because the guard could not understand him anyway. All that counted was the body and the tone of voice.

"Come here, you disgusting ignoramus," he murmured seductively, giving one breast an extra shove to make it quiver. "Come gawk at this, you malingering creep." He was getting into the feel of being an unwilling woman.

The guard obliged. Then he brought out his key and unlocked the door. This was almost too easy! But of course it was the game, and anything in the right ballpark sufficed. So probably Walter's modest endowments didn't matter; the guard responded to the offer regardless.

The door cracked open. Obviously the guard was suspicious, but willing to risk it. "Present bosom," Walter whispered to Bad Girl. "Lean forward toward him."

Bad Girl did exactly as directed. The guard looked. "Let us both out, and we'll give you a terrible time," Walter said dulcetly. Then, to Bad Girl: "Step into him. Embrace him. Kiss him. Hold it as long as you can."

She did as directed. Walter squeezed out with her, and also tried to embrace the guard, who seemed satisfied to have two women caressing him. But Walter's hand went for the key in the guard's pocket. He got it during Bad Girl's kiss.

"Keep caressing him," he told Bad Girl. "Guide him to a private chamber where he can undress you, and keep close to him." Of course nothing would happen between the two, because they were both game constructs. But it would keep them out of circulation for a few minutes, and that should be all Walter needed.

Bad Girl guided the guard toward another chamber, following Walter's instructions. She couldn't do anything else; that was her limitation as a game figure. So she had been effectively taken out of play, along with the guard.

Walter used his key to lock the cell he had been in. There was no protest from inside; the game characters didn't care. They reacted only to the player's direct stimulus. Then he surveyed the hall.

There was only one other guard in sight, and he was snoozing. The game was getting downright cooperative, now that he was pushing its buttons.

Walter set himself, then ran his hands through his hair, making it unruly. He pulled his blouse out of his waistband and unbuttoned it all the way, so that it hung loosely on him. Then he slammed his hand against the wall, to make a noise to wake the guard. He ran down the hall, hair and blouse flying back behind him. "Help! The women have found a hole in their cell!" he cried. "They're getting away!"

The guard jerked awake, took one look at Walter, and charged toward the cell. A door at the end of the cellblock opened and the matron appeared. The original guard came out of another chamber, trailed by Bad Girl.

"I'm the spy! They're getting away!" Walter screamed as piercingly as he could. "Through the wall! Stop them!"

The game figures had to obey. They all ran for the cell, and the second guard unlocked it. They opened the door and charged in.

Walter ran up behind them and pushed the door shut again. He locked it, again. It was a good thing the game figures hadn't been programmed to reason, or they would have wondered how Walter had gotten out, with the door still locked. They would also have realized that he was not identical to Bad Girl, the true spy. In fact Bad Girl herself should have realized it, but she too had been stampeded into the cell.

Walter didn't bother to unlock any other cells. There was nothing in them but game figures. Instead he walked on down the hall, around the corner, and to the stairs he had seen. He descended them. At the bottom was another locked door, but his key unlocked it. He went through, and found himself in another ward.

A guard approached. "Prison break upstairs!" Walter cried. "Guards held hostage! Go help them!"

The guard dashed upstairs. Either he was one who happened

to know English, or the game hadn't programmed him to not understand it. Walter was alone again.

He walked through the ward, unlocked the door at the far end, and found another stairway leading down. He followed it to the locked door at its base, unlocked that, and walked out of the castle at ground level.

The set turned to cardboard. The score box appeared:

```
PLAYER: Walter Toland

LEVEL:  Journeyman

SCORE: 5   OPTIONS
```

He had never thought to check that box, on this level! Quickly he touched OPTIONS and made the box permanent. He had probably done things the hard way, when the right option could have simplified the procedure. At least now he knew that he had gotten five points for this success. How many did it take to get to the next level?

He would find out. He spied the special inter-set door and used it.

four

HERO

Baal found herself exactly where she had been when she exited the game. She was in the Journeyman anteroom, with the brown-skinned character statue True Blue before her, and her hand extended toward the screen to set his hair color. If she had quit without saving, she would have had to start over. That would have been a pain, though now that she had been through the Novice set, she could have done it again readily enough. Well, maybe not; she might not have gotten the same collection of challenges, and one of the new ones might have killed her. So it was best to stay with what she had.

She made the hair black, and the stature large. This wouldn't affect the figure's actual performance; it was only cosmetic. But a big brown man was about as anonymous as she could get.

So now she had the physical form, and that was all she could do. The other qualities were defined by the game, at this level. Each level allowed the player more leeway and gave him a more complicated challenge, and Journeyman was still lowly.

She walked down the hall and opened the door. She

saw a lovely scene beyond, with a fairyland castle. This should be fun! And fun was what she wanted right now, because her real life wasn't.

She stepped through, and she was in it. She saw the castle much more clearly now. It was large, with high battlements, and from the highest turret flew a small pink flag. It had a moat up against the wall, and somewhat farther out a beaten path surrounded it.

She stood with a group of five other men. They seemed vaguely familiar, and in a moment she realized that they were actually animations of the three male types: True Blue, Joe Blow, and Doodoo. The other True Blue was white, and wore metallic armor and a sword. One Joe Blow was brown, the other yellow, and both carried clubs but lacked armor. The two Doodoos were evidently servants, and had neither armor nor weapons.

She herself was in armor, and she wore her own sword. Apparently the ones with swords were the leaders, and the Joe Blows were followers.

But what was her challenge? Well, she could ask. This was the equivalent of invoking the game's Help option, and was fair play. "True, what is our present situation?"

"We have trekked for days through the almost impenetrable jungle," he replied. "Now at last we have reached the hidden castle where the Evil Sorcerer has confined the lovely innocent damsel Princess. He will marry her, much against her maidenly will, at noon today, and force her kingdom to support his foul activities. You are her only hope, Sir Knight; you must penetrate the castle defenses and rescue her from a fate worse than death. Then of course you will be able to marry her yourself, and reap the personal and social benefits accruing."

Baal began to wonder whether she had been smart to take a male character. Marry the damsel?

But of course the round would end when she rescued the girl; they would not get to the marriage. This was only a game, however real it seemed. Indeed, it was substantially more real than the Novice settings had been, and that was good; it would be easier to lose herself in this. So why not be a handsome man, rescuing a beauteous Princess who had never heard of diabetes?

Baal judged by the elevation of the sun that it was about eight in the morning. So she had about four hours to get the job done, or lose. What would happen if she ran out of time? Would she just be booted from the setting, or would some horrendous thing appear to swallow her whole?

Well, she could ask. "What happens if we don't rescue the damsel in time?"

True shrugged. "The Evil Sorcerer will achieve control of her power the moment he marries her. He will use it to ensorcel all those who might oppose his nefarious designs. They will all die."

"But can't they just hide?" she asked.

"The ensorcelment will cause them to commit suicide."

Ouch! She was playing this game as a flirtation with suicide, but she didn't want to be compelled to do it by default. She preferred to go down fighting, or maybe to find reason to truly want to live.

They walked toward the castle. Suddenly there was a pounding noise, and the ground shook. "Hide!" Baal said, and they dived into the bushes.

That was just as well, because what passed before them was a monstrous dragon. It was about eighty feet long, with a serpentine torso thickening into a four-foot diameter at the center, and it had several pairs of stout legs assisting its motion. Its head was reminiscent of the world's ugliest alligator, with tusks. And, yes, it was breathing fire.

Baal reminded herself that this was not ridiculous. This was a game setting, and anything was possible. If she got near that dragon, it would burn her up, literally.

So how were they going to get past it? Baal was not inclined to tackle it with her sword. Maybe in romantic fantasy stories the hero could walk up to a dragon and slay it with a stab, but she did not see herself as that type of hero. Even if she had a magic sword that could slice cleanly through the dragon's scales, she would not be able to get close enough to do any damage without getting toasted. Unless—

"Do we by chance have flame-resistant armor?" she inquired.

"Our armor will not melt," True replied laconically. "But we will."

So much for that. She wasn't surprised. Why set up a challenge that was easy to nullify?

She watched the dragon from the bushes. It seemed to have a broad path circling the castle some distance out, and it slithered constantly along that path, alert for intruders.

"Perhaps we can sneak across while the dragon is on the other side of the castle," Baal said.

However, she suspected that there would be a catch to any solution that simple. Caution was best. So she examined the region more carefully, moving from bush to bush to get the best view. She saw that the trees and bushes resumed inside the dragon's path, providing some cover, but that there were many avenues for the dragon to follow there. So if someone got across, but the dragon smelled him, the dragon could pursue him well enough. Probably the dragon would pass that region before the person made it all the way to the castle anyway. Even the slightest ill-timing would be disastrous.

And what of the castle? Surely there were armed sentries, who would cry the alarm and bring the defendants with their arrows and spears. Even if there were not, how was a person to get into the castle? It was a stone edifice without windows at the lower reaches.

Well, first things first. There had to be a way, and not too difficult, because this was only the second level of what she understood was a five-level game. She just had to figure it out. There was a river that passed close to the ramparts. That was no doubt the water supply. It had not been wholly diverted into the moat; it merely kissed the base of a wall and meandered on out again, playfully. The dragon's path crossed it at two places, where neat, solid-stone bridges had been built. Probably the castle denizens used those bridges too.

Which meant that the dragon didn't attack them. Because otherwise they would have no way to come and go. There had to be some way for them to let the dragon know that they were friends rather than enemies. And therein might lie the key to entry.

"Maybe it's all a bluff," Baal said. "Anyone who crosses with assurance is not molested. So we'll try it." She turned to one of the Joe Blow characters. "Walk boldly down to that bridge and cross, as if you have no fear," she said.

"I have no fear," the man agreed, and walked down.

They watched from cover as he approached the bridge. The dragon had just passed it, so it was a good time to cross. He crossed and proceeded in toward the castle.

The dragon abruptly stopped. Then it turned around and slithered rapidly back to the bridge. It spied the man. It aimed its snout and fired out a long jet of flame.

The man went up in smoke, literally. He screamed, and his arms waved wildly, but the flame was unrelenting. In a moment nothing but a pile of ashes remained.

"I think that wasn't the way," Baal remarked. She was schooling herself not to overreact; that was not a man who had been killed, but a game construct in the form of a man. It was worth no more concern than a fallen chesspiece. Still, her heart was beating, and she knew that it was her real heart she felt, not that of the heartless game character she was animating. That had been a fantastic but uncomfortably realistic killing. She even caught a whiff of scorched flesh, as if the errant wind had brought it to her. The odors the game equipment could produce were limited, but in the ambience of the scene, this was effective. She felt like retching.

But something bothered her. The dragon had not smelled the man. It had stopped, then turned, as if aware that something was going on. Had smell been the factor, it would have stopped the moment the man set foot on the bridge. Instead it had delayed several seconds, then changed its mind. Why? Something else must have given it the clue.

Could someone in the castle have seen the figure, and somehow signaled the dragon? That seemed unlikely; the bridge was out of sight of the castle, because of several shielding trees. And how had the signaling been done? Baal had seen nothing. Of course she had not been watching the dragon closely, until it stopped and turned. How had it known?

Baal realized that she did not dare try the crossing herself until she knew the answer.

She saw no better way than sacrificing another piece. She felt guilty, but reminded herself again that these were not real people. She had to use them to win her game, or she would be the one who got demolished.

"Doodoo, go down and cross that bridge," she said to the closer of the two. "Try to time it so that the dragon doesn't see you."

The farther Doodoo got up without question and walked to the bridge. He waited for the dragon to pass, then crossed. This time Baal watched the dragon closely.

A flicker of light played across the dragon's scales, then touched its near eye. Immediately the dragon stopped, reversed, and charged after the man just stepping off the bridge.

Baal shielded her eyes with her hand. "Oh, no!" she exclaimed. "The dragon's going to get him!" But under the cover of her hand, she was looking around at her own men. Because that spot of light that had touched the dragon had been on the near side, which meant that a member of her party had a mirror. There was a traitor in her group!

She saw no mirror. Whoever it was must have hidden it the moment the dragon responded.

But she could figure it out anyway. Because it was dishonest to be a traitor to one's own party, and only Doodoo could be dishonest. And now she remembered that the wrong Doodoo had gone out to the bridge. She had spoken to the nearer one, but the farther one had gone. Because the nearer one had not chosen to respond. Because that one was the traitor, who served not Baal but the game, as a threat.

So now she knew. But how could she plan anything, if the traitor was going to mess it up? She needed to be rid of that person. But not openly, because it was surely to her advantage to have the game not know she had caught on.

She pondered, and managed to think of something that might work. She turned to True.

"I think the personnel of the castle must have something to let the dragon know they're all right," Baal said. "So they can cross the bridge without getting burned up. We need to find out what it is. Then we can get it and use it to pass the dragon."

No one commented. Baal realized that while they would respond to her direct questions or directives, they ignored anything else. She had to take the initiative, since she was the only member of this party who cared about the outcome of the quest.

"Are there any people associated with the castle who are outside the dragon's path?" Baal asked True, not expecting any meaningful answer. She was just setting it up for a search.

"I believe there are," he replied, surprising her. That suggested that she was on the right track. "I heard some voices by the river."

"Then we shall check the river, remaining hidden," she decided.

They proceeded cautiously in the direction True indicated. Sure enough, there were two young women bathing and frolicking in a shallow bend of the river. They splashed each other and laughed, heedless of the nearby dragon path.

Baal watched and listened carefully as they sneaked closer. After a while, the girls repeated their actions and laughter, exactly as before. They were on a programmed cycle. Probably everything in this setting was similarly programmed, waiting for the player to interact with it. So while this was a more sophisticated challenge than those of the Novice level, it was of a similar underlying nature.

Now to get clever, she hoped. "We need to find out what those girls have that stops the dragon from bothering them," she said. "It doesn't seem to be anything on their bodies, for they are bare." Indeed, they were nymphlike, with flowing waist-length hair, large breasts, narrow waists, and long firm-fleshed legs. Baal would love to have a body like that, even a diabetic one. "So it must be something they know or do. A code word, or a gesture. A signal that the dragon understands, that identifies them as friendlies."

She paused, but there was no response. "So we shall have to ask them. But I don't think they will tell us. So we need to do it subtly. We need to engage them in conversation, and persuade them that we are friendlies too, perhaps from another castle. Then maybe they'll let the information slip."

Still no response. She couldn't tell whether she was on the right track or the wrong track. However, it didn't matter, for she had something more devious in mind. "We are men, and they are women," she said. "So we shall pretend to be romantically interested in them. That may distract them from our real intent. I will go with one of you, and we shall try to separate the girls and charm the information from them." Now the key. "Doodoo, you and I will do it. I think you should be good at deceiving a woman."

The man could not evade this directive. Indeed, he probably didn't want to, because he needed to be near Baal to mess up her plan. He accompanied her down to the river, upstream from the girls, who were now in their third or fourth cycle of innocent frolic.

"We shall have to strip, so our foreign clothing doesn't give us away," Baal said. She found that she was less concerned about exposing this alien male body than she would have been about her own. She wondered whether it could react as a real male body could. She had no idea how to test that, and wasn't sure she wanted to. There was a certain emotional pain associated with the thought, because all that she knew of sexual love she had experienced with Tyson, and that had led to disaster.

They stripped and entered the water. It was of a pleasant temperature, as seemed reasonable, considering that the girls never seemed to get cold.

"Now we shall pretend we are bathing and swimming and playing, as they are," Baal said. "You see if you can lead your girl upstream, and I'll try to lead mine downstream, so that we can separate them and question them without giving ourselves away. If you get the answer before I do, then come back downstream to tell me."

Doodoo nodded. She knew that he would not actually question the woman; the moment he was out of sight he would revert to some cyclic behavior. Baal, as the player, would have to get the answer herself. That was fine.

They played the game, splashing water at each other and yelling as they drifted downstream. Soon they came in sight of the women, who broke off their banter to gaze at them.

Suddenly Baal pretended to notice the others. "What have we here?" she exclaimed. "Lovely maidens! I wonder if they would like some company?" She wished she knew more about standard male lines; she wasn't sure her improvisation was effective.

But the girls were responsive. "Oooo, men!" one cried.

Baal approached the dark-haired one. The maiden was standing waist-deep, her perfectly shaped breasts heaving delicately. Baal fought down another surge of jealous regret. If she could only have a set like that, she could conquer a portion of the world! Meanwhile, she was glad that she too was waist-deep, so that her male part did not show. Because a real male would surely be reacting sexually, and she was not. "Come dally with me, pretty maiden," Baal said, extending her hand.

The girl tittered, then swept her hand through the water, splashed Baal, and dived away. Baal followed, relieved that the girl was going downstream. She seemed to be of the Bad Girl type, which was good; a Royal Lady would hardly consent to play naked games with strange men.

In a moment Baal caught up. She realized that the girl really was not trying to escape; she was making a mere feint of it. She wanted to play a game with the strange man. She stood again, expectantly.

But Baal did not really want to play that game. She wanted to get the girl farther downstream, out of sight of the other girl and the spy. How was she to do that?

She decided to extend the game. She caught the girl's hand and tugged her downstream. "Let's get out of sight of the others," she suggested.

"Why?" the girl asked.

She had to explain? This was taking noninitiative a bit far! "So we can kiss, and you-know," she said, somewhat awkwardly.

"Ooooo, yes!" the girl agreed, sweeping into Baal's inadvertent embrace and kissing her on the mouth.

Baal, surprised and dismayed, fell back into the water. Now she wondered: if a real man were playing this character, how would he behave with this girl? Would he make a real sex game of it? This seemed to be what the girl was programmed for. If they had sex, would it be fulfilling? These were not real bodies; indeed, the girl was only a figment of the game's imagination. How could they have meaningful sex?

Meanwhile the girl was hugging her, and Baal felt the firm wet breasts against her chest. This was awful! She did not want to indulge in male-female sex. Not while she was in a body of the wrong gender. She was even less inclined to female-female sex, regardless of body. But it seemed that this was part of the girl's programming.

It could be a trap. If the player wasted his attention on sex, then he wasn't making progress toward rescuing the Princess. Maybe the girl would even turn out to be one of the Princess' handmaids, and she would tell the Princess what had happened, and the Princess would refuse to be rescued by this sullied man.

So now she had a rationale to avoid doing what she didn't want to do anyway. That was satisfying. "Let's swim on downstream, to get really private," she suggested.

That was a mistake. "Why?" the girl asked again.

"Because we can't do more than hug and kiss, where someone might come and see us," Baal explained.

"Yes we can," the girl said. She wrapped her arms and her legs around Baal's body.

Apparently if a male character was with this girl, sex was what she was programmed for. There wasn't anything else to do with her. Could this be the way the average man saw the average woman? A creature crafted for sex and nothing else? She was appalled at the notion, but was not sure it was in error. Maybe it was that way in male fantasy, and this aspect of this game setting had been programmed by a man.

Baal decided to give her stated plan a try. She forced herself to kiss the girl, who responded eagerly. "How do you stop the dragon from burning you?" she asked after a moment.

"Oh, the dragon doesn't scorch friends," the girl said, rubbing herself against Baal's body.

That was almost getting interesting, physically. And that realization alarmed Baal even more. So she gave up on the questioning. She just had to get away from this creature.

"I see the bridge ahead," she said. "Let's swim under it."

"No, that's out of my territory," the girl said.

Baal realized that she had been on the wrong track, in her diversionary questioning. There was no way for the girl to pass the dragon, because the girl wasn't a real person. She was just a game figure, assigned to be a distraction in one section of the river. She never went to the castle. Only the player and his companions did that. So probably the dragon scorched anyone who tried to cross its path. *There was no secret dragon-nullifying thing or signal.*

How lucky that she wasn't depending on that anyway. So it was definitely time to get on with her real plan. "Well, I want to swim," Baal said. "What will you do if I go near the bridge?"

"I'll scream for the dragon," the girl said.

Baal kept being surprised by the directness of some of the answers. The game figures didn't volunteer anything, but neither did they hold back when asked.

"Well, then, I will just swim in the river here," Baal said. "Maybe you should go back and join the others, who must be kissing and hugging and more."

The girl just stayed where she was. After a moment Baal realized what the problem was. She rephrased her suggestion. "Go join the others, upstream."

Then the girl went that way. Baal knew that the others were simply waiting for the player to return and bring some action, and this girl would do the same the moment she was out of sight. That was fine. Baal just didn't want the girl watching what she did next.

She swam slowly toward the bridge. Then she took a breath and dived under the water. She stroked swiftly with the gentle current, passing under the bridge, keeping a layer of water above

her. When she reached the other side she came up and looked
back.

There was no dragon. She had succeeded in crossing the line
without alerting it. She had also gotten rid of the spy in her
group.

She considered briefly, and decided to stay in the river. Whenever it passed in direct sight of a window or turret of the castle,
she would swim underwater again, avoiding discovery. She had
evidently found a game-approved entry route.

She approached the castle. The wall looked forbidding; there
was no place to scale it, and no place to get in if she could scale
it. The only entrance at ground level was the front gate, and that
was no good. How could she just walk around and in, without
being spied and speared?

But there must be a way for the castle to draw water from the
river, and maybe she could get to that spot. The river actually
washed the base of the castle at one point, where it connected to
the moat. If there was an intake under the surface—

She took a breath and dived. It occurred to her that since this
was a game figure, with no actual life of its own, she could probably dive without holding her breath; her own natural body was
not underwater, after all. But she didn't want to try it right now,
in case she had guessed wrong. It was just possible that if she
dived underwater, and breathed, the game would assume that she
was breathing the water, and therefore drowning. No sense wash-
ing out that way, pun and all.

She had guessed right about the intake anyway: there was an
opening several feet below the surface. It wasn't even barred.
There was room for her to enter. She swam in and up in the
darkness, and in a moment her head broke the surface.

She breathed, as quietly as she could, and felt around while
she waited for her eyes to adjust to the gloom. She seemed to be
in a well. That made sense: the inhabitants could simply drop a
bucket down and haul up the water.

Then she made out the rim of the well. It wasn't far above the
water level—just enough so that the river at flood stage would
not overflow into the castle. She ducked down, then stroked
strongly up, and reached as high as she could. One hand caught
the rim and held.

She got the other hand up on the rim, but wasn't able to go

farther. She knew her hands would slip if she tried to haul the rest of her body up. So how was she to proceed?

The bucket! The bucket should be sitting near, and it should have a rope attached, and the rope should be anchored so that it couldn't accidentally fall into the well. She could haul herself up on that rope.

She slid her hands around to the left, and soon felt a loop of the rope. She grabbed it, hauling it down, until it got taut. Then she drew herself up to the rim and flung a leg over. She felt her torso getting painted with the grime of the floor, but she made it up.

So now she was in the castle, but she was filthy. Well, that was readily remedied: she dropped the bucket down into the well and hauled up water. She doused herself with it, getting clean again.

But she still had a problem: she was naked. She doubted that the castle personnel would ignore a naked man who was walking the passages. She needed clothing.

Could she ambush one of the castle denizens, knock him out, and take his uniform? That was the way it was done on TV adventure shows. But she had doubts. Just how easy would it be to waylay a man, or to knock him out, without making a commotion that would attract others? And would his uniform fit her? Still, she had to have something.

Or did she? She was an intruder, and might be recognized as such the moment anyone saw her. The castle personnel surely knew each other, and would spot a stranger instantly regardless of his clothing. So maybe her nakedness didn't matter; she had to stay out of sight anyway. The effort to waylay a guard might be no more than a time-consuming dead end.

So she shook herself dry as well as she could and stepped cautiously along the passage leading from the well room. She was lucky no one had come while she was getting herself in order.

Lucky? The luck of the game was treacherous! She had better prepare for the bad breaks it would surely throw at her, at its convenience.

So she explored the passage carefully, discovering its crevices and nooks. There was a mop closet with a door which could be closed. Farther along there was an intersecting passage, which by the smell led to a privy: a place to defecate, or to dump the buckets of defecant collected elsewhere in the castle. It was amazing how much realism was possible in the game! She held her nose and explored it, finding another nook where she could probably hide if she had to.

She proceeded slowly, making note of every hiding place as she went. And suddenly it paid off. There was the wavering light of a lantern, as someone came down the main passage. Baal ducked into the mop closet, and the person went by, the lantern swinging from one hand, an empty bucket in the other. That meant he was going to fetch water, because otherwise the bucket would have been full, and smelly.

She waited for the man to return with the water. Then she followed him, as closely as she dared. The light made it easy to spy the alcoves and intersections.

He proceeded up a flight of stairs. She decided not to risk a close pursuit there; she waited for him to get clear. Then she moved up the stairs to the next story.

This one was considerably less gloomy. Indeed, the man had put aside his lantern and left it on a rack for the next person to use when braving the dark cellar. She could move much more rapidly without colliding with anything. But by similar token, she could be seen more readily by anyone who happened to pass this way.

Well, she would have to be alert, and to use her ears. She listened carefully, and found she could hear sounds scattered around the castle. Someone was talking in one chamber, and someone else was perhaps eating, and someone else—that was possibly a couple in bed, doing what they chose with each other. More likely all of it was on a cyclical pattern, waiting for some interruption by the player.

She continued skulking through the shadows, getting better at it. Other castle personnel did pass, but she eluded them with increasing ease. She was almost getting comfortable with this. Maybe she just was better able to let go of her inhibitions here in the game, concealed as a man.

But now she had to locate and rescue the Princess, who was in the highest chamber of the castle. Baal realized that that simplified her problem: she did not need to figure out the complete layout. She needed only to get to the highest point, and the Princess would be there. However, she would have to bring the Princess back down and out, so she had to note and memorize the best spots to hide.

She found stairway after stairway, making her way up. There seemed to be only one way up, so that was fairly frequently traveled. But most of the castle personnel were content to remain in their chambers, waiting for the player to come in and jog them out of their routines. She passed the dining room, and the servants' quarters, and sewing rooms and storage chambers. As she got high the population and activity thinned, and then she found a guard at the next staircase. This was the forbidden section of the castle.

How was she going to get past that guard? Well, she could try to sneak up on him and conk him on the head. That was probably the game-determined way. But she didn't much like violence, even in a mock setting like this. Normally, as a woman, she did not consider violence to be an option in handling problems. Now she had the body of a man, and it was all a fantasy setting with no physical consequences, but that didn't make it all right. There had to be a peaceful way.

Could she distract him? Suppose she called out something, so that he would come to investigate, and she could slip past and up the stairs without him knowing? That seemed good. But what could she yell? Well, something that would interest him enough to investigate.

She set it up carefully. There was a deep alcove whose cobwebs indicated that no one had gone into it for ages, so the guard probably wouldn't either. She could hide in that. She went beyond it, cupped her hands by her mouth, and made ready to call out that a nude nymph was in an empty chamber. If that didn't bring the guard, he wasn't realistically programmed.

She inhaled—and discovered that she couldn't speak. She was trying to, and surely doing it in life, but the sound was not coming through to the game. She had lost her voice! What was the matter?

Then she caught on. There was no nude nymph; it was a lie. And her character was True Blue, who was completely honest. He could not tell a lie.

This was interesting. She had had no idea that the game could read minds and enforce a code of ethics on an unwilling player. Did it have a lie-detector circuit it used to analyze her brain waves? But maybe it wasn't that sophisticated. Maybe it just refused to allow True Blue to speak in a manner he wasn't programmed for, and kept an ongoing file of relevant facts. Maybe.

The net effect was eerie, regardless. She had learned something important about the game. Diversion was all right, but not an outright lie.

But there was something true she could yell. There was no nude nymph, but there was a naked man. So she cupped her mouth again and inhaled. This time it worked: "There's a naked man here!" she cried. Then she ran silently for the alcove, which was between the chamber and the guard.

It worked. The guard walked to the chamber to investigate. Baal slipped out and hurried on her toes up the stairs. By the time the guard realized that he had been fooled, she was on the next floor and out of his sight.

Would the guard notify his superior about the incident? Probably not. He would assume that he had been the victim of a practical joke, and shut up about it. At least, that was what a real guard would probably do, so this game-figure guard should be programmed for much the same. She had found a game-approved way through, and she was gratified.

There was one more stairway. This one was a spiral, leading up to the highest turret. Where the Princess was imprisoned.

Baal hurried on up. At the top was a tiny landing and a locked door. Oops—how was she going to get that open? She hadn't thought to get the guard's keys.

Keys? But if the guard had them, then anyone else who came here would have to bring the guard along, to unlock the door. The stairs were too narrow for two abreast, and the landing was barely big enough for two. If the Princess came out, that would be three. Surely they took her out every so often, to give her a bath or something, so she could be suitably clean and dainty for the Evil Sorcerer to marry. So there must be a simpler way. Why bring the lout of a guard up here at all? He might try to take advantage of the captive maiden, ruining her virtue before the Sorcerer got at her.

Baal looked around. She saw an opaque curtain that didn't seem to cover a window. She drew it aside. Sure enough, there was the key, hanging on a nail in a nook. Since only authorized personnel were supposed to be up here, no special security was required.

She took the key and used it to unlock the door. She pushed it open and stepped inside the chamber. There was a bed, and on it lay the Princess. It had to be the Princess, because she wore an ornate robe and a golden circlet on her lovely head.

"Hello, Princess," Baal said. "I am here to rescue you from a fate worse than death."

The maiden lifted her head from the pillow and turned to get a good look at her rescuer. Her lustrous eyes widened. Her rose-like mouth opened. Her perfect bosom heaved. Then she screamed. It was the world's most piercing scream.

Too late, Baal realized her mistake. The Princess saw a naked man coming toward her. She must believe she was about to be ravaged. Naturally she screamed.

There was a clamor below. The guard had heard, and probably others, and they were coming to investigate. What escape was there now? There was no hope of making it down the narrow stairs; she would only meet the guard coming up. If she managed to conk him on the head, despite her objection to violence, his body would still block the staircase, and in any event others would be hard on his heels.

Her desperate eye fastened on the window. It had nice little lace curtains the Princess had fashioned. There were no bars on it. That could be the way out.

"Princess!" Baal said. "I really *am* here to rescue you! But we'll have to use the window."

The Princess merely continued screaming. It seemed that she could not see past True Blue's naked midsection. Damn that literal programming!

Baal pondered, knowing that she had only moments to save her situation. Could she rip the sheets from the bed and fashion a crude rope to climb down from the window? No, that would account for only a few feet, and this chamber was about a hundred feet high. Anyway, it would be easy for the archers to pick them off as they dangled. And how would she carry the Princess, and still have her arms and hands free to hang on to the rope?

Baal went to the window and looked out. She saw lovely scenery. Then she looked down. She got nauseous. A hundred feet had never seemed so far! There at the awfully distant base of the castle was the loop of the river.

The river! Just how deep was it? She had swum through it, but hadn't tried to probe the bottom. Could it be deep enough?

A guard burst in the door. No chance now to salvage the situation. That last mistake, with the Princess, had spoiled everything. All Baal could do was save herself, hoping that after that she could find a way to rescue the Princess and win the game.

She scrambled out the window and let herself drop toward the river. If it wasn't deep enough . . .

It wasn't. Her feet struck the surface of the water, and then jammed into the muck of the bottom. She found herself buried in darkness.

She reacted claustrophobically. She scrambled upward, but got nowhere. She tried to breathe, but could not. Instead a terrible pressure came down on her, crushing the life from her. She felt it ebbing, ebbing . . .

If this was death, it wasn't her idea of fun.

The scene stabilized, but it wasn't much of an improvement. Now she was locked in a coffin, with gloom surrounding her. Just the faintest bit of light wedged through a crack. Then that too shut off, as there was the sound of dirt landing on the box. She was being buried!

She screamed, but knew that she could not be heard. It didn't matter; she kept right on screaming.

Then she found herself standing in the character-selection hall. The score showed that she had no points in the Journeyman level.

And she hadn't even had time to think about what her seeming act of suicide felt like!

five

**P
O
L
I
C
E
M
A
N**

Walter stood in the anteroom, considering the list of games. It seemed that as a Survivor-level player he had a choice. There were many, but their bare titles did not tell him enough. There should be a way to get further definition, so he could make a more informed choice. Well, he would experiment, and in due course find it.

He noticed one titled Metropolis. Well, that should be relatively familiar territory. He touched it, and the screen showed a cast of characters. It also showed a list of other players in this game. There were no names there except his own, though. Good enough; he could have first choice of characters. There was also a clock, showing half an hour and counting down. It must have started when he entered this game, since he was the first player. He had plenty of time, and he would be satisfied to wait, after the rigors of his Journeyman-level game.

So what character did he want, this time? He had tried Bad Girl before, and that had been all right, but there were problems being in the wrong sex that he preferred to avoid now that the game was getting more serious. So it would be a man this time. In fact he would

go for the top, and take True Blue. Might as well have the pleasure of being a real man, for a change.

He touched Blue. Nothing happened. Then he realized that he
had first to select a game character; he had more choice than before. So he found an easy one: a policeman. Then he touched
Blue again, and the character definition choices appeared on the
screen.

APPEARANCE: COLOR, HAIR, STATURE
MENTAL: INTELLIGENCE, CREATIVITY, DISCIPLINE
SITUATION: CLASS, LUCK, PERSUASIVENESS
PHYSICAL: STRENGTH, REFLEXES, ENDURANCE

And this time he saw that he could define all of them. There
was a pitcher of fluid, and cups set by each of the listed traits.
Evidently this was the destribution mechanism: pour in as much
of that trait as he chose, at the expense of the others. That should
be interesting.

He made True Blue like himself, before his accident: brown
hair, brown eyes, tall, with good physique. Blue looked better
than he had, but he couldn't change the actual features of the
modeled face. Maybe that would become possible at a higher
level of the game. It hardly mattered, since it was all only a figure in the game.

Now for the character traits. How did he get the fluid out of
the pitcher and into the cups? Experimentally he touched the
pitcher, and it moved. It was a picture, but it responded to his
touch. Okay.

What he really wanted was a person like himself. But he realized that the game had no way of knowing his inner nature; it
had to be told. So he would have to do a self-analysis, and hope
he was reasonably objective. For the purpose of the game it
didn't matter any more than his appearance did, but for himself
it did.

So what was his nature? Before it had become irrelevant in
life as well as in the game, because of the accident? Walter considered, and realized that for the first time since the accident he
just might be able to look at it halfway objectively. Because this
was a game, not reality. It didn't make much sense to figure this
gave him freedom to think, when he hadn't been able to do it before. His mind was always free, wasn't it? So maybe it was just

that enough time had passed so that he could distance himself from it. Whatever the rationale, maybe he could do it now. If he didn't pause to reconsider.

Walter Toland had always wanted to be a policeman. He had been the Cop in Cops & Robbers as a child, and had rooted for even the corrupt cops in movies. Undissuaded by realization of the danger and pay scale and restrictions, he persevered through courses and physical education. He was not the smartest boy, but neither was he stupid, and when he worked hard he could make B's. He was tall but not solid, so he went out for sports and ultimately bodybuilding, and though he was just average in those too, he was a fairly formidable man on the street. Against a trained boxer he was in trouble, but very few folk he encountered were trained. Guns he could take or leave; it was the uniform and the responsibility he liked. So he learned to shoot, but hoped never to have to use his weapon against a man.

He had to take a job where he could find it, which meant moving to another city. His actual service as a cop slowly eroded his enthusiasm, but he persevered. Community relations were bad, because the police were predominantly white while the neighborhood was shifting to black and Hispanic. He tried to be fair, but he was viewed with suspicion simply because of his office. He was locked into what had turned out to be a largely thankless chore.

Then his life changed. The onset was seemingly insignificant. He had to go to a marital dispute in his own immediate neighborhood. That was one of the worst kinds of calls, because all too often both sides wound up blaming the policeman. The fact that it was in walking range of his apartment made it worse; the chances were that he would be recognized, and an irate plaintiff could start harassing him with calls. In this section it would be a white couple, middle class, which meant there would be pride and concealment and avoidance, which could be more difficult to deal with than outright meanness. But duty was duty.

It was a case of spouse abuse. The man had beaten his wife, and the woman had phoned in a complaint. He was Conway Minke, a middle-level executive in manufacturing. She was Lori, a housewife.

"It's all a misunderstanding, Officer," Minke explained. "My wife is temperamental."

"You hit me!" Lori flared. "You knocked me into the wall! You can't do that!"

Walter looked at her. She was petite and pretty in her outrage, with long straight black hair now somewhat disheveled. There was a forming bruise on her cheek. "Will you swear out a complaint?" he asked. He did not like wife beaters, and this seemed like a fairly clear case.

"No," Minke said.

"Yes!" Lori said almost at the same time.

So Walter took the man in. There was no immediate trouble. Conway Minke seemed stunned that his wife had actually carried through on the complaint. But the evidence came in during the next few hours: she had been struck on the head, thrown into the wall, and had sustained a mild concussion. The doctor was clear about the diagnosis. Unlike most women, she remained stalwart, testifying against her husband and obtaining a restraining order. He had to move out, but still provide support for her while she pursued the avenues of separation and eventual divorce.

All of which was out of Walter's bailiwick; he was only the arresting officer, and apart from routine paperwork and a court appearance on the plaintiff's behalf, he had nothing more to do with it. He was well on his way to forgetting the incident, when it abruptly became immediate again.

He recognized the address when he got the call. That domestic violence complaint. The man was supposed to stay well away from the house, but of course they seldom did. He would have to go and warn the man away, and arrest him if he didn't stay away. Somehow the abusive ones were the hardest to steer off their destructive course; they seemed to feel that it was their right to beat up their women, and they resented any interference.

Sure enough, the man was there, using a tire iron to bash at the door. He could readily have gotten in by this time if he had used that weapon to bash out a window, but naturally Walter would not tell him that.

Minke spied the approaching police car, and hurried back to his own car. He was gone by the time Walter came to a stop. That was typical of such bullies; they preferred to beat up on women. But Walter had noted the license tag, and recognized the man from the prior contact; that sufficed.

He went to the door and knocked, gently. The woman had evidently seen him too; she opened it immediately.

"Thank God you're here, Officer Toland!" she exclaimed. She was prettier than he remembered her, perhaps because she was no longer quite as disheveled and bruised. He had always had a hankering for small, shapely women, but they had not returned his interest. "He was threatening to kill me!"

That too was typical, and too often was no bluff. Sometimes Walter regretted being a member of the male sex. "But I think he will not return today," he said reassuringly. "He knows that we will be alert for that."

"Yes he will!" she exclaimed. "I know him! He can't stand to let me live my own life." She turned huge dark eyes on him. "Officer, what will I do? The law isn't protecting me! I mean, you're here, you're a good man, but you can't stay, and then *he'll* come back!"

"I really don't think—" Walter started.

"Test it, Officer Toland!" she pleaded, standing close. Her nice bosom heaved, causing an illicit thrill to run through him. If only this were a real situation, just the two of them, instead of a grubby routine police call! But he had no business even imagining anything of the kind. "Drive away, circle the block, come back, see if he isn't right back here! He's watching, waiting for you to go, so he can have time to get me. He knows you can't stay here forever. He doesn't care about anything else, just so long as he gets me."

It really hadn't seemed that bad before; Conway Minke had been relatively polite. But it was never possible to tell. Walter couldn't be sure she was wrong. The best thing to do was to prove it, and get on about his business.

"All right, Mrs. Minke," he said. "I will depart, and return quietly in a few minutes. If he is here, I will deal with him." This might be unprofessional, but he wanted to please her, because of his foolish private fancy.

"Oh, thank you so much!" she exclaimed, squeezing his hand gratefully.

He returned to his car, made some notes, then drove away. He gave it a reasonable interval, then returned along another street. He expected to reassure her about her fear, and that would be it.

But Conway Minke was there. This time he had gotten half-way smart, and was bashing in the window. Lori had been right!

Walter turned on his siren as he came up, giving warning. The man stopped immediately and ran for his car. Walter turned on his loudspeaker. "Halt!" he said.

Of course it did no good. The car's tires squealed as Minke drove away.

Walter should have radioed so that the fugitive could be intercepted, but he didn't. What was holding him back?

The door opened and Lori came out. "See? See? I told you! He doesn't care about the court or the law or anything. He just wants to get me, and he will, he will, if he isn't locked up!"

"We can't keep him locked up," Walter said. "He'll be out on bail in an hour. Perhaps you should go to stay with a relative, until this can be straightened out."

"I don't have any relatives," she said. "Not that I could go to. That's why I couldn't leave him before. Now it's out in the open, and there's nothing holding him back."

"Then maybe I can get you a referral for a home for battered women."

"It's full," she said. "I checked. Anyway, he knows where it is. He'd go there, and they couldn't stop him."

She was right; he remembered now. Such facilities were always overcrowded. That said something ugly about the priorities of society, but didn't do her any good. "Maybe we could take you into protective custody," he suggested, though he wasn't at all sure that a judge would go along with that. He was acutely aware of his inability to help her in any significant way.

She smiled brilliantly. "Yes! Oh, yes, that's wonderful, Officer! I'll go with you right now. Is your house nice?"

"I didn't mean—"

But she was already running back into her house to fetch her things. Helplessly he followed her in. This was, he realized belatedly, why he hadn't radioed to intercept Minke: he had wanted to deal with Lori directly. Privately. Just the two of them, in her house, for just a few minutes. So that he could fancy that there was something more than a routine call. That wouldn't have happened if he had gotten involved in a run-down.

Soon she reappeared with a suitcase. "I'm ready, Officer Toland. Take me away."

"I meant to the police station," he said lamely. "To see where you might go."

She met his gaze. "No you didn't."

Oh, God! She had seen through him! She knew how she appealed to him. She was desperate, so she was using him, but he was helpless against it.

Wordlessly he led her out to his car. He took her the short distance to his apartment. "You know this isn't according to the book," he said.

"It's the only way I can be safe," she replied firmly.

"Maybe tomorrow we can find a better place for you to stay," he said.

"Maybe," she agreed in a tone that indicated her willing disbelief.

He left her there, gave her a key, and resumed his rounds. He knew he was crazy to do this, but he couldn't help himself. He'd never had a woman truly interested in him before, and though he knew this was disaster, he couldn't help himself. The thought of her in his apartment thrilled him.

He reported that Conway Minke had attacked his wife's residence twice, and fled when challenged. The wife was all right. They would assume that she remained at the house, and that things had settled down. The judge might revoke Minke's bail and confine him to jail temporarily. But things were so busy that the judge probably wouldn't get around to it. The case would be lost in the shuffle. No one cared where Lori Minke was. No one except Lori—and Walter. For now.

When he finished his shift and returned home, he found a meal waiting for him. Lori had made herself busy in his bachelor kitchen, doing a better job than he ever had. But he hardly noticed the food. He was too distracted by Lori herself.

She was in a sheer negligee, and looked breathtaking. He had thought she had a good figure; he had underestimated the case. She had a perfect figure, for his taste.

But he was not so dull as not to challenge it. "What are you up to, Mrs. Minke?"

She was helping him out of his jacket, brushing close. "Lori," she corrected him.

"Lori," he agreed numbly. "I—I said you could stay the night. For protective custody. Only—"

"Only it's not official, Walter," she said. "I have a better way. Let me just move in with you. I don't have money, but I can pay." She opened her negligee to show her bare breasts.

No doubt now: she was trying to seduce him. So that she would have a place to stay. It probably didn't mean anything to her, emotionally; she was just doing what she had to, to achieve comfort and safety. He knew it was wrong, and that he was a fool to allow it. But he also knew he couldn't turn it down.

She took his silence for the assent it was. She continued to undress him, until he had to respond. Then she pulled his head down and kissed him. Then she led him to the bed, and drew off her negligee.

That was the beginning of the best night of his life. They had hot, fast sex. Then they dressed somewhat and ate. Then they made love. When he woke in the night, and found her still with him, close, he felt desire again, and immediately she accommodated it. The whole thing was a glorious experience.

But in the morning some semblance of reality tried to intrude. "You must find a better place to stay," he said.

"There *is* no better place," she replied.

"But you're a married woman!"

"Not any longer than I can help it." She approached him. "Do you want me to seduce you again?"

"They'll think I took advantage of your situation."

"Who needs to know, Walter?"

"This isn't right!"

"But is it wrong?"

He couldn't argue with her. "You are free to go whenever you want. You know that."

"But I don't want to go, Walter. You're a much better man than my husband, in every way."

He didn't believe her. He did hope he was better than her husband, because he wasn't an abuser. But he didn't trust her belief. She was just using him as a convenient haven, and forthrightly paying for it in the coin she possessed. As a married woman who had dealt with a difficult man, she had a pretty good notion how to handle a man. The difference between what she was doing and prostitution was mainly one of nomenclature. He ought to insist that she go elsewhere. But he knew he wasn't going to.

"I have to go to work," he said.

"You want to do it again before you go?"

"No!" But that wasn't true. "I mean, yes, but that wasn't what I was trying to say. I have to leave you here, and I don't know what you can do. I normally leave my apartment locked—"

"But you gave me a key. Walter, leave me some money and I

will grocery-shop for you. There's a store within walking range. I think I know what you like."

"But people will see you!"

She smiled. "There's only one I fear, and he won't know where I am. I know some people in the neighborhood, but they won't know I'm not home. I can manage."

So it seemed. She was competent and independent. Her husband had gotten out of control, so she was doing what was necessary to eliminate him from her life. Still he had misgivings. "I could get fired, if—"

"Are you planning to beat me up?" she asked.

"No! I just meant—"

"I know what you meant. What *I* mean is that I won't complain unless you mistreat me, and I will comport myself in such a way that no one else complains either. People will know you have a woman, but no one will complain. It isn't their business. They know that police officers have private lives too." She smiled. "Now come, let me do for you now, and I'll be ready for you when you return. When you get dissatisfied, tell me to go, and I'll go."

He looked at her, still not at ease. She opened her negligee, and his resistance dissipated before it could solidify.

His day was routine, but not his thoughts. Just how foolish was he being? Would he return to discover his apartment cleaned out, and a sarcastic note scrawled in lipstick on the bathroom mirror? He had given her fifty dollars for groceries; was it money thrown away? No; she had given him sex galore, for which he would have paid more than that. Even if he never saw her again, he would count himself ahead. One night of illusion; it was certainly worth it. Unless he lost his job because of it.

Unable to let it be, he phoned his apartment. Normally he would get the answering machine. If she was there, she shouldn't answer. So it was pointless. But he called anyway.

He got the machine. So he left a message. "Lori, if you're there, this is Walter. I hope you're okay—"

Then she picked up. "Hello, Walter. Everything's fine. I wouldn't answer for anyone but you, of course. Do you mind cruising by my house, just to see if anyone's there?"

"I'll do it," he agreed, relieved and excited. She hadn't taken off!

When he returned home, she was ready, as she had been be-

fore. She did not wait for him to ask; she brought him to the bed
and gave him the utter delight of her body. Then she served him
a meal of far better quality than he was used to. She had evidently shopped well.

"Oh—here's your change," she said, giving him three dollars.
"I'm afraid I splurged a bit, but there's enough food to hold us
for several days now. I hope you're satisfied."

"I'm satisfied," he said. "This is like a dream. It's as if I died
and went to heaven, and you're an angel to make me happy.
But—"

"But it's temporary," she said. "Until I get my divorce and settlement. Unless we have a more permanent arrangement by
then."

"You've been mistreated by your husband. You should be
afraid of men. Instead—"

"I love men," she said. "I just made a bad mistake with one.
I don't judge others by him. I knew you were a nice man from
the start; I could tell by the way you acted. Now I'm proving it.
I'm not just giving you a good time; I'm having one myself."

He believed it because he wanted to believe it, knowing himself to be a fool, but not sure just what kind of fool.

So it was for the following month. Walter was in a sexual paradise, and falling in love with Lori despite his common sense.
She was *the* perfect woman for him. He knew she would leave
him when she got her divorce and settlement, because she
wouldn't need him anymore, and he schooled himself to be ready
for that separation, but he knew he wasn't. He just hoped it
would continue forever.

Then Conway Minke finally figured out where his wife was
staying. The man had evidently tried to locate her via her divorce
lawyer and gotten nowhere; the lawyer himself didn't know
where she was hiding. But neighbors did, and as the chain of information slowly spread, Minke managed to get a line on it. He
phoned and left a message on Walter's answering machine: "I
know where you are, Lori. Come back to me and all will be forgotten."

The message electrified Lori. For the first time since the crisis
that had brought her to him, Walter saw her frightened and
shaken. "He's found me! I have to get away!"

"But you still don't have anywhere to go," he pointed out.
Nervously she agreed. She remained. She was afraid to go out

to shop, or to answer the phone. But though she still tried to, as she put it, do for him, the seeming spontaneity and joy of it were gone. The honeymoon, as it were, was over. Walter knew that he would never have his ideal woman back unless he found a way to get rid of Minke. Then, if he did, she would be free—to leave him. If she wanted to. He had never been sure of her real feelings.

Had she set him up for this? To fall in love with her, and kill her husband for her? He didn't think so, but couldn't be certain. Certainly he wasn't going to commit such a crime on her behalf. Yet if Minke should come after her, and Walter should intercept him in the act—

Minke did come. Lori saw his car from the window, and phoned Walter. The message was relayed: a desperate woman wanted him to call home. If others in the police force knew his situation, they did not speak of it.

Walter didn't call. He raced for his apartment. As luck would have it, he was close by; he got there in two minutes. Sure enough, there was Minke's car. Walter parked behind it and charged in. He heard screaming and crashing, and knew that the man was trying to break in. He drew his gun.

He came to the hall and sighted down it. Minke was there, trying to jimmy open the lock. That was useless, because there was a dead-bolt.

"Halt!" Walter called.

Minke saw him and bolted down the hall, away from him, where there was another exit. Walter had him covered, but didn't fire; it was not a matter of life and death, and a shot would not be justified.

He paused to call to Lori. "I'm here! I'm going after him!"

"Be careful!" she cried from inside.

He was careful. He did not charge blindly after the man. He paused at the corner and listened before quickly stepping around it. He made his way cautiously on out. By that time Minke's car was gone.

But Walter had had prior experience with the man. So he didn't depart immediately. Instead he holstered his gun and walked down the block, checking to see where the man might hide, waiting for Walter to drive away. The car was probably circling the block, slowly, seeking a place to park for a few minutes. If Walter could find it—

He reached the intersection and peered around. He did not spy the car. But it was probably still in motion nearby.

This was a one-way street, with parking on both sides. He saw an open spot on the far side, the only one. That could be the one the man would take, when he got here. So Walter would just get there first, and wait.

He started across the street. Then the car appeared, as if from nowhere. It was Minke, trying to run him down!

Walter's first thought was to duck back the way he had come. But his inertia was forward, so he could move faster that way. He broke into a run, but the car was too fast. It was going to catch him!

He dived out of the way. The hood of the car caught his hip and sent him spinning through the air. He did a forward rolling breakfall, protecting his head and shoulders, but he knew already that he had taken a bad hit. Then he came to rest on the pavement, half against the wheel of one of the parked cars. He must have hit his head, because then the world fuzzed out.

Walter realized that he had relived the whole sequence. Now he stood before True Blue in the game anteroom, trying to decide what array of characters to give the man. He had accomplished very little, really; he still hadn't truly analyzed himself.

He shook his head. Might as well finish the memory, painful as it was. He had been picked up and taken to a hospital, where they had labored diligently to save his mobility, but it was no good. Minke had evidently returned while Walter had been unconscious, and run over his legs repeatedly. They were such a mangled mess that the doctor would only shake his head, promising nothing. Walter had only partial control over the natural functions in that region, and had to use a catheter to urinate. The pacemaker governed his heartbeat, because ancillary damage to his system had made his heart subject to fibrillation. He required modern technology to survive.

His career as a police officer was over. So was any other career that required any walking at all. So was any sex life to which he might have aspired. That, he realized, had been Minke's real objective: to destroy his rival sexually, in case he should survive. It seemed he had succeeded. There had been some nerve damage, and nerves did not readily heal. Technology wasn't able to restore that particular function. Walter could have the urge, but performance seemed beyond reach. Minke had fixed him almost perfectly.

Lori had left him, of course. He had assumed that she had indulged sexually with him so often because she was trying to keep him satisfied to have her with him, prostituting herself. Now he learned that she really did enjoy it, and did not relish the prospect of caring for a man who could no longer perform. She was polite about it, even kind, but she had to go. Where she went he did not know; she just disappeared from his life.

After he got through the surgery he spent a longer period learning the use of the wheelchair, and care of himself. Insurance covered it, but insurance could not make him whole again. It was an entirely new world, from the wheelchair; he could no longer even cross the street unless there were suitable ramps at the curbs, or helpful people. His old apartment was no longer feasible, because it wasn't equipped for wheels. Everything had changed.

So it was now three years after the "accident." Minke had been arrested and sentenced and had served his time and was out. Overcrowded prisons meant that the nonserious offenders had to be released early, and Minke was regarded as nonserious by everyone except Walter. The man had no further animus against Walter; his revenge had been even better than the murder he had attempted. Minke even had another woman, whom he surely mistreated. But not Walter. Women had been excluded from his life. All because of his foolishness of the moment.

Yet, he reflected, it had been a glorious moment. For the first time he had lived with a woman, a truly responsive one. Even without the sex, it would have been great. If he had known the eventual cost of it, he might have turned it down. But more likely he would simply have shot Minke, and damned be the consequence. It might have cost him his job, but gained him his health—and perhaps the woman too. It would have been worth the gamble. If he had known.

He had gone through what the psychologist called the normal stages of adjustment: denial, anger, bargaining with God, grief, and resignation. He had learned to cope. He had redeveloped bladder control, so no longer needed the catheter. But the colossal frustration of being less than a man, and the boredom, remained. He had read books, and watched movies endlessly, but there was only so much that vicarious experience could do for him. Until he had obtained the equipment for this new type of game, that raised vicarious experience to a new level. It was supposed to be interactive with other players, in its upper stages. Could that substitute for the drabness of his remaining life? It had seemed worth the try.

So okay, here he was, and he had used up about twenty-five minutes of his half-hour wait. What did it matter exactly what character traits his dummy character had? He would just spread the fluid evenly between the cups, and see how the game played, this time.

Then a notice appeared. GAME CANCELED OWING TO LACK OF PLAYERS. NEXT GAME SCHEDULED IN 35 MINUTES.

Walter grimaced in disgust. He had wasted his time here. Well, not exactly; now he had reviewed his history, and had a better handle on it. The psychologist had told him that he would know he was making significant progress when he was able to do that. So he was making that progress. But he remained a paraplegic.

Well, he might as well take time out from the game, and return in half an hour. If Metropolis was filled, he'd try some other setting. It hardly mattered, at this stage.

He reached up and touched the OPTIONS choice on his screen, then QUIT. SAVE? it queried him. That reminded him of the religious query, Have you been saved? Computer technology gave it new meaning, or perhaps merely clarified it. Because if you exited a computer program without saving, you lost it all. He didn't want to start over with the Novice-level challenges, so he touched YES.

A new message flashed. ERROR. CAN NOT COMPLETE DIRECTIVE.

Huh? All he had done was try to quit and save.

Very well. He'd quit without saving. It wouldn't kill him to come up through the ranks again. He touched CLEAR ERROR, then QUIT again, then NO to the SAVE query.

ERROR. CAN NOT COMPLETE DIRECTIVE.

What was going on here? How could it be impossible to quit? Quitting was the one thing you could always do.

But as he tried it repeatedly, he realized that this was the exception. He couldn't quit from inside the game—and because he was in it, not looking at it via a screen eighteen inches from his face, with a keyboard, he couldn't disconnect by pulling the plug. It seemed ludicrous, but he was trapped in the game.

Gradually it dawned on him that this was serious. If he didn't get out, he would be unable to feed himself. He would starve, or rather dehydrate, because fluid loss was a much swifter threat than food loss.

Actually the nurse who checked on him every day would discover him and unhook him manually from the game, and then bawl him out for getting himself into such a scrape. But she wasn't due for eight hours. He had cranked up in the morning, and she came in late afternoon. He could get pretty uncomfortable in the interim.

Well, if he was stuck, he was stuck. He might as well play the game.

He checked the other choices, and saw one that might be interesting: Princess in Castle. That might even be fun, if the Princess was beautiful. There were already several players signed up for it, so probably the good parts were already taken, but he didn't need a good part. He just needed something to play, until he could figure out how to exit the game, or until the nurse came and got him out. Still, what did he care about a fantasy adventure? He was an ex-cop, not given to that sort of thing.

Then he noticed one of the names on the player roster. BAAL CURRAN—the same one he'd seen before. The guy must have passed his Journeyman test and made it into the Survivor level. Walter didn't know him, of course, yet it was the one halfway-familiar thing here. Maybe they could meet in the interactive game, and compare notes.

So he touched PRINCESS, and watched the screen change.

six

PRINCESS

REPEAT? the screen inquired.

Baal considered. She had washed out of her first Journeyman setting, but she had actually come pretty close to success. If she had done everything the same, but covered up before speaking to the Princess, she should have succeeded in gaining her cooperation and rescuing her. Why not try it again now, while the experience was fresh in her memory?

So she touched REPEAT, and walked to the door again. She stepped through, and there she was at the beginning of the Princess sequence. The others did not seem surprised to see her; they of course had no memory of her prior effort, because they weren't people at all. She could run through this a hundred times, and it would make no difference to them. It was like playing a song over and over: the song didn't care.

They ran through the business with the dragon and the nymphs in the river. Baal tried to keep the same pace, because she didn't know what might happen to change things if she deviated too far, and she didn't want to find herself in an unfamiliar situation. She wanted to win this game, so she could progress to the Survivor level, where it was supposed to get really interesting.

When she made it to the Princess' chamber, she took down the curtain hiding the key alcove, and fashioned it into a temporary skirt. So this was a male character; so what else could she do? At least it would cover up what had freaked out the innocent damsel last time.

"Princess," she said in a low voice. "Do not be afraid; I may look strange, but I have come to help you."

The Princess lifted her head and looked. She saw nothing of what she had seen before, but she evidently suspected it was there. "Who are you?" she asked nervously. "Another servant to prepare me for my fate worse than death?"

"No. I am the Hero, come to rescue you from that fate. But I must warn you that it will not be easy to escape this castle."

"I would rather die than remain here in dire captivity!" she declared passionately. That could not be literal, since she had not thrown herself from the window to die, but Baal saw no point in arguing the matter.

"Then let me explain what we must do. I found my way here by swimming in the river, and we can swim back out. But clothing will only get in the way. I had to leave mine behind, and you will have to do the same."

"Oh, I could never do that!" she exclaimed, putting one hand to her heavily alarmed bosom.

"I fear you will have to," Baal said. She was beginning to appreciate why some men lost patience with some women. "Unless you prefer to wait for the Evil Sorcerer to marry you and undress you shortly after." That was a bit cruel, but it seemed that the Princess needed to be persuaded.

"Oh!" she cried faintly.

"You see, it is known that Princesses do not go naked," Baal said. "So if anyone should spy you in that state, they would assume it was a serving maid. Nudity is the perfect protection."

"But my honor!" she protested.

"Your honor?"

"It would be severely compromised if any man were to see my innocent body."

And Baal was in the form of a man. This promised to be difficult. She could have done without the skewed definition of honor, where it seemed it related to sights rather than actions.

But this was a different world, and had to be handled on its own terms.

Baal pondered, then tried something chancy. Would the game allow it? "I may look like a man, but in truth I am not what I seem. I am a woman who has been placed in the body of a man. After I rescue you, I will revert to my natural form. So your honor will not be compromised if I see you."

"Very well," the Princess said. She stood and began removing her apparel. She was of course a Royal Lady, and as she stripped it became apparent that she was as well constructed as any nymph.

Surprised at this ready acquiescence, Baal couldn't help inquiring, "That makes it all right?"

"Of course. I thought you were going to tell me to use my apparel to cover my head, so no one could recognize me."

"And that would have been wrong?"

"No, that's the standard ploy."

These game constructs were certainly literal-minded! Maybe she should simply have asked the Princess how to make their escape. The game figures weren't supposed to offer constructive advice, but if she had phrased it as a review, to be certain they had things straight, it might have worked.

"Now I must disrobe myself," Baal said carefully, remembering how the Princess had reacted before. "Remember, I am not really a man, and my temporary body has no more relevance than that of a statue. There is no part of it that need concern you."

"Of course," the Princess said bravely.

Baal found herself quite nervous about removing the makeshift skirt. This female was a game construct, but she was realistic, and if she was programmed to freak out anytime she saw a certain thing, this game would be lost again. But there was no way to find out except to try it. So she nerved herself and removed the skirt.

The Princess stared. "What a weird apparition," she said distastefully.

"Yes, I can hardly wait to get back to my own body," Baal said, relieved that the reaction was no worse. She had succeeded in detuning the girl's freak reflex. "Now we must go quietly downstairs, and we must try to hide whenever someone comes. I will guide you. Do not say anything—and particularly, do not scream, for that will bring guards running. Then they would see you, and it is best that as few see us as possible."

"Oh," the Princess repeated in her faint fashion. She had accepted the idea of Baal seeing her, since Baal wasn't really a man, but a guard might be an honor-shattering disaster even if he didn't recognize her.

Baal led her out and down the winding stairway. But as they approached the bottom of the spiral, Baal remembered the guard. How were they to get by him this time? She couldn't use the "naked man" ploy, because that would bring the guard up the stairs, and there was no place along the stairs to hide. They had to get beyond the guard before the ploy would work, which made it useless.

Would she have to resort to violence, after all? Baal still didn't like that. There had to be a nonviolent way.

She paused. "There's a guard ahead," she whispered to the Princess. She wished she could throw her voice to the side chamber she had used before.

Then she had an idea. This was a realm of magic, because the dragon was a magical creature. Could people work magic? Could voice throwing be possible here?

If she tried it, she would probably mess it up. She had no experience with magic. But the Princess was a native.

"Princess, are you able to throw your voice magically?" Baal asked.

"Of course. That is one of the first things we learn. Sometimes it is necessary to give a servant an order when the servant is in another part of the castle."

Good enough! "Then throw your voice to the chamber which is to the side of the base of these stairs. Say 'Eeek! The naked man is back, and there's a naked woman with him!' "

The Princess did not question this, since it was a specific directive and it was true. She was not programmed to be discerning enough to realize that such a voice coming from that chamber would be deceptive, as the naked man and woman were actually on the stairs. She glanced down.

"Eeek!" a feminine voice cried. "The naked man is back, and there's a naked woman with him!"

Baal stared. Two things amazed her. The voice really was coming from the chamber below—and the Princess' mouth was closed. She wasn't speaking with her mouth, but with her magic.

"Hey, I'm not falling for that again," the guard below retorted. "Go away, you practical joker."

Ouch! Even game figures learned from experience, if it was in the same sequence.

But what else was there? Maybe they could up the ante. "Can you make a male voice too?" Baal asked the Princess.

"No, that would be unmaidenly."

"Well, then, can you pretend that the woman is talking to the man, saying 'Take your hands off me, you brute!'?"

"Yes, I could do that."

Always fairly literal-minded! "Then do it."

The Princess did it, and it sounded so realistic that Baal herself almost believed that there was a woman there. Then, prompted by Baal, the Princess continued the monologue. There was a pause between utterances, but that was all right, because they were presumably in response to silent actions by the man.

"If you don't stop, I'll tell the guard!"

"I'm sure the guard is a nicer man than you are."

"Eeeek! That tickles!"

That did it. The guard went to investigate.

Baal and the Princess scampered down the stairs. Baal crossed to the next staircase down, and started to use it. Then she realized that the Princess was lagging. Baal turned, and saw the Princess standing at the foot of the circular staircase, looking in the direction of the chamber.

"What's the matter?" Baal cried in a whisper, which was a talent she hadn't realized she had.

"I hope the guard doesn't hurt her."

"There's no woman there!" Baal said. "She's just your thrown voice! Remember?"

"Oh, yes," the Princess said, remembering. Still she stood there. Because Baal had not actually told her to move.

"Come here!" Baal said. "Hurry!"

The Princess obeyed, running to the lower stairs. Her hips swiveled and her bare breasts bounced, and suddenly Baal realized why men liked to watch running women. The breasts called attention to themselves, their separate motions drawing the eye in, and men were partial to breasts. Of course it helped to have breasts like those of the Princess, which were impossibly full yet firm. It would have been pointless for Baal herself to run naked; her natural body lacked both the substance and the firmness.

But in the game, she could have a perfect body. It might not be real outside the game, but it would be a pleasure nonetheless. Next time she would select the best female body available, and revel in it. She had entered this game to flirt with death, but now she realized that she wanted to flirt with life too. Life as it might be without her limitations. Life as it might be for one of the beautiful people. So it was illusion—so it could still be fun for a while.

Meanwhile they were moving down the stairs, getting away from the guard. But they weren't safe yet. There were about seven more floors to go, and a number of randomly walking people in the halls.

In fact Baal heard one approaching as they reached the foot of the staircase. "Quick—we must hide in a closet!" Baal whispered, drawing the Princess toward one of the memorized sites.

They made it, and the person passed without noticing them. Then Baal became aware of something else. She was jammed up against the Princess' lush body. She had no sexual interest in it, but realized that if she had been in the Princess' body, up against True Blue's body like this, she would have found it quite intriguing. Make that one more thing she wanted to try in the next setting!

They emerged from the closet and hurried to the next stair. They got safely down it, and down the following one. Then, abruptly, they had a problem.

A castle denizen approached from one side; Baal heard the footsteps of a man. So they ran for a hiding place around a corner—and there was another figure, a woman. A castle matron. There was no way to avoid her; they were both in plain sight before realizing.

"Cover your face with your hair!" Baal told the Princess. "So they won't recognize you." The maiden had lustrous long tresses, of course: the kind that took hours of attention each week. The Princess obeyed, and Baal did likewise, for True Blue had the handsome locks of this archaic fantasy setting. Together, anonymous, they charged on by the woman.

But the woman saw something other than their faces. She screamed. "There's a man! There's a woman! They're na-na-naked!"

Immediately there were footsteps from other directions. Baal realized that she had found an even better way to bring folk run-

ning than the ploy of screaming "Fire!" instead of "Robbery!"
Just scream "Naked Woman!"

But then something coincidental happened. "Stop that!" a
man's authoritative voice snapped. "The topmost guard has
turned in two false alarms of that nature. The humor is wearing
thin."

"Who's that?" Baal asked the Princess as they sped for the
next hiding place.

"The Evil Sorcerer!" the damsel replied, horrified. "Throwing
his voice."

"Well, he did us a favor this time." Baal wondered at that;
since when did the game start covering for the players? But she
realized that she had been lucky. The game would allow someone to be fooled by voice throwing once or twice, but after that
prevented it. She had benefited from the prevention. That had to
be a fluke.

They made it down to the cellar. Baal explained how they
would have to go down into the well and then dive under the
wall and out into the river.

"But I can't swim!" the Princess protested.

Oops! This hadn't occurred to Baal. But she remembered that
half of all folk in the world today could not swim, so it was reasonable that the Princess couldn't. What now?

"I'll just have to teach you," Baal said. "First, you will have
to hold your breath. Then you cup your hand, like this, and—"

She broke off. She heard footsteps approaching!

"Just hold your breath and hang on to me!" she said. Then she
grabbed the Princess around her slender waist and jumped into
the well. The plunge took them under the surface; she waved her
free hand through the water, found the wall, slid her fingers
down, and found the bottom rim. She hauled herself and the
Princess down and kicked her feet, driving them forward. Then
she braced against the outer wall and pushed them out into the
river. They were free of the castle!

Well, almost. They still had to get out beyond the dragon's
path. In fact they still had to get out of the depths and breathe
some air.

They bobbed to the surface, but only Baal breathed. The Princess was still holding her breath. She did not seem to be in any
particular distress. Since she was merely a game figure, she

didn't actually have to breathe; still, for realism it seemed better. "Breathe!" she said in the Princess' ear.

The Princess breathed. Baal held her up, then instructed her to hold her breath again, so she could haul them both to the shore. The Princess obeyed without question.

They climbed out on the shore away from the castle. Baal knew she should feel tired, after that effort, but she didn't. That was because her body hadn't really done it; this was all game activity, with no more actual substance than a dream. Still, its threats were real on its terms, as she remembered from her death in the prior session.

There was a cry from the castle. "The Princess is escaping!"

They had been discovered! Someone must have checked the Princess' chamber and realized that she was gone. Then someone had spied them emerging from the river. The chase was on!

But they had a head start. "Run," Baal said. "This way!" She set off up the side of the river.

The clamor in the castle increased. Baal glanced back, and saw guards boiling out of the front gate. But they were on the other side of the river.

An arrow sailed over Baal's head. Uh-oh! "Get behind a tree!" Baal told the Princess.

But when they were behind the tree, they couldn't run for freedom. Meanwhile the guards were bringing up a boat from somewhere. They would soon cross the river.

Baal cudgeled her brain for an idea. All she came up with was one that required a considerable act of faith.

There was no time to think of anything better, because inaction would have much the same effect as wrong action. So Baal stepped out from her cover and called to the guards. "If you fire any more arrows at us, you risk hitting the Princess, and then your master will be very angry, because he doesn't want to marry damaged goods." Would the guards buy it?

"Come on," she told the Princess. "We have to get past the dragon's line before the guards cross the river." Because once the guards crossed, they could grab the Princess without hurting her, and drag her back to her fate worse than death.

They ran again, in plain sight and range of the archers. But no arrows fell around them. The ploy was working!

As they came near to the dragon's path, Baal veered back to the river. They could dive under the water and cross the line the way she had before, with the water drowning out the smell of them.

Then the Princess stopped running. "What's the matter?" Baal asked, pausing.

"The guards—they have seen my body!" the Princess said. "My honor has been sullied! I must die of shame."

Baal sighed inwardly. They had too little time to waste on the discussion of the philosophy of a superficial definition of honor. She had to settle this immediately.

"No! The guards are too far behind to fire their arrows safely. If they're out of arrow range, they're out of honor range. Just keep far enough ahead, and they'll never see enough to sully you."

"Oh." She was buying it. Apparently the game accepted any reasoning that seemed persuasive.

They resumed their run toward the river. But their loss of time hurt. Now the boat had reached the bridge, and guarded their access there. They couldn't use that route.

Meanwhile the dragon was coming along its path, breathing fire.

"Maybe we can cross before it gets here!" Baal said, though she didn't quite believe it. "Run!"

They ran directly for the dragon's path. But the dragon spied them and accelerated. It was going to intercept them!

It was too late to call it off; the dragon had its eye on them, and would follow them back and scorch them anyway. So they just kept on running.

They reached the path just ahead of the dragon. The dragon inhaled, ready to send out its flame. It was way too close to miss.

But the flame didn't come. Baal looked, and saw that the dragon had stopped. It was merely watching them pass.

Then not one but two explanations burst on her mind. Number One: the dragon didn't dare hurt the Princess either, because that would ruin her for the Sorcerer. Number Two: the dragon was programmed to attack only those folk who tried to cross from outside, who were by definition intruders. Those inside were by definition friends. That was the simplest way to do it.

They passed beyond the path. They had made it! Indeed, the score screen appeared, showing Baal Curran with five points. There was a door set in the trunk of one of the larger trees. The castle, river, and dragon became cardboard. She could exit the setting now, with her new status achieved.

She looked at the Princess, who stood with her bare bosom heaving gently. She alone seemed still to be real. If Baal were a true man, she would be interested in doing something with that maiden, before quitting the game. But that was not the case.

"You are free," Baal said. "Go back to your native kingdom, and be happy. I am glad to have rescued you."

"But aren't you going to play with me before you go?" the Princess asked plaintively.

What was this? Was the Princess being offered for the champion's pleasure? Or was it a secondary trap? Baal hardly cared to gamble, and would have felt the same even if she had been a man.

"No, as I told you, I am a woman, merely using a man's body. I came to rescue you, nothing else. So you may do as you please now."

"You are rejecting me?" the Princess asked. "After you have tarnished my honor by seeing and touching me naked, so that I have no choice but to oblige your vile lust, you are throwing me away?"

This was weird! Had the maiden forgotten the significance of Baal's explanation? Or had she never properly understood it? Probably it was simply that she was programmed for a certain reaction at a certain stage, and prior stages became meaningless. "I'm afraid I am," Baal said.

"Oh!" the Princess declared, a tear falling from one eye. "I am undone! Spurned after my honor is gone!" Then she too became cardboard.

Baal stared at the figure, feeling strangely guilty. It was almost as if she had sentenced the Princess to death. How could a game figure have any feelings?

It had to be mischievous programming. But Baal's curiosity was getting more persistent. What *would* have happened, if she had tried to—to do something with the lovely maiden?

She gazed at the cardboard creature, bemused. She had wondered before whether it was truly possible to indulge in sex in the game. Now she seemed to have had the confirmation. Maybe it had been a trap, and if the Hero had indulged, he would have been disqualified. But she didn't think so. The Princess had seemed to be quite ready for it, forgetting the prior reassurances about the player's actual gender. If Baal had really been a man, she surely would have indulged. It seemed that not only was it possible, it was expected.

Baal found herself intrigued. There had been a time, about an hour ago, when she would have been repulsed.

She walked to the door and opened it and stepped through. She was back in the anteroom—only this time it was a different one.

WELCOME, SURVIVOR, the big screen said. YOU MAY NOW PLAY IN ANY OF THE LISTED SETTINGS, WITH OR WITHOUT OTHER PLAYERS DEPENDING ON FACTORS IN FLUX. POINT BALANCE MAY BE POSITIVE OR NEGATIVE. BECAUSE SURVIVOR LEVEL IS INTERACTIVE, SETTINGS MAY BE SAVED ONLY AT PLAYER'S RISK. AN EXITED ROLE IS FAIR GAME FOR ANY OPPOSING PLAYER. POINTS ARE SCORED OR LOST ONLY BY DEATH OF PLAYERS AND BY BONUSES.

Baal considered that. This level was getting serious! She had won her way through the prior level without killing anyone, though she had lost two game characters. When she had lost, she had not lost any points. This time she would have to get into violence. Death was only in the game; still, this was a rougher course. It wouldn't be enough to kill mere game constructs; she would have to kill other players, or be killed by them.

Well, this was after all the Kill-o-byte game. It specialized in killing. It kept murderers in prison entertained, as well as ordinary folk with secret passions. It was *the* way to indulge illicit agendas without breaking the law. If it got too hot for her, all she had to do was exit it and not return.

She looked at the list of settings. One jumped out at her: Princess in Castle. That was the one she had just been through! Only now it was a Survivor set, instead of Journeyman. The rules and action would be more advanced.

One section of the screen listed the players already committed to this setting. There were five. The more the merrier, she knew, but she preferred a relatively quiet game. Just Princess and rescuer, ideally. Since there could be as many as fifty characters, five was at the low end. There was a screen clock, showing that this game would start in another ten minutes, and run for four hours.

Ten minutes? That gave her time to exit and get her booster shot. Then she would be good for the duration.

So should this be the one? Well, she was infernally curious about an aspect of it, and it should be better to start this level with a familiar setting than an unfamiliar one. So she would try it, this time taking the character of the Princess, and see what happened. At worst she would get killed and lose a point.

She touched PRINCESS. Immediately the screen showed a new list: that of the cast of characters. She could choose to be any of them, male or female. Unless someone else had chosen it before her. Even the Evil Sorcerer. She had never encountered him in the Journeyman version of this setting; he had just been a remote background figure. Now she saw that he was an available role, which meant that he would probably be active on his own behalf. Not just an irate voice. He would probably be able to do magic, but there would be some kind of constraint that prevented him from interfering directly with the Hero.

She touched the Princess as a character. To her surprise, she got it; no one else had taken it. Good enough. Now it was hers, unless she failed to make it back in time for the start. Then she would forfeit a point, as if she had been killed at the outset of the game. That was no good!

She saved and exited. She checked her blood and gave herself a shot. She was okay. She reset the helmet and re-entered the game. There were still three minutes to spare.

Oops—she had selected her character, but hadn't defined it. She had to hurry!

Appearance was no problem; she gave the Princess lovely long dark hair and the same figure she had had as a game construct. Also a beautiful low-cut gown to display that figure. She remembered the advice of Miss Piggy: if you've got it, flaunt it. She would have it, for this scene.

But now she had to tackle MENTAL, SITUATION, and PHYSICAL. A crystal decanter appeared on the screen. It was filled with golden fluid. Each listed quality of the character had a crystal goblet. What did this mean?

Then she remembered the explanation in the manual: she had to distribute the fluid to the cups, and the more she put in any one cup, the stronger that quality would be. But by the same token, less would be left for other qualities.

Oh, if only she had left herself more time for this! She had too little time to consider. She would just have to slop it in halfway randomly. But that could be disastrous.

She looked at the choices:

MENTAL: INTELLIGENCE, CREATIVITY, DISCIPLINE
SITUATION: CLASS, LUCK, PERSUASIVENESS
PHYSICAL: STRENGTH, REFLEXES, ENDURANCE

Well, she was a Princess, so she didn't need much in the physical side; her lovely figure would have to serve instead. Her situation was already defined to an extent, but persuasiveness could be useful, and luck. As for the mental qualities—she wanted them all.

So she touched the picture of the decanter. It moved with her finger, as if she were carrying it. She tilted it over the INTELLIGENCE goblet, and the fluid spilled in, filling the goblet about halfway. She moved the decanter to CREATIVITY and poured some more. She gave less to DISCIPLINE, on the assumption that she would be mostly locked up anyway and not need to exercise it. Then she moved to PERSUASIVENESS, and tilted too much, almost filling it.

Only a little remained in the decanter. Her time was running out. She splatted a few drops in each of the remaining goblets. Then, with only thirty seconds remaining on the clock, she ran for the door at the end of the hall. She flung it open and stepped through.

She was in the lofty turret chamber she had seen before. But it was a painted scene, with a cardboard bed and chair, and a picture of a view in the window.

Then it turned real. The game had begun, on schedule.

It should be a while before the Hero fought his way into the castle to rescue her. Meanwhile she could enjoy her new appearance. Baal went to the mirror set in the wall and inhaled. Her full and perfect breasts bulged from her décolletage. She angled her head. Her lustrous tresses fell across her shoulders and caressed her awesome cleavage. She whirled, and the skirt of her gown flung out to show a bit more of her shapely legs. Oh, rapture!

She remembered how the game-figure Princess had acted, when Baal had had the aspect of a man. Endless protestations about sullied honor, then a direct sexual come-on. It was evident that sex was a part of this game. It might be vicarious, but it was bound to be better than any prospect she faced in real life with her real body. So she intended to be reasonably demure at first, but she would not protest unduly when the Hero rescued her. She would find out just what this fine body could do in that regard.

seven

S
O
R
C
E
R
E
R

Walter looked at the list of characters for the Princess setting. There was the Hero, of course, and the Princess. Also a plethora of minor ones: castle guards, serving wenches, laborers, farmers, assistants to the Hero, and frolicking nymphs. Walter wondered why any player should choose any of those minor roles. Surely there were more points to be won in the major roles. If they were all filled, other players might simply move on to another setting, with better roles still open.

He touched HERO. Sure enough, it was taken.

Then he spied the dragon. That was a role? That could be fun! This was evidently a fantasy setting where magical creatures roamed.

In fact now he spied the Evil Sorcerer. Well, obviously there had to be one for a setting like this. No one would want that role, of course.

Walter smiled. He touched it. It should be fun to be the bad guy for once.

Then he considered the character types. Could True Blue assume an evil role? He might, but his uprightness might be a liability. Doodoo was surely the appropriate type. But Walter wasn't satisfied to be that obvious. So he took the intermediate type, Joe Blow. He should be decent, but not perfect. He might lose out as the evil figure for the setting, but perhaps some imagination would bring him through.

Walter considered appearance and character traits. He decided to make Joe Blow as much like himself as he could, as he had with True Blue in the aborted Metropolis setting. Tall, brown-haired, and so on. Then he pondered the nine other qualities. He had intended to spread the fluid evenly between them, before, but now he wasn't sure that was wise. He wanted intelligence, creativity, and discipline, but maybe persuasiveness would be better. So he poured the PERSUASIVENESS cup full, then distributed the rest of the fluid more or less evenly between the others.

Then he reconsidered. He had assumed that his own intelligence and other qualities, of better or worse nature, would translate into the game character, but it was evident that they wouldn't. Was he dooming himself to stupidity, weakness, and lack of gumption? Could he repour some of the fluid?

He touched the PERSUASIVENESS cup, and it lifted and jiggled. Hastily he set it down again, lest he spill some of the precious fluid. The cup was brimming, and he would probably lose some when pouring.

On the other hand, why not try it this way? He needed to know just how much control the character-set qualities exerted. If he turned out to be a moron, he would know better next time. He might as well experiment, since he had so much time to pass. What had gone wrong with the game's Quit option? Was it a glitch that would clear itself in time, or was it a defect in his particular computer system? Maybe he should wash out of this setting early, and try to quit again, and it would be okay. So his severely unbalanced distribution of traits might be best, because it would show him just what counted, and boost him quickly on out of the setting.

He saw the door at the end of the short hall. Only five minutes remained to the start of the setting. He might as well enter it early, and get his bearings.

Then a flicker caught his eye. Another name had just been added—no, there was no name list here, only a number indicating the total number of players participating. It had been six, and now was seven.

Walter paused, considering. Was the roster of the names of

players "outside"—available only to those who had not yet committed to this setting? When he joined this Princess setting the anteroom had not changed, but maybe his status had. So now he could not know the name of the new player, just that there was one. Why was it set up that way?

This also demonstrated that this was not a common chamber. Other players did not appear here. Because the newest entrant must have come and perused the list of settings, and chosen this one, and must even now be choosing his character and the traits of that character—while Walter's anteroom remained empty except for him. Since this was all a construct of the larger game, another window in the screen as it were, that was no problem to understand. But why was it done this way? Could he step out, as it were, and look at the list of names, then step back in? He suspected that he could not; that he would lose his place the moment he left. The game wouldn't like having players step in and out at the last moment. Maybe some players were prone to stepping out if they didn't like the identity of later players. So perhaps they could pause, and exit the larger game at this stage, but would have to return to this particular spot by its starting time, or forfeit.

Now there were three minutes. It was time to go to the door. What would happen if he didn't? Why was a door necessary? Surely the game could change the scene around him when the time came. Probably that's what would happen. The door was just for those who wanted to enter the setting early. Once they did, they would be locked in, unable to change their minds. So if any were unsure, they would remain in the anteroom.

The screen flashed again. HERO ROLE VACATED; OPTION OF TRANSFERRING.

The player for the Hero had stepped out! So it did happen. The total number of players in this setting was now listed as six again. The game was offering the role to another player in the game. It reminded him of the way airlines offered passengers bonuses to be bumped, when they had overbooked. Could Walter himself transfer?

Before he could decide, the screen flashed once more. HERO ROLE FILLED. Another player had beat him to it. Or else a new one had entered, because the number was back up to seven, and now eight. Then nine, and ten, as the time wound down to less than a minute. Why were so many coming in so late? They would know that it was too late for good roles. They would barely have time to get their characters set up. Unless they were experienced players who knew exactly what traits they wanted, and could do it in an instant.

Ten seconds. He started for the door, then stopped. He might as well find out if his conjecture was correct. So he waited—and as the clock reached zero, sure enough, the scene changed.

He was in an elegant chamber with a four-poster bed, wide desk, full-length mirror, and fancy tapestries on the walls. A deep woven rug covered the floor. The Evil Sorcerer evidently coddled himself.

He walked to the mirror and gazed at his figure. He was himself, as described by his choices for Joe Blow, and did not look evil. He wore an ornate robe which enclosed his body from neck to feet, and, yes, a somewhat pointed magician's hat. He was every inch the Evil Sorcerer.

But just exactly what did this character do in the setting? He had better find out soon.

There was a book on the desk. A compilation of spells? He went to pick it up. Indeed, on its ancient crinkled leather was printed ANCIENT EVIL MAGIC. Inside were spells, one to a page, listed like recipes. Indeed, some *were* recipes, for potions of love, hate, strength, youth, knowledge, and the like. Others were merely descriptions: how to see around corners, how to fly, how to hypnotize instantly with a glance, how to hurl fireballs, and how to call down a plague of noxious ailments.

Walter nodded. This was good stuff! But there had to be a catch, or the Evil Sorcerer would automatically win all his encounters. How could he find out what that catch was?

He looked at the mirror again. It occurred to him that this was a fairy-tale setting. There were certain standard devices. Could it be?

He went to it. "Mirror, mirror, on the wall, what's the catch to this all?"

A face formed, replacing Walter's reflection. "O Evil Sorcerer, the catch is that all thy magic has been expended in the takeover and control of this castle. Thou canst not perform any magic without freeing some denizen, who will then immediately seek to do thee ill or free the Princess."

Walter had never had any use for fantasy, but already he found himself liking this mirror. It promised to be a most useful source of information. "Are you also constrained only by my magic? Can I trust you?"

"I am thy magic possession, requiring no constraint; I serve thee loyally throughout and may be trusted."

"How can I be sure of that?"

"If ever I lie to thee, I will crack asunder. But I take pleasure in lying to all others, because I am of course an evil mirror. I delight in showing comely damsels as fat old harridans, and in insulting the servants. So didst thou craft me to be, O my master, in thy foul intellectual image."

Walter decided to take the mirror at its word. "What is my mission in this setting? That is, what do I have to do to win?"

"Thou must marry the Princess thou dost hold captive, at noon. Only then will her power to resist thee be ended, and when she is wed to thee, her powers and those of her kingdom will be joined to thine, and thou will be supreme over all."

"I hold her captive? How did that happen?"

"Thou didst approach this castle in the guise of a wandering noble, and once within its protective ramparts thou didst kill the knight in charge and enchant every person within it except the Princess, whose nobility alone sufficed to resist thee. Now all serve thee, and keep her confined to the highest turret chamber."

"So this is *her* castle!" Walter exclaimed. "Not mine."

"True. Until the nuptial, when it will be thine by conjugal right."

"And what about the Hero?"

"He must infiltrate the castle and bear away the Princess before the noon hour. Then he will win the bonus points."

"Bonus points?"

"At this level points are earned in two ways. Each opposing player thou dost kill counts one point, and costs him one point. If thou dost possess the Princess at high noon, thou dost also gain a bonus of one point for every player in the setting. Since there are ten players this time, this means ten bonus points toward the twenty-five required to achieve Expert level."

"And if the Hero rescues her, then he gets the bonus?"

"Correct. And if the Princess escapes both Hero and Sorcerer, the bonus is hers."

"The Princess can kill players too?"

"Indeed. But she is but a maiden, so prefers not to sully her hands with violence, unless there is no other way."

"And every person any of us kills gives us a point?"

"Not so, my master. Only the players thou dost kill. Game figures count for naught."

"How can I tell a player from a game figure?"

The reflection formed hands and spread them. "There is no easy way, O evil one, apart from the major characters of Hero, Princess, and Sorcerer, who are required to be players. But if a castle denizen thou hast ensorceled tries to betray or kill thee, then surely he is a player who has taken the place of the real denizen."

So he would not know the difference, and would have to be alert against any other person he encountered. "Suppose there had been only three players? Only a three-point bonus?"

"Even so, my master. This is why more players will come if a game already has several. They quest for the larger jackpots."

Walter was intrigued by the anachronistic term "jackpot." Actually it might derive from a pot with a jackrabbit: a good meal for the hungry. So maybe it was after all consistent. "But why do they accept lesser roles? I mean, a castle denizen can't rescue the Princess, can he? So what's the point?"

"It is true that a mere denizen can not achieve much at the outset. But if he kills the intruding Hero after the Hero has taken the Princess, then that denizen becomes her rescuer and is eligible for the bonus. Similarly, if one of the Hero's companions kills the Evil Sorcerer, he can assume the role and recover the Princess for the bonus."

"But that means that both the Hero and Sorcerer are targets!" Walter said. "Other players will try to kill them instead of rescuing the Princess."

"Thou didst ask for the catch," the mirror reminded him.

So he had. So now Walter knew the underlying rules of this setting. He had to fight off the invasion of the Hero and his minions. The advantage of taking a minor role was that the player was less of a target, and might have a better chance of winning the bonus in the later stages of the episode. Evidently there were players who preferred to wait until they could see which games had the most other players; then they would join, taking whatever roles remained, gambling for the larger bonuses. He could see the dynamics of interactivity shaping up. Why play ten games, winning two or three points in each, when the bonuses of two games might provide the same point total?

But points could be lost at this level too. Everyone who died lost a point, and there would be only one real winner. So this was also like a lottery, with the many losing somewhat, while the few won big.

But he couldn't just remain holed up here. He had to get out and defend his position. Otherwise he risked being surprised by a killer player.

"Mirror, you said that all my magic is taken by the need to control the castle personnel," he said.

"Indeed."

"Then how can I use it to forward my cause?"

"That is thy main problem, master. To use thy magic, thou must free one or more denizens, who will then turn against thee, and be forever thine enemy. I may not instruct thee in how to handle this; it is thy challenge to win or lose."

"Forever my enemy? You mean I can't recover control by ending my spot magic?"

"True, O my master. Thy magic, once invoked, remains thine to use or ignore, as thou dost choose, for a period of but fifteen minutes. Thine freed enemies remain to harry thee, until thou dost kill them or they kill thee."

"But suppose I invoke my magic and it turns out not to be as useful as I expect?"

The face smiled grimly. "Tough obscenity, master."

Walter pondered. Invoking magic seemed to be a losing ploy, since it was temporary while the losses it incurred were permanent. This might not be sensible, but it seemed to him that if he had the power of magic, he ought to be able to use it. It was likely to be a safer risk than going physically into the fray. So he would just have to make his quarter hour of power count.

He looked in the spellbook again, turning its pages. Flying— that should be useful. And invisibility. And invulnerability to physical weapons. Oh, there were many goodies here! But each one he invoked would cost him a castle denizen, and that would be mischief. If a denizen happened to be a player, he might come to kill the Sorcerer right away.

But maybe there was a way around that. "Mirror, can I send any denizens away from the castle?"

"Thou canst, master, but when they leave the castle environs, they will no longer be subject to thy enchantment, which holds sway only within."

That was perfect! Except, perhaps, for one detail. "When I take enough magic to do a spell—can I select which person loses control?"

"No, master. That is random. The one freed may be relatively harmless, or may be critical. Thou mayest know him only when he takes action."

So he couldn't send a denizen outside, then turn him loose when he was about to be lost anyway, where he would be relatively harmless. Too bad. He would just have to gamble that he could spot any deviants and eliminate them.

He studied the spells for flying and invisibility. Both were simple. The one for invulnerability was a bit more complicated, but still could be done verbally. All could be put on Pause with a word, and renewed with another word. It was nice magic. Whether it was worth its price was another question, but he was determined to use it this once regardless. In real life he couldn't even walk, let alone fly, and he wanted to have at least this much experience.

Walter reviewed the three, then tucked the book into an inner pocket of his robe and invoked the first. This required a word and a gesture done together. The magic wouldn't work for anyone else, because it was defined for the Sorcerer, so it didn't matter if any denizen saw or overheard the invocation.

"Invulnerable," he intoned, making the requisite hand sweep. He felt something close around him, like a metal vest. A timer appeared on his floating screen, counting down from fifteen minutes. That lent a sense of urgency, but he was determined not to be panicked. He had to use his spells well.

Just to be sure, he walked to a closet and found a broom. He swung the handle of the broom at his own foot. It bounced off without touching the foot, and Walter felt neither discomfort nor rebound. But in real life it was hard to know what his feet were doing anyway, so that wasn't sure. He tried putting his hand against a projecting nail on a beam, and it wouldn't touch. He was protected.

"Invisible," he said, making the appropriate gesture. And saw his reflection in the mirror disappear. He looked down at his body and could not see it. Good enough.

"Flight," he said, making the third gesture. He saw the blank mirror descend, and the ceiling coming down. He had floated up from the floor, possessing no weight.

Quickly he spread his arms and made swimming motions through the air. He moved rapidly in the direction he wanted to. Air swimming was much faster than water swimming. In fact it was flying; it surely would not have worked like this if he had merely been weightless.

He flew to the casement window and opened it. This chamber turned out to be about halfway up the castle, or perhaps fifty feet. It overlooked the shorter trees nearby, and offered a good view of the moat and adjoining river. Was he sure he wanted to trust his magic enough to step into the air? If it decided not to work outside the castle . . .

"Hey, mirror!" he called. "How far out do the spells work?"

"As far as the setting extends, master," the mirror replied.

Well, either he trusted this or he didn't. Walter stepped onto the sill, then did a dive out.

It was glorious. He sailed over the small trees and around the castle. He flew out to the track the dragon had worn, that circled the castle and crossed over two bridges. There was the dragon, pounding along, watching for enemies, fire and smoke streaming from its nostrils. Pity the creature who got in front of that!

And the enemies were there. A group of men were busily chopping down small trees and limbing them. A framework was forming. Was it a huge shield? No, it looked more like a catapult. Were they going to bombard the castle? That didn't seem to make sense, because the Princess was still in it. Suppose they lofted a stone and it crashed through the Princess' high turret, killing her? Where was the bonus then?

But as he studied it, he saw that the emerging structure wasn't even aimed at the castle. It was aimed to intersect a turn of the dragon's path. It was the dragon they were going after!

But after they eliminated the dragon, they still had to win their way into the castle. The denizens would fight, because they were under the control of the Evil Sorcerer. All but three of them. Something more was required.

Then Walter saw three nymphs bathing in the river. They were shapely bare girls, laughing and splashing each other. But one of them wasn't staying with the others. She was swimming downriver toward the castle, evidently having passed under the dragon's bridge without getting torched. She had to be a player, and therefore an enemy. Maybe she planned to sneak into the castle, and open a door for the others. This could be a well-coordinated campaign.

However, there was no need to let it happen. Walter landed and brought out his magic text. And paused, disgruntled. He couldn't see it!

So he walked to some shrubbery where he could hide. Then he nulled the invisibility spell. The book came into view along with his body. He flipped to the page covering fireballs. He rehearsed the spell silently until he was sure he could do it. Then he walked to the catapult.

"Hey!" someone yelled. "Who's that?"

Oops—he had forgotten to restore his invisibility! He did that, and ran a distance so that the others couldn't close on him. Then he addressed the catapult. "Fire," he said, making the gesture.

A fireball appeared, the size of a basketball. It sailed at the catapult and splatted into the wood. It exploded, setting the wood afire. Never mind that it was freshly cut green wood; this was magic.

Appalled, the Hero and his cohorts stared at the fire. "Get water!" the Hero cried. "From the river!"

"With what?" another asked.

That baffled them; they had no buckets.

"The Evil Sorcerer!" the Hero exclaimed. "This is his doing."

That was Walter's cue. He nulled his invisibility spell. "Ho, ho, ho!" he laughed, and took off. "You oafs will never win the Princess!"

One of the men brought out his bow. Walter quickly reinvoked his invisibility spell and veered to the side. His invulnerability should protect him, but he wasn't inclined to test it. This incident had been fun, but there was no point in pushing his luck too far. He had not poured himself much luck, after all.

He returned to his chamber and landed before the mirror. He nulled all his flying and invisibility spells. His screen showed that only five minutes had passed. It had seemed longer, because of the excitement of the experience. "Mirror, what's the situation?"

"Three denizens were released. Two went to the Princess' chamber. The third came here to assassinate thee."

"Oh? Where is he now?"

"Right here," a man said behind him. "Die, miscreant!"

Walter whirled, ready to defend himself. The man was coming

at him with a sword, swinging it at Walter's head. There was barely time to duck. But when he did duck, the man swung again, backhanded, and this stroke was impossible to avoid. Walter gave himself up for lost.

The sword struck his shoulder, and bounced off. Walter didn't even feel it. Then he realized that he still had the invulnerability spell. He had forgotten about it, since it didn't interfere with his standing on the floor or his dialogue with the mirror.

"Accursed sorcery!" the man cried, amazed and frightened.

"That's right, miscreant," Walter said. "I am invulnerable. You can not hurt me."

The man threw down his sword and dropped to his knees. "Spare me, O great leader, and I will never betray thee again!"

Brother! But at least it was a solution to the immediate problem.

"Return to your duties," Walter said, and the man dutifully departed. There was no point in punishing him, after all; he was just playing the game.

Walter turned to the mirror. "How did I handle that?"

"Not well, master. Thou shouldst have killed him, since he became thy enemy when he came to kill you, and remains so. Thou couldst have won a point."

The thing was right. He was making mistakes, and those were bound to catch up with him before long. This was no chivalrous exercise, it was an every-man-for-himself melee. The man had tricked him into giving up his advantage. Because in a few minutes Walter's magic would be gone, and then he would be vulnerable.

So what he needed to do was get smart. The key was the Princess; he didn't know who most of the other players were, but she was sure to be one, and he needed to maintain possession of her in order to win the bonus. So what could he do that would ensure that, before the Hero or one of his minions infiltrated the castle and got to her?

He glanced at his screen. He still had seven minutes. Whatever he did would have to be done quickly. The two other denizens were probably trying to break down the Princess' door right now.

Break it down? They belonged to this castle. They probably had a key. And they served the Princess. She would probably go with them willingly. He was in worse trouble than he thought.

"Mirror, what is the status of the Princess?"

"Two men are nearing her chamber. They have been delayed by the guard, who serves thee." The face paused, looking surprised. "Correction: the guard killed one and gained a point, but the other killed the guard and is now starting up the final flight of steps."

So he still had time. But why would the Princess go with the Evil Sorcerer, instead of the denizen who served her?

Well, his character was strong on persuasion. Why not use it?

Quickly he checked the door to his chamber. It wasn't locked. He locked it and set the bar in place, so that no one could enter during his absence. He had been a fool not to do that before. Had he returned, stopped his three spells, and tried a new one, the castle denizen could have clobbered him. It was better to have no one else in this suite.

Next he checked the Sorcerer's closet. There was a fair array of costumes hanging on hooks. As he had suspected, the man often enough had occasion to go about in disguise. It was the nature of evil folk.

He selected what he presumed was a traveling minstrel's outfit: black tights with a codpiece, voluminous white blouse, flat cap, and pointed slipper-shoes. There was no musical instrument; probably the Sorcerer conjured one when he needed it. It didn't matter; Walter had no particular aptitude for music anyway. He just needed to look as unlike the Sorcerer as possible.

He adjusted himself before the mirror. He ran his fingers through his hair, messing it. That helped. He could be mistaken for a Hero's assistant.

Then he thought of something. "Mirror, those spells—is the time continuous, or does the clock stop when I'm not invoking them?"

"It is continuous, master. Thou hadst better get a wiggle on."

Damn! But he could see why the time could not be saved. A smart Evil Sorcerer would invoke his spell of invulnerability only when in danger, and make it last the whole game. He would fly only when there was a barrier he couldn't navigate by foot. And turn invisible only in the presence of enemies. Fifteen minutes of magic would be a decisive advantage.

He walked to the window. He now had just five minutes left. He reinvoked the other two spells, then flew out again. This time he stayed close to the castle, spiraling up until he reached the window of the Princess' chamber. It was open; indeed, she was standing at it, pensively gazing out. She was absolutely lovely, with long dark hair, an excellent figure, and a dress which showed off that figure to extreme advantage.

"Princess, hear me," he said.

"Eeeek!" she screamed, stepping back in affright.

He entered and landed on the floor before her. He nulled the flying and invisibility spells. "Princess, fear not," he said. "I am a man who means you only well."

"You used magic!" she exclaimed.

He smiled. "How else could I get here? By fighting my way through all the castle minions?"

"But Heroes don't use magic," she protested.

"But Heroes can borrow spells," he said. "Come with me, O beautiful creature, before we are discovered. I know a place where they will never think to seek us."

She looked at him, considering. She might have objected, but he was overflowing with persuasiveness, and she had to yield to it. "Very well, stranger; I must trust you. But first tell me your name."

"In life I am Walter Toland."

"And I am Baal Curran."

"Baal!" he exclaimed. "I thought you were a man!"

"You saw my name on the register for the setting? No, I'm female, though I have played a male part in the game."

"And I have played a female part. But I like my own gender better."

"Yes. Well, Walter my Hero, let's get on with it."

"I must carry you. If I can bear you out the window, I'll be able to fly with you."

He approached Baal, and she acceded gracefully to being picked up. His arms held her legs and upper torso, while she put an arm around his neck. When he glanced down he found himself gazing right into her deep décolletage. That almost made him reel. What a beauty she was!

"When you get an eyeful, wink," she said.

"Oh, I couldn't bear to shut out a sight like that, for even that long," he said gallantly. He knew that it was all crafted by the game, but the unexpected glimpse had sent a thrill through him of a nature he had not felt in recent years. But he had no time to waste. He invoked the flying spell.

It was no trouble. She became as light as he, and he hovered in the air of the chamber. Then he invoked the invisibility, and they both disappeared. It seemed that the spells applied to anything he was in close contact with.

There was a sound beyond the door to her chamber. The denizen had arrived, and was unlocking the door! Walter knew he should kill the man, but his screen showed only ninety seconds remaining. He had to get her out of here now.

He flew with her to the window—and something bumped. "Ouch!" Baal exclaimed in his ear. "My foot hit the sill."

"My deepest apology," Walter said, trying to hide his urgency. If the magic ran out while they were in the air, they would both perish. He nulled the invisibility so he could see her limbs and get her safely out the window. But that brought back the royal distraction of her body. The skirt of her gown was riding up, so that her smooth round legs showed above the knees, and her décolletage was buckling, so that her globular breasts now showed at three-quarter rondure. What a sight!

"Actually it didn't hurt," she confessed. "It just sort of bounced off harmlessly. I expected it to hurt, so I reacted. I apologize."

"I have a spell of invulnerability," he explained. "It affects you too, while you are in close contact with me."

The denizen burst into the chamber. He spied Walter and quickly nocked an arrow. It flew—and bounced off harmlessly.

"So I see," she murmured appreciatively.

But he had a job to do. In just over one minute. He navigated her through the casement, actually closing his eyes when her bare legs spread to get past the obstruction one at a time, so that he wouldn't lose all thought of what he was doing. She might be a game construct, but she looked and felt like the finest woman since Lori. He could fall right out of the sky if he let himself be dazzled by her body now.

The denizen cursed and fired another arrow, with no better effect. Walter took a certain peripheral delight in the man's frustration. So did Baal; she tittered.

They got through, and he reinvoked the invisibility and straightened up and flew right. He spiraled down around the castle, while she oohed and aahed at the experience. Her arm tightened around his neck. Then he felt something at his face. It was her invisible face. In a moment her mouth found his, and she kissed him.

This time he did lose control. He dropped like a stone. Baal screamed in his ear. That jolted him back to business, and he got his spell in order and stopped their fall. The screen showed ten seconds left. He headed for his window, but there wasn't quite time enough. The clock reached zero just before he reached the sill.

But they didn't fall. Instead, the clock reset itself for twenty-five seconds. His flight continued. They reached the casement, and he managed to get them inside without banging anything.

He set her on the floor, closed and fastened the window, and then felt his flying lightness end. The two of them also popped into sight. But what had happened to extend his time?

Then he realized that he had not invoked the three spells together. He had used invulnerability first, then the other two. There might have been twenty or thirty seconds between those invocations. The clock had started with the first. Only when it had expired had it reset itself to show the remaining time for the next spell.

He had been lucky, again. But luck could go two ways, and he wanted no more of it.

Now it was just the two of them, in his nice suite.

"Where are we?" Baal asked, looking around as she straightened out her robe. He was sorry about that; now that he could afford to look at her body without crashing into a window or falling out of the sky, the view was gone.

"This is the Evil Sorcerer's suite," he said. "They may look everywhere else, but they'll never look here."

"Oh, how very clever!" she said. "But suppose the Sorcerer returns?"

Dangerous question! Walter doubted that any amount of magical persuasive power would persuade the Princess that her best interest lay with the Evil Sorcerer. But he didn't have to tell the truth about that, because he had selected a character type of imperfect integrity. For Joe Blow, the end of being with a beautiful woman justified the means of a small deception. Now was the time for his most persuasive lie.

"I hope I have arranged a distraction for him that will keep him occupied for the rest of the setting," he said. "If he doesn't check your turret chamber and find you missing, he may remain distracted."

"A distraction?"

"I arranged to have him encounter a most attractive woman." That much was true.

"Oh, he won't be distracted by that," Baal said. "His mission is to marry me at high noon, and gain all my power."

"But that's a matter of politics and expediency. His romantic inclination may be elsewhere."

"You are very persuasive," she said. "But I'm not sure this makes sense. The setting is for only four hours, while his real romance will be in the real world."

"Not if he seeks romance within the setting, because he lacks any such interest in the real world."

"Yes, folk do that," she agreed. "I understand some men get no farther than the nymphs in the river."

"I saw them. I can see the temptation. But I had to rescue you."

Baal shot an oblique glance at him. "So you passed up the nymphs? Perhaps you will find some way to console yourself after that disappointment."

Was there a suggestion there? The Princess seemed smarter and more aware than he had expected. "Speaking for myself, I find your presence to be all I desire. You are the very model of my ideal woman."

She blushed. "You know I'm not this way in real life. I chose to be pretty, here."

"Of course. But you chose well."

She blushed again. It was surprising how human this game figure seemed. "Are you trying to seduce me, sir?"

Now Walter blushed. "I apologize if I gave that impression. I'm just trying to have possession of you—uh, to win the bonus points—"

She took a breath, as if briefly considering something. "Because if you are, I'm amenable."

He stared at her. "I don't think I understand."

"This is just a setting in the game. Everyone wants to win points. But I'm just here for fun; I don't expect to become a master player. I'm curious about just how—how far it is possible to—you know. That's really why I chose this role. To find out what is possible. When a woman is beautiful and available. If we have to wait three hours anyway."

"But you don't know me!"

"Yes. We're like ships passing in the night. We may never see each other again in the game, and surely never in real life. So it doesn't matter who we are. We're just Princess and Hero."

Walter was wickedly intrigued. He had never expected the Princess to broach such a thing. But her body, faked up as it might be, fascinated him. Just how far *could* game characters go?

Still, he was not at ease. "I think there are things I should tell you first."

"Oh, don't spoil it by telling," Baal said.

"I have to. I have a character who can lie, to a degree, and I have misled you. I am not the Hero."

She stared at him, her mouth forming a sweet O of surprise. "That magic! You mean you're—?"

"I am the Evil Sorcerer. I'd love to possess you, in the other sense, but I fear that would be cheating if I do it before noon."

"The Evil—you're joking!"

"I'll prove it." He faced the mirror. "Mirror, tell her the truth."

The face formed. "He is the Evil Sorcerer, cutie. A fool, to be sure, but nevertheless the Sorcerer."

Baal laughed. "You know, you had me fooled, Walter! What a ploy! I should never have come with you. How will the Hero ever find me?"

"I hope he won't. That's the idea in the game."

"But why did you tell me? I was ready to—"

"That's *why* I had to tell you. My character may be dishonest, but I'm not. I just didn't want to use that particular deception to get close to you. Romantically, I mean. Because that's something beyond the rules of the game, I suspect. Something, well, real."

She looked around. "The door and window are locked? And you have magic? I'm captive, no matter what I do?"

Walter sighed. "I'm afraid you are. I wouldn't have deceived you, if I'd realized what you had in mind."

"Why not? I mean, why this ethic in real life?"

"I—I've been unlucky in love. It's not something I care to mix in with deception. Even a fake romance, even fake sex, if it's possible—I'd rather not have it under a false pretense. I know this is just a game, but, well, maybe I don't exactly know why it bothers me, but it does. I'd far rather have you love me than curse me, but not for a lie."

"You could rape me."

He was appalled. "I would never—"

"It's only in the game. I understand it happens."

"I don't care where it is! That's out." Then, as an afterthought: "But since you can quit at any time, how could there be rape? You could simply vanish from the scene."

The mirror took that as its cue. "That is not the way it works, master. If she quits in the middle of a scene, her body remains here, without volition. Then thou canst rape her when she's unconscious, or kill her, preventing her from coming back to the role. So she loses, either way. Maybe if she stays for the rape, she will get a chance to kill thee, and get even that way. It is all part of the game."

Walter whistled. "This is more of a game than I thought! Maybe there are players who come for this sort of stuff, but it's not for me. Not even vicariously."

Baal nodded, not seeming displeased. "Let's put it this way. Obviously the Evil Sorcerer lured the Princess here to have his evil will of her. It doesn't matter what she feels about it. She's captive. She was a fool to walk into this, but she did, so she pays the penalty. There's not even much point in her screaming or crying, because the chamber must be soundproofed. She could try to fight, but he's got muscle and magic. So she's caught like a fly in a trap. Everyone will know what she's in for."

"They will know wrong. I will leave you alone."

"But I said I was willing."

"Before you knew I wasn't the Hero."

"Yes, but since I'm in for it anyway, I might as well enjoy it." She began to remove her robe.

"You're *not* in for it anyway!" he protested, unable to take his gaze from the exquisite body she was unveiling.

"You aren't seducing me," Baal said carefully, "so I'm seducing you. It's fun being daring and wanton here."

"Princess, I like thee," the mirror remarked.

Walter wrenched his eyes up to her serene face. "Despite the fact that—"

"It's only a game. One fake man is as good as another. Here I have a body to madden men's minds, I want to use it while I can. I wouldn't do this in real life, but this isn't real life. For the purpose of the game, you can tell others that I screamed and fought. Okay?" She stepped out of her bra and panties and stood naked before him. She was glorious.

Walter capitulated, as he had with Lori. "Okay," he agreed

weakly. "As long as you feel that way." He removed his own clothing.

His anatomy was all there, but it didn't react. He looked down. "Damn, I hoped it wouldn't be this way," he muttered.

She came and embraced him. "Maybe this will help."

He felt every part of her torso. He longed to do more. But he couldn't. The impotence of his real body carried through to his game body.

"You have to do your part, you know," she reminded him.

"I want to. Oh, how I want to! But it seems I am unable." He saw the face forming on the mirror. "Don't say a word, glassface! I know I'm an impotent sorcerer."

"Just how unlucky in love have you been?" Baal asked.

"It's a long story. I don't want to bore you."

She considered. "Suppose I bore you with my story first, then you bore me with yours? Then we'll know each other better, and maybe it will change."

"Okay," he said, relieved.

"We'll lie on the bed together and do it," she said.

"I will like that."

They lay on the capacious bed, and she began to talk.

eight

ONSET

Baal was ten when it went wrong. She had been a reasonably good fifth-grade student with the usual complications: teachers who didn't understand creative spelling, parents who didn't understand the importance of slumber parties, and friends whose folks let them get away with twice as much as Baal ever could.

Then her best friend got into trouble, experimenting with a drug that made her feel good though her grades were bad. Baal in her naivete told her parents, who told the school principal, and Steps were Taken, and suddenly Baal's best friend was her worst enemy, who wouldn't have spoken to her even if further association wasn't forbidden. And Baal was frozen out: she had Told, and was therefore ostracized. If only she had known!

She felt terrible. Her schoolwork suffered, and then her grades. Gradually, seeing her humiliated, her classmates relented; other things were happening, and the group attention span was limited. But somehow she didn't feel better. She had to urinate frequently, which was odd because she had never had that problem before. Then she got thirsty. Terribly thirsty. She kept returning to the water fountain to drink and drink, until she was awash. Then she had to use the bathroom again. She thought she would die of thirst, fifteen minutes after gulping down all the water she could hold. But no matter how much she drank, her mouth felt dry. She lacked the energy she had once had, and she felt slightly nauseous for no reason. This time she had the sense not to tell anyone, and she tried to act as if nothing were wrong. She dragged her way through, making up excuses for her declining performance.

Her skin got dry in places, and chafed, especially in the bathing-suit region. She got a terrible itch, making her fidgety uncomfortable. She was afraid to scratch it in the classroom, because of where it was, but when she was alone she just about rubbed herself raw. What could she do? Pain was better than the intolerable itch.

She was losing weight. She had been a bit overweight, so this didn't bother her. She wasn't dieting or anything, just shedding pounds. Oddly, this didn't make her feel lighter; she was just as tired as she had been with the extra weight. Maybe it was only some kind of flu, and she would throw it off. Why look a gift horse in the mouth? Thinner kids were more popular.

She made a valiant effort and managed to haul her grades up just enough to get through the critical tests. But her malady was worse than before. Her vision blurred. She had glasses that helped her read, but the blurriness remained despite them.

Something else happened that seemed irrelevant at the time. Her mother complained that she must be dumping something in the toilet, because it was so hard to clean. All Baal had put in it was urine. Lots of it.

There was a kind of sequel at school. "Hey, did you spill fingernail polish remover on yourself?" a girl asked.

"I don't use nail polish remover," Baal replied.

"Yes you do," the girl insisted. "I smell it on you. On your breath, even. Maybe you swallowed the bottle!" She laughed.

Baal laughed with her, letting it be a joke. But it was another mystery. Later she asked a friend: "Does my breath smell like nail polish remover?"

"It sure does! What have you been eating?"

After that, Baal was careful not to breathe in anyone's face. Even so, there were some remarks about a fruity odor. She wished she could just stop breathing when others were near.

Then her nausea intensified, and she started vomiting—and couldn't stop. Her stomach retched up everything and more, and kept on heaving. Through the night it continued, with her unslaked thirst demanding water, and her stomach casting that water out soon after she drank it. When she sat up to drink more, she became so dizzy that sometimes she fell back on the bed, feeling as if she were sinking into an impossibly deep abyss. She had a vision of a black wall that stretched into infinity, marking the void, and she was heading into it.

Her folks at first thought she was reacting to something she ate, and that her illness would pass once her system was clear of the bad food. But as the night passed with no relief they became alarmed. Finally they hauled her up—she was now too weak to stand on her own—and walked her to the car.

Things faded in and out. She noted with surprise that she could not walk straight, as if she were a drunk in a movie, being tested by police. She would have laughed, if it had been funny. Finally her father simply picked her up and carried her.

Then she was aware of the car moving. That was all; it was like a brief dream scene, with no connection to anything else. Where were they going?

She came to again when someone was sticking a needle into her arm and doing something to it. The sudden pain had wakened her. She tried to pull her arm away, but they were holding it tight. And someone else was holding her legs and pushing something into her body. That hurt too. She remembered the health-class discussion on sexual abuse, and realized that this must be rape. It was right in the forbidden region. She tried to protest, but then she was unconscious again.

She didn't dream, exactly. It was more like being in a deep sleep, with no bright lights or ethereal music or any of the other effects the movies advertised. It was just darkness, and every so often some far voices, which later turned out to be her family members holding a death watch while she was in the coma. Later she would try to laugh about it: "I thought a coma was a period with a tail, used to punctuate a sentence. I guess I got punctuated, or at least punctured." But it never was a laughing matter. She had always hated getting stuck with needles.

When she came back to life, hours or days after being put in the hospital, her first impression was of a TV blaring the international news. She didn't care about the news, and wished she could turn it off or change the channel to a cartoon program, but she couldn't reach it. She was in a little cubicle, and there were tubes galore poking into her body, and beeping and humming of all kinds of electronic boxes all around. She just lay there, trying to make sense of it all. Her last clear memory was of vomiting in the night at home, and feeling awful. Now she still felt pretty bad, and the tubes didn't help. Was she the captive of alien monsters, who were pinning her to a board like a butterfly so they could do any dreadful thing they wanted to her?

Then a nurse came in to test a sample of her collected urine. It turned out that her faint rape memory hadn't been exactly that; they had run what they called a catheter into her bladder so as to be able to monitor her fluid output while they got her rehydrated. It seemed that was important. Now she peed through a tube. It was weird, but it saved her having to get up to do it.

"Oh, you're conscious!" the nurse said, as if she had just discovered something unusual. "I'll tell the doctor."

In retrospect, Baal wished the nurse hadn't told the doctor, because that was the beginning of the real horror. The hospital had batteries of vampires in medical frocks, and every one of them came to stick in another needle. Baal began to long for the abyss.

In between stickings she was told scattered bits of what was going on. It seemed that at one point they had feared a cardiac arrest, and gotten ready more torture machines to use just in case her heart stopped. At another point her blood pressure had dropped very low, and it seemed that this was another bad sign. Baal wondered whether this was at the time when she had felt herself sinking down deep. "You could have died," her mother said, horrified. Someone else said that if they had waited a few more hours before bringing her in for help, she could have died regardless. Another said that she had a raging yeast infection, which had been fed by the sugar in her urine. That was what had made that intolerable itching down there. They were cleaning that up with medication and topical treatment. That was the silver lining in this cloud: despite the tube in her, the itch was mostly gone.

But what was wrong with her? As soon as she started to feel as if just maybe there was something to be said for living, the doctor told her—and then she realized that she had allowed herself to hope too soon. For what she had was what they called Type I Diabetes, otherwise known as Juvenile Onset, or Insulin

Dependent, Diabetes. In simple language, high blood sugar. It was because her pancreas had lost all of its ability to make insulin, which her body needed to get the blood sugar into her cells. She hadn't even felt any symptoms until the insulin-producing cells, called the islets of Langerhans, were ninety percent gone, and then it was too late. What she had just suffered was a diabetic coma, or full-blown ketoacidosis, complicated by severe dehydration. To prevent this from happening again, she would have to take several shots of insulin a day, every day of her life.

Baal screamed. She jammed her eyes tight shut and kicked her feet. They tried to reason with her, but she put her hands over her ears and just kept screaming until they went away. No way was she going to accept the notion of getting stuck every day!

But they would not relent. The Doctor came to talk with her, and the Nurse-Educator, and the Psychologist, and even the Dietitian. They all had their says. It was confusing to get so much information all at once; her poor head was spinning. But gradually, finally, she came to adjust to the terrible fact of it. Not only would she have to get stuck, she would have to do it to herself. She would have to prick her own fingers to draw blood, and jam what seemed like long needles into her tender flesh at least twice a day. And she would have to go on a diet that prescribed not only what foods she ate, and how much, but when she ate them. No longer could she have seconds, or skip a meal. She had to be in lockstep with her schedule. Or else.

Or else what? she demanded defiantly.

Or else her health would suffer, and she might even die.

She fought it, in her fashion. It just wasn't fair. What had she ever done to deserve this burden? To be inflicted with a severe lifelong disease?

She blamed her parents, because it was genetic: it was their faulty genes that caused this to happen. She thought they would object, but the funny thing was that they accepted the blame; their guilt was manifest. That, oddly, made her feel guilty too, because she remembered how the doctor had explained that no one was responsible for his genes; he inherited them. How could they have known of the bomb lurking in their genes?

Anyway, there was supposed to be some kind of virus involved, that set it up, so that later a person got diabetes who otherwise wouldn't. Sometimes there were identical twins, and one got it and the other didn't. It was complicated, but meant that it wasn't right to blame her parents. Yet she did. She knew it was unreasonable, but she couldn't help it.

She felt guilty herself, for not catching on sooner that something was drastically wrong. If she had said something, made her folks take her in to the doctor as soon as it started—

She felt hopelessness. There was just so much inconvenience in the required new living pattern. She was boxed in, unable to leave it behind even for an hour. It was like an albatross hung around her neck. And the terrible long-range threats of it: renal failure, which meant maybe losing her kidneys, which meant not being able to pee at all, and having to have a machine clean her blood instead, because that was what kidneys did: clean the blood. Loss of digits or limbs—like getting gangrene in a foot and losing toes. She would have to watch her feet carefully, because she couldn't feel as well when things were wrong with them. Any little thing going wrong, like a wart or chafed skin, could lead to infection, which could lead to worse. And strokes or heart attacks. And blindness. That was the one that really scared her. What would she do if she couldn't see? How could she watch TV?

But these were all more distant than the matter of getting stuck. Pricking her fingers four times a day, forever? Just to find out how bad her blood was? Her poor fingers were going to be scarred for life! How could she stand it? And the awful needles for insulin injections—she kept coming back to that, almost savoring its horror. Surely this was a torture of hell: to have to stick yourself, again and again.

Her return to school was another shock. Her best friend refused to come near her, for fear of catching "it." The girl turned to her new best friend, and giggled, pointing at Baal. Baal was crushed. The teacher interceded at that point, and explained that diabetes wasn't contagious. And no, it wasn't possible to get AIDS from this needle. But the friendship never quite recovered. Baal had been rendered Different.

No, it just couldn't be! God wouldn't do this to her. Surely she could make some bargain, do something special, so that she wouldn't have to endure this punishment.

But God did not relent. This was her cross to bear. So finally, reluctantly, she came to accept it. She knew that her life had been changed forever. Never again would she be the carefree girl she had been. Discipline would be her watchword from now on.

This chain of reactions occurred over the course of time. By the time it was complete, she was out of the hospital, back home, and on her diet. But her misadventure was not over. She discovered that it was expensive to be diabetic. The monitor was costly, and the ongoing charges for test strips, syringes, and insulin were a burden on the family. They had been planning on a summer vacation; that was canceled, because they needed the money for the treatment. No one blamed Baal for that, but she felt guilty, knowing what the others were sacrificing.

There was one more shock. Once her body started adapting to having insulin by the needle instead of from the pancreas, which was the organ that normally made it, it used it pretty well. Sometimes too well. The pancreas produced only just the right amount of insulin to do the job, never too much, but the needle lacked that judgment. When she exercised too vigorously it brought her blood sugar level down, and then the insulin brought it down further. She became weak and shaky, but also sweaty. Her vision blurred, but not the same way as before. Her stomach felt fluttery, yet she was suddenly hungry too. She was getting sleepy, though it wasn't bedtime, and she felt confused. Despite her sleepiness, her heart was beating rapidly.

She looked around, realizing that something was wrong. She burst out laughing, which was odd, because she saw nothing funny. In fact, in a moment she feared she would be crying.

"Baal!" her mother said, alarmed. "You're pale as a ghost! Check your blood!"

She got her equipment, stuck her finger and checked her blood, and discovered that her sugar was way down, too low. Lower than she had ever seen it before. She was going into insulin shock—the opposite of ketoacidosis. But she knew what to do. She quickly drank some sickly sweetened orange juice and sat down, trying to steady herself. She made a mental note: she preferred candy to this stuff, and henceforth would use that instead.

In just a few minutes she started to feel better. Her symptoms faded. The sugar in the juice was going right to her blood, bringing up its level, and her blood was getting it to her cells. She had gotten by her first Insulin Reaction. It had been scary. A normal person was in blood sugar balance, while the diabetic wasn't, because the shots couldn't match the responsiveness of the pancreas. So the diabetic person could act irrationally, doing things he knew didn't make sense. Just as she had been doing.

After that she watched it, when exercising. She always made sure she had some food on her, just in case. Now she knew that if too much sugar was dangerous, so was too little; either one could wipe her out. She had it under control, but it reminded her strongly of her situation. Her hopelessness. It was, she thought, like nuclear war. She had felt horribly insecure when she first realized that all her world could be wiped out in an instant by a bad war that someone else started. Now that insecurity had come again, closer. Now she knew she could sicken and die. Diabetes wasn't a distant, emotionally neutral word to her. It was the end of her spontaneity. She couldn't just dash off with a friend to do something fun. Not if it was time for a meal. She had to stay home and eat, or else. Her rigid schedule felt like a straitjacket. She thought she had adjusted to it all, but she kept returning to the awful futility of it. Did she really want to live this way?

She learned how to do what she had to for herself. The finger sticking wasn't too bad, once she got the hang of it. She had a spring-loaded device. All she had to do was put the side of her forefinger against it and touch the button, and it popped the stylet, which was really a tiny knife, into her finger and cut it just the right amount. When a drop of blood welled out, she put it on the end of a blood glucose strip, waited a minute for it to react, then put the strip into the optical monitor. If it gave her a readout between 60 and 180, which stood for mg/dl or milligrams of glucose per deciliter, she was okay. If it was outside that range, she wasn't. She had to do this four times a day, just before breakfast, lunch, supper, and bedtime, and record the values on a record sheet. It was almost never under 40, but often over 180. That wasn't too bad, if it wasn't too far over. But it was a pain of another sort, keeping those records.

In fact it was such a bother that after a while she stopped doing it. She didn't tell her folks, of course. She just made up reasonably good figures and put them down, and told her folks that the figures were good. That much was true: the figures *were* good—because she made sure they were. Later the psychologist would explain that a chronic (that was to say, unending) disease like this tended to distort a person's behavior, so that someone who would ordinarily have been in control acted irrationally.

Another word for it was Denial. She didn't want to admit that anything was wrong with her, and since a spot blood test would show that she had high blood sugar, she just didn't make that test. That way she could pretend that she was perfectly healthy.

The diet she was able to live with, because her family had to get on it too. The doctor had impressed on them that this had to be a family matter. So they all ate healthful foods, and Baal was privately gratified to see that her father didn't like some of it any better than she did. Of course they probably cheated when she wasn't around. But that was all right, because she was cheating too.

Actually, she cheated in both directions. The diet wasn't fixed merely in type and amount, it was fixed in time: she had to eat the same amount at exactly the same time each day, because otherwise it wouldn't be coordinated with her insulin. She might have a lot of insulin and not a lot of blood sugar, which could lead to shock, or it could be the other way around, which could lead to coma. But she wasn't always hungry when it was time to eat, and sometimes she was starvingly hungry when it wasn't time to eat. That required the kind of discipline she had never practiced before, and she hated it. Again she felt the loss of the spontaneity of her existence. That was something she had never realized she had, and now, too late, she understood how much she valued it. She was a child who could no longer afford to be childish.

In addition, there were special temptations that were just plain off her diet, and that really rankled. The thing was, she could give up many things, but at age ten she had not yet come close to filling her lifetime quota of candy. Candy was full of free sugar, and free didn't mean free, it meant that that sugar jumped straight into her bloodstream and wreaked havoc, or whatever it did. But she just couldn't resist. Candy was just soo good. She couldn't stand to limit it to the few times she was threatened with low blood sugar shock. Temptation was always at hand, because she carried the candy with her, in the form of her emergency "shock troops." So she ate it on the sneak, and didn't say anything about that either. She knew she could stop some of the temptation by carrying some kind of candy she didn't like, such as black licorice, but she couldn't even bring herself to do that.

The funny thing was that it didn't seem to make much difference. She was able to function as long as she took her insulin shots. What she didn't choose to understand was that she was taking bad risks, and perhaps doing harm that wouldn't show up until later. Her blood sugar level was probably running way high, maybe several hundred, instead of down around one hundred where it belonged. Well, maybe she did understand in a way, because she felt ashamed—but still she couldn't stop cheating. Her shame made her value herself less, and it showed in the increasing sloppiness of her dress and manner, but really, what was the point in caring? Her life had not been all that great before, and her malady had ruined whatever chance it might have had to get better.

Her guilt about cheating did not ease. It found new ways to torment her. She pictured herself, after thirty years, telling her mother that she had lied on all her blood tests. Then her mother would cry and sink down in a swoon and die of grief. Baal knew this wasn't a realistic scenario, but it always brought tears to her eyes. And changed nothing.

There was something else that really griped her, when she caught on to it. She had liked to play computer games, the kind that required quick reflexes and precise judgment to thread through the monster-ridden mazes on the screen. She had improved a lot with practice, and had been making higher scores—until the diabetes. Now she tried to play the same games to distract herself from her misery, but they didn't work as well and her scores were lower. She had her ups and downs, as always, but both were beneath her prior norms. Finally she realized what the problem was: her reaction time was slower than it had been. Even when she was feeling decent, physically, she just wasn't as good as before. The games proved it. Her folks tried to tell her that she was really as good as ever, but she knew it wasn't so.

Then she went to a summer camp for diabetics. It was called Camp Needlepoint, and she dreaded it. Who could stand a place with a name like that? But the Doctor-Nurse-Educator-Psychologist-Dietitian-Lawyer-Indian Chief and who knew what else in the team had convinced her parents that it would be Good For Her, and she was stuck with it, pun and all. Separation from her parents was difficult, because she really needed their support in her illness. They never let her forget her shots, and though she griped about being reminded, she knew she had to take them. Suppose she got really lax, away from them, and spun way out of control, and died? She just didn't feel safe away from home. The psychologist called it Separation Anxiety. What did he know about it? She looked up the term and learned that it usually applied to two-year-old children, which meant that she was being called childish. As if she didn't have reason to be anxious.

But she had to do it, and to her amazement it turned out to be great. Because everyone there was a diabetic, and they all had to prick their fingers and give themselves shots, and some of them were way worse off than she was. Baal had to take two shots a day, while others ranged from one to three or even four. Baal used moderate doses, while some others had to have large ones. They were all different, yet all the same; each kid had his own set of symptoms, his own ways of reacting when he got out of balance, yet each was also very much a member of the diabetic community.

She made friends there. It was easy to do, because of the common bond of diabetes. Nobody had to hide it. In fact they all did their blood tests and shots together. A game could be halted for that purpose without anyone getting impatient. If someone had to stay up a bit late for the next shot, nobody yelled "Turn off that light!" It was so great to be in that ambience of understanding!

There was another thing about these friends. Outside, Baal had never been quite sure whether a friendly person was that way because he or she liked Baal, or because of merely feeling sorry for her. Here at the camp, that was no question at all. They were all in the same boat. That didn't mean that everyone necessarily loved everyone else; there could be rivalries, arguments, and even fights. Boys were boys, often as obnoxious as ever. But diabetes itself was never an issue.

That led to a wonderful discovery. Romance was possible here. She was only eleven, but she liked dances and dressing up, and she saw that the older kids were really getting into it, even holding hands and kissing. It was as if they had to do everything they were going to do in two weeks, because then camp was over and they had to go back to blah home and isolation. So even young ones became quite social. Baal started going with a boy, Barney, who wasn't at all like the popular image of the name. Nevertheless he got teased about being short, fat, silly, and not too bright, and he, tall, thin, and serious, seemed to like it. Baal knew, as they all knew, that there was lots worse teasing than that, outside. She really liked him, and the last day of camp she kissed him, and they promised to get together again at camp next year, and to write to each other meanwhile. But his family

moved to another region, and he was sent the following year to
a camp closer to their new home, and Baal never saw him again.
However, next year she was twelve, and then thirteen, and
though she really wasn't much to look at, as her regular schoolmates had impressed on her, she did just fine at camp, and had
a new temporary boyfriend each year. But after the first year she
didn't make foolish promises, and neither did the boys. Two
weeks really was all there was. Even the oldest kids tried not to
get too serious, because they did not want to marry and have
children who might get diabetes mellitus. It was better to marry
a nondiabetic, with the hope that the children would never have
to use a needle. She learned later that many *did* marry, and had
healthy children. But the risk remained, and Baal herself resolved to marry normal if she possibly could.

There were some who were cheating, too, though it wasn't
easy to do here. However, they were clever; in fact Baal learned
new ways to cheat, that the counselors weren't quite up on. Baal
didn't cheat, at camp, because she would have been ashamed of
getting caught. So she was well controlled, while some others
were not. She saw how those others could get in trouble, not
with the counselors or other campers, but with themselves. One
boy splurged on soft drinks, not the diet kind, and exercised vigorously by playing volleyball. "It balances out," he explained.
"I'm using it up." But something went wrong, and he went into
ketoacidosis. That caught everyone by surprise, because normally the buildup was much slower; there should have been time
for him to be aware of the problem, check his blood, and take a
shot to bring it down. It looked worse from outside than it felt
from inside because it made Baal remember her own experience.
She was surprised that he didn't seem to lose consciousness; that
was when she learned that ketoacidosis did not necessarily mean
unconsciousness. It could be deadly, nevertheless.

They got him to the hospital, and the report came back that he
would make it. The counselors explained that while it was true
that exercise normally brought down the blood sugar, so less insulin was needed, sometimes things got out of control and it had
the opposite effect. So the boy had built up higher levels of sugar, until it was too much. If he hadn't been here at the diabetes
camp, where they were super-quick to recognize the symptoms,
he could have died. As it was, it scared Baal straight, cliché as
that sounded, and she resolved never to cheat on her own diet or

figures again. To that resolve she was reasonably true for six months.

As a result she came to feel emotionally better about herself, as well as feeling physically better, at least while she was at the camp. She was more completely in control than ever, and hoped to remain that way. She felt that she was a better person than she might otherwise have been, because of the discipline required. She was probably also healthier than she would have been without the disease, odd as that seemed, because she knew that the foods which were bad for her were also bad for regular people, but they ate them anyway. The same went for exercise: it benefited regular people too, but few regular people bothered to do it regularly. There was an irony: the regulars weren't regular! The doctor confided that there were doctors who had diabetes too, and that as a group they lived longer than those who didn't have it. She had laughed, thinking it was a joke, but it wasn't. But when she asked another doctor about it, he looked puzzled; he was doubtful that it was true. That was when she realized that doctors could have differences of opinion. That notion had never before occurred to her.

So in its way, the dread needle was her friend. Not only did it allow her to live and function normally, it made her appreciate the pleasure of being well. It really wasn't so bad, getting stuck twice a day, once she got used to it. Sure it hurt, but she knew exactly how much and where, and it was under her own control. It hurt less when she did it rapidly; in fact she got so efficient that she hardly noticed the pain. She even got so that she could block off the pain in the region of her abdomen where she normally gave the shots. It didn't work anywhere else, but there it was as if she were numb, as if someone else were getting the needle. She just filled the syringe the right amount, wiped off the place with a cotton swab dipped in alcohol, pinched up the skin, and almost threw the needle through the flesh. Then down with the plunger, out with the needle, and another swipe with alcohol. She had two main sites for injections: the outer thighs and the bit of fat at her waist. A shot took effect faster in the thigh, so if she needed quick action, that was where. But she used that site only if she had to, because it did still hurt. What had once freaked her out had become routine. She just had to be sure to move the needle a bit farther over each time.

She actually used two kinds of insulin, which she mixed:

twenty units of NPH and five of regular. The NPH stood for Isophane, but that was too complicated to remember, so she thought of it as No Pee Hard, which was as good a description as any. The NPH had an action curve that resembled a slug crawling across a twenty-four-hour chart, with most of the action in the middle. The regular had a curve like a horse dropping, rising right up, rounding off, and dropping steeply back down in the space of six hours or even less. So it was the regular that mostly took care of the sugar rush of breakfast and the similar rush of supper, while the NPH spread out and took care of lunch and snack and carried on through the night. It was a pretty good system. The second shot even gave her some freedom—not much, but some—because if supper was late, she could move her shot late to accommodate it. The kids on three shots had even more freedom that way. So while it wasn't nice getting stuck more often, it did have its compensations.

So she settled in, after getting her early kinks worked out, both the physical and the emotional ones. She read the manual and caught up on all the material that had sort of sifted through her brain and out again, when presented in a big lump. She had been frustrated at first by the deluge of information the hospital folk had dumped on her, as if she were a Dumpster taking in trash, but now it didn't seem that complicated. Her folks thought she had adjusted well, and perhaps she had, but it was to a certain extent a mask. Underneath she was angry at being caught by this albatross. She could handle it—but why should she have to? Life was so much simpler for other people. She also felt sad, very sad; in fact too often she was just plain depressed.

There turned out to be a faint silver lining to the cloud: sometimes it enabled her to get out of unpleasant chores, such as rough phys-ed. She found that her dreams were more interesting than they had been, too. Her dream adventures could get very strange and sometimes even frightening. Usually they were very dramatic, in the manner of a restricted movie, but they tended to have sad endings. Since she sort of liked sad endings, that was okay, provided they didn't get too bad.

She had heard at camp that it was okay, gradually, to stop the regular blood testing. It was one of those things the counselors didn't admit, but was common knowledge among the kids. So she followed that course, on her own, because it made sense. Her four fingerpricks a day became three, then two, then one, and finally she had to do it only when there was a question. She could tell by the feeling of her body how it was doing.

But the increasing freedom allowed her to get into trouble. She tried to keep her glucose levels down low, toward the ideal, and sometimes she played it too close. Once she was trying to study, and she just couldn't concentrate, though there was a big test coming. Her vision kept blurring. So she tried watching TV for a while, and it seemed so real she thought she was in it. But she was also depressed. When there was a sad scene, the tears ran down her face, and she thought it might be nice just to die. Her mother said something to her about snacking on Brussels sprouts, and she said sure, that would be good. Then her mother said, "Baal! Check your blood." Because Baal hated Brussels sprouts, and when her tastes got confused, that was a signal of low blood sugar. So she got up to fetch the stylet, and staggered and almost fell; her strength was much less than she thought.

The blood test showed that she was down to 24. That was way low. No wonder she was having trouble; there wasn't enough glucose in her blood to keep her body going properly. Then she remembered that she had forgotten her snack, so that the insulin was bringing her glucose down too far. For an ordinary kid, missing a snack didn't make any difference, really, but to her it did. She could not afford to forget; that NPH just kept working regardless, around the clock.

There was an ugly scene following that. Her mother, concerned that Baal could have gotten so low without warning, thought there might be something wrong with the insulin or the blood tests. She asked to see the past week's records. Baal, having quit pricking herself, had not bothered to fake up the records, so couldn't produce them. She tried to explain, but her folks would have none of it. "How could you?" her mother asked, shocked and hurt. "This is denial!" her father said angrily.

They dragged the story out of her. Not the whole of it; just for the period she had let her fake records lapse. She had to suffer through a good lecture on how she was *never, ever,* to stop or skip her blood tests without the doctor's written say-so. Anyone who thought she could keep track of her blood levels, either high or low, by the feel of her body was deluding herself; she might think they were in the normal range, but they could be running over 400 or, as had happened, 24. Any kids at camp who were doing it were existing in a state of denial, deluding themselves.

Baal knew it was true. She was mortified. She swore never to skip another blood test. And to that second resolution she was reasonably true. For three months. But she never, ever, forgot again to keep up the fake records; she learned to make them up in advance, just in case.

Even when she was stable and experienced, she could encounter pitfalls. Once she was riding her bicycle, and bounced over a rock, and the front wheel popped loose. She took a spill and bashed her face and arm. She had to have stitches in her cheek. All that was unpleasant enough, but it wasn't the first time she'd managed to bash herself up. It was her father who took the real hit: their insurance refused to pay on the medical bill. The company claimed that it was known that diabetics suffered sieges of low blood sugar that impaired their judgment and coordination, and that this must have been the case. Thus her accident was a complication of her diabetes, and therefore excluded by the policy. Never mind that Baal's blood level had been around 150 at the time; their definition gave them their out.

"If something fell out of an airplane and hurt her on the ground, they'd say it was a complication of diabetes!" her father said, furious. It was plain bad faith on the part of the company, but it would have cost them more to try to sue it than they could have gotten from the claim, and they would have been up against the company's hired-thug lawyers and probably lose anyway. They looked for other insurance, but other companies had similar restrictions. The doctor said that he had not before encountered a case as egregious as this one, and probably another company would be more reputable. Baal felt like telling him he was in a state of denial, but she didn't quite dare.

Baal moved on through school, making generally good grades, and she was active in sports too. Every so often someone would remark that it was almost as if she were a normal person. She concealed the hurt such remarks gave her. She also concealed her pain at being tacitly excluded from the romantic aspect of the social life. Boys just were not much turned on by the notion of dating a girl who stuck needles in herself. There was a diabetic boy in her class, but he never approached her, and she knew why: he didn't want to be teased about going with his own kind any more than she did.

Now she was back to the present. "So now you know what's behind the character," she said. "Certainly no princess! Not any lovely woman, even. Without my illness, I'd be nothing much anyway."

Walter looked at her. "What do you look like, in a general way, in real life?"

She shrugged. "Fair, blond, ruddy-cheeked. I was a bit chubby, until my illness took it off. Just like most diabetics; we're a type. But I'm not beautiful or shapely. You wouldn't care to look at me twice."

"Wait till you hear *my* story," he said. "Then we'll see who wants to look at whom."

That, amazingly, was a very positive response.

nine

INTRUSION

"So that's my story," Walter concluded, lying beside her on the bed. "Yours and mine—I can see similarities in the way we each suddenly lost our regular lives. But I think I'm worse off than you are."

"I think you are," Baal agreed. "No wonder you can't do it. If I'd known, I wouldn't have—"

"You didn't know. And I hoped it was possible. In the game. I've healed a bit; I do get feelings of that type sometimes. Maybe they're just futile dreams. My mind—oh, my mind is eager, but the body just doesn't respond. I'm really sorry I couldn't do it with you." He paused, thinking of something. "Look, it *is* only a game, and there's time left, if you want to find another man—"

"No, I like you," Baal said. "You understand what it's like to be rejected. I think that's more important than the other."

"I appreciate that. Even from a game character."

She ran a hand over him. "I wonder whether it would be possible in real life."

"I doubt it. The nerve is damaged. I hoped that nerves didn't matter here."

"Maybe they don't. This is where imagination counts for more than reality."

"How I wish it did! But the equipment picks up physical reactions, and mine isn't there."

She considered. "I don't know a lot about it, but isn't it possible—I mean, to—to get it started physically?" She was starting to blush.

"You mean if I touched myself in real life, and got a reaction, so I could have one here? This is possible; there is reaction to local physical stimulus. But I'd have to leave the game to do that."

"Gee, why don't you quit here, and do it, and come back. I won't kill you while your character is inactive, I promise, even if it does give me the chance to win the bonus if no one recaptures me. I'm really curious."

Walter shook his head with real regret. They had reached a surprising level of intimacy in a short time, and not just because they were lying naked together. "I trust you, Baal. But I can't do it. I'm locked into the game."

"Locked in?" she asked blankly.

"When I tried to quit, all I got was an error message."

"That's not supposed to happen! A player can always quit. Maybe it was a one-time glitch."

"Maybe," he said, hoping.

"Try it now. Just call up your private screen and try it. Maybe it will work."

"My private screen's hovering off to the side. I found out how to make it stay."

"Oh, you don't have to have it in your way all the time. Didn't you read the manual? You can flick it in and out as you wish."

"No, I thought I'd try the game blind. I must have done something wrong, and messed up a circuit. Now I can't get to the manual. But I can touch the Quit option."

"Do it," she said, as if this were the most thrilling possible thing.

He touched QUIT. The error message showed. "Still there."

"Here, show me."

"Show you?"

"Touch OPTIONS, then REVEAL. Then I'll be able to see your box."

He did so. There were new options, including the one she had named. He touched it.

"Okay now I see your box," she said. "But only you can operate it. Touch QUIT again."

Walter did so. The error message flashed: ERROR. CAN NOT COMPLETE DIRECTIVE.

"Wow, you're right," she said. "You've got a glitch, all right. Must be a defective copy."

"But how do I get out?" he asked plaintively.

"I'm not sure. Maybe you'll have to signal HELP. There're supposed to be game experts on duty to give on-line assistance in case of emergency."

"Okay." Walter touched OPTIONS, then HELP.

ERROR. CAN NOT COMPLETE DIRECTIVE.

Baal stared at it. "There is something definitely wrong here, Walter."

"Now she tells me," he muttered, smiling weakly.

"Maybe my own HELP will work," she said after a moment. She moved one finger cryptically in the air, touching her options. "OPTIONS—HELP—oh, this is just pages from the manual," she said, frustrated. Her eyes moved as she skimmed through the material. "It doesn't seem to address this particular problem."

"Just like a manual," he muttered. "Covers everything except what actually goes wrong."

"I guess this is the first time their Quit has malfunctioned. It says for any other problem, contact the proprietor at 800 KILLOBYTE."

"That's a nine-digit number," he pointed out.

"The last two digits are the Help extension," she explained. "It's really 800 545-5629 extension 83."

"Can you call from here?"

"No. My phone line's taken up by the modem for the game."

"You should be able to buzz them, since you're obviously connected. There are signals constantly going from your phone to their mainframe and on to my phone. A simple alarm signal should light on their big board."

"Let me see. Ah, here it says for emergency assistance hold down the HELP button."

"That would be the word on your screen," he said. "Let me try mine first, just in case." He tried it, but got the same error message. His HELP was inoperative.

Baal tried hers. She waited a moment, then read a message, and looked disgusted. "It says YOUR EQUIPMENT IS IN

PROPER WORKING ORDER. PLEASE RECHECK YOUR HELP OPTION TO ALLEVIATE CONFUSION ABOUT THE RULES OF THE GAME."

"It's not your equipment in question," he said, similarly disgusted.

"The idiots," she agreed. "How do they expect an inoperative system to contact them?"

"Programmers don't actually use the things they program," he said. "I've seen it many times. The most elementary errors go through, and the company—any company—doesn't seem to care."

"I guess you're right. Well, maybe I should quit, and then use my phone to call in a complaint on your behalf."

"But it's not your problem," he protested. "You shouldn't give up your chance in this setting to—"

"I told you, I'm not here to score points. I'm here to flirt with death, and flirt with you too, I guess. Though now that I know your situation, I can see that I don't have much to complain about. You need help, and I'd like to help you."

He smiled. "You are very generous to the Evil Sorcerer."

"I'm generous to a person in need."

"You know, I could get to like you, Baal." It was an understatement, but he tried to pass it off as offhand.

She laughed. "Here we are lying naked on the bed, and you say that!" She looked around. "Maybe we should exchange phone numbers and addresses, if there's something here to write them down." Then she looked startled. "What am I thinking of! We can't take any written notes out of the game."

"We'll just have to memorize. I can remember such things well enough; it comes from my training."

"So can I. It comes from learning how to keep records. Okay, here's my Chicago address and number." She gave them.

"I'm in Atlanta," he said. "Here's mine." He gave his data.

They worked on it, each memorizing the other's information.

"Say!" she exclaimed, excited. "I just remembered something. The manual mentioned a special effects situation, and I wonder whether that could mean—" She hesitated.

"Sex?"

"I'm still a little shy about saying it. Let me check my screen." She poked at the air again. "Yes! There's a Special Effect Invoke option. Maybe that's it."

"About time," the mirror said. "Thou wouldst not let *me* tell thee that, master, thou fool thou."

"But we've already established that I can't—"

"No we haven't, Walter," Baal said. "We were trying it without invoking the sex program. It must be turned off normally, so players don't have sexual sensations at the wrong times. So suppose we—"

Walter looked at the mirror, beginning to hope.

"Go for it, master," the mirror said.

"Show me the way," he said. "I'm doubtful that it can make any difference, but I would be phenomenally grateful if it did."

She told him where to find that option on his screen, and he touched the right option. Suddenly he felt a tingle in his genital region; something had come alive.

Baal did the same. "Oh, that's different," she said. "What about you?"

"There's something," he agreed.

She moved over and embraced him, pressing her body to his in the places where it counted. He felt the pressure. This time he reacted. It was as if she were touching his physical body, and it was responding despite the inability of his own brain to send that directive.

"It's working!" he exclaimed. "The game is doing for me what I can't do in life."

"It's those hot pants," she said. "They can really stimulate you where it counts." She moved against him again. "Oh! I'm getting it too."

"Master, danger comes," the mirror said.

"Tell it to wait," Walter said, luxuriating in the delight of the embrace.

"I hate to say this, Walter," Baal said. "But you know there are players out to kill you. If you get killed, you'll be out of this setting, and I'll have to try to fight off rescue by a rapist."

He sighed. "Okay, mirror: what's the situation?"

"One of the traitors who got released from thy power has informed the Hero of the Princess' whereabouts. He is approaching this chamber with the traitor and a henchman."

"The Hero!" Baal exclaimed. "That's trouble!"

"It sure is," Walter agreed. "He's surely a better fighter than I am, in the game. He'll be tanked up on strength, endurance, and luck. I'd better try magic." He grabbed for the book of spells.

Baal, meanwhile, scrambled back into her outfit. "Get rid of him, Walter, and then we'll resume where we left off."

He hoped so. He leafed through the book. "I don't suppose you are allowed to make a suggestion, mirror," he muttered.

"I thought thou wouldst never ask! Try illusion."

Walter turned the pages, looking for that subject.

"Illusion?" Baal asked "What good is that?"

The mirror was silent. "Talk to her," Walter said.

"If he makes it seem that the two of you are elsewhere," the mirror said, "then you can remain here."

"What do you care where we are?" she demanded.

"Here I can see thy succulent maidenly body in the throes of love."

She colored. "I'll put a drape over you!"

"Easy, Baal," Walter said. "The mirror likes to tease people. I did direct it to talk to you, remember."

"Well, it's got an evil mind!"

"Thank thee," the mirror said.

Walter found the place. "There's a spell that will make it seem that this chamber is empty. But that will last only fifteen minutes, so if we can't direct them elsewhere, they'll catch us when it expires. We need hours, not minutes."

"We need to send them on a wild-goose chase," Baal said. "Can you do that, mirror?"

"Naturally, damsel. However, thou didst mention something about a drape—"

"Okay, no drape!" she snapped. "You'll help?"

"If my master so directs."

"I so direct," Walter said immediately.

"Then have the damsel open the door—"

"What?"

"So that it will seem thou hast fled the chamber with the Princess. Direct me to speak to the intruders. Then invoke the illusion spell."

"I so direct you," Walter said as Baal unlocked the door. Then he invoked the spell.

Nothing happened. "Hey, they're coming," Baal said, peeking out the window in the door. "Is the spell ready?"

"I invoked it," Walter said. "Mirror, what's wrong?"

"Nothing, master. Merely ignore the intrusion."

"But they'll see us!"

"I doubt it, master."

Baal came close to him, nervous. "Are you sure you can trust that mirror?"

"O ye of little faith," the mirror said sadly.

Walter picked up the sword left by the denizen who had attacked him. "I guess I'll have to try the old-fashioned way. You run and hide."

"No, I'll stay and try to help you." She glanced at his body. "Maybe you'd better get dressed, though."

Walter realized that he had been distracted by the problem, and remained naked. He took a step toward his clothing—and the Hero appeared at the door, wrenching it open.

"Hold, Evil Sorcerer!" the Hero declaimed, striding in with sword in hand. He was the very picture of a righteous Hero, unsurprisingly. Two of his men crowded in behind him, also bearing swords. The Hero glanced around. "Where are you?"

Walter felt extremely awkward, standing naked with his sword. But what choice did he have? He hoped the Hero would prove to be as clumsy as Walter was with this weapon. "Here, stupid."

The man continued to look around blankly. "Search the chamber," he told his men. "Maybe he's hiding in the closet."

Baal's mouth dropped open. "They can't see us!" she exclaimed.

"They can't?" Walter asked, hardly believing it.

"Naturally they can't," the mirror said. "Thou didst invoke thy spell of the illusion of emptiness, remember? Go dally with thy damsel on the bed while I dismiss these varlets."

"I guess it's true," Walter said, watching the men pass right by Baal to search the closet and bathroom chamber. "The game has phased us into another state, so we can see and hear each other, but they are oblivious."

"It's magic," she agreed, sitting on the bed.

"Ho, Hero!" the mirror cried. "What be thy business here?"

The Hero whirled, thinking it to be another person. He saw the face in the mirror. "What's this?"

"This be the Evil Sorcerer's magic mirror, of course," the mirror said. "I guard the premises in my master's absence. Surely thou hast better things to do than ransack his premises!"

"Where did he go?" the Hero demanded. "Does he have the Princess with him?"

"My master went where thou canst not follow, miscreant," the mirror said. "Didst thou not note the open door?"

"Don't tell me where I can't follow!" the Hero said.

"He did take the Princess with him, being of a mind to ravish her charms early."

The Hero winced, seeing his game bonus in peril. "Where did they go?"

"There is a secret passage in the cellar leading to the dragon's lair. He means to take her there, and if she marries him not on the spot, he will feed her to the dragon."

"He can't marry her till noon!" the Hero protested.

"He can with her consent," the mirror replied. "Think ye she will give it not, seeing the alternative?"

"A coerced consent isn't binding!"

The figure in the mirror shrugged. "In any event he will ravish her; for that he does not need her consent."

"Her magic should protect her from that."

The face in the mirror winked with evil implication. "Perhaps she be not quite so reluctant as she claims."

"We'd better get to that secret passage!" the Hero cried, striding from the chamber. His minions followed.

"Thou canst not find it!" the mirror called after them. "He will use a spell to mask it!"

"That won't last more than fifteen minutes," the Hero called back.

"He will not even invoke it till thou and thy running dogs get close!"

"So we'll wait!" The Hero was gone.

The mirror grinned. "That will hold them for at least an hour, the fools," it said. "Now canst thou lock thy door again and have at the damsel."

Walter looked at Baal. "Are you interested?"

"Yes! Then I'll go to see what they can do about your glitching system."

"I thought that was what we were going to do on the bed."

She laughed as she locked the door and threw off her gown again. "That too." She joined him on the bed.

He kissed her and embraced her. Her body felt exactly like a real one. He found himself reacting as before. "Oh, Baal, it's wonderful to be able to do this again, even if it's all illusion!"

"It's not illusion, it's surrogate," she said. "It's wonderful to have this type of body to do it with."

"But you know that I don't even have a plain body, really," he reminded her. "In real life I'm paralyzed."

"But here you're not." She kissed him again, and stretched out against him.

"Hey, schnooks!" someone said.

Walter and Baal jumped. Had one of the Hero's minions gotten back into the chamber?

It turned out to be the mirror. But neither the voice nor the image was anything like its prior presentation.

A robot straight out of a cheap science fiction movie stood looking out at them. Red lights flashed where its eyes should be, and it had tractor treads instead of legs.

"What the hell is this?" Walter asked.

The robot vanished, to be replaced by the mirror's normal face. "Are you addressing me, master?"

"Yes! What's this idiotic robot doing in your image?"

"This is a rhetorical question, master?"

"Forget it," the robot said, reappearing. "The mirror can't perceive me, because I'm not part of the setting. I haven't been logged in. I preempt it when I choose, and the stupid thing doesn't even know, because it's just a programmed prop." The lens-eyes peered at them. "What are you doing with honeybuns there?"

"You're not part of this setting?" Baal asked. "Then get out of it, you bucket of bolts."

"In my own time," the robot said, its eye lights staring at her torso. "I have to tell something to Walter, here. So don't get your precious bare boobs in an uproar."

Baal showed a flash of princessly anger. She swept up a pillow and threw it at the machine—and the pillow plopped harmlessly against the mirror. The robot image laughed.

Walter was disgusted. "The thing's a ghost!" he said.

"I told you I'm not part of this setting," the robot said. "So to it, I'm a ghost, sure. It doesn't matter. What counts is that I can talk to you, cripple."

Walter reined in his temper. This thing evidently knew something about him, and not just his name. In a moment he made the connection. "The Quit error—that's your doing?"

"Hey, smart man! Yeah, that's my virus. I set it loose, and it locks onto the next player who logs in. Then he's mine."

"You mean it's essentially random?" Walter asked. He knew the technique from his police work: when a criminal started talking, keep him talking. Not only could it yield useful information, it allowed the phone line to be traced, or the backup crew to close in. "Then how do you know anything about me?"

"I looked you up, of course, dodo," the robot said. "I can learn anything about anybody, just by going through the lines. When I know enough, then I come and say hello. So hello, deadcrotch."

"You learned that I am paraplegic," Walter said evenly. "What else?"

"That you're a cop. Or were, before you walked in front of that car. That was a real stupid thing to do, you know that? To go in front of the car of the guy whose wife you're diddling. Sure he ran you down. You deserved it."

"He did not!" Baal exclaimed.

The robot glanced at her again. "I guess you're giving him more than your buns, huh? But it's a fake body, right? You're really some homely bitch."

"He seems to know about me, but not about you," Walter murmured. "Don't let him bait you."

"Who cares about her?" the robot said. "I came to see you, cripple."

"And what is your business with me?"

"I just wanna tell you you're stuck with me. You can't get rid of me and you can't get out of the game. What do you think of that, A-hole?"

"You want my company?" Walter asked, bemused.

"Yeah. I like company. It amuses me. So now go ahead and diddle the doll; I'll watch."

Walter had adjusted to the notion of the mirror watching, because it was a thing rather than a person. But this was different. "Who are you?"

"I'm Phony Phreak, but you can just call me Phreak. With a *P-H.*"

"Phreak," Walter agreed carefully. "And you're not in this game, you're just here to kibitz."

"You got it, man."

"What's your interest in me? I mean, why me and not someone more interesting?"

"It's the challenge. I take the first who follows me in. It can be anybody. Maybe a woman, even." Phreak laughed, but it sounded forced.

"And you just wait until there's something interesting going on, and then you move in to watch?"

"Yeah, pretty much. Takes me a while to locate the character in a setting, is all. I didn't know you were screwing a doll. How'd you get her to go for the Evil Sorcerer?"

"So you're not really a robot," Walter said. "You're a human kid, male, maybe fifteen years old, and in trouble at home."

"How'd you know?" Then Phreak did a double take. "You tricked me into telling!"

"I've dealt with your kind before," Walter said. "You're a kid with attitude."

"Yeah, and watcha going to do about it, bareprick? Arrest me?"

"You know that if you took a role in the game, you could do it yourself," Walter said. "With a woman. You could take a Hero role and pretend to be nice, and you might even fool her. Why bother to watch without participating?"

"Nah. I'd have to log in. Then they'd catch me."

"He's sneaking into the game!" Baal said. "So they can't charge it to his phone. He's a game hacker."

Walter nodded. "Why don't you do that other business we discussed, while I talk with Phreak?"

Baal's eyes met his. "Yes, I don't think we're going to have much privacy right now."

"What're you talking about?" Phreak asked.

"Maybe I'll explain it to you," Walter said. "Maybe I won't."

Baal looked troubled. "Walter, suppose I can't get back before this setting's out?"

"I'll enter the next game alphabetically following your name. You can follow me there, or wait for me to come out."

"What's her name?" Phreak asked.

"You don't need to know," Baal said emphatically.

"I'll find out." Phreak walked to the wall and through it, disappearing.

Baal scooted over to Walter and quickly kissed him. "I'll tell them about him. If anyone else comes, hide my body under the bed."

"I'll try to stay here to the end of the setting," he said. "But if we have to meet in the next setting, how will we recognize each other? I mean, we won't look the same."

"Code words, maybe," she said. "Like, one of us says 'My hair is red,' regardless what color. And the other says—"

" 'If yours is red, mine is blue,' " he finished. "But if someone overheard one of us, and happened to give the right response—"

"Then we'll have a follow-up. Something more descriptive. Like 'Needlepoint' for me—"

"Or 'Wheels' for me! That should do it. Then we can verify with further dialogue."

"Yes. Kiss me again." She met him more than halfway, delightfully. Walter reminded himself that he hardly knew her; it was foolish to like her. But he was getting foolish.

Phreak reappeared in the mirror. "Baal Curran," he announced. "She's the Princess in the Castle. It's on the list."

"No it isn't," Walter said. "They don't identify names with roles."

"But I've seen the other players around. You two are the new ones. So I got it by elimination. You can't fool me, you smooching jerks."

Baal was poking the air with her finger. "Farewell, Walter," she breathed, then sank back on the bed, apparently unconscious. She had quit.

"Hey, she's gone!" Phreak said. "You going to diddle her body while you got the chance?"

"No, I'm just going to talk with you." Walter got up and started dressing.

"Why'd she want to quit just now?"

Now Walter wanted to keep the kid occupied as long as he could, so he would be here when Baal returned, in case she had news what they might do about him. "Maybe she just wasn't thrilled to have you watching her smooch."

"Well, I'll be with you when she comes back, so I'll see it anyway. She's got to know that."

Walter shrugged. "Perhaps her reason is on the list. Why don't you look?"

"You're pretty damn smart-mouthed for a cripple!"

"Too bad you're not smart for a teen."

The robot's eyes glowed brighter. "That's a lie! I'm smart! I'm real smart!"

"And you're a high school dropout," Walter said, making a likely guess. "That's smart?"

"There wasn't nothing in school for me! I'm smart where it counts. In phones and computers and games. I made the virus that caught you, didn't I?"

Walter had heard of the type. They *were* smart—but limited. They locked onto one thing, and could verge on genius in that, but were inept in most other respects. They wangled free rides in phone and computer networks, costing companies thousands of dollars, and messed up files. Sometimes they messed up whole systems, and then the costs escalated to hundreds of thousands or even millions of dollars. They could be very hard to catch, because they were adept at bypassing electronic checkpoints.

But why was this one fooling with him, Walter? So it was random; it remained pointless. And the business of locking him into the game—that might be clever programming, but it was also crazy. What could the kid gain from such a stunt?

"Go ahead," Phreak said. "Ask me why I'm messing with a zilch like you."

What was the best way to handle this? What would make the kid stick around for the next hour or so? Perverse logic might do it. "As you explained, it was random," he said. "I just happened to be the first to log on after you loosed your virus. I might have been doing something interesting with someone, but she has now vacated the game, so I have reverted to dullness. I can see how the mystery of a new player could be intriguing, but now that you know my situation, you have to be getting bored. You know I'm just going to stay here and wait for the Hero to find me. Is this worth it for you?"

"Sure it is, meathead. I got all the time in the world. I'll get to know you pretty damn well by the time we're through. Then I'll go on to some other dope and get to know him. That's how I get my kicks."

So Phreak got his jollies by thinking he was superior to someone else. Someone who couldn't avoid him by quitting. It was like trapping a bug under a glass and poking it. But what happened to the bug after the kid got tired of playing?

Maybe he could find out. "So when you're done with me, will you nullify the virus, so I can go home?"

"Nah! You'll be gone on your own. That's part of the game. To see how long it takes before someone comes and unhooks you manually. Course that'll mess you up in the game, 'cause when you exit without quitting it can't log you out. You're neither saved nor dumped; you're in limbo. Chances are the game bosses won't let you in again, at least not without a hassle. But that's your problem; I'll be bugging somebody else."

"My nurse will check on me at noon. That will be before this setting ends."

"No she won't, sport."

Walter laughed. "You can't stop her, sport! She's like clockwork. She'll be there."

The robot's eye lights blinked. "I see you need educating, smart guy. What do you think I was doing, while you got all set up with boobsy, here? I was running down your line and checking out your ID. I got your work record, your credit history, your insurance policy number, everything. I got the case history on Conway Minke, your whore's hubby. So I know how you kept darlin' Lori in your room all that time. Shapely tart like that. You must've screwed the bejesus out of her! And now you can't screw nothing. Ain't that an irony!"

"What's your point?" Walter asked grimly.

"I got your nurse's number too. So I called her, and told her you wouldn't need her today, so not to come. I gave her a song-and-dance about how you were going out for the day with an old friend, so you'd leave your place locked up. I gave her enough background crap on you so she knew I was legit. So she said okay, she'd cancel it. She won't show, chump."

Walter stared at him. "You're bluffing."

The robot shrugged. "Wait till noon and see. Fool yourself awhile. But you ain't leaving this game, buster."

The kid could have done it, Walter realized. He had the information. The nurse, suspecting no evil, would believe. She would skip today's visit. He was stranded in the game.

"And this is your idea of fun," Walter said. "Trapping someone in the game, and then sticking around to watch him squirm?"

"You got it, creep. Some of them get pretty crazy after a while. I had a woman begging me to let her go. Said she'd do anything. Boy, I wish I'd been solid then!"

"Well, I'll just disappoint you by taking a nap." Actually Walter wanted a pretext to think about this new development. His Quit glitch was turning out to be worse than he thought.

"Suit yourself. Meanwhile I'll go tell the Hero you're here with the bare Princess."

"Sure—and get me killed so you can't mess with me anymore."

"I'll mess with you all I want, moron! You think you can get out of the game by getting killed? It's only the setting you lose that way."

Walter ignored him. He lay on the bed beside Baal's inert game body and closed his eyes.

"You asked for it, jackass," Phreak said, and faded from the mirror.

Ouch! Walter had thought the kid was bluffing, because he wouldn't want the setting to end so fast. But of course he could just track Walter down in the next setting and continue his harassment. So he didn't mind ending this one. Maybe he would keep exposing Walter to hostile elements in other settings, just to wipe him out and make him mad. He was evidently the kind of person who was satisfied with negative attention, just so long as he got some kind of attention.

Walter hauled the Princess off the bed and shoved her under it, as she had requested. But it probably wouldn't do any good, because Phreak would tell. So the prize of the dead Princess would go to the Hero, after all.

He paused to peer at the body, before dropping the bedspread down to conceal it. This one had not turned into cardboard, perhaps because it was a player, not an empty game figure, and because it wasn't yet finished. Baal had simply put her game body on hold during her absence. It still looked and felt exactly like an exceedingly comely young woman. The woman who had been about to revive what he had thought was forever lost: his physical sexual response. Thanks to her, he now knew it was possible, in the framework of the game. That was a wonderful discovery.

He lay on the bed again, pondering. If he was trapped here indefinitely, what about his body? He had to eat and drink. He could survive for a day and night, but suppose Phreak called the nurse again, to stop her from coming the following day? This could be a death sentence!

But maybe that was Phreak's game. To convince his victim

that he was going to suffer physically from hunger, thirst, and natural functions, so that he would have to do whatever Phreak wanted. And Phreak might have perverse tastes. He couldn't actually touch a player, but he could demand that the player do weird things. Like a weak man with a gun, Phreak could revel in his feeling of power over another person. The bug under the glass, getting poked. And Phreak could act indirectly, by telling other players, who would come to kill the victim. That was what was happening now.

In fact Phreak was just making his point. He would wash Walter out of this setting, to prove he could do it, and force Walter's cooperation in another setting. He was establishing that he did have control over the bug, even if he couldn't touch him directly. Much as he would do if it happened to be a wasp under the glass.

So what could Walter do about it? Well, he had already taken action, by sending Baal out of the game. If she could alert the game proprietors, and if they could do something about it, then Phreak would be put out of commission. So time was on his side as much as it was on Phreak's side.

But hadn't Phreak done this with other hapless players before? Why hadn't one of those others taken this route to stop him? That suggested either that they hadn't thought of it, or had tried it and it hadn't worked. But maybe they had thought of it, but not had another player to send out. Cooperation of this nature among players must be rare, since each won points by killing others. So Phreak had no prior experience with this ploy. Walter hoped. Phreak might be a sitting duck for whatever the proprietors had in mind.

Meanwhile it might be smart to ready another spell or two. Walter looked in the book.

There was the sound of running feet in the hall. Then Phreak appeared, in the mirror. "Better get ready, dodo! They're coming for you!"

So the kid had done it, and the Hero had listened. He had fought his way back through whatever castle denizens remained loyal to the Evil Sorcerer. And the Evil Sorcerer hadn't readied a defensive spell. He should have done that first, so as to be ready. His mistake.

He took up the sword and stood ready to fight the old-fashioned way as the Hero burst in. "So you tricked me, Sorcerer!" the Hero cried indignantly.

"And you listened to a game-crashing freak to gain an unfair advantage," Walter retorted.

"I thought it was another trick!" The man came at him with the sword.

Could he reinvoke one of his prior spells? That would free another castle denizen, but would be worth it if it worked. He paused to set up the spell of invulnerability.

Nothing happened. Then the Hero's sword was swinging at him. He tried to bring his own up to parry, but was too slow. The blade sliced into his left shoulder.

There was a jolt of pain. Probably a stiff electric shock, but it felt just like a literal wound in this context. Appearance and imagination counted for a lot.

He swung his own sword, viciously, at the Hero's head. But the man countered, and knocked Walter's blade away. Then he rammed the point straight at Walter's face.

There was another shock. This one was to his head. Then there was a worse one at his chest. Walter spun into oblivion, the pain tearing at him.

After a horrible moment that was also an eternity of agony, Walter became aware of a dark cell. His screen flashed: his score was now minus one in the Survivor level. He had wiped out.

But where was he? There seemed to be no scene or setting. This wasn't the anteroom either. It was just nothing. Just a place where his heart was beating out of control.

It was probably the game's notion of death. A time of nothingness. Maybe for some there was a scene of Heaven or Hell, depending on their religion and state of grace. But he had listed NO PREF in the box for religious preference, so he had nothing when he died here. It made sense.

What didn't make sense was the ferocity of the death scene. His heart was really hurting!

Then he realized what must have happened. The game had given him a shock at the chest to signify the failure of his heart when he died. But he had forgotten about his pacemaker. There had been some damage to his nervous system above the waist, and his heart could fibrillate on occasion. That game shock must have affected his pacemaker! So instead of keeping his heartbeat steady, it had sent it *into* wildness.

Gradually it settled down, and Walter relaxed both physically and mentally. That had been an ugly session. He would have to avoid such shocks in the future, until the position of the pacemaker could be corrected. It must be sitting right under the section of the wrapping that delivered the shock. A shock that was surely harmless to any ordinary person, but potentially deadly to Walter.

But how was he going to get it corrected, when he couldn't leave the game?

ten

HELP

Baal got out of her helmet, gloves, boots, and wrappings. She checked her blood: it was in good shape. Indeed, she felt good, because she was needed and she had a mission. She liked Walter, and wanted to help him.

Now to do what she could, quickly, before that awful Phreak character got away. She would call the local police and report him—

She paused. How could she report a character whose real name and description she didn't know? The police would ignore her. And why should they believe her, even if she had better information? They must get hundreds of false accusations every week. And it wasn't even the business of the local police; Phreak could be anywhere in the country, or maybe in the world.

Then she had a better idea. Why not call Walter's city, and have the police or hospital send someone out to unhook him from the game equipment? She had his number, thanks to their exchange of information just before Phreak had manifested.

She removed the phone receiver from the modem, hung up, then dialed Walter's number. She got a busy signal. Then she cursed herself for her idiocy; of course it was busy; he was locked into the modem and the game! It was the Atlanta police she had to call.

She got the number from Information and called. Only to get the brush-off; the police had been advised that someone was trying to harass Walter Toland by phone, and to ignore any odd calls. Therefore they asked her politely not to call again.

Phreak had really fixed him! She couldn't take direct action, because the hacker had anticipated such an effort and spiked it before it started. Phreak hadn't known it would be her trying to help Walter; he had just fixed it so that no one would be taken seriously. This must be routine for him. So she was stymied despite having Walter's information.

At least she could contact the game proprietors, as they had agreed. That would have to be enough, because it was, as it turned out, her only avenue. 800 KILLOBYTE.

She hung up the phone, then lifted it again and dialed the number and extension. It rang and rang, interminably. They must have many calls for help, or too few lines. Finally there was an answer—and a recorded message. "KILLOBYTE. All our lines are busy at the moment. Please wait."

She waited, drumming her fingers impatiently on her knee. She needed to alert them before Walter finished the Princess game and went to another setting, so she could readily find him again. Every minute hurt.

At last a live person came on the line. Baal poured it out, knowing she should be terse and clear, but unable to stop herself. "My friend is caught in the Killobyte game, and he can't get out. There's just an error message when he tries. He can't get Help either. You have to fix it, because he's paralyzed and if he doesn't get out so he can take care of himself—"

"What is his name?" the woman asked briskly.

"Walter Toland."

"What is his game number?"

Oops. There was one bit of identification they had forgotten to exchange. "I don't know. I just met him in the game, and—"

"There is such a name in our file. What is your name and number?"

Baal gave the woman her information. "But I'm not the one in trouble. I'm trying to help Walter. You have to—"

"We can not act on a complaint by someone other than the complainant," the woman said.

"But he can't get out of the game!" Baal exclaimed, frustrated. "He can't make his own complaint."

"Let me explain. If we were to act on information from noncomplainants, we could be subject to legal action. We have no way of knowing whether the complaint is valid or a practical joke."

"Practical joke! It's Phreak whose playing the joke! He's got Walter trapped and won't let him go."

"Did you say a freak?"

"Phreak, with a *P-H*. That's what he calls himself. He's got some kind of virus—"

"Let me alert my supervisor."

Well, maybe that was progress.

After another delay, a man came on. The lowest workers always seemed to be women, and the supervisors men, in any business. "You have had contact with the Phreak?"

"That's what he called himself," Baal repeated. "He's a game-crasher, using the form of a junky robot. He just appeared in the magic mirror, and regular players can't touch him, literally. He's obnoxious as hell."

"We know of him. What setting did you encounter him in?"

"Princess in the Castle. I was the Princess, and Walter Toland was the Evil Sorcerer. We—" She hesitated, not wanting to say exactly what they were doing.

"We have been after Phreak for three months. Ever since we put Killobyte on-line. He is a computer hacker who has wreaked continuous mischief."

"Well, now he's doing it to Walter. So if you can just reverse that virus—"

"We are unable to track the virus. He keeps it limited and specific. It self-destructs when we try to extract it. The kid is a genius in virus design, and we can't touch his programming. What we need is to catch Phreak himself."

"I guess so. But meanwhile can't you cut the connection to Walter, so that he can get out of the game?"

"We could. But we prefer not to."

"What?"

"Let me explain," he said, exactly as the woman had. "Our target is Phreak. Catching him comes first. Your friend can remain in the game a while longer, serving as a focus for Phreak's attention, so that we can pin the hacker down. If Toland exits the game, Phreak will immediately go elsewhere, and we will lose our chance to nab him."

"How long will that take? To nab him?"

"Tracing a clever hacker is difficult. It requires many hours or even days, and some lucky breaks along the way. We can't do it at all at present, but we hope to be able to change the situation and make it possible."

"How will you do that?"

"That depends on you."

"On me?"

"We need your assistance, because you are the one who knows Toland."

"Actually I don't know him that well. We just talked in the game."

"But you will be able to locate him again?"

"I hope so. But you know Toland's game address; I mean, he's logged in, isn't he? So you can send in one of your own people, can't you?"

"We could, but Phreak can sniff us out from far away, just as smart criminals can spot undercover police. He's better at this than we are, though it embarrasses us to admit it. So it has to be someone natural. Someone Phreak has checked and knows is just another innocent player."

Baal sighed. "That's me, for sure."

"Then it depends on you. We will give you a patch, which you will take to Toland. When Phreak comes to harass Toland, you must touch the matrix and invoke the patch."

"Touch what? Invoke what?"

"Phreak's virus is actually a small program that modifies part of the large game program. Our patch is another modification, of a different nature. It will have the effect of connecting Phreak to Toland, locking him in as long as Toland remains locked in. Phreak will assume game stature, and be bound by the rules of the game. He will have to remain in the same setting as Toland, because of the lock. That still will not enable us to trace his home station immediately, but it will nullify him. He will be able to escape only when Toland does. Maybe this time he'll let slip some hint, and we will be able to locate him."

"So he'll have to nullify the virus," Baal said.

"Actually he can't nullify it from within the game."

"He can't? Then how will Walter get out?"

"You or Toland will have to persuade him to give one of you the applicable vaccine code. Then you can exit and apply that code from outside. That will free both of them."

"Suppose Phreak won't give us the code?"

"Then both of them will remain in the game indefinitely. Actually someone will come and sever the connection manually, eventually. If that happens with Phreak too soon, we will lose him. But if, as we suspect, he is at an isolated station, where no one checks on him, it may become an endurance contest."

"You mean Walter will have to outlast Phreak in the game?"

"Yes. While we try to spot Phreak's connection. Of course if we do trace it, we will send a representative to disengage him, and turn him in to the local police. There are charges enough against him to put him away for some time."

"This all sounds horribly uncertain."

"Catching a clever hacker is an uncertain business. However, once you patch him, you will be able to track him. Simply watch your screen until you locate him."

"Why not send a representative to unhook Walter, so that at least he can get out?"

"Because that would also free Phreak, and Phreak is the one we want."

"You mean you'll just let Walter go to hell, so you can catch Phreak?"

"I wouldn't put it that way."

Baal tried to argue, but the man was polite but inflexible: they wanted Phreak, and Walter was their tool, and they would not let him go if it meant letting the hacker go too. She had to go along with them to get any help at all. It was better than nothing. So she stifled her objections and said she would do what she could.

"Very good. We have learned some things about Phreak that might help you. He may be claustrophobic—afraid of confined spaces—and he doesn't like snakes. At least we have no evidence that he's ever entered a setting featuring either tight tunnels or reptiles. That may be coincidence, of course."

"Big help," she said somewhat sourly.

"It could be, if you patch him. He may leave your friend alone if your friend enters a deep-sea-dive setting or a narrow cave exploration."

Baal realized that the information could indeed help. So she apologized for her hasty judgment. At least these people were willing to listen to her and try to help Walter, even if their help carried a price tag.

"And if he says anything about where he's based," the man said, "you tell us as soon as you get out. We'll get him arrested, and then he won't bother anyone in the game again."

"That will be nice," Baal agreed, remembering how Phreak had interrupted her love scene with Walter. She was surprised at herself, in retrospect; she had never been that forward with a man. But there was something about the game; it liberated a person's inhibitions, because it was so much less real than it seemed. There was also something about being beautiful, as she wasn't in life, and knowing that she was a truly attractive creature. She had wanted to score before midnight struck, as it were, when she turned back into plain Jane. She wished that interruption hadn't come; she might not have the nerve to act that way again.

That was all there was to it. Baal got back into her gear and re-entered the game. The patch was with her; they had sent it to her station, and on her screen there was now one more option: PATCH. She would touch that when she was in physical contact with Phreak's image.

She returned to her saved role. Immediately she found herself in action. The Hero was facing her as she sat on the bed, and he was trying to get her dressed. His hands were clumsily touching both public and private parts of her body.

"Hands off, varlet!" she shrieked. "I am no serving wench to be handled thus."

"Ha! You're back," he said. "Get yourself dressed, Princess, unless you want to walk through the castle naked. What the hell were you doing, hiding nude under the bed while you quit the game?"

"I was taking a break from a boring time," she retorted. "And it didn't get any more interesting when you came on the scene. What happened to the Evil Sorcerer?"

"I killed him. Now I'm rescuing you."

Walter had been killed! She hadn't expected that. She had thought that she would rejoin Walter here. But with Walter out of it already, she had to get out too, so she could join him in the next setting. She couldn't afford to delay too long, because it might have a close starting time, and she would be unable to get a character, or might even miss the setting entirely. Then where would Walter be?

So what exactly was her situation here? She pondered while she donned her robe, so as to avoid being handled any more by the Hero. In a moment she had it. The Evil Sorcerer had been killed, which meant that the denizens of the castle had been freed of his enchantment. So they had reverted to their natural loyalty, which was to the Princess. The Hero was no longer the savior, because when given the choice, the castle denizens preferred to keep her as their Princess rather than lose her to some outsider. There was a hefty bonus at stake, for one thing. So they were poised to rescue her from the Hero, who was now under siege in the Sorcerer's chamber. Indeed, any one of them who rescued her from the Hero might now have the opportunity to take possession of her, and retain it at the end of the setting, getting the bonus.

But her situation had changed. She did not want to be "rescued" by either side. She wanted to get out of this setting, in a hurry. How was she to manage it?

There was only one way. She had to get herself promptly killed. How was she to manage that, when both sides wanted to preserve her alive? She couldn't simply attack the Hero and force the issue, since he was nominally on her side and not an enemy. If he tried to rape her, she could defend herself, but he showed no such intention. She was obliged by game protocol to be the helpless female prize, doing what the Hero told her, as long as he was trying to rescue her. There was very little prospect for death there.

Then she thought of a possible way. Maybe she could make him think she had changed loyalties, so would be too much trouble to haul out of the castle. Then he might kill her for the single point she represented, and to deny the bonus to any other player.

"You were a fool to kill him, you know," she said. "Now you're in trouble, with all my loyal servants reverted."

"They were all against me anyway," he muttered, glancing out the window. "What difference does it make, what peasants I have to fight through?"

He had not had the experience with this setting that she had had. He didn't fully appreciate the nuances. That was good. "But a number of them no longer served the Evil Sorcerer, because he had used his magic several times."

"I know," he said, though it was evident that he hadn't thought it through before. "The bastard torched my catapult."

"So some of them were trying to rescue me, while others still served him. The castle was a house divided. Now it is a house united, against you."

"But if I had let him live, he would have used magic on me. He was more dangerous than all the rest of them."

"Surely so. Now I am the dangerous one, because they serve me. I do not care to go with you."

"What the hell are you talking about? I'm rescuing you."

"From what?"

"From the Evil Sorcerer, of course."

"Who is now dead. Therefore I need no further rescue. You may ride with our thanks off into the sunset."

"Like hell I will!"

"Then begone, intruder."

He stared at her. "What's this? You sweet on the jerk, or something?"

"Yes. He won my heart, and we were lovers."

"Hey, that's not in the script! You're supposed to hate him!"

"The script is malleable. He charmed me, and I loved him. If you try to touch me, I will kill you." She looked for her knife, but it had disappeared. That was unfortunate, because it made a bluff of what she had intended seriously.

"Well, I'm not going to touch you. I'm going to rescue you. So just shut your mouth and come along."

Damn! He hadn't been bluffed, and she couldn't attack him as long as he didn't attack her. Because he was nominally a friend until he proved himself otherwise. She would have to go along with him. None of her castle denizens would try to kill her either. She seemed to be doomed to be rescued.

Then she thought of a better idea. She had a perfect princessly pretext. "I don't believe you!" she declaimed. "I am grief-stricken by the death of my lover, and I shall not be comforted. I shall end my poor life forthwith." Then she ran fleetly for the window.

"Hey!" the Hero said, caught by surprise. He tried to intercept her, but she straight-armed him and hurled herself at the glass. (Glass? This must be a more modern castle than she had real-

ized.) It shattered, and her body sailed halfway gracefully out
into the air. She had done it! She had committed suicide—which
was why she had gotten into this game in the first place.

Then she looked down and saw that it might not be far
enough. She could be badly bruised but not quite die. So she
quickly formed herself into a dive and managed to strike the
earth headfirst. That should at least break her neck.

It worked. There was the literal shock of game-death, worse
than the prior one, because they were set to become more intense
with repetition, discouraging players from casual demise. Then
she was in the death cell, in the darkness. She was dead and
buried.

In this Journeyman level, death did not put her immediately
out of the setting. It put her in the coffin for a minute, and then
she would have the option of trying the same role again. Each
death would put her in the coffin longer, until the tenth one
would lock her out of the game entirely, forcing her to reregister
and start again at the Novice level. So death was not a thing to
seek, if a person wanted to prosper in the game. But in this case
she had had reason, and she didn't regret it.

The coffin faded away, and she was back in her game anteroom. She voided the Repeat option, yielding the character to
whoever else might want it, and considered alternative settings.
There were her choices, ranging from utterly mundane to wildest
fantasy. And the next one following her name, alphabetically,
was Beirut.

Oh, no! There was a warning in the manual about that. It was
the most violent of all the regular settings, being eclipsed only
by special ones such as Torture Chamber or Shark Bait. It was
supposed to be a magnet for the most ambitious (read:
bloodthirsty) players, who wanted to make a big killing and vault
into the Expert level. She didn't want to be in it, and she was
sure Walter Toland didn't either.

But it was the one they had agreed on, and they would never
find each other otherwise. So she had to do it. And Walter had
to do it too. In fact he surely already had done it, since he had
been killed in the Princess setting before she returned. The listed
starting time was five minutes away; she had been right to suicide, because she would otherwise have missed it. As it was, her
choice of roles would be severely limited.

Then she thought of the obvious: she checked the roster of players already committed. There was Walter Toland! So he had made it. But what part had he taken?

She checked the list of characters. She knew there were hundreds, because there were hundreds of players' names, and still about twenty roles remaining to be filled. Even as she looked, the list was shrinking; more were signing up. So she focused hurriedly on the females, having concluded that she preferred her own sex, especially now that she had found an interesting man.

And there was only one female part remaining: an Israeli spy. She took it, perforce. But immediately her screen had a question: what faction had this spy infiltrated? Baal, having no time to really think about it, picked the closest she might have some hope of understanding: the Christian. Then she quickly defined her character's attributes, making her not too pretty, but strong on luck and intelligence. She would need those qualities!

Then, hardly a minute before the start, she went through the door. She was in the setting.

She found herself in a chamber vaguely resembling the interior of an airplane. There were painted windows at the sides, and a cardboard pilot in the front. The center was piled with packages. A mail route?

She looked down at herself. She was as she had defined her character to be: ordinary as a woman, with fairly bright red hair. She was in greenish military clothes, and combat boots, with a pack on her back. A pack? That was a parachute!

In her hands was a kind of valise. On it were printed the words DIPLOMATIC POUCH, and below these, in words stamped in the manner of meat grading, READ ME. But she could not read it, because the valise was made of cardboard, having no depth or content.

Then the minute was done, and the scene came to life. The pilot moved, and the chamber jerked. She had to grab onto a handhold set in the upper wall to prevent herself from being bounced around. It *was* an airplane, or rather a helicopter.

She didn't know how long she had before the copter got where it was going, so she wasted no time. She opened the pouch, which was now full-fleshed, and pulled out the single envelope within. It was addressed, simply enough, to **ISRAELI SECRET AGENT**.

She opened it and read the sheet. Fortunately it was in English, though it surely would have been in Arabic or some other language in real life. The settings of this game did have to make some concessions to the limits of the players.

YOUR MISSION, SHOULD YOU CHOOSE TO ACCEPT IT, IS TO RESCUE THE AMERICAN HOSTAGE HELD BY A NOMINALLY INDEPENDENT FANATICAL SHIITE SPLINTER GROUP, ACTUALLY THE HIZBOLLAH, OR "PARTY OF GOD." THE ISRAELI GOVERNMENT WISHES TO OBTAIN INCREASED FINANCIAL AND MILITARY SUPPORT FROM AMERICA, AND BELIEVES THAT THE RESCUE OF THIS HOSTAGE WILL FACILITATE THAT. THE MARONITE CHRISTIAN FACTION WILL COVERTLY COOPERATE, IN THE HOPE OF RECEIVING FINANCIAL AND MILITARY SUPPORT FROM ISRAEL. SPEAK FIRST WITH THE PATRIARCH OF ANTIOCH.

She glanced up for an instant—and the paper burst into flames. Damn! What important information had she lost? She would have to make do with what she had read, but it was frustrating. Who was this Patriarch from Antioch? Some secret Israeli who would have more information for her? Where would he be?

She looked out a window, which now was real instead of painted. She was in a mountainous region, evidently heading toward the city of Beirut. Where from? She doubted this copter could have flown directly from Israel. More likely from somewhere in Syria, which she remembered was close to Lebanon. But didn't the Syrians hate the Israelis? Also, she saw the shore of the ocean to the rear; that suggested that it had come from the opposite direction. Maybe it didn't matter, as long as it got where it was going.

But the city she saw ahead did not look devastated. In fact it was more like a country town, with low houses with stone walls and red roofs. There seemed to be scattered through it theaters, restaurants, hotels, and even something with a sign flashing CASINO. This couldn't be Beirut, could it? Maybe it was a neighboring port town.

As the helicopter flew low and slow, she saw the changing types of vegetation near the town. It shifted dramatically with the altitude. There seemed to be bananas and citrus trees mixed with the palms on the coastal plain. The foothills just beyond featured olive groves interspersed with almond, apricot, and peach groves.

On the higher slopes of the mountains were apple, pear, and cherry orchards, connected by stands of pine. Maybe they were cedars; she remembered the Biblical cedars of Lebanon, so valued for ship timbers.

The looming mountain they approached was capped by a towering statue of the Virgin Mary with her arms outstretched. That was a Christian artifact, for sure! The helicopter came down to earth there. There were buildings, but this was obviously no great city. Could it be where the Patriarch lived?

The pilot shut down the motor and opened the door. "Carry a bag," he told her gruffly. "So you look like a worker."

Baal picked up a bag and jumped down out of the door. She caught her balance and looked around. She was in a fairly barren field, beyond which were what looked like small stone and wood houses. This was a mountain village with terraced farm fields where there were goats and chickens. Beirut? No way! Had she somehow gotten into the wrong setting? Yet the Secret Agent message had mentioned the Maronite Christian faction, and there was that statue.

Two forbidding-looking men were there. They were black of hair and dark of eye, with broad faces and seemingly somewhat pointed skulls. Both wore blue jeans and T-shirts. This surprised her again; she had expected elaborate native costumes. Since the game could craft any clothing it wanted without difficulty, these must be reasonably authentic. She wished she knew more about the Beirut area.

They seemed startled to see her, but recovered quickly. "Put on this coat," one told her, holding it out. "We must not have you seen in foreign uniform."

Baal didn't argue. She was aware that any overt difference in appearance could mark a person for death, in a place like this. But why hadn't she been provided with an appropriate uniform for her mission? There were already mysteries here, in everything but the language. In real life these men would have been speaking Arabic or something else, but that wouldn't work for the game.

"Where is this?" she asked.

"A Maronite village overlooking the port city of Jounieh, north of Beirut," one of the men replied. "Thus is where we come to escape the strife of the civil war."

There was the sound of a string of firecrackers going off. One man stiffened and fell. "Down!" the other cried.

Baal was already throwing herself to the ground. The surviving man brought out a huge pistol and fired back in the direction of the shots. Baal checked herself and found that she carried both a knife and a pistol. She doubted that either would help at the moment. Meanwhile the helicopter pilot dived into his craft. In a moment the engine was revving, and the horizontal blades were turning.

This was where they came to relax?

More men appeared at the edge of the field. More shots were fired. These were, Baal hoped, rescue troops. After all, if this was a Maronite stronghold there should be many friendlies here.

The copter took off. It lifted only a few feet, then moved swiftly across the terrain as if keeping its own head down. Then it exploded.

Baal and the Maronite gaped at the ball of flame and smoke. "Lord, they're playing hardball!" he muttered.

"How could someone plant a bomb this close to the beginning?" Baal asked.

"More likely one of the attackers had a grenade launcher," the Maronite replied. "Or a rocket."

"So he made a point taking out the copter pilot, while the others tried for us," Baal said.

"Yes. Maybe they meant to shoot down the copter before it landed, but were late. They certainly intended to stop you from reaching us. But I see that our men have taken care of the situation." He got up, and helped her to stand.

Indeed, there was a cluster of men around several bodies strewn on the ground. The enemy party had been killed.

But Baal wasn't quite satisfied, as they walked to join the others. Surely the enemy party had known this was a suicide mission. If three of them killed three others, then got killed themselves, they'd only be breaking even. As it was, they had killed only two, so they had suffered a net loss. Even if they had killed four—the two Maronites, the pilot, and Baal—they would have gained only one point. Unless they thought they would get away with their own lives, which seemed unrealistic. So this raid didn't seem to make a lot of sense. Except to stop her, the agent, from performing her mission—by killing her at the outset. That was a chilling notion.

The Maronite hurried her by the dead men, professing sympathy for her sensitivities. It seemed to Baal that an Israeli agent should be tough enough to handle the sight of death, but she herself hardly cared for it, even in the vicarious manner of the game. She did sneak a peek, and saw one of the slain men lying faceup, his mouth open in a rictus of terminal agony, eyes staring up. That was bad enough; she could not tell the difference between this and reality. Indeed, she already felt as if she were really in Lebanon, with real death uncomfortably close.

They entered a building. "I must speak to the Patriarch of Antioch," Baal said.

The Maronite turned to stare at her. "This is impossible. You must consult with our military leader, and explain your mission to him."

"No. Only the Patriarch of Antioch." So it seemed that they did not know her mission, and that it was best for them not to know. Maybe they didn't know her origin either. Obviously it wouldn't be secret if she started telling it freely.

"You don't understand. You can't see the Patriarch. He is our supreme religious authority. He does not involve himself in day-to-day political maneuverings."

"Well, he is the only one I'll talk to," she said. "Obviously someone is extremely eager to see that I don't make this connection; that should suggest its importance."

He looked flustered. "I will see what can be done. Here is your chamber." He showed her to a small upstairs room with a single bed and a barred window. It looked more like a prison cell than an accommodation.

She stepped inside. She decided that not all players knew much of what was going on. When this one checked, he would discover that she was supposed to be shown full courtesy and cooperation. Then she would get to see the one her orders required. "Make it quick, please." Because she had to get on into the city, so she could find Walter. The best way to do that was to insist on performing her setting mission rapidly.

He closed the door on her. There was a click. Suddenly suspicious, Baal tried the handle—and found that she was locked in.

Was this for her safety? She didn't trust this. But in a region as dangerous as this, all doors might have to be locked.

She removed the heavy overcoat the Maronite had given her and laid it on the bed. He had said it was to conceal her foreign uniform, but was that really it? Maybe it was really to conceal the fact that she was female. The Maronites had looked startled when they saw her, and that shouldn't have been the case if they had come to meet an Israeli agent; maybe they had expected a male. What was the role of women, here? Surely subservient. However, in Israel women had more rights, and she was Israeli.

She went to the barred window and looked out. It faced onto an interior courtyard. No exit there.

There was a sound behind her. Baal whirled. A closet door was opening. In a moment a shrouded figure emerged.

It was a man, and he carried a stout iron bar. He turned to her, lifting the bar. "Quick, Israeli," he said. "You are being betrayed. You must go out the window." He strode toward her.

Baal acted before she thought. She dodged out of the way as her hand went for the knife.

The man moved past her, toward the window, the bar swinging. Baal drew her knife and jammed it into the man's exposed side. He emitted a pained scream and collapsed. Blood came out and flowed across the floor.

Baal's heart was thudding. She had made her first kill! The man hadn't turned to cardboard, so was another player, which meant she had a point. Indeed, the little screen at the edge of her vision showed her setting score: +1. Her total Survivor score was now 0, because of the -1 she had registered when she suicided as the Princess.

But how had he gotten in, with the door locked? He must have been there at the outset, waiting for her. He had known her identity, because he had called her "Israeli." An enemy agent? That didn't quite make sense, but she wasn't sure why. So she cudgeled her brain, which was supposed to be smart, trying to figure it out.

Suddenly her mind was spinning with alarming notions. That shoot-out on the field—how could the enemy raiders have known about this secret mission? Surely the copter landing was one of a regular series, delivering packages every day. So the enemy should not know—but players could know. Yet that too wasn't quite it. The enemy would have had to take hours to infiltrate the Maronite stronghold to ambush the helicopter—and the setting had been in progress for only minutes. So even if some players had played this setting before, and knew about the agent, they shouldn't have been able to get there in time. Yet obviously they had.

And now she was locked in. With a man hiding in the closet. That was what made her mind race. Suppose the Maronites weren't the friends they were supposed to be? Suppose they didn't want to cooperate with the Israeli agent, but couldn't refuse, because they needed Israel's support, or at least its lack of enmity? Suppose they arranged to get her "accidentally" killed on the field, and when that didn't work, by an ambush from the closet? If she had tried to flee, he would have caught her as she tried to use the door, and clubbed her. She had surprised him by acting like a skilled agent, and efficiently attacking. Surprised him? She had surprised herself! But her character was smart and lucky, so she had done a smart and lucky thing.

But what now? If the Maronites intended to kill her, she wasn't safe. What could she do?

She went back to the body and put her hands under its shoulders. She exerted herself and hauled. It moved more readily than she had expected; the game didn't make sufficient allowance for the lesser strength of women, so in effect gave her the power of a male. She hauled it to the closet from which the man had come, and jammed it in. She shoved the door closed. Then she looked for a cloth, found none, so used the coat instead. She mopped up the spread blood, turning the coat over to get a fresh side when it got soiled, then turning it inside out. When she had done all she could with it, she dumped it in the closet on top of the assassin's body. A stain remained on the floor, and there seemed to be no bathroom or water in her room, so she couldn't scrub it out. However, there was a small rug, and it was large enough to cover the stain. The evidence was gone.

Now what? She remained alive, but still locked in. She would be best advised not to remain in the second state, if she wished to remain in the first state.

She saw the assassin's bar beside the bed, where it had rolled when he fell. It was a sturdy four-foot length. Her intelligence flashed again. That would do just fine to pry out the window bars. It was a crowbar.

Then something else occurred to her. The man had been heading toward her, lifting that bar. She had assumed he was going to strike her. But she had been standing before the window. Could he have been heading for that, ready to pry it open? She remembered exactly what he had said: "Quick, Israeli, you are being betrayed. You must go out the window." She had thought he meant that he was betraying her, and would throw her out the window. But now she realized he hadn't really had a threatening expression on his face. Could he have been warning her, and about to pry open the window for her? That was at least as good an interpretation as the other.

He could have been her ally. And she had killed him.

As a secret agent she might not be exactly shining.

But she had scored a point by killing him. Shouldn't she have lost a point for killing a friend? No, not necessarily, because by the definition of this setting her only friends were the members of her own faction, the Israelis. Here, as in real life, things were not necessarily as they were defined. She had probably gotten a point for killing a technical enemy rather than a real one.

Baal gritted her teeth and picked up the bar. She put it to the window bars and threw her weight into it. They were rusty and weak; they gave way. Soon she had bent a hole through which she could crawl.

Should she get a sheet from the bed and twist it into a rope to climb down? No, for three reasons: it would take too long, she was only on the second floor, and there was no sheet or blanket on the bed.

She tossed the crowbar out first. It clattered on the ground below. She hoped nobody heard it. Then she put her hands on the spread bars, put one leg up, the other leg up, and squeezed her hips through. Good thing she had chosen an ordinary female form instead of a wide-hipped beauty! This body was more like her own, except for its red hair, and it did have its advantages.

She squirmed around, shifting her grip, and let her body down outside the window. Her strength, again, was beyond what it should have been, making this easy. When she was stretched out, hanging from the bars, she let go and dropped. It was only about three feet to the ground.

She picked up the crowbar. It could be useful again. No one seemed to have been looking, or to have heard her. That was probably because of her body's high luck quotient. Now where?

Her outfit differed from that of the locals. It would be a dead giveaway. The Maronites had been right about that. Her intelligence was more than adequate to come to that conclusion. So she needed a local uniform. Would her luck help her get one?

She pondered a moment, and decided that fast, decisive action was her best bet. She would have to give herself the maximum opportunity for good luck. Maybe the game helped those who helped themselves. Maybe that was why she hadn't been provided with local clothing: to force her to be competent at the outset.

She ran to a recessed doorway, but did not open the door. Instead she used the shelter for what bit of privacy it afforded, and stripped her clothing. In a moment she stood in underpants and bra. She hid her pistol and knife under the pile of clothing. Then she hefted the crowbar, opened the door—this one wasn't locked, fortunately—and stepped inside.

She was in a hallway that seemed to lead on through the house to the outside. But she didn't go through; she checked for side doors, found one, and opened it.

There was what seemed to be an office. A man in camouflage fatigues and an olive-green headband sat at a desk. He looked up as she entered, and his eyes widened. Astonished at the sight of an almost naked woman, in a region where women tended to be secluded or veiled, he did not manage to speak.

She assumed what she hoped was a provocative pose, the crowbar concealed behind her. She inhaled. Now she could have used the buxom figure. "Hi, handsome!" she said, walking toward him as sinuously as she could manage.

But her luck could not be stretched entirely out of shape. The man opened his mouth, ready to shout.

Baal charged across the intervening space, swinging the crowbar. She clubbed the man across the side of the head. There was a satisfying thud. He fell forward across the desk. He was unconscious. Perhaps dead; she had forgotten her unrealistic strength; and just about crushed his skull. His two eyes seemed to be squeezed together, and blood was dribbling from his nose. *Damn* this game realism! He did not seem to be breathing. Yes, he had to be dead.

She glanced at her screen. Yes, the setting score now read 2. She had been an effective killer again. Was that something to be proud of?

No time to be squeamish! She had just made another point, and only the figure was dead, not the player. There was an odd satisfaction to this kind of killing, just as there had been to game sex; its lack of complete reality allowed her to be far more casual about it than she could ever be in real life. In fact she was beginning to understand the supposed thrill of killing she had read about. No wonder so many folk liked to play Killobyte: it gave them the kind of emotional wallop that perhaps nothing else could.

She yanked the man's fatigues off him. She pondered his masculine undershorts, then pulled them off too. To hell with the modesty of a dead enemy man! She put the shorts on herself, over her panties. Now if she had to strip again, she might even be able to fake it in shorts.

She put his heavy T-shirt on over her bra. She wished she had some way to strap down her breasts, so that she could seem masculine-chested instead of feminine-breasted, but there was no way at the moment. Then on with the fatigue shirt and trousers. They would probably be way too big, but—

She paused, astonished. They fit perfectly! Yet the man's body was significantly larger than hers. How could this be?

In a moment she had it: the clothing wasn't real, any more than the setting bodies were. They were all constructs of the game, fashioned from electronic images and responses. So one size fit all, in clothing. What she donned fit her, by definition. Even his boots. It did make sense. Still, she felt lucky again.

She found the man's military headband on the floor, and tried it on her head. It too fit perfectly. She looked at herself in a mirror, and drew her hair back. There were rubber bands in a desk drawer; one of those held her crude ponytail in place. She would have to hope that her cap concealed it well enough.

Then she marched boldly out of the office. She went to her pile of clothes and fetched her knife and pistol. Then she walked on through the hall and out the far door. Could she bluff her way out of the Maronite fastness and make her way to Beirut? Could she accomplish her mission of freeing the American hostage? Could she find Walter? Could she nail the Phreak with the patch? She didn't know, but she certainly intended to give them all her best college try.

eleven

PHREAK

Douglas Wannington was a dedicated man. He was a good provider and capable husband. He believed in his religion, and as the years progressed, so did his faith. Unfortunately his religion was unorthodox. In fact there were those among the ignoranti who called it snake worshiping. This was not true. The snakes were not worshiped, they were regarded as vessels of evil. They were used as an ultimate test of faith. The believer whose faith was strong enough could handle a poisonous snake without getting bitten, and if he did get bitten, he could deny the effect of the toxin.

Each year those who sought advancement in the hierarchy of the religion proved themselves against the snakes. The snakes were never hurt, but neither were they tame; they were freshly caught for the purpose, and after the ceremony they were set free. This was so they could inform their brethren that the minions of evil were neither feared nor heeded, and that their worst were harmless against the minions of the true faith.

Douglas had successfully handled the snakes for six years, and he handled them again this year. But when one rattlesnake made a threatening pass at a novice

worshiper, Douglas lifted it up and demonstrated how not to fear
it. How not to be governed by its malice. He held it stretched
across his loosely enclosing hands, over his head. And the rattlesnake bit him on the forearm.

He set it down gently. "It may strike, but it has no force," he
said, and all were comforted by this demonstration. He declined
any treatment; indeed, he ignored the bite entirely. They completed the ceremony in good order, the others never realizing
how much he was hurting.

Douglas' faith must have been imperfect, because within an
hour of the ceremony he died. There was a hostile outcry from
local radicals, and an unkind article in the local paper, but no
member of the church would testify and the case was written off
as an accident.

This misfortune left Douglas' wife Paige in an unkind situation. She was an intelligent upper-class woman, and reasonably
independent, but her husband's religion had decreed that women
should know their place. In the interest of the first flush of a love
that was to weather somewhat in later years, she acceded. As a
result her education had been wasted, and she had focused on
homemaking and volunteer work. Now, abruptly, she had to support the family, and she was not prepared.

Paige did her best. She took a clerical position, and performed
it competently. She was in line for promotion when news of the
earlier fate of her husband reached the employer. Snake worshiping? No accusation was made, but an unrelated reason was
found to include her in the next layoff. Actually Paige had not
cared for her husband's religion, and had disassociated herself
from it the moment he died, but that seemed not to matter. She
was, it seemed, indelibly tainted by association.

She took another clerical job, the best available. She was a
comely woman, and it turned out that the office manager had
hired her with this in mind. The way was open for rapid advancement, for one who was sufficiently obliging and discreet.
Paige was discreet but not obliging, and the way was then open
for rapid dismissal. This was not in accordance with the rules of
employment but she was learning the ways of the real world.
She didn't try to lodge a complaint, and thus obtained a favor-
able referral letter.

She mustered what remained of their estate and moved to a far
city. There she was able to get a decent job, but the hours were

awkward, for it was the swing shift. She stayed with it, and settled into a dull kind of security. Until she came down with leukemia, suddenly it seemed, and was gone.

Paige had been a good mother to their son Timmy, who was bright but irresponsible. He had shown a flair for electronics, even at the age of eight, and was forever assembling devices whose purposes were obscure. He had built his own computer from a cut-rate kit, and learned to use a modem so that he could communicate with other computers. The modem was a device that converted his computer's digital data into a series of tones to which the phone lines were responsive. The phone didn't care whether it was speech or music it transmitted, or some weird combination. The phone company didn't care either, so long as the bill was paid.

Ah, yes, the bill. Timmy had caught on early that the phone cost money. The longer a call took, the more it cost. His mother got upset when the phone bill was high, and she also got upset when she called home to make sure he was all right, and couldn't get through. What was he to do? Because Timmy really needed to be on-line, and not for just a few minutes at a time.

For Timmy Wannington was as awkward socially as he was bright electronically. He was extremely shy. The teasing by schoolmates about his father and snakes had only aggravated it. Timmy feared snakes, for himself and for his parents. He had dreamed that a rattlesnake rose up before him, monstrous in size and savvy, and said "I'm going to bite you, Timmy, and you'll die. I'm the snake who got Adam and Eve kicked out of the Garden of Eden, and I'm going to get you kicked out too." Then the snake had indeed bitten his father, proving its evil power, and Timmy's fear was confirmed. He jammed folds of paper in all the crevices of his room, trying to make it snakeproof, but he could never be sure it was effective. At night the ghost snakes came in anyway and wriggled across the floor in great awful coils, just daring him to put a foot down. There were some places he didn't dare go even in daylight, because there might be snakes, and night outside was impossible. He had to keep a light on at all times, so as to be able to see the snakes if they were there. But other kids didn't understand, and he quickly learned to shut up about snakes. Indeed, he learned to stay away from other kids, and from most adults too, because none of them could re-

ally be trusted. Any who approached him got that snake look in
their eyes, and he knew their nature.

But it was no fun home alone, either, especially when his
mother took the night job. The snakes kept the house under constant siege, always lurking just out of sight around the corner.
Except when the phone was on. Then they retreated. There was
something about the phone line that frightened the snakes.
Maybe it was because it connected to all the world beyond, and
they were afraid they would get sucked into that line and shot
into some far place. Maybe it was because there were people on
the line, hundreds of people, and none of them wanted a snake
there. So Timmy spent as much time on the line as he could,
connected to other computers, just exchanging remarks.

This was the thing about that: Timmy wasn't nearly so shy
when on the line. Because all the others on the line liked computers and phones too, and many of them didn't get along with
other kids either. They understood. And because there he wasn't
a scrawny ugly little brat of a kid with no friends and a father
who had been killed by a snake and a mother who mostly wasn't
there. He was a personality on the net. It was just great.

But when the phone bill got high, his mother laid down the
law: cut it out, or she'd have the phone removed. That was a fate
worse than death. He couldn't live without that connection.

Then his on-line friend Sidney came to his rescue. "Gimme
your address, and I'll send you a letter. Do what it says, and
you'll be okay." So Timmy did, and Sidney did, and the letter
came. It introduced him to the concept of hacking, which meant
really understanding how the net worked.

It turned out that what he needed was a blue box. It wasn't actually blue; it was a distant descendant of the original Blue Box,
and was a good deal more sophisticated, but its principle was the
same. This was a device that made an invisibly high note, or
combination of notes, that gave free access to the line. The box
could enable him to dial anywhere in the world, without being
charged for the call. He could remain connected as long as he
wanted, without ever worrying about the cost, and his mother
would never know.

Timmy had to have that blue box! But it cost money he didn't
have. Desperate, he braved the neighborhood and invaded a
house when its family was away, and found some money. It
wasn't enough, so he had to make repeated raids, terrified all the

time, before he got enough. Then he sent for the box, to the address Sidney had given in the letter, and in due course his blue box arrived.

It worked. He was thrilled. At first he used it cautiously, afraid that the calls might after all be getting charged to his mother's phone. But after a month he knew they weren't, and he was free to go on-line virtually all the time he was home and awake. It was glorious. He was a hacker! He even had a special name, because of course he couldn't use his own. So he became the Phony Phreak, or simply Phreak for short, and that was how he logged on. Soon everybody knew him by that name.

Then trouble came at home again. His mother had tried to call home repeatedly, and found the line continuously busy. She had finally called the company and verified that the phone was not accidentally off the hook; there was activity on it. Fearing a huge phone bill, she came right home. It was useless to reassure her that there would be no big bill; she knew nothing about his kind of electronics, and in any event would never have countenanced the blue box. So he promised to keep the line open, so she could call in without obstruction.

He went for advice to the hackers, and soon had the answer. They explained how he could reprogram the phone to signal him when an incoming call was coming, even when he was on the line. Then he could switch to that line, as if just picking up the receiver, and talk normally. Not only would his mother not know, it would make it possible for him to switch rapidly from one caller to another, or even to put two other callers in touch with each other through his phone. It was like magic.

This initiated the heyday of Phreak's early career. He lived on the line, all the time his mother was at work, and there were no charges for the phone. When his mother called, he switched lines and answered, saying that yes, he was doing okay and yes, he would remember to take out the garbage, and meanwhile he was just playing with his computer and having real fun. Reassured, she would hang up, and he would switch back to his real life on the network.

Actually he was not really off-line when his mother was home. He obtained technical manuals about the equipment and operating systems, which he read with fascination. There had been a time when his prime reading interest was science fiction, and he still enjoyed it, but now his most intriguing challenge was to find the holes in the larger system so that he could exploit them for free access and information. He learned how to break into restricted nets by ferreting out their key passwords. But it was better to sneak in without a password, in such a way that the net never even knew it had been invaded. Military nets, for example, were extremely finicky about intrusions. Some of the business nets, in contrast, were foolishly lax. He could fairly readily break into a bank's records and mess with its accounts, or learn the license tags, unlisted phone numbers, or credit histories of his neighbors. He refrained from the temptation to transfer funds to his mother's bank account; she would know immediately that something was wrong, and would inquire, and that would be mischief. He refrained similarly from changing his recorded grades at school. What could he gain thereby? It was better that he be considered stupid there, and thus beyond suspicion.

But in time this palled. Phreak wanted action and excitement, and just sneaking around unobserved or exchanging greetings with other hackers wasn't enough. He craved physical interaction, but not the kind that his mundane existence offered. He didn't want to be a skinny awkward homely kid who was always chosen last for team games and who inevitably embarrassed himself socially. There were some kids his age who were getting interested in girls, and they could joke with the girls and get along. Timmy Wannington could only stare and blush. The girls treated him with the same contempt the boys did. He told himself he hated them, but actually he would have liked to be accepted by them, knowing it was impossible. His hatred was really of himself, his horrible incapacity.

In the net, however, Phreak was respected. He had been able to break into some elite systems, and to prove it by providing their passwords to other hackers. If there was a system that balked others, Phreak would tackle it, and in time he would find a way. Of course that way might be rapidly closed as the proprietors caught on. But that was part of the challenge: to outwit the proprietors despite their best efforts. To let the proprietors know they had been had. Sometimes he even left a signature on one of their computers: PHREAK WUZ HEER. Then he and other hackers would watch with glee as the proprietors scurried around the net like ants, trying to run down the source of the intrusion. When they succeeded in closing the hole, Phreak would break in again, and leave another taunting message.

The question was how could he get physical experience and excitement, with his net identity? As Phreak he would be respected. Men would look up to him, and women would find him fascinating. But the net wasn't physical. How could Phreak get a body?

Before he solved this problem, his mother died. This came as more than an emotional shock. He was abruptly without family. He remembered how the terrible poisonous snake had risen up to threaten him, and that this time it had bitten his mother. They said it was something else, like cancer of the blood, but he knew. Now he was the only one remaining, and the snake would be after him alone. It had horrible patience, and would lurk eternally, waiting for that one tiny careless moment when he wasn't on guard, and then it would bite him too and he would die in agony. His dread grew, and he could find relief only in the comforting folds of the net. Now the net was his family, his only safe haven.

He was shipped to the closest relative equipped to take him, an aunt who was well off but emotionally distant. Her husband was away most of the time, a driving executive. The man tackled the problem of thirteen-year-old Timmy in a businesslike manner: "You stay out of my face and I'll stay out of yours. You do whatever you want, but if it causes trouble for me or your aunt, you'll be packed off to reform school. Got that?"

"All I want to do is go on-line with my computer."

So he was given a private line and a phone allowance of a hundred dollars a month, within which he had no trouble staying. He was scrupulous about attending school, knowing that his situation could quite readily degenerate, and the rest of the time he stayed home and absolutely did not bother his aunt. Because she knew no more about computers or hacking than his mother had, and he wanted to keep it that way. All he needed from his aunt and uncle were food, a place to sleep, and ignorance. They gave him that.

Sometimes he thought about his father and mother. They had tried to do what was right for him, but they had been busy with concerns of their own. That was why he had gotten into concerns of *his* own. It was as if they had excluded him from their real interests, so he had excluded them, and in due course they had faded from the scene. He really didn't miss them; he just feared the snake that had killed them. A psychologist might have had another opinion about that, but there was no such specialist in

the circuit. At least that remained unchanged; it didn't matter
where his physical location was, it only mattered how he logged
on.

But life outside the net was no better than before. All the students at the local school were strangers, just as had been the case
with the school he had left. They didn't know about his father's
religion, which helped, but he didn't know how to relate to them,
so it made no difference. He was alone, in this plane of reality.
It was a good thing he was self-sufficient, in his true existence
in the net. If only the dullness didn't keep creeping in and spoil-
ing it.

Then he discovered virtual reality. At first it manifested
merely as small test projects, little scenes to show the effect.
How the images were three-dimensional, and interactively responsive, so that a person animating a figure within them seemed
almost to be there. If he stood in a room and turned, the scene
turned as it would in life. If he picked up an object, the object
moved in his hand. If he threw something, it described a realistic
trajectory: in ordinary words, it went where he threw it. This was
a way to be truly in the scene. Here was his answer; he could
have a body within the net, through virtual reality.

Soon the old computer games were being adapted, and new
ones were appearing, to exploit the effect. Realistic travelogues
were crafted, so that when a person viewed a tour of Scotland,
he actually seemed to be climbing the steep slopes of the high-
lands and sailing across the firths. When he stood by the bank of
Loch Ness, he saw the distant shrouded head of the monster lifting from the water. When the wind blew, he saw the skirts of the
bonnie lasses rise around legs that looked completely round and
real. So it was with any country, and Phreak, like everyone else,
soon became a seasoned virtual traveler.

The introduction of the "wrappings" added a new dimension
to the experience. They were more than just things to wrap
around the arms, legs, and torso, of course; there were solid
gloves and boots, and a sort of chastity belt for the crotch region,
and a complicated helmet with patches for the eyes and ears. The
helmet sent stereo pictures and sound. It was really a complete
little monitor for each eye. Now a person could not only see and
hear the places he visited, and cause things to happen, he could
actually feel them. He could pluck a Scottish flower and feel its
stem, and sniff its fragrance. He could dip his toe in the chill wa-

ter. He could hug the bonnie lass and feel her slender yet full body against him. This led almost instantly to a new class of tours, as the erotic industry leaped into the act. Phreak perused several of these with interest, because they provided just about the closest approach an excruciatingly shy fourteen-year-old boy could make to the real thing.

But there were complications. He had to get the wrappings to put on, and they cost money. More than he had, even just to rent them. He finessed that by leasing a set, using money from an account he had arranged that his aunt didn't know about. It never occurred to her that a kid who maintained a C-/D+ average in school, sitting alone in his room, staring at a computer screen, could arrange for money to be diverted from a carelessly supervised business account to an anonymously held local account, which could in turn be billed for the things Phreak ordered. As usual, he was careful not to educate her. His anonymity was increasingly important, because there was now a warrant out for Phreak's arrest—if the authorities could ever find him.

He got the wrappings, and learned how to put them on. He dared use them only when he was sure he would be alone in the house for several hours. But the complications didn't end there. To use the wrappings, and become a participant in one of those tours, he had to log in formally. Because when he just flitted anonymously around the net, he could not get the necessary bodily feedback. The program had to be zeroed in on him, so it could send its sensations to his equipment. That meant he could be traced. That was dangerous.

So he compromised. He arranged to visit another hacker on a weekend. He took the wrappings along. He used the other hacker's computer, and logged on with his identity. The deal was that he would let the other hacker use the wrappings, after he had done so himself. He got connected, and took the tour of "The Worst Little Whorehouse in Texas." This was a relatively simple program, available as a stand-alone entertainment, but that was more expensive than sneaking into it on the net, even if the store had been willing to sell this restricted program to an underage snot.

It was some experience. It seemed as if he were right there. The woman looked completely real. When she approached him and touched him, he felt her hands. When she embraced him, he felt the whole length of her body against his. Even her two soft titties. It was weird and wonderful. When she kissed him, he felt her warm lips touch his. When she undressed, he saw every part of her, and he could touch it too. She would do anything he wanted. All he had to do was tell her, or touch her in a way that suggested his wish. Soon, naked, she lay on the bed and spread her legs. "Come on in, honey," she said.

The trouble was that it seemed *too* real. When he took off his clothes he got all embarrassed, and his body wouldn't react. Not even in emulation. So she might as well have been a mere picture, for all the good it did him.

He saved and exited. He explained the situation to the other hacker, who was two years older. "It's so real, I just can't—it's like I was really there, and I knew she'd just laugh at me when I couldn't get it up."

"Let me go in, then," the hacker said. "I'll ream her, for sure."

So Phreak got out of the wrappings and put them on the hacker. He made sure the gloves and boots were on okay, then lowered the helmet on the hacker's head. He tied the strap down around the chin, and adjusted the small fine mesh which projected up from it to mask the mouth. "You can talk and breathe okay, but when you purse your lips they'll touch the mesh, and then you'll feel what it sends."

"Like what?" the hacker asked, uncertain about this detail.

"Like kissing." Then he set the earpieces and goggles on the man's face. He was ready to go.

He watched the hacker pick up the experience. The tour had been saved, which meant that when the person returned to it, he would start exactly where he had left off before. The program didn't know that they had swapped out people. So now the hacker was standing there naked, staring down at the pretty whore, with her naked body and her legs spread invitingly.

"All *right!*" the hacker said, and his body quivered. The gloves and boots were anchored, so there wasn't any real motion, just some flexing of the muscles in place. But Phreak knew the hacker was getting down on her and doing his thing. The super-realism didn't bother him at all.

For a moment Phreak felt like snatching up a hammer and bashing at the hacker where it counted. He was crazy jealous for the other's experience. But he knew that all he had to do was get into the wrappings again after the hacker was through, and he could have at the whore all he wanted. And he knew that if he did go back, he would wimp out again. He just wasn't ready for what he wanted so much to do. The failure was in himself.

In due course the hacker emerged, drawing his hands from the gloves and unstrapping the helmet so he could see the real world again. "Wow! That's better than the real thing!" he exclaimed. Then he glanced down at his crotch. "But I think I gotta clean up."

Damn it, he was going to do it! Phreak started to get back into the wrappings as the hacker removed them.

Then the screen flashed a message. WHOREHOUSE PROGRAM USE CHARGED TO FOLLOWING ADDRESS: and it gave the listing for the hacker's system, complete with its phone number and house address.

Phreak stopped right where he was. The thing logged the computer automatically! He didn't dare use it at home, because then it would become a matter of public record. He couldn't afford any such record. For one thing, his computer was not legally registered anywhere. So when the program tried to track it, it would fail and that would set off an alarm he couldn't afford. Because there were ways to track things, especially when there was a formal log-in, even if it was a spurious identity.

But he could still do it here, since this was not his own system. It might be his only chance.

So he set himself up again, while the hacker took a shower. He started from the beginning, walking in the entrance foyer of the whorehouse and asking for a girl. This time he took a different one, afraid the first might recognize him, though of course they were only tour constructs, fashioned from recordings of live women. They had no memories because they had no personalities.

But when he entered the whore's chamber, it was the same one. He realized that the choices in the foyer were fakery; this was a one-whore setting, and whatever girl was picked brought the client to this same one.

She looked at him, "What, back again already?" she asked.

Terrified, Phreak hit the Quit button before he realized it. She had recognized him! How could that be?

But the hacker explained it readily. "My system is logged in. The program recognized the duplication, not knowing that two different people are using the same system. So the whore was programmed to take note, as a real one would. It means nothing.

Go back and diddle her good. She's one helluva screw. I swear, you can feel every throb."

But Phreak was too shaken. He just wasn't cut out for this kind of realism. Ashamed of his incapacity, he did not return to the whorehouse. He hated himself for it even as he made the decision.

Thereafter he explored new programs the safe way, unlogged. He continued to use the wrappings, because he needed them to translate his physical motions into setting motions. But because he was unlogged, that was all he could do: move around and look. He couldn't participate. Instead he broke into the programs, and watched others use them. Thus he saw many men visit the Worst Little Whorehouse to service the same whore. Each man looked the same, because each had to use the program's male mockup figure. It was a reasonably robust, handsome man fashioned after a bygone movie star, with the word PROP written across the back. However, he seemed to function well enough, going through programmed motions with the whole figure. There was a sameness to it, and Phreak realized that the experience was a lot less individual than the men outside realized. It was, indeed, artificial sex. Still, Phreak was sorry he hadn't been able to do it himself, and he hated the men who did it so readily.

In due course he managed to invoke part of the programs despite being unlogged. He had discovered that sight, sound, and touch had separate circuits, and only sight and touch were secure against unlogged players. Probably the proprietors figured that no one would get much of a thrill just wandering around, being heard without solidity. Being an auditory spook. He was like a wraith, walking through walls from setting to setting, unable to operate any of the game devices or to feel any of the effects.

That, however, was enough, for a while. He could spy on anything, and he could indeed pretend to be a spirit, and speak with regular players. Some thought he was a legitimate game manifestation, particularly when it was a haunted house setting. So he had a certain amount of reality. Until they caught on, and ignored him. He couldn't do much about a player who ignored him, because he couldn't actually touch anyone or anything.

He tried making up weird personalities, to startle players. For example, he worked up a crude ferocious ape voice that was a startling contrast to, say, the girl in the Worst Whorehouse. He had a Green Martian voice he would use in a thoroughly mundane setting. These had the advantage of concealing his identity so thoroughly that no one would ever know what his real voice sounded like. But after a while these voices became known, and players would tune them out.

Phreak became increasingly cynical as he ranged through the net. He discovered that many others might ignore him if he was polite, but they seldom did if he was impolite. Since he liked interaction, he became increasingly obnoxious. It was a whole new frontier: making other networkers react. They couldn't do anything about it, because he was too clever to be traced. It sure was fun to see them try, though.

When he was fifteen the major new virtual reality games started coming on-line. Some were relatively simple, such as golf, in which a player could stand at the first green and tee off, and the ball would go exactly where he hit it. Except if there was a wind blowing; then the ball would veer to the side if he didn't allow for it. Then he could ride his go-cart to that site and play again. It was just exactly like real golf, on a recognized golf course. Since Phreak had never been a fan of golf, he lost interest in a hurry. Some were more fiercely interactive, such as basketball, where the player could animate the figure of a six-and-a-half-foot man with big sure hands and try to make him score. Several players could join to form a team, passing the ball back and forth as they drove past the game team. Or enough players could enlist to make up both teams, and they would have a completely real pseudo-game. It might be far from star quality, but it was evidently fun, and easy to arrange. The team players could be from all over the world, with no physical traveling necessary. Indeed, regular teams were soon formed, playing each other in a forming league, and bets were made on the outcomes. They had names like the Virtuals, Virtuosos, Virulents, Viriles, or the Viruses, every name beginning with the letters *VIR*. There were even female teams named the Virtues and Virgins. But Phreak wasn't much interested in basketball either.

Then the structured role-playing fantasy games appeared. The first were adapted from existing computer games, with similar challenges and input, but with the virtual reality effect. For the first time a player could seem to be in the arena with a dragon, and if he killed the dragon the blood flowed richly, and if the dragon killed him, he felt the pang of physical death.

Soon the second-generation fantasy games appeared: those

that were crafted from the start with virtual reality in mind. The most significant of these was called Killobyte, as in Kill-o-byte, the computer game that killed. Points were scored by killing other players, once the introductory exercises were navigated. There were five levels: Novice, Journeyman, Survivor, Expert, and Master. The first two were really for practice; it got serious once the players were experienced, and the challenges were considerably more challenging. Phreak labored on his programming, and found a way to break into the default character aspect: he could animate the game figures that weren't being used, provided he didn't try to take them out of their immediate settings. That way he could talk, gesture, and even touch real players, without logging on, because the game circuitry thought his actions were just part of the automatic piloting. It was limited involvement, but a vast improvement over just being an anonymous voice.

This was the game Phreak had lived for. He knew it instantly. But he still didn't dare play it legitimately; there was too much phreaking on his record, and the police would put him away for an eon if they ever ran down his identity and caught him. That would be the end of him; he couldn't stand confinement or isolation from the net. They drove him literally crazy. So he played it his way: by breaking in as a kibitzer and driving the legitimate players crazy. The trouble was that they soon learned simply to exit when he appeared, leaving him without satisfaction. So he went to his books, and finally worked out a device to solve the problem. It was a small program like a virus, which he could set to infect the system of a particular player. The virus would lock the player into the game, so that he could not exit. Then Phreak could harass him to his heart's delight.

This became his life: making acquaintances in the game and teasing them until they escaped by having someone outside disconnect the equipment. When he caught a woman he would make sexual comments, delighting in her embarrassment. In this way he recovered the sexuality he had lost by not being able to log on. When he caught a man he found other ways to set him off. Sometimes the dialogues were almost friendly. But he knew better than to trust any of them. There was a woman who tried to sweet-talk him into telling his real identity, saying that then she could meet him in person and really give him a good time. He had been foolishly tempted, but had demurred—and then she had been so angry that he knew it was a trick. She would have set the police on him, for sure. That would have been the end of him, because he would have been thrown in prison, alone, with no computer or modem, nothing at all to do. Then at night the snakes would have come, destroying him. He knew they would. That was why he couldn't stand to be alone without light. The snakes had gotten his father, and then his mother, and were constantly slithering around his house, silently watching, waiting, flicking out their forked tongues, keeping their poison potent. Some were huge, able to bite his head off. Others were small, able to squeeze through the tiniest crevices. Those were the most dangerous ones.

Actually there were snakes in the Killobyte game too. But here Phreak was ghostly; nothing could actually touch him. He could jump from the animation of one default figure to another, as fast as he had to. So he could laugh at the snakes. But he didn't. He stayed well away from them. If there was a snake, he just cruised elsewhere for a while, and returned when it was gone. He didn't let the players know that, though. Because if they knew, they would go to settings with snakes, and escape his attention.

Now he was with Walter Toland, a crippled policeman who promised to be a lot of fun. He had acted to stop the man from getting out of the game soon, so there should be many hours, even days of activity. The Princess scene had been fun; it was sheer luck that he had caught them having sex, the best possible time. Now the man was game-dead, and about to start on a new setting. The one he and the girl had agreed on was the next word after her name. That would be Beirut.

It would take him a while to locate them, because he couldn't go into the death cell to watch Walter. Death cells were bad places, where there might be snakes. So he would just head straight into Beirut and look around with his prey monitor. Soon enough he would identify the various players, and lock back onto the policeman. It was mainly a matter of getting close, then listening to them talk. Players could look like anything, depending on their game figures, but they usually sounded like themselves. Their voices were piped straight through. So now that he knew Walter's voice, he would lock on as soon as he heard it, and identify the game figure it belonged to. Players could have the game modify their voices, but that was a special option that the novices seldom knew about, and the experienced ones seldom told them. Walter Toland would keep his own voice, for almost sure.

Phreak smiled, though no one could see it. He expected to have good fun in Beirut. It was just about the most vicious of all settings available at this level, with truly wholesale killing.

twelve

BEIRUT

Walter found himself back in the game antechamber. The coffin had faded away, and his heart had settled back to normal rhythm, this time. He hoped Baal had been able to find help, and that it would come before he got himself killed again. Because there were only so many deaths he could suffer here without truly dying, and he wasn't ready for that.

He looked at his score. Minus one. He had gotten himself killed, and he hadn't killed anyone else or won any bonus. But that was hardly his concern at the moment. He would have to become a much sharper player, if he didn't get rescued soon.

He thought about Baal. She had been beautiful, of course, but that was because of the game figure. He tried to nullify her appearance in his mental picture, since it wasn't relevant, and couldn't quite. Whatever she was in life, he liked her. That was foolish, of course. But this was the game, and in this context they could associate. He hoped to see her again, and not just because his life perhaps depended on it.

He looked at the list of settings. The next one after her name, had her name been a game, was Beirut. It started in twenty-five minutes. He hoped Baal returned to the game before then, but was afraid she wouldn't. So he would enter that setting, and do his best to survive until she appeared. If she didn't appear, he would just have to enter it again. What scared him was his suspicion that there could be many editions of each setting, starting at staggered times, so as to accommodate players at any hour. Suppose each of them entered Beirut, but not the same one?

He touched the setting, then studied the list of characters. There were hundreds! This was one big one, which meant a huge bonus, and probably very lean and hungry players. What would be the best way to survive in such a situation?

He would try to choose an insignificant role, then be excruciatingly alert. He knew that the real-life Beirut had descended from a playground of the rich and famous to a hell of constant combat. A dangerous place to be, but his training and experience as a policeman should serve him in good stead there. He would just have to school himself to be unscrupulous and paranoid about the intentions of those around him. If he was on guard against every other player, he might stop those who did try to kill him.

The available-characters list was shrinking. That meant that other players were snapping up roles, even this far before the start. If he wanted any choice at all, he had to make it soon.

But there was one thing he had to ascertain first. How many female roles were there, and which ones were likely to be available for Baal, assuming she got to this setting in time?

He saw that the cast was overwhelmingly male. That figured, because in the Middle East the status of women was abysmal by Western definition. They mostly stayed at home and bore babies. He believed that this was one reason this region of the world was relatively backward: it failed to exploit the potential of its women. Israel had more independent women, and was the dominant power of this corner of the world. But he was no political expert, and wasn't about to argue that case and maybe show off his ignorance. He saw only ten female roles out of a total of two hundred and eighty; five were Israeli Army personnel, and three of them were wives of prominent male figures. One was an Israeli spy, and one a hostage.

A female hostage? Were there any of those in real life? Maybe it didn't matter; this was not real life, and the game could set up its situation any way it wanted. So maybe this was its way to add in a female role. That was probably the one Baal would take, if she could, so he would look for her.

What was the best inconspicuous role that would allow him to look for the hostage? He didn't know. He saw that one option was Map, so he invoked that, and his screen became a map of the city of Beirut. The main portion of it seemed to be about four miles square, with a green line wending through the center in a general north-south manner. South was the airport; west and north was the Mediterranean Sea. An inset map showed the country of Lebanon, with Beirut about in the center of its seacoast. The Litani River wended its way through the center of the country, staying clear of Beirut. Down the seacoast was Sidon, and farther down was Tyre. Those names Walter remembered from Biblical history; they were the ancient Phoenician cities whose trading ships explored the Mediterranean. Alexander the Great of Macedonia had deemed the conquest of Tyre to be his greatest exploit. Walter wondered how the folk of Tyre felt about it. An inset in that inset map showed Near East Asia, with Lebanon south of Turkey, north of Israel, and west of Syria. Today it was the least significant of nations: a real come-down from the ancient days.

He peered at the city itself. The green line was labeled GREEN LINE, and it seemed to divide the territory of the Maronite Christians from that of the Moslem factions. But the Moslems were by no means united; there were the Sunni, Shiites, Palestinians, and Druze. Even those were not united; the Shiites were divided into the Amal and the Hizbollah. Syria's presence was marked to the east, and Israel's to the south. Walter wasn't sure how it was in life, but in this setting it seemed that all eight factions—one Christian, five Moslem, and two foreign—were clustered in or near this one city. Each was of course out for itself; each wanted to achieve power over Beirut. Whichever one achieved that power in the course of the twelve-hour action would get the bonus to split among its members.

That bonus was formidable. One point for each player, which meant two hundred and eighty if every part was filled. But each of the five hostages was worth five points, rather than one point, bringing the total to three hundred. The schedule showed that the leader of the winning faction would get fifty bonus points, and his five chief lieutenants ten each, and the rest would be divided up between all the members of the faction. If two or more factions collaborated to win, the bonus would be divided among the larger number of players, and each would receive less. So it seemed that it didn't pay to make alliances too freely. This was bound to be one rough, tough session!

The number of players assigned to each faction differed. Each had at least twenty-five, but the Palestinians—whose military arm was called the Palestinian Liberation Organization, or PLO—had fifty and the Maronite Christians, whose military arm was the Phalanges, had seventy-five. So if a player wanted to be on the team with the biggest advantage, he would join the Maronites—but his bonus would be only a third as much as if he had won with the Sunni Moslems.

So what was his best bet? He didn't care about bonuses, but about simple survival, and the chance to meet any female players in the setting. He remembered when the PLO, given sanctuary in Lebanon, had then tried to take over the country; Israel had finally invaded and driven the PLO out. It must have managed to come back, though, to have such a substantial presence. Unless the game didn't approximate reality at all. So was the PLO a safe group to be in now? Or was Israel a better bet? It was hard to tell; so much depended on the immediate situation.

The roster of available roles was shrinking, while the roster of named players was growing. One faction was filling up quite rapidly. Walter considered that one. It was the Druze, whose territory was just south of the city, in the Chouf Mountains. They had twenty-five players, and didn't look any different from the other factions. What was so special about them, that all but three—two—of their roles were already gone, while only five Sunni were taken, and ten PLO? Did somebody know something?

Another Druze role went. Walter decided to gamble that the takers were not fools. He touched the last Druze role. This was a simple militiaman, which was a suitably lowly role.

Now he had to define his character. He wrestled with common sense and lost: he chose True Blue. So he would be fundamentally honest and straightforward. He just preferred that, even if the ability to lie was likely to be an asset here. He had used persuasion in the Princess setting, and it had helped him persuade the Princess to go with the Evil Sorcerer. In fact it had even encouraged her to try to seduce him. She would have succeeded, if they had thought to invoke the sexual subroutine before the Phreak had appeared to mess it up. So he would fill the cup with that quality, and spread the rest across STRENGTH, REFLEXES, and ENDURANCE. That might leave him sort of slow mentally, but in an action-adventure setting like this maybe brains wouldn't count for much.

Physically he made the figure as much like himself as possible, hoping that this would help Baal to recognize him. Actually she had only seen his Evil Sorcerer figure, so maybe that wouldn't help.

He needed to know more—a lot more—about this setting. How could he learn it? The information given by his screen was quite limited. He had of course been aware of Lebanon in the news over the years, but had seldom paid much attention. He understood that Beirut had once been a playboy city. Then the Lebanese civil war had come, and things had been downhill ever since. Israel had invaded once, and Syria had invaded at least once, and President Eisenhower had sent in American troops once to stabilize the government. But what had happened in what order, and with what effect? He didn't know.

He still had fifteen minutes before the setting started. Since there seemed to be no more to learn here, he might as well enter it early. Maybe he would be able to learn more from what he saw, even if it was cardboard.

He walked to the setting door and stepped through. He landed behind a cardboard-stone barricade overlooking a picture of a terraced mountain slope. Far beyond, tiny in the picture, was a city. That must be Beirut, and this must be a fortification in the Chouf Mountains, so he was looking north.

He turned around. Behind him was a picture of a house. It was at the top of the hill, surrounded by a mini-tiered vegetable garden. Some chickens scratched in the dirt beside it, and there was a young goat in a nearby pen. To the sides were pictures of other houses and other terraces. Below were what appeared to be olive groves. It seemed that the Druze were industrious folk who made the most of their terrain.

He looked at himself, to see what costume he wore, but he was just the naked True Blue, because the setting hadn't started its run yet. No clues there.

Still, there must be some way he could get a better notion how to proceed. He inspected the pictures closely, knowing that they

would come to life when it was time, and that the present detail
was reasonably accurate. He saw a road leading to the city, the
obvious route to travel. But when every hand was turned against
every other, the obvious might be dangerous. So he looked elsewhere, and found a trail winding behind houses and foothills.
That would be a more private way to travel. The house behind
him had stout walls, and evidently could be defended from attack. He checked the path leading to it, noting places where ambush was possible.

And he spied a man in hiding. He barely showed in the picture, but it was definitely a man, and there was the suggestion of
a glint of metal by him. A rifle? Was that a friend or a foe? Probably a friend, if this was the Druze bastion, ready to shoot whoever might shoot Walter. But he didn't care to gamble on that. So
he moved out of that man's line of sight.

He searched and found other hidden men. There must be many
of them scattered through this scene. Why? He was getting nervous.

Then he realized that they were not players, but game constructs. Because players didn't turn into cardboard. Anything that
became cardboard was under the control of the game, and was
strictly part of the supporting cast. With two hundred and eighty
players, there was no need for direct action by the game constructs. They were just there to make it look authentic.

Still, this was one way to tell the constructs from the players.
Any that were visible in the paintings were constructs. If he
could note and remember their positions, he would know that
anyone he encountered who had not been in a painting was a
player. It was the players he had to be wary of, because they
were real people who had notions of their own.

He had had training in noting details, as a policeman. Now
perhaps he could make it pay off. Because he did not really care
whether he won or lost, but how he played the game. Specifi-
cally, he did not want to get killed again. Not until he was able
to exit and move his pacemaker, so that death was not so likely
to be literal.

He completed his survey of constructs and fixed them in his
mind. Now he was ready to play the game. He didn't know exactly how he would get into the city and search for that female
hostage, but maybe he could volunteer for the assignment. It

would surely be dangerous, which he didn't like, but it was his most likely way to find Baal, which he had to do.

His timing was good, because suddenly the setting came to life. The terraced scenery became breathtakingly real. He took a step beyond his solid-stone wall, going into the region of the picture, and encountered no resistance. No reason why he should; the picture was a game construct too, replacing the game-constructed scene he was experiencing now. Neither stage of it was truly real; only his body, locked in its wrappings in his house, was real.

He looked again at his body. Now he wore baggy pants gathered at the ankle, hanging low at the crotch, and a loose-sleeved shirt. On his head was a red and white checkered headcloth. This was the local uniform?

He looked down across the terraces, and saw a woman. She wore a blue dress, with a diaphanous white headcovering. That was as different from the familiar as his own clothing, and that was reassuring.

He saw motion. It was another militiaman, like himself, except that he wore a white knitted skullcap. Not a construct. The man was going to a neighboring house on a higher slope. Why? Wasn't he on guard duty, just as Walter was?

Farther away there was another man, also walking toward that house. Another player.

Walter remembered how rapidly this section of this setting had filled. People had chosen this early. Surely they had something in mind. Walter wanted to know what it was. His police sense of the unusual was sharpening.

So he did likewise. He walked toward that house, keeping an eye on the man who was closest to it. He would act exactly the way the man did. If the proceedings turned out not to be of interest to him, he would go his own way, hoping to accomplish his private mission.

As he got closer, he saw that men were approaching the house from all around. This was definitely some prearranged deal. The men had come here, and now were meeting. The house was a large one with three stories, but simple and unobtrusive.

He entered the house. He found himself in a large room with a central pillar. Others were talking, introducing themselves to each other; now Walter was certain they knew each other outside, because they were recognizing each other's first names.

They might be in unfamiliar bodies, but it was a familiar group. They must have planned their campaign before entering, and now would proceed with extreme efficiency. Obviously they were out to win, and to achieve a big bonus at the expense of the other players who weren't organized. He had just happened to get into it.

The room filled. There were no women. A man standing by the pillar called for attention. He wore a flowing black robe, and on his head was a ruby fez with a wide white cloth wrapped around it. A chain around his neck bore a pouch. He was evidently the leader. "The count is now complete. All twenty-five of us are here. Bradford, make your report."

There was a silence.

"Bradford?" the man repeated. "We need your report on who is playing elsewhere in this setting, so we know what we're up against."

Walter realized what had happened. He had inadvertently messed up their plan. They would catch on to him in a moment, and he wouldn't be able to get away, so he had better make an immediate confession.

"I fear I have taken Bradford's place," he said. "I did not realize that I was interfering with your project."

There was a general groan. "A stranger!" someone said, disgusted.

"Murphy's Law," another said.

The leader oriented on Walter. "Who are you?"

"I am Walter Toland. I was the last to enlist in this company."

"Because Bradford was to wait until all the other roles were filled, before entering," another man said. "I knew that was risky."

"Why did you come here?" the leader demanded.

"That's complicated to explain."

"Don't temporize!" the man snapped. "If you came here to sabotage our effort, we'll simply kill you and take the penalty. Tell us what brought you here, and make it quick."

No doubt of it now! He had blundered into a conspiracy. They certainly could kill him, in game terms, and he couldn't afford that, for a reason they didn't know. He would have to give them the story as concisely as he could.

"I am a paraplegic in real life," he said. "I entered the game for diversion. But a joker named Phreak locked me in." There was a reaction; several of them evidently knew that name. "I have a pacemaker, and when I get game-killed, it affects that, and puts my heart into fibrillation. I don't know how many times I can game-die without really dying. So I am in serious trouble; I can't quit and I don't dare die. A woman I met in another setting said she would help me; we agreed to meet in the next setting alphabetically after her name. That happened to be this one. Then I saw that the Druze faction roles were going rapidly, and thought I'd find out why. I'm sorry I got in your way. I just want to survive until I can find that woman, and I hope she has found a way to get me out."

"Who is the woman?" the leader asked.

"Baal Curran. She's diabetic."

"What setting?"

"Princess in the Castle. She was the Princess; I was the Evil Sorcerer. I got killed before she returned to the setting."

"How is she going to help you?"

"By quitting the game and calling the proprietors. We hope they've heard of Phreak, and know how to deal with him. He'll probably come here to bug me some more."

The leader looked around. "Anyone able to verify or refute any of this?"

"I saw the name Baal on a Princess roster," a man said.

"It's the way Phreak works," another said.

The leader paused, then lifted his head. "Okay, we'll chance it. Our plan's in place; the names of others was only to be sure that no one was setting up a counterplan to stop us. We can do it as we are." He looked at Walter again. "We're out to win big bonus points, which can push several of us into the next level. We have a plan to take over the city and hold it. Are you with us or against us?"

"I don't care about the bonus," Walter said. "You can have mine. I just want to survive and find Baal."

"Every member of the faction gets the bonus, alive or dead," the man said. "That's not the issue. Will you work actively to help us win, or do we have to lock you up for the duration so you can't betray us?"

"You can't trust a deal made under duress," Walter said. "My word would be meaningless."

The leader smiled grimly. "That's an honest response. Suppose we help you find your woman?"

"For that, I'll deal," Walter said. "I'll do anything you want. Except lie or cheat—my character can't do those things."

"It's a deal. What skills do you have that might help us?"

"I'm a former policeman. I have street experience. I know how to use a gun, and how to disarm a man quickly."

Now the leader grinned. "I think we lucked out. How can we recognize your girl?"

"When one of us says 'My hair is red' the other will reply 'If yours is red, mine is blue.' Regardless of actual hair color. Then to follow up, one will say 'Needlepoint,' and the other will say 'Wheels.' We figure we won't get those responses by chance."

The leader looked around. "Got that, men? Just say 'My hair is red' if you meet a woman—" He broke off. "She'll take a female part?"

"I hope so," Walter said. "If she makes it in time, and any are left. I thought she might be the female hostage."

"Okay. You go with Leon. Do exactly what he says. Remember, we expect your complete loyalty, as long as you're in this setting. The Druze are honorable when dealing with each other, and we depend on that. There are no traitors among us."

A man forged through the crowd toward Walter. "I'm Leon."

"You know your assignments," the leader said to the rest. "Move out."

The men piled out of the building. Walter and Leon remained. "You know the city layout?" Leon asked.

"I saw the map. I don't know every street, but I have a notion where the Green Line is. I also studied the visible territory before the setting started, so as to be able to reach the city without traveling the obvious road. I assume that enemy factions will be ready to attack what comes along the main road."

"Smart man. You'll like our mission. We're going to infiltrate the Hizbollan and see if we can rescue a hostage. It's damn dangerous, but if we get one alive, the country that hostage is from will support us, and that could tip the balance if it's close. So if your girl's a hostage, she could help us win."

"I hope so," Walter said. "But remember, I don't even know for sure that she's here. Her name wasn't on the roster when I entered. I hope she'll see my name, and know. But if she didn't make it back in time—" He shrugged.

"The boys will try your code exchange on any female player

they see. If one responds correctly, they'll spread the word. You'll know soon enough."

"That'll be great," Walter said. This was an unexpected development, and he was grateful. It greatly improved his chances of finding Baal.

"Now we'll take my van into the city," Leon said. "But first we'll change into peasant clothing, so we won't be known."

"Won't that make us targets for other Druze?"

"No. We're coordinated. They'll let my van by. Once we're in the city we'll be on our own, though."

Leon showed the way to a separate chamber where there was an assortment of clothing. The players could not have assembled this; it had to be provided by the setting. So it was one of the assets on which players could draw, if they had the wit. These players could have checked such things out in prior sessions, and now were ready to use them effectively.

They changed, and Leon helped Walter do it properly. They donned jeans and jackets, as well as cowboy hats and crossed bandoleers of ammunition. All indications of Druze membership were removed. Leon put on an armband bearing a hammer and sickle, and Walter a beret with a red star. He was conscious of the man's unobtrusive watching. It was obvious that these organized players did not trust the stranger, perhaps fearing him to be a spy for another faction. There would have been no time to set up such a thing within the setting, but if there were other preplanned efforts, one of those groups could have sent a man to infiltrate the Druze effort. So Walter was under suspicion, necessarily. Why, then, were they letting him in on the effort to rescue a hostage? How could they be sure he wasn't going to try to help the Hizbollah, by betraying the Druze attempt to rescue one of their hostages?

They went to the van. There was a wagon loaded with fruits and vegetables from the surrounding terraced fields. "We'll load these in to sell our wares on the city street," Leon explained. "However, we'll also be smuggling in ammunition for our other men." He went to an alcove where supplies were stacked. "Put this in first, then cover it with vegetables."

Walter looked around. This was a depot with a considerable amount of equipment. Much of it seemed to be Russian-made, which the Druze had probably obtained from the Syrians, or through the illegal weapons market. There was probably more that he wasn't being allowed to see.

Walter picked up a box. He glanced at the writing on the outside, then sniffed it. He paused. "Leon, I told you the truth. I'm playing straight with you. But I don't think you're playing straight with me."

"What are you talking about?"

"This isn't ammunition. This is explosive."

"How could you know that?"

"I told you, I was a policeman. I had to know enough to recognize trouble. I never had to defuse a bomb, but I had to know one when I saw it. This is TNT. It's not considered powerful by today's standards, but there's enough here to do a fair amount of damage, especially if packed around cylinders of propane and hexogen, which I see you also have here. That's a sophisticated explosive compound that multiplies the force of the blast several-fold."

"Maybe they need explosives," Leon said.

"Where are the detonators?"

Leon tapped another box. "Here."

Walter looked at him. He slid his hand down to his pistol, on the side away from the other man. He drew it and held it behind him. "These aren't remote. They're wired."

"I suppose so. I don't know much about it."

"This stuff won't rescue any hostages. It will simply blow us up when anything sets it off."

Leon looked at him. "What's your point?"

"This is a suicide mission, isn't it?"

"Maybe it is. So what? Every player gets his share of the bonus for being on the winning team, even if he doesn't make it to the end of the session. He loses only one point for dying, and could win seven or eight points in the bonus. It's a good deal."

"Not if I die in life as well as in the game."

Leon nodded. "That's right. You did say you could be in trouble. But this is the mission."

"Your leader said that the Druze are honorable among themselves. You are not being honorable."

Leon looked angry. "Listen, you weren't supposed to be here. You're a party crasher. We don't owe you anything."

"I'm a Druze. I signed up in the manner prescribed. You are the ones who conspired to make this setting something other than routine. You owe me fairness within this faction, because we made a deal."

Leon reached for his pistol.

Walter brought his right hand around from behind. It held his own pistol. "I could have shot you in the back at any time. I could shoot you now, even if you draw, because I can see that you have not had the experience with such weapons that I have. I believe I could shoot your pistol out of your hand, though that's a foolishly risky trick shot. But I'm not, because I'm trying to play by the rules. Why aren't you?"

Leon paused, aware that he had lost whatever advantage he might have had. "We don't owe anything to a spy."

Walter smiled grimly. "If I were a spy, I wouldn't be challenging you now. I'd wait until I saw exactly what you were up to. Or I might take the explosive and blow us both up before we could do any damage to my side. But I'm not a spy, I'm a man who may truly die if I get killed in the game, and who needs to find a certain woman in order to get out of it." He put his pistol away. "Now, I can help you in your mission, but you have to play straight with me. I think I have more at stake than you do."

Leon shook his head. "We took a long time to set this up. I don't see why we have to cut any stranger in."

"It seems you were stuck with cutting me in the moment I displaced your man in this setting. I'll get my share of points whether I live or die. Meanwhile I'm willing to help you if you help me. Your leader agreed; are you reneging?"

"Our leader put you in my charge because he didn't trust you," Leon said. "Because I'm the one who's supposed to see to security."

"So this business about Druze honor is meaningless?" Walter asked. "Maybe the real Druze have it, but not you imitators in the game? When you make a deal you don't mean it?"

Leon was plainly nettled. "We do mean it! We use Druze history and culture to recognize each other when we're in disguise. We studied it a long time. But you're not—"

"Not a Druze? I think I am as much of one as you."

The man relented. "Maybe you are, at that. Okay, so you don't want to get killed. But my mission in the city is to find any hostages, and bomb a hole in the building where they're kept. The chances of getting killed are excellent."

"But less if the others on my team are with me," Walter said. "And I can help more effectively if they trust me."

"And I have a mission to accomplish," Leon said. "I guess you're right: it's better to work together, and maybe you'll help us win. But there's much you have to know, or you'll get killed by a Druze as readily as by an enemy. So come along, and I'll fill you in while we ride. Are you a quick study?"

"Yes, when my life is at stake."

They loaded the van, then started out. Walter drove; he was the one who wasn't trusted, so Leon's hands were free to draw a weapon if necessary. They used the back roads Walter had seen in the picture. They had to move carefully, because the surface was uneven and their cargo touchy. Good plastic explosive could not be detonated by accident, but this was probably second-rate, and the game programmer might have assumed it was like dynamite, subject to stress by heat and wear. They were able to talk as they rode, because there was only token noise programmed into the van.

"The Druze are a small Moslem sect that started in 1016—that date's important, so remember it—when al-Hakim, who was the sixth Fatimid caliph, announced himself in Cairo, Egypt, as the earthly incarnation of God. Maybe outsiders don't believe him, but we Druze do. We know that God has been divinely incarnated into a living person at various times, and Jesus of Nazareth was one, and Mohammed another, and al-Hakim was the final one. Know what a Druze does when he hears someone say otherwise?"

"He kills the idolater?" Walter asked.

"No. He does nothing. Because infidels simply don't know the truth. We don't want them to know it either. When we are living among others, we worship as they do, whether they are Moslem, Christian, or Jewish. We follow their forms, but they are meaningless; only in our hearts do we know the truth. Know what we do when a convert comes?"

"Run him through basic training in the catechisms?"

"No. There are no converts. The only Druze are those born to Druze parents, and they remain Druze throughout their lives. So anyone who says he changed religions—"

"Got it. A Druze may profess another religion, but an outsider can't profess to be Druze."

"Right. In fact no one will claim to be a Druze, because the real ones are hiding, in the city. So kill anyone who says he's a Druze. If it's not convenient to kill him, don't trust him. A real Druze will profess some other religion, but he'll know all about al-Hakim. If anyone mentions him, but gets the name wrong, or any of the facts of his incarnation wrong—"

"Kill him," Walter said. "You're right: I wouldn't have lasted any length of time. And I see why you folk don't trust outsiders."

"Yes. In private we call ourselves the Muhwahhidan, or Unitarians, and we refer to our faith as the Tawhid. We also call ourselves the Sons of Benevolence. Druze don't pray, feast or fast, or hold any religious services. Except for the *uggal,* or 'enlightened,' privileged class, and none of us here belong to that. We're *juhhal,* or 'uninitiated,' in the deeper mysteries of our religion. Only our leader is uggal." He frowned briefly. "Actually he should be juhhal, because all political leaders are chosen from this class, but there was a complication and he had to be uggal. So technically he's just advising us." He shrugged. "Mental separation will do for us; that's the most important. But those of us who can live in our colony in the Chouf Mountains are blessed. We have seven principles, which have fancier formulations, but in essence amount to honesty with each other, mutual protection and assistance, the belief in the divinity of al-Hakim, satisfaction with what we are, submission to God's will, and we try to keep separate from those who are in error. Also from demons. We don't use wine, tobacco, or profanity. We believe that souls transmigrate and gain status as they progress. And that's it; we fight to defend our way of life, and man for man we have the best fighting force in Lebanon."

"So if you die defending your faith, Heaven is assured?"

"Not at all. We do not believe in a Judgment Day. The number of souls for believers and nonbelievers was fixed at the moment of creation, and these souls transmigrate."

"They do what?"

Leon smiled briefly. "Reincarnate. Go to new people when the old ones die. So what others call judgment, we call the end of the soul's long journey, when it reaches full development. So we don't breed fanatical martyrs, though we can fight as well as we need to."

"You know," Walter said as he assimilated this, "I think I like the Druze philosophy."

"It does grow on you."

"Are there any Druze lying in ambush in this vicinity?" Walter inquired.

"No. All our men are moving into the city by different routes, with a few guarding our mountain home. Why?"

There was a faint flash. Walter drew his pistol and fired into the window of a house they were passing. There was a scream.

"Question answered," Leon said. "You saw the glint of his gun barrel as he brought it to bear. You seem to have a talent for this."

"I have had experience on the streets, as I said. In the game I don't have to be cautious or read anyone his rights. That simplifies things considerably."

"Well, you just earned yourself a point."

They rode on. Walter watched one side of the road, and Leon watched the other. Anyone was a potential enemy here. But they continued to talk.

"God himself—is he like the Christian concept, or the Moslem?"

"Actually Druze includes elements of Judaism, Christianity, and Islam, as well as Gnostic, Persian, and even Neo-Platonist elements, but probably is closest to Islam in concept. We believe in one God, who is not to be defined or understood, who renders impartial justice. We revere Hermes, Pythagoras, Plato, and Plotinus as well as Adam, Noah, Abraham, Moses, Jesus, Mohammed, and of course al-Hakim. We don't proselytize. We keep our teachings secret."

"But surely there are times when strangers have to verify that they are Druze before they can have a dialogue," Walter said. "You don't want to be shooting each other by accident."

"Well, the Druze Star helps. Recognition of al-Hakim includes recognition of Hamza and his four ministers, called the Five Dignitaries. Each dignitary is associated with a color, and sections of each color make up the Star, which is often displayed in Druze areas. Our flag has the green of Hamza in a triangle, with the other four colors in horizontal stripes. Or there may be five vertical stripes painted on the bumpers of Druze trucks and cars."

"So if I encounter someone I think is a Druze, and I want to confirm it, I can mention some private aspect of the religion and see whether he picks up on it."

"That is our system. But we hope not to have to make much

contact that way, and indeed, we mostly recognize our forms, which we have crafted to be individual. I resemble my appearance in life, except that I am older there."

"Is that usual? To duplicate your real appearance?"

"Yes. First-timers go for the most impressive figures, but the experienced ones prefer to play themselves. It makes recognition easier."

They reached the outskirts of the city, and had to slow down almost to a crawl. The sound of gunfire in the background became constant. "Don't show your weapon unless you mean to use it," Leon said. "In fact don't show it *when* you use it, if possible."

Walter looked at the city. He remembered again how it had once been a resort area, with rich tourists and many splendid edifices. Now it was a sprawling ruin. Buildings were missing roofs, walls, or even entire stories, and the streets were lined with rubble. He saw that each driver was a law unto himself, using any part of the street he chose without much regard for other traffic. He saw two cars meet in a narrow side street; one looked like a Mercedes and the other a Jaguar, but their drivers were scruffy bearded men, hardly rich tourists. The cars had probably been stolen. There was no room for them to pass each other, and neither car would back up. Then one man pulled a gun, and at that point the other did back up, grudgingly.

They slowed to pass a checkpoint. This was the Hizbollah section, and the Hizbollah were of course suspicious of anything coming in from the south. But the Hizbollah were evidently already locked in a struggle with the Amal to their west; that was the direction of the sound of gunfire. There were a number of farmers entering similarly; Walter and Leon were in a line of loaded vehicles.

The guard made only a cursory inspection: he lifted out a nice ripe fruit from the van's stock, and kept it. He waved them on by.

But just a little farther along they had to slow again. Someone was selling newspapers by a barricade made of a trashcan flying a faction flag. The price, translated into familiar money, was two dollars. "We don't need that," Walter remarked.

"But we'll buy a paper anyway," Leon said.

"That little sheet? It isn't worth a tenth the price!"

"Consider it a donation, or a highway toll," Leon said, nodding to the side. Walter looked, and saw three men in jeans and T-shirts lounging there across the street, casually holding AK-47 automatic rifles. Oh.

So they bought a paper, and went on, unmolested. The other drivers did likewise. But the pace of traffic remained maddeningly slow. It would have been faster just to walk.

Then another man appeared, walking by their vehicle. "Ah, there you are, cripple!" he called, spying Walter.

Walter groaned. Phreak was back.

Three heads turned to look at the man. Those of Walter, Leon, and the checkpoint guard. The other people ignored it. "How did you know me?" Walter asked.

The man grinned. "I didn't, dope, until you responded. I've been checking all the Druze militiamen on the list, knowing you were one of them. That's as much as I can get from the game listing."

Walter realized that he and Leon had just given themselves away to the guard. The people who hadn't turned were game constructs, possessing no free will. Had Walter kept his face straight forward, the guard wouldn't have known. In fact, Phreak wouldn't have known either; he hadn't recognized Walter in this guise, so had used one of the oldest tricks in the book: calling his insulting greeting to every Druze militiaman he found. Somehow he had known who was Druze despite their attempt to conceal their identity.

Now the guard was bringing his gun to bear. Walter shot him before he could complete his orientation, and the man slumped by his stall. Two points for Walter.

But of course now the Hizbollah knew that an intrusion was occurring. In a moment they would converge on the sound of the shot. And Walter and Leon were still stuck in the traffic. It didn't matter that the rest of it was game construct; it was solid in terms of the setting.

"Ho! Ho!" Phreak cried gleefully. "Here he is, you jerks! Come and kill him!" He danced around, pointing at Walter.

Leon shot the Phreak. The man fell. But in a moment another man, who had been an obvious construct, left his routine station and came to the van. "Nyaa nyaa, you can't get me!" this one cried in the same voice.

"He just animates constructs," Walter said. "He's the Phreak I told you about. We can't kill him because he's not logged on. But he can interfere with us by calling the enemy's attention to us, and that's exactly what he's doing."

"We have a problem," Leon said.

That seemed to be the understatement of the hour.

thirteen

Baal thought she had gotten away cleanly. But then an alarm sounded. They must have discovered either her empty room or the dead guard. They would be after her in a moment.

She looked wildly around. There ahead of her, parked in front of the building, were several cars. Could she drive one of those? Yes, surely she could, because vehicles tended to be simple in the games: no complications such as ignition locks or low gasoline levels or foreign controls. If a person knew how to drive, she could drive a game car. She hoped.

She ran to the first car, reaching it just as there was a shout from the building. She yanked open the door and scrambled in, tossing the crowbar in back. She was relieved to see that the steering wheel was on the left. She got herself behind the wheel, put her hand on the ignition key, turned it—and nothing happened except a buzz.

Men were boiling out of the building and charging toward her. She couldn't possibly outrun them. She had to make this car go. What was wrong with the machine?

Then she realized that she hadn't buckled the seat belt. Trust the game to be safety conscious, even in its most dangerous setting! She didn't know whether real Maronites buckled their seat belts or merely trusted to God to protect the Chosen, but here she had to do it. She jammed the belt across, and as it clicked into place the buzzing stopped.

She turned the key. This time the motor came to life. Just as the first man reached the car.

She stepped on the accelerator, gunning the motor. But the car didn't move. Now what was the matter? Oh—the handbrake was on. She took it off and goosed the motor again—and still the car didn't move.

Meanwhile the man was yanking open the passenger side door, the same one she had used. Why hadn't she thought to lock it after her! He bent to stick his head inside, reaching for her with one hand.

The motor roared, and yet the car didn't budge. What was the *matter* with the car?

It wasn't in gear. How stupid could she get? She reached for the lever, to go from park to drive, without really looking; she was too busy trying to avoid the man's grasping hand as it approached her shoulder. She clutched for her knife with her left hand.

Her right hand came into contact with the lever, but when she tried to move it down, there was only a horrible grinding noise. *Now* what?

Then she saw that it was standard shift. The kind that had to be put into gear. She knew only automatic shift. She was sunk.

The man's hand closed on her right shoulder. She hauled out her knife and rammed the point into the side of that hand.

He screamed. He must have gotten a marvelous shock there, augmented by the sight of the stabbing blade. But he was still half inside the car. Meanwhile the other men were arriving. What had seemed like minutes was actually only seconds, but seconds were enough. One was about to open the door on the driver's side.

Baal used her knife hand to strike the lock button. Then she looked desperately at the floor beside her feet. How *did* a manual-shift car work? There was the gearshift, which really was something like the selector for the automatic shift. But because it wasn't automatic, the motor had to be disengaged before it could be used. The clutch! That was what did it. That must be that other pedal to the left of the brake.

She jammed her left foot on that pedal, then hauled down on the gearshift. This time it moved into place. She goosed the motor again—and yet again the car failed to move.

The man grabbed for her again. She whipped the knife across and stabbed at his face. He drew back, exclaiming.

Meanwhile the clutch hadn't done it, after all. She lifted her foot—and suddenly the car lurched forward. And stalled.

Oh. She had to let the clutch go after shifting. And not too fast. Okay, now she knew.

Meanwhile the man had been hauled down and dragged the few feet the car had traveled. That helped, though his upper body was still inside.

She turned the key to restart the motor. The car jumped forward and stalled again. Oh—it didn't want to start in gear. She tromped on the clutch and turned the key again, and now the motor started cleanly. Then, profiting by experience, she let the clutch up slowly.

The car hesitated, then nudged forward. The motor didn't stall. She was getting it! She was driving a manual-shift car!

The man tried to scramble into the car. She shifted the knife to her right hand and gave him a literal poke in the eye. She was getting the hang of vicious fighting too. He cried out and fell back out. But her tally in the screen did not increase; she had not killed him. Too bad. She leaned over, reached across, and tried to pull the door shut. But her seat belt restrained her; she couldn't reach it.

Something loomed ahead. She was trying to drive into a telephone pole! She jerked the steering wheel and managed to avoid the obstruction.

She accelerated, and the car speeded up, but it wasn't going fast enough. The men were running alongside, trying to get in again. Didn't this thing have any velocity? The motor was really racing.

Oh. No automatic shift. She kept forgetting. It didn't take itself into the higher gears.

Okay, now do this right. Down with the clutch pedal, so. Then the gearshift stick. Where did it go? Surely not back into neutral. What were its positions?

She tried them all, moving the stick any which way it would

go. She found one slot up and to the right. She let up the clutch—and the car started moving forward faster. She had found a higher gear!

Thrilled, she aimed the car down the road and picked up speed, leaving the man behind. Then she got smart about the open door. She swerved left, and the door swung open; then she swerved right, and the door swung closed and latched. Remote control!

Then she looked ahead, and saw the start of a steep descent. She was up in a mountain, and the level terrace extended only so far. She jammed on the brakes, managing to slow down enough so that she didn't go leaping off the mountain.

But now the pursuers were getting smart too. The cars behind were coming to life. She saw them in the rearview mirror. It was amazing how well even such a detail worked, considering that this was all a game animation. It was getting easier to forget that this wasn't really Lebanon, or a real car. Part of her hadn't forgotten, because in life she never would have killed a man by klonking him with a crowbar, or stolen a car while stabbing a man. She was still acting more freely and violently than normal, and experiencing the illicit thrill thereof. Increasingly she was getting into the spirit of this adventure. She was being a wild woman, beating back the mean men. What a glorious feeling!

The car behind was catching up. Baal knew she had to get back to business. First she had to escape the Maronites. Then she had to go rescue a hostage. Then she had to find Walter Toland. Somehow. Because he was the one who really needed rescue.

She swung right, around a corner, finding a more level street. There was pressure on her left side. That was just the wrappings giving her a selective tingle, but it certainly felt as if she were being pushed by centrifugal force. Her vision and mind helped translate the small sensations into an overall experience, and it was realistic enough. She couldn't make high-velocity right-angle turns here any more than she could in a real car.

The following cars made the turn and gained on her again. She stepped on the gas, but though the motor roared the car didn't go that much faster. One of the pursuing cars was coming up beside her, trying to force her to the side of the road.

Oh. The gears. She pushed down the clutch pedal and tried for another notch in the invisible pattern of the gearshift. She found one. She let up the clutch, and the motor engaged. She moved faster, with less engine stress. She was in the top gear!

She accelerated, but the other car kept pace. It was the same kind of car, and probably better driven. How was she going to get away from it?

Well, this was war. She fumbled until she found her pistol. Then she pumped the pedal, moving ahead a little. Then she rolled down her window. When the other car matched velocity again and moved across to shove her car, she poked the muzzle of her gun out and fired. Through the window of the other vehicle.

The pistol bucked in her hand. Glass shattered. The other car veered, crossed the road, and clipped a telephone pole. It continued on until it crashed into a house. It burst into flame. Her screen registered a tally.

Now, wasn't that nice! She had just won another point. But if they succeeded in pushing her off the road, she would be the one to crash and go up in the fireball. Fireballs were evidently easy to come by, in the game. But she didn't want to be in one.

The other car was still coming. And there might be more of them heading in to cut her off. How was she going to get away? She didn't want to let one come up beside her again, because next time they'd be firing through *her* window. She had gotten as far as she had by surprising them, but her store of surprises was about gone.

Fortunately she was coming down off the mountain now, and was no longer in danger of sluing off the road and rolling down the slope. She picked up speed.

The road was headed into the city. Not Jounieh; she had headed out away from that, going south. So she must be coming to Beirut, where the real action was. She saw the thickening houses and buildings ahead. Was that good or bad for her? She hadn't had a chance to review the situation of this setting. She knew that there were several factions, each of which controlled its section of Beirut and fought the others. Where did the Maronite section end? Did it matter?

Now there was other traffic. But the other cars didn't try to interfere with her. That meant they were game constructs, there just to make it look normal. But it also meant she could be caught in a traffic jam. That could be the end of her, because the Maronites would just fire into her car until they killed her.

Unless there was a way she could use the game constructs as interference. If she got them between her and the pursuit, maybe she could leave the Maronites in the traffic jam and get away.

She tried it. She reminded herself firmly that this was a game setting, and not real life. Anybody she killed here didn't really die. *She* wouldn't really die if she crashed. She could afford to be really wild.

She veered out of her lane, passing the car ahead. There was too small a gap in the opposing traffic, but she pushed her luck and squeezed in without having a head-on collision. It definitely helped her, knowing it wasn't real. It gave her much increased nerve. After all, she was supposed to be strong on luck and intelligence, so now she was giving her luck the chance to help her.

The Maronite car tried to follow her, and couldn't; the gap had closed. But she knew it would catch up soon, if she didn't keep squeezing past other cars.

She spied another chancy opening, and took it. Again her luck held, and she squeaked through. Her heart was racing, and she knew that wasn't any game manifestation; she was at a high fever, bodywise, because part of her really was scared by these daredevil gambles. It was like riding the roller coaster: she knew it was ultimately safe, but it was crafted to seem unsafe, and so it was manageably scary.

But the traffic was getting thicker ahead. Soon she would be locked into the channeled flow, with no chance to squeeze out. That was no good. She had to keep her options open, or they would close in on her and kill her. Already that flow was slowing, and she had to struggle with clutch and shift to return to the middle gear. As she did so, she wondered whether the setting was realistic in this respect. In most cities traffic got congested, but this was a city at chronic war with itself; there shouldn't be routine traffic, should there? There weren't exactly white-collar jobs waiting downtown. Maybe a regular city had been used as the template, and some programmer had forgotten to delete the thick traffic.

However, this was the scene with which she had to deal. So she would deal with it.

She abruptly took a right turn onto an intersecting road that headed back out toward the country. There was little traffic here, so she was able to move at full speed.

It took the pursuing car a while to reach the intersection, so Baal got a good lead. But that would do her no good if she didn't exploit it to lose the Maronites.

She tried. She took a left turn, hoping the other car wouldn't see which one and would cruise on past. There was a settlement here, with several streets. These were fairly clean, without cars. This must have been a subdivision, deserted when the trouble started. She turned left again, before the Maronites caught up to the first turn. Then she saw an open garage, and on impulse swerved onto that drive and pulled into it. She could hide until they gave up and went home!

She braked hard to stop—and the engine jerked and stalled. Oh, that nonautomatic drive again! She should have shifted to neutral. Well, she could start it once more, when she needed to.

Meanwhile, she might be better off outside the car. At least she could stretch her legs, for whatever good that might do her, considering that in real life she couldn't move out of her boots and gloves.

She detached the seat belt, opened the door, and got out. She looked at the side of the car—and saw what looked like a bullet hole in the side. They had fired at her, and scored, but not in a vital part, so she had not been stalled or blown up. But it had been a closer call than she had thought at the time.

She tried the door into the house. It opened, and she entered. No one seemed to be here. Even in Beirut, folk had to earn their living, and they couldn't simply stay home and relax. This was of course merely a game-construct family anyway, which was why she felt safe exploring; even if any of them had been home, they wouldn't have reacted to her. They were like the paintings and cardboard figures at the beginning and end of a setting's activity. Even when they seemed three-dimensional, they weren't. And this ordinary, undamaged suburban residence was probably another careless leftover from the template. The game programmers just hadn't expected anyone to turn randomly off the highway and randomly hide in a house. That would probably change as they got more experience in esoteric settings.

She decided that she had used enough time. The Maronites must have thoroughly lost her by now. She could emerge and go her way. Where was that? On into Beirut, the center of town, where maybe somebody was hiding the American hostage.

How was she ever going to find that hostage, since the folk

who were supposed to give her directions had turned out to be her enemies? That left her pretty much blank. She couldn't just walk into a library and look it up!

Or could she? Who was to say she couldn't research for information she needed? There could be devious devices in the settings, as she had discovered as the Princess. Such as that magic talking mirror that wanted to see her perform the act of sex. Some programmer must have gotten his jollies programming that lascivious prop. But it seemed to have helped Walter, and therefore her. So why not a library here, with exactly what she needed? Her character was smart, so could think of something like that, and the game would probably honor it.

So where was she to find a library? She needed a street map of the city, with public buildings identified. A tourist guide! And maybe she knew where to look for that.

She cast about for a telephone. But here her luck petered out; there was none. Therefore no phone book. But maybe there was a phone booth in the neighborhood. That would do as well. Because the phone book should list a tourist station or a library, and have enough of a map to enable her to find it.

She returned to the garage and the car. She peered out to see whether the Maronite car was anywhere close. It wasn't. She got in, set her seat belt, and turned the key.

The car lurched forward, crashing into the wall of the garage. Damn it! She had forgotten its archaic gearing again. This might be just a garage emulation, but she didn't like messing it up. She used the clutch and shifted into what she trusted was the central neutral gear, then tried again. This time the motor started without trouble.

Now she had to find reverse. Where could it be? She tried every direction the stick would go, but all speeds were forward. Where had they hidden it?

Frustrated, she stared at the knob on the stick. Now she saw that there was a design on it, with numbers. That was the pattern of the gears! And there to the side was "R"—for reverse.

But when she tried it, it didn't go. There was no path where the diagram indicated. Had they left reverse out of this car? No, that would take extra game programming, and they wouldn't have bothered.

Then she remembered something she had seen once: someone pushing down on the gearstick. Could that be it?

She tried it. The stick went down—and then it did go into the reverse channel. She had pieced it out.

She eased out the clutch, and the car backed smoothly out of the garage. To think that most of the trouble she was having probably wasn't meant to be a challenge at all! They must have assumed that anyone who chose this setting knew how to drive a standard-shift car. Well, she knew how now, and sometime when she was back in real life she'd try it, just to see how well it worked.

She reached the street, turned, stopped, and shifted out of reverse, which was easier than shifting in. She nudged forward, still peering all around. The way seemed to be clear. Good enough.

She moved slowly down the street, looking for a telephone booth. There should be one somewhere in this settlement. And there was; she found one by a small store.

She parked by it without stalling, got out, and checked for the phone book. There it was, and it did indeed have a general map and listing of points of interest. She studied the map avidly. It showed Beirut as half a peninsula, with the Mediterranean Sea on the west and north. There was a green line bisecting it, and on that line was the National Museum. The east part of the city was marked MARONITE CHRISTIAN, while the west was divided into several Moslem groups. To the south was a section marked DRUZE and beyond that PALESTINIAN. Those were the main factions. There were six crossing points, the main one being at the National Museum. What happened if someone decided to cross somewhere else? Maybe she would find out.

Where were the hostages? They weren't marked. Would a library list them either? She doubted it now; hostages were hardly fixtures of the landscape. So maybe her bright idea wasn't as good as she thought.

So then where should she inquire? Israel? She was after all an Israeli agent. But Israel would be a long way to drive, assuming she could get through. There should be other Israelis here—but where were they? How could she approach them? "Hey, I'm one of your agents. I botched my mission, so now if you'll just tell me where the nearest hostage is . . ." That did not seem conducive.

Or should she just give up on her nominal mission and search for Walter instead? It wasn't as if she owed anything to this set-

ting or the team to which she was assigned. She had been sent
in like a lamb to the slaughter, and she was lucky to be alive.
Yes, she would go for her real mission, which included nailing
the Phreak once he showed up. If that made Phreak tell Walter
how to quit the game, then he would be all right.

But where could she find Walter? That was just about as big
a riddle as the hostage. In fact he just might *be* a hostage.
Wouldn't that be something, if she quit looking for the hostage,
and it was Walter! So she would continue looking for the hostage, but mainly for Walter.

She returned to the car, and this time got it started without accident. She held the map of Beirut in her mind. Which faction
was most likely to be holding a hostage? Or were none of them
actually holding hostages, and all of them wanted to rescue hostages from someone else so as to get support from the nations the
hostages were from? She wished she had had more time to get
background on this setting.

Then she had another idea. The map had marked some embas-
sies, and one was the American. Suppose she went there and explained her mission and asked for their help? How could they
refuse it? They might not be able to do anything much themselves, but they should be happy to provide her all the information she might need. That information should be just as useful in
locating Walter as the American hostage.

Feeling better, she drove toward the street on which she had
entered this community. She would have to find her way to the
main city and on to the U.S. Embassy in West Beirut, but
she could do that. As long as she managed to remain clear of the
Maronites.

She turned onto the road. Then she saw a car starting up. The
Maronites had set a watch on this road, waiting for her to reap-
pear, and she had blithely done it! She should have stayed well
away from it, and found some other route.

She gunned the motor and shifted up. Maybe she could get far
enough ahead to make another turn and lose herself, as she had
before. Or something.

Then she saw another car coming from the opposite direction.
She knew it was a Maronite; there was really nothing else it
could be. They were closing the pincers on her, and this time she
had no way out.

But maybe she did. She was accelerating even before she re-

alized what was on her mind. It was a game called Chicken.
Never in her crazy dreams had she thought to play it, but suddenly in *his* dream she was going to. Because it was the only
way out.

She aimed her car right for the oncoming vehicle. "Here're the
rules," she muttered as if talking directly to the other driver. "We
approach each other at top speed, and the first one who flinches
is chicken. Great game, eh?"

But a better game for her than for them. Because she had to
be free to pursue her mission, and she would not be free if they
caught her. In fact she would probably be dead if they caught
her. So she had nothing to lose, really. While they had plenty to
lose. It was a case where the player with the weakest hand had
the strongest motive, because he had the least to sacrifice.

"Chick-chick-chick-chicken!" she teased, feeling wild and
wonderful. She had entered the game to flirt with suicide, and
now she was doing it in style.

The other car looked uncertain. It wavered. She corrected her
steering to remain targeted directly on it. She wouldn't let it wea-
sel out! She would make it crash, or turn tail and flee. She would
teach these people not to mess with her. Oh, what a thrill!

The other car swerved so violently that it lost control. It went
careening off the road, and Baal sailed blithely on, winner and
owner of the road. "I knew it!" she cried. "You're chicken!"

But the car behind her kept coming. She couldn't get rid of it
that way. There was nothing she could do now except keep racing ahead as fast as she could. Maybe she would find a way to
shake the pursuit. Or maybe she would lead it right through the
city and into enemy territory, where it would have just as much
trouble as she.

She skewed around the corner of the intersection, and headed
back toward the highway where the traffic was. The traffic was
thinner now, she saw; maybe the morning rush hour was over. So
she just might be able to do something with it.

In fact she might be able to play a variant of Chicken here too.
She couldn't scare off a game-construct car, because it would
drive exactly the way it was programmed regardless, and would
indeed crash head-on if she challenged it. It had way less to lose
than she did, after all, because it was nothing, just a figment of
the game's imagination. But she could take risks with construct
cars and force the Maronites to do the same, lest they lose her.

She had already proved that they had less nerve than she did, in this situation. She could keep on proving it, or die. Since she had already taken out several of them, she would be ahead on points.

Of course she didn't want to die. She wanted to help Walter, and that meant finding him. Then when Phreak found him, she could nab Phreak with the patch. If she didn't accomplish that here in Beirut, she would have no idea where to find Walter, and indeed, she might never see him again. So she had a lot to live for. But she had to pretend that she didn't, so as to have the advantage over the Maronites. At least until she managed to lose them.

She careened into the intersection, narrowly missing a car. The Maronite car had to slow, because there simply was no room behind Baal. It squeezed in three cars back. Score one more for the chicken!

But she couldn't rest on her laurel. She had to keep working at it, or the Maronite would find a way to catch up. So she watched for her chance, and pulled out to pass the moment there was a too-small gap in the opposing traffic. She squeezed back in her lane so tightly that she thought she might have lost some paint. Now she was four cars ahead.

The city proper developed around them. That brought stoplights. Baal didn't trust them; the Maronites might catch her when she stopped. So instead of stopping, she pulled out to the right and bumped along the skirt of the road. She saw a gap in the cross traffic, timed it, made a mental prayer, and shot across out of turn. That really left the Maronite in the dust!

For the moment she was free of direct pursuit. She proceeded into the city, bearing west, because the U.S. Embassy was near the coast on the north side of West Beirut.

She thought of Walter, as she had a number of times. Of course she was trying to help him, but now she realized that it was more than that. He was a chance acquaintance, another player, who lived so far away that she would probably never meet him in life. The game was their only practical contact. They didn't even know what each other looked like. He was a dozen years or so older than she, and confined to a wheelchair. But she liked him.

There it was. She liked him. Why? Did it make any sense? She was attracted to him. That was why she had been willing, nay eager, to have game sex with him. And why she wanted so very much to rescue him from the peril he faced.

Could it be that he was the first person she had encountered who really needed her for something? If so, once he got free of the game, that would be over. Or would it? He had thought sex was over, for him. But in the game it was proving to be possible. Of course he could do it with another girl, in the game. But she was pretty sure he wouldn't. She was the one he had started with, and she was the one he would want to finish with. So he needed her for that too.

But outside the game, what was there? Nothing, really. She had to be realistic. They might have a fun time in the game, but that would be the extent of it. Still, she couldn't help wishing it weren't so. The thought of being with a man confined to a wheelchair didn't bother her. After all, she was used to medical liability. Others might find that a strange attitude, but what did others know? There were qualities about Walter that truly appealed to her. So maybe it was unrealistic, but she had license to dream.

Then another description came to her: rebound. She was on the rebound from Tyson Blunt. That explained the rapidity with which she was getting interested in Walter. The alternate reality of the game detached her from true reality and gave her leave to love foolishly as well as to act foolishly. So she should watch herself. Still, when all the reconsideration was done, she did like Walter.

Now that she was able to relax, she became aware of a developing problem. She had had a booster shot of insulin during the game, which should have carried her through for the duration. But she hadn't reckoned on the excitement of the chase, literally. She had been fighting for her life, killing people who sought to kill her, and her pulse had been racing. That meant a higher rate of metabolism, which in turn meant that her body needed less insulin. She needed some sugar to balance that out, lest she run the danger of insulin shock.

Well, that should be no problem. She could park in some obscure spot and exit the game long enough to eat something sweet, then pick up where she had left off. It would take only a minute, because her sweets were right beside her body.

She saw that during her distraction of thought the nature of the city had changed. Now at least it was programmed correctly: with bombed-out buildings and rubble on the streets.

She turned off the main street, looking for a suitable alley. She could have done this when she was at the house, had she realized. She should have, because she was supposed to be in touch with her body whether she was in real life or the game. She just hadn't been paying proper attention.

Then she saw something in the rearview mirror. Another car was coming. A construct? If so, she could ignore it, or at least just stay out of its way. But if she let it get close and it was a player, she could be right back in trouble.

Maybe she could verify it. She turned onto a quiet residential lane where cars were parked along the sides. She watched the rear. In a moment the other car turned too. She turned again— and it turned again, following her.

The sugar would have to wait. The Maronites were after her again. Maybe they had been watching the traffic, and spotted the one car that did not stay in the flow. There was no physical way to tell a player car from a construct car, because all were in effect pictures in the setting. But they could be distinguished by their actions. She should have found a way to slide out of the flow without being obvious. Live and learn—too late, as usual.

She accelerated, trying to lose this new pursuit. But it stayed right on her tail, closing the distance. All of them seemed to know how to handle their cars better than she did! She still had some uncertainty shifting gears, and every so often got the wrong one.

Well, there was always Chicken. She headed west and started fishtailing through the construct traffic. But there was more room here, making it less dangerous, and the Maronite car stayed right with her. It was going to overhaul her soon, and she didn't seem to be able to shake it.

She tried going flat-out. She passed other cars at a high rate. Then most of them turned off, and she kept going straight west, with the Maronite still closing the gap. In a moment they would begin shooting at her. She tried to swerve back and forth, to make herself a more difficult target, though even in game emulation that was a scary business. Her pulse was racing again, and her body was using up more sugar. That had the incidental effect of making her increasingly wild. She had to get free, so she could stop for that brief time she needed.

Suddenly she saw barricades ahead. It was the Green Line, physically barring crossover. She swerved to the right, avoiding it without stopping. It was too dangerous to stop! But there should be a crossing point soon.

She followed the line, cruising past its jury-rigged fortifications. There were empty shipping crates, broken concrete slabs, railroad ties, steel girders, and just plain heaps of earth. Anything at all to block passage.

Then she saw a crossing. There were checkpoints on either side, with armed men. Those would be snipers.

She turned away. But only to circle the block and come at it more directly. She accelerated right down the alley. Maybe surprise and determination would get her safely through.

As she zoomed toward the crossing, she saw that someone had anticipated her and set crates out to block the way. But she was going too fast to stop, and anyway, she needed to get into the other part of the city. So she just kept moving, playing chicken with the barricades.

She struck them. Wood flew and clattered around her. The car bucked as its tires went over a fragment. She clung to the wheel, having no alternative.

She saw snipers on the far side taking aim at her with their rifles. If she ran the gantlet she'd be dead! So she veered to the side, aiming directly for the snipers, and mowed them down at high velocity.

Then she was through. The Maronite car gave up the chase; this was enemy territory to it. Unfortunately now the folk of this section took up the chase. These would be the Sunni Moslems, and she suspected that the name had nothing to do with their disposition. They would not greet her with any sunny smiles. Not after losing one—no, two—of their gunners to her hurtling vehicle. She had seen the score change on her screen.

All she could do was keep moving. The U.S. Embassy should be somewhere ahead, and she could charge into that and be safe. She hoped.

In a few minutes she found it; her luck was holding. She screeched up to its gate, jammed on the brakes, stalled the motor, and leaped out. She ran through the gate into the compound.

She saw a man. "I need sanctuary!" she gasped. "I'm an Israeli agent!"

He looked surprised, as well he might, but he gestured her to

an office. She ran into it and stood panting. Oh, she needed that
sugar! She felt the insulin taking a stronger grip, making her feel
light-headed.

In a moment an official arrived at the office. He wore jeans
and T-shirt, but she realized that this was pretty much the standard uniform for all factions here. "Tell me your situation, sir,"
he said in clear English. That was not surprising, because this
was the American Embassy, and anyway, all the players spoke
English, regardless how it would have been in the real Beirut.
Verisimilitude had its limits.

Baal realized that he took her for a man, because she was in
the uniform of a male Maronite Christian which pretty well covered her female attributes. She was going to correct him on that,
but some innate caution restrained her. This city was deadly dangerous throughout; as a woman she would be asking for even
more trouble than she was in already. So she kept her voice
husky and her clothing secure.

She poured out her story, the game version. Could they help
her find the American hostage? She knew that the embassy personnel couldn't take any direct action, but if they gave her the information, she could do what had to be done. And meanwhile,
was there a men's room? She didn't explain that she didn't need
it for its normal purpose; no player did. But it would guarantee
her a few minutes of privacy, during which she could exit the
game and take care of her sugar. Others did much the same with
respect to natural functions: they entered a game bathroom, then
exited to the real one. It was a useful convenience.

"Of course," the man said. "This way."

But then Baal remembered something. This setting was supposed to be the Beirut of approximately 1988; she had seen that
date on the phone book. She didn't know enough about the city's
history, but was sure that the violence had started long before
that year. Hadn't all Americans vacated the premises long before? In that case, who was here?

In fact was this the embassy at all? She had assumed it was
because it looked classy, but now she realized that she had made
an inordinately foolish assumption. This was more likely some
other building entirely. Which meant that these people were not
Americans at all.

She saw men standing at the side halls along their way. They
did not look threatening, but neither did they look reassuring.

Who occupied this estate? Who else but the Sunni Moslems, maybe.

They came to what looked like a truly elaborate bathroom complex, the vestige of a bygone affluence. Probably the local folk didn't use it at all, even as a takeoff point for game exits. She walked in, and discovered a palatial antechamber, and beyond it the room with toilet stalls.

So if these weren't Americans, what had she done? She had blabbed her game mission and foolishly gotten herself trapped in the heart of another enemy. The Sunni Moslems wanted to win too, and they well might use her information to further their cause. They were unlikely either to help her or to let her go.

Was there any way to get out of this self-imposed pickle? She doubted it but thought she had better make the effort. She didn't want to be the captive of the Moslems any more than of the Christians. She just wanted to find Walter and the Phreak and patch the latter and be with the former. After that, well, she would improvise.

She needed to exit and get some sugar. Surely her blood was getting low, which accounted for her reckless driving and idiotic snap decision to enter this building without verifying its nature. But if she did exit, she might return to find herself the captive of the Sunni. She couldn't take the chance. She had to try to escape immediately, before they expected it.

She hastily explored the chamber. There was a fancy window with opaque glass. What was beyond it? She didn't know, but would have to gamble that it was a way out.

She had left her crowbar in the car. Too bad. What else could she use to break that glass? She looked frantically around the bathroom. All she saw was a row of toilet stalls.

Come on, her character was supposed to be smart and lucky. There should be a way, for that sort.

She had a notion. She entered a stall and put her hands on the back of the toilet. She lifted the heavy ceramic lid to the water tank. Was that solid enough to bash through the thick glass? She would just have to find out.

Then she thought of something else. They thought she was male. Could she fake them out by turning female? Maybe she could bash out the glass, then hide in a stall, and they would search for a fleeing man outside. Then she could go out the regular door as a female, and maybe reach her car before they caught on.

It seemed chancy, but luck could make it work. She would give it the old college try.

She carried the lid out to the window and set it down. Then she stripped her uniform efficiently away. But what did she have that was female? She couldn't try it nude. That had been a ploy in the Princess in the Castle setting, but here in Beirut there were no naked nymphs. In fact the women were so heavily clothed they almost disappeared.

Well, she would try to make do. She drew her knife and used it to slice away the lining of her jacket. She used that lining to fashion a crude blouse. She didn't have any needle or thread; she would just have to tuck the material into her waistband and hope. She cut off the cuffs of the trousers, making them halfway feminine. She fluffed out her hair and used a length of cloth to make a bow. The boots just wouldn't do; she would have to trust the heavy socks to resemble slippers.

Baal gazed at herself in the mirror. She was now certainly feminine, but no way was she Moslem. But maybe the players wouldn't realize that a Western woman was out of place here. Not right away. If her luck were phenomenal.

She tucked her knife and pistol into her waistband under her blouse, picked up the toilet tank cover, and heaved it into the window. The glass shattered with a satisfying crash. This might all be computer simulation, but it was excellent. Someone must have tried this ploy before.

She ran to the stalls, then realized that she had left the remnants of her clothing on the floor. She reversed course and swooped it up. Then she went to the middle stall and entered. She climbed up on the toilet so that her feet would not show, and stood balanced with the bundle of rags in her arms, facing the stall door.

Barely in time. Men charged in, summoned by the crash. "He broke through the glass!" someone exclaimed. "Surround the building!"

They charged out again. When Baal thought they were all gone, she stepped carefully down, set the rags on the back of the toilet, and marched out of the bathroom.

"Well," a man said as she passed through the doorway. "So

you did try that ploy. And you seem to be female too. That's a bonus."

Baal turned to face him. "You're too smart for me," she said. "But if you will let me go, I'll show you what's in my blouse." She put her hand to her waistband, reaching under the blouse.

"I'll see more than that anyway," he said, reaching for her.

She whipped up the knife and stabbed him in the belly. As he looked down, surprised, she jerked out the knife and stabbed higher, this time catching him in the throat. Then she stepped back so he fell on the floor instead of on her.

She glanced at her screen. Her score for the setting now stood at six.

She was getting mercilessly efficient! Just as the game enabled her to be far looser about sex than in life, it also made her able to kill with barely a qualm. She would have to think about the implications. Was the game corrupting her? Would it eventually make of her a creature without conscience?

But she couldn't waste time on such thoughts. She had to get out of here. She hauled the body to the side, trying to put it out of sight. Then she hurried along the hall toward the front door. No one seemed to be around at the moment. Could this actually work?

She opened the front door and stepped out, hoping to see her car. Instead she saw two men with rifles pointed at her.

"Move and you are dead," one of them said. She had no doubt of his sincerity.

She stood absolutely still as the man approached. He frisked her efficiently, locating and removing her knife and gun. If she had had the sense to step out with gun drawn, or to look before she exited—but she had been too eager to get out and find the car. She had brought her downfall on herself.

"What are you going to do with me?" she inquired as the man tied her hands behind her. She wasn't sure whether she should have made a break for it and made them kill her. What would he do with a female captive? Foolish question!

"You're a hostage now," the man said. "I wonder what the Israelis will pay for you? You had better hope you're worth a premium unharmed."

She had sought to rescue a hostage—and become one herself!

fourteen

PATCH

Phreak danced before Walter Toland, pointing him out to the Hizbollah troops. He didn't care whether the man lived or died; he was simply showing him who was boss. If Toland got killed he would have to enter another setting, and another, and Phreak would find him no matter where. Eventually he would realize that there was no escape, and would become tolerable company.

The other Druze, the one who had tried to kill Phreak, faced forward and pretended to be a game construct. That was okay; Phreak didn't care about him. Toland was his toy for this game.

The Hizbollah appeared. Phreak pointed again at Toland. Toland, stuck, drew his pistol. "I'll attract their fire," he told his companion. "You proceed with the mission."

The other man nodded and moved slowly out of the vicinity. Toland took aim at the nearest Hizbollah and fired.

"Oooh, that's going to make them mad!" Phreak called, delighted. "They'll really gun for you now!"

But the Hizbollah had some caution. "What's that load you're carrying?" one shouted.

"A fruit-covered bomb," Walter Toland called back.

The guard hesitated. He knew that a car bomb could take out a fair chunk of a city block.

Walter encouraged his hesitancy. "And one stray bullet could set it off." He continued to drive forward in the slow traffic.

"I think you're bluffing," the other Druze said grimly.

"I'm trying to give you a chance to get away," Walter said. "Now that Phreak's found me, he'll never quit. My usefulness to your cause is at an end. But you can continue your mission. I'll try to distract them so that you can get out unobserved. Then you yell about the danger of the bomb, and fade into the crowd. Maybe you'll be able to get this van back after they take me away."

The Druze looked at him without speaking. He wasn't sure Walter meant it. Neither was Phreak. How good was the man at bluffing?

"Hey, don't let him get away!" Phreak cried. "He's bluffing! He doesn't have any bomb!"

"Who are you?" a Hizbollah man demanded, clapping a hand on Phreak's shoulder. "You're not one of us."

"He's a game-crasher," Walter said from the van. "Nothing he says can be trusted."

"You're probably all in this together," the Hizbollah said. "We'll take you all in." His hand hauled back on Phreak's shoulder, as other Hizbollah closed in.

Phreak did what came naturally: he vacated the body. He had to use a game-setting body in order to make himself seen and heard, but he did not dare do anything substantial, such as bashing a player. Because that would make a game record, and too many records would be his undoing. Each record was a footprint, and the game proprietors could use those footprints to track him down. If he killed someone, the game would try to register the kill to a nonexistent player, and that would set off alarms galore.

So he mainly used his mouth. He had a good mouth, so that was all right. And he could stay out of personal trouble by skipping from one game-construct figure to another. Any figure that was in the scene, he could animate without alerting the game proprietors. Sometimes there was only one, like the mirror in the Evil Sorcerer's apartment. But here there were figures all over the place.

He oriented on the one in the car immediately before the Toland van. All he had to do was focus on it, and his perception jumped to it. Then he could make it do anything he wanted, and the game program never knew the difference. So long as it didn't directly change the game.

He put his head out the window, looking back at the van. When he was sure that Walter was looking, he put his arm out too, sticking one finger sharply upward. He was going to rag the man until he made a mistake and got himself killed. Then he'd track him down in the next setting, and the next, never letting him loose. It was easy to do: he just checked the rosters until he found the name, then entered the setting and tuned in his special prey monitor. That was a spot on his simplified screen that glowed. When it was faint, the prey was far across the setting; it brightened as he got closer. It wasn't effective at close range, but he could handle that. In this case he had found Walter in the Beirut setting, as a Druze. That had narrowed it down to twenty-five players, and that was as far as he could take it. Maybe someday he'd rework his program to be more sophisticated, so he could track a player right down to his single assignment.

Then he had gone into the setting, animating one construct after another, looking around for players. When he found one, he yelled "Hey, Walter!" or somesuch, and if the man answered, bingo. Those who responded with confusion or blank stares were wrong players. Of course the players he nailed tended to get smarter as the game progressed, making location more of a challenge, but he always ran them down eventually. That was the fun of it.

The Hizbollah were hauling away the construct he had just vacated. They thought he was faking. It didn't matter. Now it was regular players messing with a construct, and any footprints made were theirs. It would only lead to confusion. That was part of the point. Messing things up was fun. He was sure it made both players and proprietors furious. But they couldn't do a thing about it, because he was way too smart for them.

Meanwhile they were also surrounding Walter, holding their fire just in case there was explosive, but not letting him get away. But his companion was leaving the van on the side the Hizbollah couldn't see.

Maybe he had better mess that up too. "Hey, watch out! One's getting away!" he called.

The Hizbollah were uncertain, but they made a game try. "Kill the ones outside the van, but don't hit the van," their leader ordered.

The Druze dived for a construct car. "Here he is!" Phreak called, pointing.

The next Hizbollah bullet struck him instead of the Druze. As his body died, he saw the Druze climbing into the car. Then the scene faded, and he had to find another body. This was like groping in the dark; the constructs had faint glows of animation, while the players had bright glows. He knew better than to try to take over a player's body; that would not be effective. So he latched onto a faint glow in the region he wanted, and opened his eyes as another body.

By this time the Druze was driving the car away. "You fools!" Phreak cried. "You shot the wrong man!"

However, they were capturing Walter. Phreak decided to shut up for a while, since the Hizbollah weren't paying much attention to him anyway, and watch what happened.

"Hey, there *are* explosives here!" a Hizbollah cried as he checked the van.

"Okay, we'll make him tell us his mission," the leader said. "Put him in with the hostages while we figure out what to do with this stuff."

So they hauled Walter into one of their cars and drove him to their secret prison. Phreak shifted to a car with a driver and followed them. They had hostages? This could be interesting.

It was—because Walter wasn't the only one being taken there. Another car was bringing a woman. They were rare in this setting, so Phreak paid attention. She wore a funny blouse and cutoff pants, and didn't look happy. How did they get hold of her? He shifted to another body, and another, until he was able to eavesdrop on two of them talking, and learned that they had made a deal with the Sunni Moslems, taking the captive the Sunni had acquired in return for leaving the Sunni border alone. They were collecting hostages, which they hoped to use to gain leverage in the setting, so that they could win.

It seemed that everybody had his angle, in this setting. The Maronites, the Sunni, the Druze all had their plans of conquest. He had passed by the PLO forces to the south, and they were marching on the city too. Meanwhile the Amal and the Hizbollah were struggling to control their part of the city. The Syrians and Israelis were marshaling their forces for possible invasion, if either could foment a pretext. This was one mean setting, and he loved it. He had watched it before; usually things got so fragmented that no faction won and the bonus was lost. Just the way it was in the real world. This time there seemed to be better organization, but the odds were still against any clear victory by any one faction. Maybe if two or three collaborated they could do it. But nobody liked to share a bonus if he figured he could do it alone. Phreak was almost sorry he couldn't get in this setting for real, game-wise, and try to score.

He followed the woman in. She wasn't all that much, physically, but that only meant that she had chosen an indifferent body. Her peculiar uniform didn't help. It looked as if she had hacked up a man's uniform and jammed it on inside out. She must have been trying to spy on the Sunni, and they caught her. Well, maybe he could have some fun teasing her after they locked her up. Mostly women wouldn't give him the time of day, not even one minute of it, but a prisoner would be different. She'd have to listen, or quit the game. She'd quit, of course, after a while. Then he'd get back to Walter.

They frisked her, but she was clean; the Sunni had taken any weapons she might have had.

To his surprise, they put her in with the male prisoner. There were five original hostages, but they were hidden somewhere else. Maybe these two would join them, after they had been tortured or otherwise made to talk. Maybe they hoped the two would talk, thinking that no one was listening. Maybe they didn't have enough secure rooms or personnel to guard them, without weakening their street warfare. So they were locked in together, and not even a guard. But it was a secure chamber.

Well, it was time to stir things up. He took over a construct who was supposed to be playing at guarding the stairs, and marched him into the chamber facing the barred cell. They would think he was one of the Hizbollah players. He drew his pistol. "So! Are you going to talk, you Druze turd?" he demanded threateningly of Walter.

Walter gazed at him through the bars. "If you kill me, you'll never learn anything about my mission," he said.

"So! You dare to talk back to me, you slime!" Phreak said. "Take that." He aimed his pistol to the side of Walter's foot and fired, hoping it would seem that his miss was accidental. He couldn't really hurt the man, of course, because that would require scoring by the game.

"Leave him alone!" the woman said.

He turned to her. "Yeah? What do you care, bitch?"

Walter squinted at him. The man was suspicious, knowing that Phreak was around, but evidently not yet sure. But all he said was "My hair is red."

"What are you talking about?" Phreak said. "Your hair is brown. You color-blind?"

The woman looked surprised. "If your hair is red, mine is blue," she said.

"That's for sure!" Phreak agreed. "Who cares what color it is anyway? It'll be red with blood before you get out of this."

Walter looked surprised too. "Wheels," he said.

"You're no big wheel, you're just a prisoner," Phreak retorted. "Now, are you going to talk, or do I have to plug you?" He aimed his pistol again.

"Needlepoint," the woman said.

"What did you call me?" Phreak demanded, turning the pistol on her.

"I apologize," she said immediately. But she did not seem apologetic. Instead she seemed oddly satisfied. Happy, even. What was going on with her?

Walter smiled. "I think she's dazed by her captivity. But I'm not. You're Phreak, and you don't dare shoot either of us. So why don't you go away before someone finds you here and shoots you?"

"I don't have to do nothing I don't want to!" Phreak said, nettled that the man had caught on so quickly. Walter was a tough customer, maybe because of his police training. He didn't spook easy.

The woman looked perplexed. "How can you talk to a guard like that? Why can't he shoot us?"

Walter grimaced. "This is hard to explain. He's a game-crasher who isn't properly logged in; he uses constructs that players aren't using, so that the game has no record of his activities, as long as he doesn't push his luck. He's here to annoy me. Ignore him."

"Like hell you will!" Phreak said, gesturing with the pistol. Walter was ruining his act.

"He's not a real player?" she asked, staring at Phreak. "He

certainly looks like one. Do you mean he's really like a ghost, so if I touched him he would be just vapor?"

"No, I'm as solid as you are, bitch!" Phreak said. "I'll prove it. Hold out your hand."

She mustered some courage. "I think you're bluffing, just as you are about the gun." She put her arm between the bars.

Phreak stepped up and slapped her hand, hard. But she grabbed onto his hand, clutching it. Her other hand stabbed at the air, as if she were trying to hit the EXIT on her private game screen. What was the matter with her?

Then he felt a kind of rippling shock, passing from her hand through his, and quickly traversing his body. Something strange was happening. So he vacated the body.

He exited the game and checked himself. Everything was in order. The bitch must have pressed a pseudo-nerve on the construct's hand and made it react. Trying to fake him out, the way he had tried to fake the two of them out. Well, it hadn't worked, and he would get right back in there and make her regret it. He'd razz her so hard she'd have to leave the game forever.

He moved back in, quickly returning to the place he'd left. He found the body on the floor; when he had vacated it, he had left it off balance, so it had fallen. No problem; he'd make it get up again, and if anything was wrong with it, he'd take another body.

He animated it—and something clamped down on him, hard. It wasn't exactly physical. It was more like a locking-in. This was weird! So he vacated it again—

And couldn't. *He was locked into this body!*

He rolled over and sat up. "What happened?" he asked dazedly.

The woman peered down at him through the bars. "I patched you," she said.

"Huh?"

"You're now logged into the game," she said. "The same as I am, and Walter is. And you can't get out, any more than Walter can."

Phreak scrambled to his feet. "Who the hell are you?"

"I am Baal, otherwise known to you as the Princess of the Castle. The one you wanted to watch engaging in sex. I went out of the game and to the proprietors, and they gave me a patch to lock you in. It ties you to Walter, so you can't quit until he does. In fact you can't even be in a different setting from him, because it gives you the same setting address as him. So now you'll have to give me the antivenin, so I can go out and use it, to free you both."

Phreak stared at her. "You're the same bitch!" he exclaimed. "In another part."

"That's right. I was looking for you, Phreak, as well as for Walter. Because I knew you'd be close to him. Now we've found each other and I have patched you. How does it feel to be hoist in your own petard?"

Phreak was having trouble orienting. "To be what?"

"Caught in your own trap," Walter said helpfully. "The petard was an early finned bomb designed to blow down a gate or breach a wall. The word derives from the Latin, to break wind. Seems quite apt, in your case."

"Listen, you creep—" Phreak started, but the gravity of his situation was sinking in. He was caught by his own virus? Then he couldn't get out to feed in the nullifying code.

"So are you going to give me the antivenin?" Baal inquired with mock sweetness.

Phreak exploded. "No, you bitch! And it wouldn't do you no good nowise. Know why? 'Cause you're locked in too. What do you think of that?"

She was set back. "What?"

"I knew you were up to no good, so I put the virus on your address before I came here. You've been locked in ever since you came back into the game. Didn't you know?"

"No, I never tried to exit after that," she said. "But I will now." She poked her finger in the air.

After a moment she looked appalled. "Oh, no!"

Phreak laughed. "So you're patched too, bitch. You can't get out of the game."

"But I *have* to get out," she said. "I need to get some sugar."

"Tough titty. You ain't going nowhere." He glanced at her, and saw that her hands were shaking and there was sweat on her forehead. She must really be nervous.

Then someone entered the room. It was a Hizbollah partisan, carrying a package. "Who are you?" he demanded, spying Phreak.

"He's one of us," Walter said, smiling with a certain satisfaction. "We're in this together."

Phreak tried to protest, but other Hizbollah charged into the room, guns drawn. In a moment they had thrown him into the cell with Walter and Baal. "Now we have three prisoners to interrogate and trade," the leader said. "Something really big must be up, to send in so many infiltrators."

"Yeah, but how do we find out what?" another asked. "We can't torture them; they'll just quit the game."

Phreak looked at Walter, then at Baal. He hated them both, but they were now in a conspiracy of silence. If the Hizbollah knew they couldn't quit, they'd start experimenting to see just how unpleasant they could make it. He didn't want to be dismembered stage by stage, even if the pain would not be the same as in real life.

"Hold 'em, then," the leader said. "We'll just have to trade them for some of our own, when we lose any. Meanwhile we've got some serious supplies to move in." The first man put his package down in the cell adjacent to the one the three of them were in, in the far corner. The large chamber had been cut into two by a row of bars down the center.

The Hizbollah left. Now Phreak was alone again with Walter and Baal, but no longer as tormentor. They had reversed the ploy, and he needed to figure how to get out. He realized that he had been a fool not to realize the nature of the trap; the bitch had tagged him with a patch, but it couldn't take full effect until he reset his system. He had done that by exiting and then coming in again. Had he just stayed in, or stayed out, he would have been all right. But he had panicked, and pulled the noose tight around his own throat.

He settled down against a wall. "So how come you're hungry, sugar-pie?" he asked the woman.

"Don't tell him," Walter recommended.

She hesitated, then answered. "He'll figure it out soon enough. I'm diabetic. I need to eat some sugar to keep from going into insulin shock." She held up a quivering hand. "When my hands shake like this, I know my blood sugar's low. Because I overdid it on exercise."

That didn't seem to make a whole lot of sense, but maybe that was part of her problem: her mind was going bad. "Ha-ha! So you're in trouble, bitch!" He turned to Walter exultantly. "You thought you'd get out of it by making me get caught too, right, schnook? But I can wait longer than your girlfriend can. So what're you going to do about it?"

Walter advanced toward him. "I believe I'll kill you," he said grimly.

Phreak laughed. "Yeah, sure, cripple! You think you're man enough?"

Walter's hand shot out, catching Phreak's arm in a come-along grip. "You forget that I'm not crippled here, while I retain my police skills. I can do what I want with you, physically." He applied pressure, and Phreak found himself going to his knees. He had thought that true pain was impossible in the game, but it seemed that though he didn't feel more than an uncomfortable tingle, the computer made his game body react as it would in life. He was helpless.

"Walter, please!" Baal cried.

Walter looked at her. "We have to get this kid to tell us the way to nullify the virus, before you go into insulin shock."

"But if you kill him, he'll only escape to another setting, and we won't get it," she pointed out.

"Yeah, smart guy!" Phreak said. "Go ahead and kill me, bunghole!"

Then Baal reconsidered. "No, I forgot. He's locked into your setting. But he might turn up in another character, where we couldn't catch him."

Then the three Hizbollah returned, carrying more packages, which they deposited with the first in the other cell. The tableau in the near cell froze until the Hizbollah left.

Walter shoved him away. "You disgust me. You don't care who else you hurt, so long as you get your cheap kicks."

"That's for sure, jerk!" Phreak agreed, stumbling in the direction he had been shoved. That happened to be toward Baal.

She caught him, but not in the way Walter had. She put her arms around him, steadying him. "Maybe I can persuade you," she said.

Phreak was suddenly aware that he was in the arms of a woman. Sure, her body was a game construct, and not the most beautiful of the types, but she was still very much female. There was an odd intensity about her, maybe from that insulin she talked about. He froze.

She was aware of it. "You have trouble relating to girls, don't you, Phreak?" she murmured.

She was one for one. Phreak stared around as if seeking help, but saw only Walter, who pointedly turned his back. They were pulling the good-cop, bad-cop routine on him, the one threatening, the other supportive. He knew he should push her away and go to his own corner, but he couldn't. Her arms might as well have been steel bands, holding him helpless though their touch was gentle, even shaky.

"We all have trouble relating, at first," Baal said. "Boys and girls. I had a lot of trouble. I still do. I know how it is. It comes with being a teenager. You weren't alone in that, Phreak. The barriers are mostly in your own mind; they aren't really put there by others."

"You're a teen?" he asked disbelievingly. She seemed impossibly mature and womanly. Her touches on him were like cold fire, making his whole body tingle. He had never been this close to a woman before, even in game emulation.

"You didn't look up my information? I'm eighteen. I came to the game because I wanted to flirt with suicide. But I'm changing my mind."

"Yeah?" It was all he could think of to say. First she had locked him into the game; now she held him fascinated. He had never anticipated either ploy. He had thought he was in control, and now he was caught like an animal with one foot in a snare, and the farmer was trying to tame him.

"Because now in this pseudo-life I'm discovering what real life is all about," she continued. "I came to play, to do impossible things, to have sex, to be irresponsible. To be free for a while of my albatross. But it's turning real in several ways, and I'm still not free."

Neither was he! "Albatross?"

"I'm diabetic, as I said. Type I. Maybe you don't understand the significance of that." She transferred her grip to his hands and stood there holding them in hers. Her grip was weak, but ultimately compelling. That horrible sweet current continued to flow, no part of the game, just the power of a woman who wanted a man's attention. He hated the notion, yet it gave him just the suggestion of the heaven such a woman represented to the man she chose. To be close to her, to have her interest, to be touched by her, known by her, loved by her. Any woman, with any man. Desire surged through him, not for mere sex, but for the whole of what a caring woman could mean to a man.

But he was not a man, he was a fifteen-year-old stripling who could only stand outside the window of paradise and gaze longingly in. He forced his mouth to work, because he wanted to continue to hold her attention. "I guess not."

"It means that my body doesn't make insulin, which it needs to process sugar so that I can function," she said, squeezing his fingers. The very weakness of her touch got to him; he wanted to support her, to be strong for her. "So I have to take it with the needle. But sometimes I get too much, and then I need more sugar to use it up. I need sugar now, Phreak, or I may go into shock and die. Already my vision is blurring, my hands are shaking, and I'm getting sweaty, as you can see. Soon I'll get confused and lose coordination. It may not show in this game figure, but I do feel it in my real body. It will get worse if I don't get out. Do you want that to happen, Phreak?"

Almost, she had him. The gossamer strands of her web were hauling him in, making him like her, making him want to help her. Oh, Lord, how he wanted her favor! But he knew it was all a fake, and that she was only using him to get what she wanted. Once she got out of the game, she'd only make more mischief, getting him deeper into trouble.

So he wrestled with the invisible strands, and wrenched himself out of her grasp. "No! You can't fool me! I'm onto you! You just want to help *him!*" He stumbled away from her, free at last from her snare. Yet it was as if a ragged section of his heart and mind had been torn away. He thought of a fox who escaped a steel trap by leaving his foot behind. What price, his victory?

Just in time, for the Hizbollah returned, with more packages, from one of which some wires dangled. They added these to the pile in the far cell. What were they up to? He saw that Walter was watching them closely; he seemed to be quite interested in their activity.

By tacit mutual consent, the three of them did nothing and said nothing while the Hizbollah were near. Their problems with each other were not the business of those other players. So they waited in tableau again until they were alone.

Baal shook her head. "Is it that you don't believe me, or you don't *want* to believe me?" she asked.

Now he rebelled against the tender snare he had so narrowly escaped. "I'm not going to help you, bitch-woman!" he shouted. "You're lying, trying to fool me. You can stay in here until you croak!" Yet at the same time he wished it could have been otherwise. That he could have had the respect of the marvelous creature he had almost seen, instead of the contempt of the enemy he knew was there.

"Well, I tried," Baal said. Her hands were shaking again, and her speech was slurring, but she was probably doing those things on purpose to deceive him. No woman could be trusted!

Walter went to her. "That patch—it just locks him into the game. It doesn't pinpoint his identity so the authorities can go to his station and arrest him?"

"That's right," she said. "I don't understand the technical aspect, but it seems the patch can only do half the job. Maybe in time they can use it to get a fix on him, but that will be too slow for me." She leaned back and closed her eyes. "Do you mind if I cry, Walter? I don't want to die, now, but I guess I can't stop it."

Walter held her, letting her sob into his shoulder. Phreak wished he could have held her like that. But it was impossible. He felt guilty, and condemned himself for that; this was the bitch who had locked him in!

After a moment, Walter stirred. "I think I have a way to make Phreak see reason," he said.

"No you don't, cripple!" Phreak retorted. "We'll all rot here together. I can outlast both of you combined."

Walter ignored him. "Give me your shirt," he said to Baal.

"You going to screw her now, chump?" Phreak demanded. Despite his predicament, he was excited by the prospect of watching, and at the same time resentful that it wouldn't be him doing it. If he had gone along with Baal, would she have done it with him? Now that he had rejected her, the prospect of what he might have lost loomed more convincing.

Baal removed her garment and sat against the wall, in her bra. Phreak couldn't help staring, though he had seen her naked before. This was a different setting, and she was in a different body. She wasn't trying to show off what she had, and that made it more enticing.

Walter tore the cloth into strips. Then he tore the strips lengthwise. He tore them again, until he had a series of thin lengths. He knotted these together, end to end.

"You going to let yourself down out of the window on that rope?" Phreak asked. "If you can get through the bars?"

Walter glanced at him. "Have you ever seen a man garroted?" he inquired mildly.

Phreak felt a chill. He had seen it on TV. "Who you planning to choke?"

"I will make this deal with you: it will not be you if you keep your mouth shut. But if I find myself unable to use this rope in the way I intend, then I will use it on you. I suspect it would not be pleasant to die of suffocation, even if it's only in the game."

Phreak suspected the same. He hadn't had to face the prospect of game-death before this Beirut scene, and now that he thought about it, he didn't like it at all. Because when a player died he went to a death cell, a place like a coffin, and Phreak had a horror of anything like that even if he knew it was only in emulation. Suppose a snake came while he was locked in? So not only did he not want to be choked to death, he didn't want to die at all. But he couldn't afford to let Toland know that. He had to bluff through, until he could get out of here without dying. Once he was away from Walter and Baal, he could try to look up a hacker and get him to feed in the null code for Phreak alone. The code could be limited to a single player, just as the virus was. But if the general code was used, it would spread throughout the system, freeing everyone and preventing any future use of the virus. Because the game proprietors would get hold of it and fathom its secrets. A hacker would understand the need to keep it limited, as was the case with any special information.

Walter continued to work on his rope, while Baal watched, seeming to know no more about it than Phreak did. What the hell was the man up to?

The Hizbollah came back again. They put the packages down and moved out. "That's the load," the leader said. "It's good stuff; we lucked out on this one."

Walter hefted his light rope. "Do we have something to weight this?" he asked Baal.

She looked up. She was getting haggard now. "Maybe my confusion's getting the best of me. What are you trying to do, Walter?"

"I'm trying to free us from this cell, so we can try to get someone else to take the antivenin code out when Phreak gives it to us."

"I ain't giving it to you!" Phreak protested.

"There's a belt on these trousers," Baal said. "Maybe if it's rolled up . . . ?"

"Thanks." He took the belt from her. Phreak hoped her trousers would fall down, but they couldn't, because she was sitting on the floor, leaning back against the wall.

Walter rolled up the belt and fastened it together with the buckle. He tied it to the end of his handmade rope. Then he went to the wall of bars between the two cells and tossed the belt wad through. It landed near the collection of packages, trailing the rope.

Walter used the rope to haul the belt back. Then he threw it again. This time it landed near a trailing wire from one of the packages. He pulled it back slowly, concentrating. The line crossed the wire, drawing it a few inches before sliding beyond it.

Baal and Phreak watched, neither comprehending what the man was up to.

Walter hauled in the belt, then threw it again. He managed to bring the wire closer. The next throw brought it yet closer. He kept on throwing, with seemingly infinite patience, until at last he was able to catch hold of the wire with his hand.

Then he set out to capture the second wire. Phreak looked at Baal, who shrugged. The two were unified for the moment in their perplexity. It was a good feeling, agreeing with her in something that didn't matter. Maybe Walter was just entertaining himself.

In time Walter got the second wire.

At last he turned to Phreak. "These are the detonator wires for the charges from the van we drove in," he said. "I can use them to set off the explosives in the other cell. The battery's already connected; I was afraid the Hizbollah were going to set it off accidentally. That will blast out this building, and free us."

"Oh!" Baal said, relieved. Then she looked again. "But the explosive is on the far side. Won't it just make a hole in the far wall, leaving us imprisoned?"

"No, it will take out our wall too," Walter said. Then he looked at Phreak. "In fact it will blow us up with the building. We will all die. Are you ready for that?"

Almost, the ploy worked. Phreak dreaded true game-death. But then he realized it was a bluff. "You don't want to die yourself, Toland! So you won't do it."

Walter met his gaze. "I don't want to die, because there's a fair chance it will be permanent. But if I don't get Baal out soon, she will die-for-real too, and I don't want that. So I'm willing to

take the risk. The game-death won't hurt her, and may give her
a better chance in the next setting. And we may have a better
chance to find a friendly player there. You can't escape me, because we're locked into the same setting. So your choice is to
deal with me in this setting, or take your chances in the next."

"You're bluffing, pighead!" Phreak said.

Walter turned to Baal. "What shall we choose for the next setting? I don't need you present when I deal with Phreak, but I'd
rather have you with me. Then you can help persuade another
player to help."

She considered, evidently forcing her brain to focus. "There's
a catchall setting called Potpourri," she said. "For players who
want to try a little of everything without being locked into any
one thing. It has slices of all the other settings. It tends to get really confused, and there're no bonus points; in fact it's an ongoing setting, always open, with no beginning or ending. You just
step in when you want to, and step out when you're tired of it.
We could meet there, in the Princess section."

"What are you talking about?" Phreak demanded. "There's no
Po-poo-ee section."

"That's P-O-T-P-O-U-R-R-I," Baal said, spelling it. It was a
crazy spelling, but she seemed pretty sure of herself. He had seen
that name on the listings: pot pour ri. He had figured it had
something to do with cooking classes.

"But suppose there are no roles open in that section?" Walter
asked.

"Just take a role in another subset and cross over," she said.
"That's what makes it so wild. It's really a joke setting, and serious players avoid it, the manual says."

"Done," he said. "We'll meet in Princess, same introductory
ritual."

"Same ritual," she agreed.

"But how will we ever locate Phreak, if there're so many
subsettings? He could hide in any."

"There's supposed to be a way to track him."

"What are you talking about?" Phreak demanded, not liking
the sound of this.

"It doesn't matter," Walter told him. "Now, are you going to
give us the antivenin code, or do you want to have it out in the
next setting instead?"

Toland seemed so sure of himself! But there wasn't anything

he could do. Not here, not anywhere. "You're bluffing," Phreak said. "So go ahead and blow us all up."

"Oh, I will," Walter said. "But I should warn you that I won't be as gentle with you in the next setting. I mean to have that information from you, and it may be easier to get in the absence of the lady."

"Yeah? Prove it, sucker."

Walter lifted the two wires. He touched them together.

There was a blinding explosion of light. Phreak felt a terrible shock. Then the light faded, and he found himself in the death cell, tight and dark.

Terror overwhelmed him. The rattlesnakes were coming! He knew it! He screamed and flailed, trying to get out, but there was nothing to break out of; the cell was intangible. It was the game's version of a padded cell; he couldn't hurt himself, he could only scream in futility and fear.

He screamed for an eternity. He felt his sanity leaking away. It was not possible to endure this isolation and darkness. Not with the snakes coming. They could come right through the coffin's lid, because it wasn't really solid, it just looked that way. He was the only one caught in it.

Finally it ended. Light formed around him. He was in the anteroom, ready to make the next choice of setting. He was shaking worse than the woman had been.

Instead of going for a setting, he called up the screen and punched the Quit option. Only to get the error message. He couldn't get out.

Well, at least he wouldn't give them the satisfaction of joining their Po-poo-ee setting. He'd hide out in something else, where they'd never find him.

But when he tried to select a setting, nothing happened. He was locked out. Because he was logged on only as a fragment of Toland's entry, not as his own. He would be dragged into the setting Toland chose. The bitch had really nailed him with that patch.

Well, there was one way to deal with Toland. He would simply have to kill him. Then the man would have no way to get at him until he was out of the setting—and Potpourri had no ending. He could hide there forever.

Well, not quite. He remembered now that players could go

right back in when they died. So dying there was temporary. But still, it would mess Toland up, and he might die for real anyway.

The one thing Phreak knew was that he couldn't handle dying himself, again. Because each death was worse than the last; the game set it up that way, making the shock worse and the coffin time longer and tighter. He would go crazy, literally. So he would do anything, fair or foul, to stop from getting killed. Until he outlasted Toland and the bitch, and got out of the game on his own.

fifteen

P
O
T
P
O
U
R
R
I

Walter felt the terrible shock of his second death, and feared he wouldn't survive it. But he clung to life, willing his heart to slow, and after an interminable time it did. This death had been worse than the last; the game had shocked him harder and made his pacemaker swing further awry and sent his heart into awful fibrillation.

It had been close. Too close. He had gambled and won, but he knew he couldn't count on another such survival.

He had indeed been bluffing, trying to make Phreak back down, but the kid had held out, and he had had to do it. Phreak had thought the bluff was about the explosive, but it was about the dying; Walter had not wanted to take the risk if he could avoid it. But with Baal going into shock, he had had to. The sight of her hands shaking, and hearing her slurring speech, and knowing that she was sinking into her own mode of death, had been decisive. She was his only friend in the game, and he had to save her if he could. Or die trying, literally.

The death cell faded and the anteroom reappeared. As he understood it, he had control, because Phreak was locked on as an aspect of his game entry. It was as if he were the engine and Phreak a boxcar; the engine did the hauling.

He looked at the choices, and found Potpourri. Good enough. He would meet Baal there by the Princess' castle, and then locate Phreak and force him to yield the information. He knew that Phreak was afraid of many things, and maybe he would be able to discover some of them, and haul the kid into a subset with some of them.

He looked for the starting time for the setting, and found none. Oh—because it was ongoing. All he had to do was find an open character and step in.

He looked at the list of players—and saw Baal Curran's name appear. She had entered the setting! But he could not tell which character she had taken, or even which subsetting she was in. The game maintained that degree of privacy, so that players could not automatically know each other's role. Except when a group took all the roles in a section, as with the Druze of Beirut.

He didn't want to wait. He needed to get back together with her, then locate Phreak. So what character should he take? Both the Hero and Evil Sorcerer had been taken; one might be vacated in due course, but he couldn't wait for that.

He scanned the subset—and suddenly saw Beirut. Then it came to him: why not take the same character he had just had? A Druze of Lebanon? That would make him immediately recognizable, especially if he made the physical description identical. And if she should think of that too, he would be able to recognize her. It was certainly worth the try.

There were a number of Druze characters open. He picked the closest match, and lined up the physical description. But this time he dumped all his fluid into LUCK and PERSUASIVENESS, on the assumption that those would do him the most good.

He stepped through the door, and was back in Beirut. But not in the prison cell, because this was a different exercise of that setting. The regular Beirut game continued, and probably he had scored some more points for blowing up some Hizbollah, and perhaps would also receive bonus points if the Druze won. But it would be some hours yet before that setting ended, and meanwhile he had important things to do in this one.

The character was where his prior one had been, standing guard. There was evidently no collusive effort here; roles remained where they were as game constructs until occupied by players. He had the advantage of knowing his way around, having just been in an identical scene with different players.

He looked around. There was no cardboard; this setting was continuously active. He walked along the path between terraces, alert for any possible enemies. He had a pistol, but preferred to have more. How was he to get to the Princess setting?

He heard the zing of a bullet passing close, and then a shot. He threw himself to the ground beside the nearest bush, taking cover. Some jerk was shooting at him!

Was it another Druze, played by someone who didn't know that Druze didn't fight each other? This was possible, because this was a free-for-all kind of setting where more or less anything went. The character would find out his mistake when he got debited a point for the killing, but meanwhile Walter would be out of it too. Of course he could step right back in again, but he might not survive the death.

He couldn't afford to get innocently killed. This was for real, for him. So he put himself into the business frame of mind, and did what he had to do. He peered closely at the spot where the shot seemed to have come from, and when the fool stood up and approached to check his kill, Walter shot him dead. He couldn't afford to mess with fools.

But he had been a fool himself, just openly walking along the path. Now he handled it like the menace it was, and moved quickly from cover to cover after checking for enemies.

He got a notion. If Leon's van remained where it had been, he could use that! Driving would be much faster than walking, and safer too.

He went to the garage, and it was there, along with the bomb makings and ammunition. Walter didn't hesitate: he loaded in enough explosive for a medium-small bomb, together with several detonators, so that he could make several little ones if he needed to. He also took an automatic rifle and plenty of ammunition. And a small rocket launcher, with several rockets. He examined the launcher carefully, to be sure he knew how to use it, because the thing would be useless if he had to fumble in a crisis. He was not about to let anything get in his way. If he had to, he would shoot Phreak, and when he returned to this setting, as he had to, shoot him again, and again, until he capitulated. Because Baal's life was at stake. He *had* to get that antivenin.

He drove the van out onto the road. No one tried to interfere with him. They were amateurs here, disorganized, probably knowing nothing about the Druze nature or religious conventions. That was just as well; it meant that he didn't have to fight his way out.

Then a bullet struck the vehicle. He couldn't have that; he had explosives aboard. So he stopped, grabbed the rifle, and sprayed the region where the enemy was hiding. He heard a cry, and the tally on his screen changed; he had scored. This was the way of daily life in Beirut: casual killing for little or no reason. Anarchy supreme.

But where was the Princess setting? He had thought the Beirut set would be smaller, to fit in the larger setting, but it seemed to be full size. So how did he get out of it? Drive into the sea?

He nodded. The sea was surely off-bounds for this set, so it could be the boundary for the next set, whatever that was. He would keep driving until he found it.

He saw a man standing beside the road, holding a rifle. Walter braced the steering wheel with his knees, poked his pistol out the window with his left hand, and fired. His third shot scored, and the man fell.

He came to an intersection and turned west. He drove at high speed through the farmland north of the Chouf Mountains toward the sea. And sure enough, when he approached it, he discovered that it was only a painting. From a distance it had looked real, but up close it was clearly fake. Since the computer could make it seem real if it wanted to, it meant that this was a marked border.

He drew up close. What now? He wasn't sure it would be smart to drive through the cardboard backing of the painting, but what else was he to do? So he nudged forward, ready to stop if it seemed warranted.

His van encountered no resistance. It passed through the painting as if it weren't there. As his body passed through, the scene changed.

Now he was on what appeared to be an American interstate highway, near a rest stop. He looked back, and saw the countryside of Lebanon: in a billboard-like painting. The setting he had left had become cardboard.

A car came slowly down the highway. Walter held his pistol ready, out of sight below the window. If the car acted the slightest bit suspiciously, he would shoot the driver. But since there was a chance this wasn't a trophy-seeking fool, Walter waited. The car passed on by, harmlessly. The driver probably didn't know how close he had come to getting shot out of hand.

He drove down the highway to the rest stop. All along it were other paintings, each showing a different kind of scene. Many sections of the world seemed to be represented, and some sections of alien worlds. All on cardboard, but surely becoming real when their pictures were entered. He would really have been interested in exploring, were he not so concerned about Baal.

He searched for snipers, and saw none. This did seem like an unlikely place. He pulled into the rest area. And there, to his delight, was a huge map, with a YOU ARE HERE marker. Now he could find his way around.

There were more settings than he might have imagined. This must be a really popular game! He scanned down them until he found Princess in Castle. He made a firm mental note of its location, then drove out toward it.

He saw another vehicle approaching. This was a pickup truck with men standing in the back. They had guns.

Walter took no chance. He pulled to a stop, scrambled to get the rocket launcher, and set it up with its rocket pointing out the window at the other vehicle. He waited.

The pickup truck veered toward him. A man in back brought his rifle to bear.

Walter launched his rocket. It was point-blank range for this weapon. He didn't even see the rocket strike; the truck went up in a ball of flame as Walter ducked down as well as he could, shielding himself with the launcher.

Four more points appeared on his screen.

He resumed driving, pulling cautiously around the smoking ruin of the truck. The Princess setting was about a mile down the highway, just one more billboard among the solid spread of billboards. In this game, it was no joke about billboards covering up the scenery; they *were* the scenery. There was the idyllic picture of the castle with the dragon path around it.

Could he drive the van into it? That was after all a medieval and magical setting, where modern technology had no place. But his position would be a lot stronger if he had his arsenal along.

He tried it. He nudged the van into the picture, and it passed through without resistance, as before. The other side was the virtual reality of the scene, and behind became the picture of the medieval landscape as it should have been had any of this been real.

There was, however, no road here. That might be one reason there weren't other vehicles in sight: they couldn't get around very well. But it could also be that no one else had thought to try anything as anachronistic as this.

Fortunately this was a reasonably tough van. It could handle some cross-country driving. He would try to be careful, because though the explosives weren't supposed to go off without the detonators, such things sometimes happened. So he chose the smoothest bumps, and used the lowest gear, handling the terrain gingerly.

Soon he came to the track where the dragon ran—and here came the dragon, a jet of flame and smoke leading the way.

Walter tromped on the brakes, and the van jerked to a stop. He couldn't risk that flame! It could set off the explosives and blow up the van and him with it.

But the dragon's eye was on him now, and it seemed to regard him as a threat. It slowed and then stopped, orienting on the van. What would a jet of flame do to his cargo?

Then he rephrased the question. What would a twentieth-century gun do to a fantasy dragon? If magic ruled here, his weapons might be useless. Still, if magical flame could blow up a van, a rifle ought to be able to shoot a dragon.

Walter took his rifle and aimed at the dragon. He fired one shot, the bullet going straight through the monster's snoot. He knew he had scored, because he saw the round hole.

But the dragon didn't seem to notice. Apparently it wasn't programmed to respond to a bullet in the head. It was huffing and puffing, making ready to send its flame. So it seemed that the dragon wasn't vulnerable to his modern weapon.

But maybe it just hadn't been enough of a jolt. Walter knew he couldn't get out of flame range in time, so he had to hope that heavier artillery would do the job.

Walter grabbed the rocket launcher. Just before the dragon fired, Walter did. The rocket smacked into the dragon's mouth. It exploded, making the usual ball of flame.

When the ball dissipated, the dragon was missing its head. The rest of it lay on the ground, twitching. His screen recorded another notch.

That answered his question. Science could prevail against magic here, if delivered in a heavy enough dose. He started the van and drove it carefully across the dragon's path. He needed to get as close to the castle as he could, perhaps even driving it inside, so that he would have its protection while he looked for Baal.

Then he had an insecure thought: suppose Baal wasn't there? He had assumed that she would be, but she might have had to take some role in another setting and make her way here, as he had. In that case he would do better to wait for her farther out.

He looked back, trying to decide what to do. And saw the dragon stirring.

Then, appalled, he saw that this was no reptilian death twitch. The dragon was growing a new head! It was coming back to life. Was he going to have to blast it again to get out? He had only one rocket left, and he might need that to get into the castle.

It did make sense. This was an open-ended setting, with no ending. That meant that its characters had to be restored to life after they died, so that it wouldn't be stripped and become meaningless. So a new player was taking over the dragon. Or maybe the old one, with a debit on his screen.

Walter decided to move on ahead, and worry about the dragon later. He hoped Baal was inside the castle. He knew she was having insulin trouble, thanks to Phreak's dastardly ploy, and he had to locate her quickly.

That brought him another insecure thought. Why was he looking for Baal? He couldn't help her, really. The only thing that would help her was some sugar for her body, outside the game, and he couldn't give her that. Sugar in the game would be useless. He needed to catch Phreak, and force him to divulge the secret antivenin code. Then he needed to convince another player to exit the game and feed that code into the system. That would free them all, and Baal would survive. He was wasting his time even looking for her now, and she had precious little time. How could he have been so foolish?

The question brought the answer: because he liked her. There was of course no future for him with her; no woman wanted to chain herself to a paralyzed, impotent man. He was also twelve years older than she was. Romance was laughable. Yet here in the game they were a couple, and however idle her fancy might be for her, for him it was wonderful. Here he could kiss her, and perhaps even have sex with her. Everything that was denied him in life was possible in the game. He longed for it. It was ironic that a game designed to give players the thrills of killing and dying was instead giving him the thrills of living and loving. But that was the case, and it was Baal he wanted to do it with. Otherwise he could simply have gotten out of his van and approached one of the nymphs disporting themselves in the river. He knew now what they were programmed for, and that they would indeed sexually accommodate any man who came to them. Killing was merely the theme of this game, not the entirety.

So his desire had blinded him to the obvious, and caused him to fritter valuable time trying to reach her. He had no idea where in this setting Phreak was. This setting was monstrous, because it embraced sample settings of all the other types. Since everything was merely imagery in the programming of the game, it could be as big as the universe. He could search for Phreak for years without finding him.

Then he remembered something from his last dialogue with Baal. He had posed the question of how to locate Phreak, and she had said that there was supposed to be a way to track him. Then Phreak had interrupted them, and it hadn't been expedient to continue that line of dialogue. Did Baal know a way to track Phreak, just as Phreak knew how to track Walter? If so, he did need to get together with her, for a practical as well as emotional reason.

He looked forward, toward the castle. His eye traveled up to where he knew the Princess' prison chamber was.

There was a hand waving from that window, holding a swatch of bright cloth. The Princess! Could that be Baal?

He realized that it could. The prior Princess might have died, or just gotten bored and vacated, leaving an opening. Baal would have grabbed that role if she got the chance, and maybe she had timed it right. Why else would the Princess be waving to a man in an anachronous van?

He put out his arm and waved back. Now he knew he would have had to rejoin her, even if it meant foolish delay. He couldn't help himself.

Now, how was he to rescue her from the castle, again? He knew the general layout of it from his prior experience as the Evil Sorcerer. But this was unlikely to be the same sort of chal-

lenge, because there was no constancy of players and no bonus
for victory. Also, he was now a refugee from another type of setting, which should completely mess up the normal course. Would
anyone even challenge him if he marched in? Should he simply
shoot anyone he encountered, to be sure no one killed him?

He decided to play it by ear, shooting only those who seemed
threatening. Maybe there would be no trouble. He drove toward
the castle, bumping over the rough terrain.

There was also the matter of getting someone to take the antivenin code out to reality, once Phreak yielded it. He wasn't sure
how he would persuade anyone to do that, despite the persuasion
in his present game character. He would need the luck aspect too.

Walter reminded himself that his game character was strongest
on luck and persuasion. Those qualities would be effective
mainly against game constructs, but there should be a number of
them around. So he would try the bold approach, and be ready
to kill anyone it didn't daunt.

He parked his van near the moat, tucked his pistol into his
belt, picked up his rifle, and marched to the drawbridge. It was
in the lifted position. There was a guard at the gate, looking
bored. Was he a construct? It was impossible to tell by mere appearance, because all the figures in the game were constructs,
with players occupying some.

"Hey, Mac, lower the bridge!" Walter called.

The guard looked at him. "Why?"

That sounded like a construct. "Because I need to get in."

"Oh." The guard went to the winch and started cranking the
bridge down.

Walter suppressed his desire to smirk. He had found a construct, and his persuasive power was effective!

The planks of the bridge thunked onto the supports. Walter
walked across. "Thank you," he said to the guard.

"You're welcome." The man began working the winch again,
to haul the bridge back up.

"Have a good day."

"Thank you, sire."

Walter proceeded to the next challenge, which was the portcullis. It was down, barring passage. There was another guard.
"Hey, friend, lift it," Walter said persuasively. "I need to get
through."

"Yes, sire," the man said, and cranked up the portcullis.

"Thank you," Walter said as he marched through.

"You're welcome, sire."

Now there was the great wooden double door, with another guard. "Open up, I need to go through," Walter said.

"And who the hell are you?" the guard inquired.

Walter drew his pistol and shot him through the face. A neat round hole appeared, showing daylight at the other side, and the man collapsed.

Walter tried to open the door, but it was massive and had no exterior handle. Was there a crank for this too? He tried to catch the center crevice with his fingers, but it was too tight. He would need a crowbar, and he hadn't thought to bring one. He looked around the guard's station, but saw nothing useful. He tried shoving it, but made no impression.

The guard stirred. Walter looked, and saw that the hole in his head had miraculously healed. He had come to life again, as happened in this variant. He got back to his feet.

He looked at Walter. "Hey, you piece of crap! You shot me!"

The same player had reanimated the figure! "You didn't open the door. Are you going to do it now?"

"Hell no! I'm going to clobber you!" The guard reached for his sword.

Walter shot him again.

Then he considered the door once more. He tried something obvious: he knocked.

In a moment the door opened. He had lucked out.

Now he was in a passage leading to the central court. From there, there should be stairs leading up and in. He had not been in this section of the castle before, but it seemed straightforward.

The court had flowers, bushes, and even small trees growing. It was an attractive place. There was even a young woman sunning herself near a fountain. Beyond her was a flight of stone steps.

Should he introduce himself? He really had no business with this woman, and she was probably a construct. On the other hand, he had to pass right by her, and to do so without a greeting might seem suspicious even to a construct.

He walked up. "A greeting, fair damsel," he said. He saw as his angle of view changed that she was nude. She was just another nymph, like those in the river, set out to decorate the premises and distract unwary players.

She turned her head to look at him. "Why?"

That was a construct, sure enough. "Farewell, fair damsel," he said, and walked past.

She got up, walked to a large hanging plate, picked up a small mallet, and made ready to strike the plate. She was going to sound an alarm! She must have been instructed to do so when any stranger entered the castle. Or maybe when any man acted suspiciously, such as not putting a move on this lovely nude woman.

He dropped his rifle and charged her, trying to intercept her swing at the plate. But his hand missed her arm, and he collided with her, face to face.

Gong! The sound reverberated through the castle. Her arm had continued to swing behind his back, and completed her mission. Now the alarm had been given.

Walter tried to disengage, but the nymph's arms clamped around him. Her face came toward his face, and her mouth opened, showing her teeth. They were pointed. He jerked his head back just in time to miss her first snap at his nose. This was no normal nymph, this was a killer creature—and he had after all walked into her embrace. What a trap!

He tried to pull her arms from around his torso, but her hands had locked together and seemed to have welded. Whatever thing this was, it would never let go.

But his own arms remained free. He used his left to shove her face away, careful to avoid the snapping teeth, while he groped for his pistol with his right. He got it, jerked it out and up, put it to her head, and fired. The bullet passed through her head from side to side, leaving a pipe-shaped tunnel. There was no blood: the proof that she wasn't real.

Her eyes widened in surprise. Then her pupils became two whirling disks, which expanded, and her face was sucked into them. Her body followed, releasing him as it disappeared into the twin whirlpools. In a moment she was gone.

Walter shook his head as he tucked his pistol back into his waistband. Some constructs were more deadly than others. Or maybe she had been a player masquerading as a dummy. The absence of blood might be merely a signal of her supernatural nature, rather than her player status. He hurried away before the nymph was reconstituted. He picked up his rifle and turned toward the flight of steps.

But before he reached the steps, a man showed at the top of the flight. He wore the robe of the Evil Sorcerer, and he held the book of spells: *Ancient Evil Magic*. His finger marked a place near the beginning.

This was trouble! Walter knew the power of those spells. He charged the steps, hoping to reach the Sorcerer before he could look up a spell and invoke it.

He was way too late. The Sorcerer made a gesture and uttered an incantation. He had evidently already reviewed a spell.

Walter swung his rifle into place and took aim. If he could kill the Sorcerer before the spell took effect—

"Adder," the Sorcerer finished.

Walter's rifle changed form. The end of its barrel hissed and turned back to look at him. The length of it writhed. He was holding a snake!

The creature struck. Walter dropped the thing and stepped back just in time. The viper fell to the pavement, hissed again, and struck at his foot. Since he was wearing heavy boots, the fangs did no harm. He shook it off and lifted his foot to crush it, literally, underheel—and paused.

This wasn't a real adder. It was his rifle, enchanted. In fifteen minutes it would revert to its original form. Suppose he squished the snake: would it later revert to a squished rifle? In which case he would have destroyed his own weapon.

He looked wildly about. Was there anything into which he could put the serpent for safekeeping? He saw no jars with lids. He might toss it into the water of the fountain, but if it didn't swim out, the water could still be bad for the rifle. He had to think of something in a hurry, because the Sorcerer was already starting another spell. Suppose he threw the snake at the Sorcerer? No, the spells probably didn't work against their originator, and it would be foolish to try to reverse them. His own experience in the role of Evil Sorcerer had shown him that there were limits either way, and one of them was that the spells never turned back against their invoker. So what to do with this reptile?

Meanwhile the nymph was reappearing in her recliner by the fountain. Her period of oblivion was over.

Walter had a bright notion. He nerved himself and pounced on the snake, his fingers catching it just behind the head. He picked it up and tossed it to the nymph. "Hold the adder safe until I return," he cried to her persuasively.

She caught the snake neatly. She had been given a directive, so she obeyed it, not being programmed to know any better. The persuasive talent of his character had prevailed. Not only did that keep the snake out of mischief, it occupied the nymph too, and with luck she would not attack him again.

"Albatross," the Evil Sorcerer intoned, gesturing.

Walter returned his attention to the man—just in time to see a big ugly bird appear. Its wingspan was huge. It flew toward him, its beady eyes orienting.

The Sorcerer had conjured an albatross to attack him? Instead of a hawk or harpy? Where was the catch?

Walter ducked, and the bird passed over his head. It looped around, somewhat ungainly in this confined space. As Walter recalled, the albatross was a sea bird—yes, now he saw its webbed feet—that seldom came to roost. There had been one in a poem—he cudgeled his memory for a moment, and to his surprise got it—"The Rime of the Ancient Mariner," wherein the protagonist had had an albatross tied to him, showing that he was in some way cursed.

Walter drew his pistol as the creature swooped in again. But he hesitated, as he had with the snake. Such birds were harmless to man, and it was considered bad luck to shoot one. This was a magical setting; if he shot this bird, would it nullify the good luck of his character? He very much feared it would. He needed that luck! So he would have to find some other way.

He ran to the fountain, gesturing. "Fish!" he cried persuasively. "Lots of fish in the water! All you can eat!" He hoped it was true. Maybe if his luck held out.

The albatross took an interest. It swooped low over the pool, then dived to the surface. Its head came up with a fish. Satisfied, it came to rest somewhat in the manner of a duck, floating, so as to have leisure to enjoy its repast.

Walter turned to face the Sorcerer again. The man was well into another incantation. But there were liabilities there, Walter knew. Not only did each spell last only fifteen minutes, it freed a castle denizen, who then would immediately go to try to free the Princess. It was not wise to use spells too prolifically. But perhaps the Sorcerer had not done his background homework, and didn't know that. He could spell himself right into trouble.

But Walter wasn't here to win points. He just wanted to rescue Baal, then see if they could chase Phreak down. Unfortunately his mission was the same as the setting challenge, because Baal was the Princess. So he couldn't shortcut it. He wasn't the official Hero, but he had to fight the Evil Sorcerer and prevail.

Could he just shoot the man? Not if the Sorcerer had invoked a spell of invulnerability. In fact, in that case the bullet might come right back to score on its source. Better not to risk it, except as a desperation ploy.

Walter ran for the steps—as the Sorcerer completed his incantation with the word "Anchor." Suddenly Walter stopped in his tracks—literally. He legs seemed glued to the floor, catching him in mid running stride. The anchor spell had anchored him.

But how was that possible? He was a player, not a construct. The magic should not work against him personally. It could affect the Sorcerer personally, when he wanted to fly or whatever, because he invoked it. But another player had to have free will. Otherwise the Sorcerer would simply immobilize or destroy all opposition and it would be no contest. He remembered that limit from his own tenure. Had the rules changed?

Maybe not. Walter reached down and braced his hands against a boot. He hauled up his foot, and it came out. He set it on the pavement and hauled the other foot out. Now he stood in his stocking feet. The boots remained anchored, but he was free. He had lucked out again. He had chosen his character traits well!

But already the Sorcerer was uttering another spell. At this rate the man would soon free all the castle denizens, which was good for Walter. Meanwhile he had to fend off all that magic, and that was too chancy. So he decided to risk a shot. He drew his pistol.

The Sorcerer finished his spell. "Angel," he said. How was he able to do them so rapidly?

An angel appeared. This was no cherubic figure, and no delicate girl. It was a Guardian Angel, or an Avenging Angel. Masculine, with a great long shining sword.

Walter was not supremely religious, but it bothered him to attack an angel. He hesitated.

The Angel didn't. He floated toward Walter. "Repent, sinner!" he cried in a golden voice, raising his glowing sword to smite the sinner.

Walter had no choice. He aimed his pistol at the Angel and fired at point-blank range.

The shot had no effect. Walter knew his aim had been good.

But it seemed that the Angel was invulnerable to mortal attack. That figured.

"Repent!" the Angel repeated, swinging the sword viciously down. Walter threw himself to the side, and the stroke missed. The glowing sword of vengeance sliced into the pavement, cutting a tile in twain and sending up a shower of sparks.

This was a one-way business, it seemed. Walter couldn't smite the Angel, but the Angel could smite him. The magic wasn't direct, but that indirect application could kill him.

"Repent!" the Angel cried again. He drew his sword from the stone and floated after Walter.

Walter ran. It was the only way to keep clear of that terrible swift sword. Yet even in this emergency he had a stray thought. The Sorcerer was going through the spells in order! Just turning pages. That was why he was so fast. All his spells had been alphabetical, in the "A" section: Adder, Albatross, Anchor, and Angel. That meant he probably hadn't gotten around to Invulnerable, and Walter could shoot him and be done with it.

Meanwhile the Angel was floating supremely after him, effortlessly keeping the pace. "Repent!" he cried, lifting the sword.

Walter realized that he couldn't escape physically. He tried something truly desperate. "I repent!" he cried, throwing himself to the ground. "I abase myself, I confess all my sins."

The Angel hovered over him. "Then give up thine evil things of the flesh," he said.

Oh-oh. That meant that words were not enough. Walter tossed away the pistol. "I give up this weapon," he said.

"Swear never to use such an evil device again," the Angel said.

More trouble. How long was "never"? If he forswore all guns, he would be prey to all the others in the game who still used them. If he got out of the game alive, would his word still bind him in life?

He concluded that he couldn't afford such a commitment. He might escape the Angel, but it would wipe him out in the game and life, and perhaps prevent him from saving Baal. "No," he said.

The Angel swelled larger and brighter. "You swear falsely? The penalty is death!"

"No!" Walter cried. "I am *refusing* to swear falsely."

The Angel hesitated. "How so?"

"I need such weapons to prevail here in the game, and I have necessary things to do here," Walter explained. "I must try to save my life, and to save the life of a woman. If I give up my weapons, I will not be able to accomplish these things, and that would be evil."

"Evil!" the Angel cried.

"You call *things* evil," Walter said. "I call *actions* evil. I repent any evil action I have ever done, and resolve to do no more, but things are only things and must not be abjured as evil in themselves. Therefore I can not so swear, lest I perjure myself and in the process wreak greater evil."

The Angel stared at him. Then he faded away.

Walter stared back at the vacant space. He had hoped only to stave off the Angel's assault while he tried to figure out what else to do. Instead, it seemed, he had abolished the Angel. By arguing the paradox of the Angel's demand: riddance of an evil thing would enable evil to prevail. Apparently the Angel had been programmed to respond to such logic. But Walter had only been arguing his case, not trying to destroy the Angel. He had, it seemed, been unusually persuasive, and lucky. It figured, he realized belatedly.

So where did that leave him with respect to the pistol? He decided that since he had reversed himself and refused to eschew such weapons, he had won his right to use it when the Angel backed off.

But already the Sorcerer was completing another spell. "Axe," he said.

A great long-handled double-bitted battle-axe appeared. Each cutting edge gleamed sharply. There was a spearlike point at the end. The axe hovered in the air for a moment, then flew purposefully toward Walter.

There would be no repentance this time, Walter knew. The axe was a dumb enchanted object, knowing only one thing: how to chop.

And chop it did. It charged him and swung itself down in an evident effort to split him into equal linear halves. He dodged aside, and the axe smashed into a tile, sending fragments flying.

Walter did what came naturally, again: he ran. But the axe had no more trouble following him than the Angel did. It was obvious that he couldn't avoid it more than a few seconds.

Could he get it to chop into something, getting itself stuck?

Maybe, if he had a really solid green sticky billet of wood. There was nothing of that nature in view. Could he get it to break itself up by striking hard objects? After seeing what it did to the stone tile, he doubted it. This thing could probably chop through anything.

Still, he had better try, because otherwise it would be his body it chopped. He dived behind the fountain, landing in the water, the axe in hot pursuit. It came down, cutting neatly through the stone pedestal and the metal pipe within it, halving both. The water of the fountain squirted away to either side.

Walter splashed out to the nymph's couch and tried to hide behind it. The axe came down and chopped couch and damsel in perfect halves. The damsel looked annoyed as she whirlpooled out.

Walter fled to the stone steps. He flung himself just around them and cowered behind. The axe cut the staircase in half. There was, indeed, no stopping it. Its long handle almost brushed Walter's head as it passed.

Acting on impulse, Walter reached up and grabbed that handle. The axe quivered with seeming anger and tried to wrench itself free, but he grasped it with both hands and hung on. At least it couldn't chop him now.

It could haul him around, though! The axe charged the wall, and Walter clung desperately, running along behind it. It made a tight circle, trying to get behind him, but he stiffened his arms and kept himself away from its business end.

The axe bucked, but Walter clung as if riding a bronc. It shook itself, but couldn't shake loose his death-grip. It dived into the pool, but he dived with it.

Then it tried to fly high. Walter's hands felt as if they were being pulled off, but this was the game; as long as he told them to grip, they gripped, and the grip could not be broken. The axe pulled so hard that it hauled him into the air, and still he clung.

The axe, like all magical things, was tireless, but it wasn't geared for this. There were limits. Walter's weight was too much for it, and in a moment it was dragged back down to earth. That wasn't much of a victory for him, because it still had more than enough power to cleave him in twain if he let go. Could he hang on for fifteen minutes? He doubted it; though his grip remained strong, his hands were sweating, making the handle slippery, and the handle would inevitably slide out in another minute or two.

That suggested that this ploy too had been tried before, and so the sweaty-hands business had been programmed in to nullify it.

He spied his pistol, lying on the tiles where he had thrown it during his session with the Angel. He had decided that it was all right to use it, since he had in effect vanquished the Angel. But it was no good to him, because he didn't have it and couldn't get it. Not unless he let go, and then the axe would chop him in half.

Then he got a notion. It was extremely chancy, but perhaps no worse than the fate awaiting him when his sweaty hands slipped off. It was a two- or three-stage ploy, and would require his very best effort. But if it worked, he just might beat the Sorcerer, and nail him before the man got into the "B" spells.

Walter timed his move carefully. Then, as the axe looped by the nymph, who was now being restored again, and the fallen pistol, he loosened his fingers and let the handle slide free. He fell to the ground, and the axe, suddenly released, soared up into the sky.

While the thing veered out of control, Walter took a roll and grabbed the pistol. He continued his roll as he tucked the weapon into his waistband. The axe was recovering its equilibrium and homing in on him again. He got his feet under himself and leaped up and away as the blade chopped viciously down, shattering the last tile he had rolled on. So far so good; he had accomplished his first objective.

He charged the wall as the axe yanked itself up and reoriented. It was a single-minded instrument, intent only on splitting him in twain. That was in a way its weakness; it didn't have any observational or reasoning processes, so didn't realize or care that he had armed himself.

He put his two hands out as he crashed into the wall, the muscles of his arms acting like springs to absorb the shock of collision. Then he rebounded, hurling himself back just as the axe chopped at the wall where his head had been. Fragments of plaster and brick sprayed out. The force of the blow was such that the blade was almost embedded in the wall, and it took just a moment for it to yank itself out.

In that moment Walter launched himself back toward the axe. He grabbed its projecting handle. Now he had hold of it again. Second objective accomplished.

The axe came out of the wall and spun like a ravenous shark to attack him again. But the effort only threw Walter around behind it; it could not chop him while he had hold of it and kept his legs out of the way.

The thing was too dull to feel frustration. It merely resumed its bucking and turning, trying to work him loose. His hands were sweating again, so the axe's strategy would be effective. Except for one thing: his counterstrategy.

Walter let go with his right hand, depending on his left to maintain the grip long enough for what he needed. With his right he drew out the pistol. He set the muzzle of the pistol at the handle just below the double blades, and pulled the trigger.

The bullet passed through the wood, holing and splintering it. Walter dropped the pistol and clapped his right hand back on the handle. Then he used his two hands to heave that handle around—and it snapped off at the weakened spot. The blades sailed on, while the main part of the handle remained in Walter's hands.

Now the axehead did a crazy dance. It was trying to orient and chop, but it had lost its leverage. Like a kite without its stabilizing tail, it spun and crashed, out of control. In a moment it had buried itself in the wall again, and this time it lacked the balance to haul itself out.

Walter turned quickly to see if he could spy the Evil Sorcerer. The man was standing there at the head of the stairs, working on another incantation.

Walter picked up his pistol again, aimed, and fired. The Sorcerer fell, a hole through his head. So he had been right: the man had never gotten to the rest of the alphabet, and had invoked no spell of invulnerability. Actually it should have given out by now if he had.

That reminded him. He looked back. There was the nymph on her lounge, holding his rifle. It had run out its time and reverted.

Walter walked back to her. "I will take that," he said.

She looked up at him. "Why?"

"Because I need it to shoot you with, when you sound the alarm."

"Thank you." She held up the rifle. His words were evidently beyond her programmed comprehension.

He took the rifle. She got up and walked to the big plate. She picked up the mallet. He shot her through the head. She fell. Then he turned and ran up the stairs, hoping to get past the Evil Sorcerer before the man came back to life. He made it. Once he was out of sight, he should be out of mind, because the new Sorcerer would have no memory and hear no alarm sounded, unless the same player came back. Since for all that player knew, Walter was waiting for him with the pistol at his head, probably he would remain clear.

Meanwhile there should be five castle denizens free, and they should be Walter's allies. Or did they revert the moment the Evil Sorcerer was replaced? It was probably safest simply to shoot anybody he saw, and rescue Baal without expecting help. So he reloaded his pistol as he ran.

He hoped he would be able to get her safely out of the castle, and that she did have some way to track Phreak. His character was lucky, but was he lucky enough?

sixteen

PURSUIT

Baal stood at the window, relieved. She had seen the twentieth-century van, and just known that it had to be Walter, because who else would be charging the castle so anachronistically? He hadn't been able to get a part in this subset, so had gotten one in another and crossed over. In Beirut, naturally, so she would be able to recognize him.

She had been lucky to get the Princess again. She had hoped for it, because it required very little action, and one thing she needed to do now was just about nothing physically. So as to let the blood sugar accumulate a bit, so the insulin wouldn't drag her into shock. She had way overdone it on excitement, in Beirut, and not realized until almost too late. As soon as she *had* realized, she had gotten just as quiet and calm as she possibly could, so as not to aggravate it further. She didn't know how well this ploy would work, but it was the best she could do. She had even worried about the amount of energy it took to stand at the window, but that much she had had to do. So she had propped herself up as comfortably as she could, and done it.

Baal glanced at her screen, and noticed something:

there were two little points of light on it. They had not been there before this setting, she was sure. Were they the signal of another glitch? She certainly didn't need that! So she would ignore them and hope that all was well.

Walter was evidently intent on rescuing her, and she wished him every success. Unfortunately, when he did rescue her, he would probably have to carry her, because if she expended the energy of walking she might use up what little blood sugar she had left. She wouldn't do him much good if she went into shock. She felt guilty for suddenly being so dependent. If only she had realized how active she was going to be, and how excited, and that she was going to be prevented from exiting the game to get sugar. Now she was stuck in a crisis that was partly of her own making.

She looked at her screen again, as if that would offer any solution. The two bits of light caught her eye anew. One was brighter than the other by several magnitudes. What did that mean? As she looked, she realized that one of the little glows was brighter than it had been before. Almost as if it were coming toward her.

Something clicked in her mind. That glow could be Walter!

She backed off, mentally, and reviewed the notion to be sure it made sense. Phreak had locked Walter into the game with a virus. Phreak had come to torment him. So how had Phreak located him? By checking the names listed for each setting, of course. But those lists did not identify the actual characters played, and some settings had a lot of territory. Obviously Phreak had some way to narrow it down. He had seemed to know that Walter was in a particular room of the castle, and later that he was a Druze. So what device did he have within a setting? The answer could be that he had a hot-cold light: something that glowed more brightly when the subject was close, and faded when the subject was distant. It might not be infallible when the subject was one of a group of people, but some observation would narrow it down.

Now Phreak was locked similarly into the game, and so was Baal. The game proprietors had said that there was a way to track him. She had assumed they meant that they would be doing it, but now she realized that they must have meant that *she* could do it. By following a blip on her screen. So now they each had lights on the screen of the other, because the proprietors had given her the same zeroing-in device. So why were there two blips instead of one? Because there were two others locked into the virus the patch was tracking. Phreak and Walter. Walter was closer than Phreak, so his light was brighter. Did that make sense? It seemed to, though she cautioned herself that it might not. Since it was the best she had to go on, she assumed that it was true. That meant that not only did she have a line on Phreak—she had a line on Walter. That could prove to be invaluable. Simply orient on one of them and start moving, and if the glow didn't get brighter, then change direction. When it brightened, keep going, getting warmer, until finally he would be in the vicinity.

But now Phreak wanted to avoid Walter, and Phreak could see Walter's blip as readily as Baal could see Phreak's blip. So Baal could pursue Phreak, but Phreak could flee from Walter. Which meant that Phreak had the advantage, because Baal could not actually pursue him until she got out of the locked chamber in the castle.

But once Walter rescued her, she would really be able to help him. Even if he had to carry her. With his van, that wouldn't be too bad. Together they could run down Phreak. She was tempted to make that literal, but it was Phreak's information they needed, not his game-death.

There was a commotion at her door. Friend or foe? She decided to be noncommittal until she was sure. For one thing, it saved energy, her most precious commodity. So she sat at the window and gazed languidly toward the door as it opened to reveal the man.

"Princess, I have been freed from the oppressive dominance of the Evil Sorcerer and have come to free thee from thy foul captivity!"

A game construct, obviously. That was good news, because it indicated that Walter was making progress against the opposition. Or did it? The loyal denizens were freed only when the Evil Sorcerer used his magic, and his magic might win the day. So she couldn't relax yet. Meanwhile, if Walter was winning through, she needed to remain here, where he could find her.

"Well done, thou good and faithful servant," she replied. "Abide with me until my Hero comes, and guard me from all ill."

The denizen promptly came to attention, standing by the door, guarding her from ill.

Soon another arrived. That meant that the Sorcerer had had to invoke another spell, which suggested that the first one had not been effective, but also that the Sorcerer remained alive, which wasn't the best news. She bade the man abide and guard, as she had the first.

A third denizen came, and joined the others. That must be quite a battle! But she remained calm, because she couldn't afford excitement. She schooled herself in faith: Walter, her Hero, would prevail.

The fourth denizen was a player. She suspected this immediately, because of his speech. "Hey, honey, we'd better get you outa here before that Guardian Angel clobbers the kook from Beirut!"

But he hadn't used the code word, so he was a stranger. "I thank thee, faithful servant. But I must wait the victory of my beloved. Remain and guard me from evil meanwhile."

"Okay, honey. Boy, you sure are cute! Do you look anything like that in real life?"

"Nothing at all," she assured him. "I am a homely thing, and sickly."

"Too bad." He lost interest. In a moment the character went blank; the player had stepped out of it and gone elsewhere.

The fifth one was another construct, this time a woman. Baal questioned her on the progress of the battle, but she was from elsewhere in the castle and knew nothing of it.

After what seemed like a long time, something odd happened. All five denizens came out of their guard positions and stared at her.

"What is the matter, loyal servants?" she inquired, quelling her thrill of alarm.

"We must confine thee here, Princess, until our master decides thy fate," the first denizen said.

Oops! That meant that the Evil Sorcerer had been replaced, and the castle denizens were all back in thrall. But after a moment she realized that this was good news: it meant that Walter had killed his man! Indeed, his blip was glowing more brightly on her screen, indicating his rapid approach.

But it also meant that these denizens would oppose Walter

when he came here. They might kill him out of hand. What could she do to stop that?

She remembered that the Princess did have a bit of magic. It didn't approach the level of the enchantments of the Evil Sorcerer, but was more than other characters had. Maybe she could use it. Let's see, what were her talents? Ah, yes: she could throw her voice.

Baal concentrated, hoping this worked well the first time. She willed a man's voice to sound from the landing outside the chamber. "Here to me at my chamber, denizens!"

It worked! The denizens, hearing it, immediately crowded out of the chamber and hurried down the winding stairs. They even forgot to lock the door.

Soon another person approached. She heard his bare feet on the stairs. Was this an enemy trying to sneak in to molest her? How could she fight him off? Was it even worth the effort, considering that this was only a game body?

She decided to defend herself with minimum effort. She took her knife in her hand, holding it concealed. She would let him strip her and get close; then, when his belly was exposed, she would make one deep stab.

The figure appeared at the door: a Druze militiaman in bare feet. "Needlepoint!" he said.

Her heart jumped gladly. "Wheels!"

He ran to her. "Oh, Baal, I'm glad you're all right!"

"Just kiss me, Walter."

He did that, and it felt a lot like love. Then he drew back. "A knife?"

She looked down at the knife in her hand. "I feared someone else might—"

"Right. Your insulin—are you okay on that score?"

"For the nonce. I have been conserving my energy. The moment I do something, I'll be in trouble, though. Just my excitement at being with you is depleting me."

"Excitement? That almost sounds like—"

"I think I love you, Walter. Maybe that's because of my low blood sugar." She was more serious than she cared to let on. Low blood sugar did mess with her emotions, but usually to intensify what was already there.

He smiled wistfully. "I don't have that excuse."

She stared at him. "You mean—?"

"I shouldn't have spoken."

She made a connection. "Because you are paralyzed, in life."

"Because I am useless, in life. I need more than a lump of sugar to set me straight. I'm an albatross."

No way! But she muted her reaction, knowing that this was not the time for foolish commitments. "I can live with that, Walter."

It was his turn to stare. Then he shook himself. "Maybe we'll talk again once you're okay. Things will be different then."

When her blood sugar was back up, and she was rational. He thought she would take back what she had said. "Will they? I don't think so."

"It's all academic if we can't catch up with Phreak. Do you have any way to locate him?"

"Yes!" she said gladly. "The proprietors set it up. My screen shows glowing blips for both of you. Yours is bright. His is dim. He's far away, off in another subset. But we can find him."

"Then let's go find him! I'll carry you."

"But suppose we encounter enemies?"

"Can you fire a pistol?"

"I think so."

He produced a pistol and handed it to her. "Plug anyone who looks dangerous. In fact better to plug anyone we see, because I think the castle denizens reverted when the Evil Sorcerer came back to life."

"Yes they did. Maybe you should have tied him up and gagged him, instead of killing him, so that my five loyal servants would have helped us."

He looked stricken. "I never thought of that! I could have made it so much easier for us."

"No, maybe not," she said, reconsidering. "Because most of the castle denizens remain in thrall to him. One of them would have untied him. Better to have a new, ignorant Sorcerer, or maybe even a construct in his place."

"I like your way of thinking. Remember: no mercy on others, until we get out to the van."

"No mercy," she agreed. "We both have too much at stake."

He picked her up and walked out of the chamber. But the winding stairs were too narrow; her head and feet projected to the sides. "I'll have to walk," she said.

"No. Let's see how strong this body is."

"But there's no room. Any way you carry me, I'll bang into a wall. Even piggyback."

"How about shoulderback?"

She considered. "The one direction it isn't tight is up," she said. "Still—"

He sat on the top step. "Get on."

She got on. Her thighs clamped around his ears. She had to tuck her billowing robe behind his head so that it wouldn't cover his face. He caught hold of her legs, his two hands clamping on and above her knees. Then he eased forward until he could heave himself to a standing position.

"Oooo!" she cried, feeling dizzy. "It's precarious."

"But possible. Hang on." He took a step down.

She put her free hand on his head to further steady herself. Then she realized that she was covering his eye, and shifted to his forehead. She was afraid that he would fall forward at any moment, but he managed to move down step by step in good order. So she concentrated on being calm, because emotion could make her pulse race as well as activity, and that was what she had to avoid.

Then she saw a man. It was a castle denizen at the foot of the stairway. She aimed the pistol carefully and fired. The thing bucked in her hand, and the denizen fell. She felt mixed thrill and horror. This was her first kill as a helpless Princess, but not as a player; which feeling should govern? Neither, she decided; she should be unemotional, as if killing were nothing.

They reached the base. "I can get down now," she said.

"Actually this isn't bad," he said. "And there'll be other stairs."

"But not so narrow."

"Maybe I just like the feel of your legs on my ears."

She squeezed his head, not arguing further. The Princess did have good legs, and she could halfway appreciate how a man would like to have them associated with his head. When there had been impromptu team sports in school, with the girls riding the boys and jousting, there had never been a lack of volunteers to be steeds. She also had a good view of things, up here.

They navigated the next flight of steps. Baal spied another denizen, and shot him. She was getting pretty callous. Maybe that, too, was because of low blood sugar. This whole adventure had an unreal quality, apart from its being a game fantasy.

"Ho, varlet!"

Baal saw that it was the Evil Sorcerer. She lifted the gun and shot the man before he could start a spell. He collapsed. "That should give us several minutes of nonresistance," she said, satisfied.

It was so. They made it to the ground floor and told the several gatekeepers to let them out. The men obeyed. Only as they crossed the drawbridge did things change, and then it was too late for the new Evil Sorcerer; they were lumbering for the van.

Walter opened the door, got down, and she slid onto the front seat. He ran around to the driver's side. He got in and started the motor. She was afraid it would balk, but it caught. He seemed to have no trouble with the standard shift.

They started out—and a fiery wall appeared before the van. "Oops—this Sorcerer isn't starting at the beginning of the book," Walter muttered. "He's making heavy spells."

"Can't we just drive through it?"

"It might set off the explosives in the van."

"Explosives "

"I came ready for trouble." He looked back at the castle. "I think the Sorcerer is angry about being killed. I'm going to have to take him out again."

"You can't go back into the castle!" she said, alarmed.

"No way. I'll do it from here. I happen to know where he lives." He stopped the van, got out, and went to the back. He brought out a contraption. "Rocket launcher," he explained, setting it up.

She watched as he fired the thing. The rocket sailed across the moat and to a middle-level window of the castle. There was an explosion. Stone flew outward, followed by billowing fire and smoke. Explosions were always impressive in the game.

"That did it," Walter said with satisfaction as he returned to the front.

Baal looked. The wall had vanished. That meant that the Evil Sorcerer had been killed, and all his evil works terminated with him. For a couple of minutes.

Walter started up and moved on through the place where the wall had been. But then they came to the dragon.

"We can't delay," she said worriedly. "Because then the Sorcerer will be back, and we aren't out of range of his magic."

"I blasted it with a rocket before," he said. "But I used my last one on the Sorcerer. I could rig the explosives, but that would take time, and I'd have to be close enough to detonate them."

"And you'd either get blown up yourself, or scorched by the dragon," she said. "Maybe I have a better way."

"Nuh-uh! I don't want you getting killed either, even if the game-death isn't your problem. I need you."

"To find Phreak," she agreed. It was important not to confuse things, when her mind was trying to blur.

"That too." Which didn't help.

She forced herself to focus on the immediate problem. "The Princess has a little magic. She can throw her voice—or even throw someone else's voice. I used it to get rid of the castle denizens before you came."

"So that's why you were in the clear, with the door unlocked! I would have been afraid of a trap, with anyone else but you."

"Maybe I can make a voice to distract the dragon."

"If you can, now's the time," he said grimly. They were driving right toward the dragon, who was waiting for them with no display of fear. To the side was the river, and the bridge they had to cross.

She concentrated. "Hey, look at those babes in the river!" a man's voice came. "Let's have at them before we raid the castle!"

The dragon's ears perked. So did Walter's. "That's you?" he asked, amazed.

She nodded, pleased. She was getting better at this!

"Eeeek!" It sounded just like a bare bathing damsel who had been surprised by a man.

The dragon charged the river, intent on this distraction. As it did so, Walter gunned the motor and the van hurtled forward, passing in the wake of the dragon. By the time the dragon discovered that there were no men molesting the water nymphs, it was too late.

"There's something to be said for Princesses," Walter remarked as they bumped toward the edge of the Princess realm. "Does that magic work beyond the subset?"

"I don't know. Your weapons worked beyond the Beirut set, so maybe my magic does too." Then, belatedly, she remembered something. "When I was the Hero, in this setting, the dragon didn't challenge me on the way out. I think it assumes that anyone going out is a friend. So maybe we weren't in danger from it anyway."

"Now she tells me," Walter muttered. But he was smiling.

They plowed through the border and emerged from what seemed to be a huge picture. Baal stared, astonished.

"Each subset is a billboard," Walter explained. "A picture, until we enter it. I came in this way."

"I was locked in my chamber," she said. "I didn't know how it's set up." She saw other billboards as they turned onto the highway.

"Can you tell where Phreak is?"

She looked at her screen. "That way," she said, pointing ahead. "Probably at the very end of the road, wherever that is."

"We'll get there quickly," he said, accelerating.

The billboards were continuous, so that no other scenery showed. She remembered a parody of the poem "Trees," about never seeing a billboard as lovely as a tree. But many of these billboards had trees in them. Each was labeled with a title: METROPOLIS, ROME, GREECE, CAMELOT, BATTLESHIP, GLOCCA MORRA, HAREM, PARADISE, HADES, and such: places and situations, each with its assortment of challenges. What a panoply!

Meanwhile the second blip was brightening. "We're zeroing in on him," she said. "But he can see your blip too, so he'll try to escape. That's why he started so far away; he's keeping your blip faint."

"But if we get close enough to track him directly, fleeing won't do him any good."

"But we still have to make him give up the secret," she reminded him. "He wouldn't do it in Beirut, and I'm afraid he won't do it here."

"I've been thinking about that. There's something he's hiding. He should have cut his losses and let us all get out of the game. He could find another victim to bug. He's not getting any fun from me now; in fact he's hiding from me. So why doesn't he get rid of me by letting me go? But he's resisting that. He also doesn't want to die, even in the game. I'm wondering whether there is something that could account for both those attitudes."

She glanced at him. "They seem opposite to me. He can stop you from killing him by giving us the antivenin code. He can also get himself out of the game that way, and he must want to do that, because he knows that the game proprietors are trying to track him down. The longer he stays pinned in the game, the more likely they are to find him. Physically, I mean. Then they'll have him arrested. He surely doesn't want that."

"He surely doesn't," he agreed. "I've encountered characters like that on the street. They are characterized by paranoia. They don't trust anyone, and they have many fears. I think Phreak never entered the game legitimately because he was afraid to experience all of it. Such as dying. That would explain why he's fleeing instead of just exiting the Potpourri setting by getting killed."

"But he can't really get away from it," she reminded him. "He's tied to you, and has to be in the same setting with you."

"True. But he could take time out by getting killed. Or he could just face me and dare me to kill him. I could kill him a hundred times, and he'd just keep bouncing back. It wouldn't necessarily make him tell me the code. Or he could get killed and come back as a character at the far side of the setting, so that I'd have to take time to chase him down again. It would be almost impossible to corner him. But I don't think he's doing that, because he has a phobia about dying, even in the game. He'll do almost anything to avoid getting killed again."

"Except give up the code," she said.

"Yes. That's what doesn't seem to make sense. What is he afraid of that matches his fear of getting killed? If I could only figure that, I'd have the lever to make him talk."

Baal focused on that riddle. Why would someone be afraid to give up a bit of information that would get him out of a trap and stop another person from chasing him? What could be worse than dying, whether in reality or emulation?

Suddenly it came to her. "Living!" she cried.

"What?"

"He's afraid of living," she said. "I mean, living the sort of life he'd have to live if he couldn't roam the games. He probably has a hellish home life, so he escapes to the games. But he's so obnoxious that no one will play with him, so he uses the virus to trap someone. And if he loses that virus, he won't be able to do it anymore."

"Why not?" he asked. "I think you're on the right track, but I don't see the answer."

"Because maybe the antivenin is just that: it inoculates the whole system against that virus, so it can't be used anymore. So he won't be able to trap any more players."

"But he'll have to use it to get free himself," Walter said.

"But he won't have to give it to anyone else. Maybe it doesn't nullify things permanently itself, but if we get it and give it to the game proprietors, they'll know how to install it throughout the game so that the virus won't work. So he'll only give it to a friend—"

"And he has no friends!" Walter said. "And maybe no one to take him physically out of the game, so he's stuck just the way we are. But he's hoping he can find another hacker who will make a deal."

"That's hard to do," Baal said. "I wish I could make a deal with another player, and have her exit the game and go to my house and disconnect me physically. But I don't think anyone would believe me, and anyone who did would probably be thousands of miles away. So I'm stuck. And so is he."

"Which means that his refusal to yield the virus to us suggests that he believes that his life won't be worth living if he does," Walter said. "Just as you said. Life as he knows it would stop."

"That's the trouble with being obnoxious. You have a life even you can't stand."

"But *your* life will stop if we don't get you out of the game soon," he said. "And mine can stop at any time, if I get killed in the game. So we have to make Phreak change his mind."

"We have to," she agreed weakly. "The proprietors told me that they think he's afraid of snakes and tight places, like narrow caves. Maybe if we can get him in a cave, he'll crack."

"Maybe," he agreed. "But first we have to catch him. I figure to keep chasing him until he can't hide anymore. Then we'll see what offers."

The highway didn't terminate. It merely reached the end of the billboards. The road continued beyond, but disappeared into a starry sky. This was the game's way of hinting that there was nothing out there for players.

The last billboard was labeled HAUNTED HOUSE. The picture was of a huge rambling decrepit mansion with broken windows and curling roof shingles. Its front door opened directly to a soiled walk leading to the highway. The moon showed gibbous behind it, looking moldy in the night sky. The Phreak blip glowed more brightly as they approached it. It would have to be that one! She had enjoyed mock haunted house shows, but had the feeling that she wouldn't like any as realistic as this one, with spooks who were genuinely deadly.

"That's where he is?" Walter inquired.

"That's where he is," she agreed weakly. "Walter, I don't know how much I can help you in there. If I get frightened, that will accelerate my pulse and run me down, just as activity would."

He considered as he parked. "I could leave you out here. But I don't know how many players are in this subset. It could take me a long time to locate him, and then he might kill me from ambush. If you get killed, will it hurt you?"

She made a wan smile. "That sounds weird! No, I can handle the game-death. In fact that death coffin is rather restful, and in that sense it's good for me. I have nothing to fear from getting killed here."

"Except that if you do die, you'll have to take a new character," he said. "If you take the Princess again, you'll be far away and locked up. I'm assuming that characters revert to their original stations when reset. Otherwise this Potpourri setting would soon become hopelessly muddled. If you take a Haunted House role, I won't know who you are. If you approach me, I might kill you again, thinking you to be an enemy."

"But I can't help you if I stay out here," she said, perversely arguing the other case. "And I *can* help you in there, by using my voice-throwing magic."

"If it works here."

She tried it. "Hey, Walter," a voice called from outside. "Why don't you kiss her?"

His head snapped around, but there was no one in sight. He turned back to her. "That was you?"

She nodded. "I'm getting better, and the magic doesn't seem to use any energy."

"Then I'd better kiss you."

"That was just to test my magic," she said.

"So why didn't you test it by yelling an insult?"

She spread her hands, having no excuse. They moved together and kissed. She thrilled to it while trying to condemn herself as foolish.

They got out of the van, tacitly agreeing to stay together. If their mission didn't succeed, at least they had this much. A summer-camp romance. They held hands and stepped into the picture.

The walk turned distastefully mossy under their feet. Each step squished. A wind came up, feeling like an unclean breath. There was a low moan as it cut around the house.

"Nice special effects," Walter murmured.

Suddenly the developing spell was broken. Special effects was exactly what it was; this was all a matter of sight and sound and trace electric tingles from the game wrappings. None of it was real.

She squeezed his hand. "Thanks."

"Maybe your magic can defuse some of its haunts," he said. "If you see a ghost, throw your voice behind it."

"Can do," she said from the door ahead.

The thrown voice triggered one of the haunts. It was indeed a ghost. It glared at the space above the doorstep. Then, spying nothing, it faded away.

"Can you do a knock?" Walter whispered.

She tried. In a moment there was a sharp rapping at the door. This triggered maniacal laughter.

"So far the effects are harmless," Walter said. "But I doubt that they remain so. This set is like a gantlet for the visitor to run. We'd be fools to play by its rules."

"What other rules are there?" she asked.

"Beirut rules." He retreated down the walk, and she kept pace. They stepped back through the billboard, into blinding daylight, and the van came into sight. She realized that it had disappeared behind them, because from the Haunted House side the painting had only a sketch of a shady nocturnal lane, not the real view.

He opened the back and lifted out a package. He got a smaller package from which two wires trailed. She had seen similar wires in Beirut: they led to the detonator. He was going to blow something up.

"But what about innocent players?" she asked.

"Isn't that an oxymoron?"

She must have looked blank, so he explained. "A contradiction in terms. Any player who survives more than a few minutes is unlikely to be innocent. He's more likely to be a successful killer. We are both killers now. We kill without compunction."

She had to agree. Conscienceless killing was the name of the game. But she was surprised to realize how far she had come in this respect.

"However," he continued, "we shall give fair warning. That may spook Phreak, which is what we want. When he moves, let me know."

He carried the packages back through the billboard. She watched as he set them against the door. He drew the two wires out until they reached the end of the walk. "Now throw your voice and tell Phreak that he has one minute to come out with his hands up, or we'll destroy the house," he said.

"He won't come out."

"Right. But he'll get out of the house. Watch your screen."

She threw her own voice to the front step. "Phreak!" she called. "Come out within one minute with your hands up, or we'll blow up the house."

The ghost manifested again, and faded again. The maniacal laughter sounded. That was all. There was no change in the bright blip that was Phreak's indication on her screen.

"Step back through the board," Walter said tersely. "It's a pretty strong explosion."

She stepped back, and he disappeared. Then he reappeared in part, his head and arms remaining on the other side. It looked as if he had been bloodlessly severed at the shoulders and neck. Then, suddenly, he pulled back, and was whole again. There was a shudder.

"Okay. Let's move in."

They stepped through. The Haunted House was on fire, with smoke billowing around it. There was only wreckage where the front door had been. Walter had indeed blown it up.

She looked at her screen. The Phreak blip was flickering. That meant that Phreak was moving. She turned, so that her screen would turn with her, and the blip firmed. "He's moving away," she said.

"He must have been behind it," Walter said. "That's okay; I didn't want to kill him anyway, just get him out of there. We'll have the advantage if we can keep him running. Maybe we can break his nerve."

Baal hoped so, because she was feeling giddy. It was requiring more of an effort for her to keep alert.

Then Walter was putting the rifle in her hands. He picked her up. "Point the way," he said.

She pointed to the left of the house. He carried her across the desolate lawn, going that way. She looked back, and saw the shady lane, with its somber streetlamps. Of course the game could put night and day on opposite sides of a wall; everything was image anyway. But it remained strange.

Then they stepped through another boundary. Suddenly they were in what looked like an enormous boardroom. Men in expensive suits were seated around a giant oak table. This must be the Boardroom subset, and they were interrupting an important meeting of the board. Several businessmen looked up as Walter and Baal appeared.

And appeared was exactly what they had done, because behind them was a paneled wall. No door, no window, no hall. They had passed through it without affecting it.

Baal became conscious of the sight they made. Walter was in Druze military uniform, while she was in her Princess robe. Both were somewhat bedraggled.

"Is he moving?" Walter asked tersely.

That much she could tell. "No."

"Then he must have donned a suit, and is masquerading as a board member."

She had to agree. "But we don't know what he looks like in this frame. He could be any of them."

"One way to find out." Walter set her gently on her feet. He took the pistol from his waistband and pointed it at the Chairman of the Board. "Who stepped through the wall just before us?" he inquired.

The man puffed out his cheeks. "You can't come in here like this and make demands!"

Walter shot him through the head. The man slumped forward, and blood began to pool on the shiny surface of the table. Walter turned to the next. "Who came last?" he inquired evenly.

The man just stared at him without reaction. "A construct," Baal murmured. "A player wouldn't have that nerve."

Walter aimed at the next. "Who—"

"Look out!" Baal cried, seeing a man farther down the table bring up a gun.

Walter pushed her away from him. They leaned in opposite directions. The bullet spanged between them.

Walter whipped his pistol around to fire at the other man, but he was already ducking under the table. Walter ducked down too, and swore. "Damn! It's solid underneath." He ran around it, but Phreak was ahead of him, scrambling to the hall and out of the room.

Walter went to the hall, but had to keep to the side so that he did not present a target. Baal looked at her screen. "He's moving away," she said.

Walter charged into the hall. But in a moment he stopped, turning back. "Big array of doors," he said, disgusted. "He could have used any of them."

He came to Baal and picked her up. "Tracking is fuzzy at close range," she said. "But he still seems to be moving away."

"It figures. And he has a gun. We'll have to be careful."

"At least now we know what he looks like," she said.

"And how he's dressed. If he pauses to change, we'll catch up with him. So we're after a man in a business suit."

They moved down the hall, trying to see whether any door had been used recently, but it was impossible to tell. Then the blip flickered. Baal turned her head back and forth, zeroing in on it. "That way," she said, indicating a section of the wall without a door.

Walter stepped through it, carrying her. It seemed that every set had its boundary, and the sides and rear bordered on other sets. When a player moved out from the center of the set, he encountered that limit, and simply passed through it; it didn't have to be at the main highway. That must be just for convenience in choosing or locating a subset instead of stumbling blindly from one into another.

Walter set her down on her feet, and she sat in a nearby chair. She looked around.

They were in a Space Station set. A curving screen behind them—through which they had just stepped—showed a distant planet against a background of stars. No one would ordinarily try to walk through such a screen; either it would be impenetrable, or it would break, putting them into vacuum and depressurizing the whole space station. No one would ordinarily walk through the wall of a boardroom complex either, when there were plenty of doors. Not even players, she suspected. What was the point?

Before them was what seemed to be the control center. Maybe this was a ship, in orbit, ready to move out to another planet. Or maybe the controls were to operate necessary appurtenances such as light collectors and airlocks and telescopes. A man was sitting in what might be the captain's seat, and another was doing something under a piece of equipment; she saw his bare legs projecting on the floor.

Bare legs? On a space station? That didn't make much sense. She wanted to say something to Walter, but he was already walking to the other side, checking for people, looking for Phreak. He was facing away from her. She didn't want to speak, because that would alert others to their presence and perhaps spoil Walter's search. Had Phreak charged right through here and on into another set, or did he remain here, perhaps lurking in ambush? In fact could he have conked a crewman on the head and taken his clothing—and the conked man's feet were the ones she saw? With others in hot pursuit, Phreak wouldn't have had much time, and might not have been able to hide the body effectively.

She looked at her screen, but couldn't tell how close or exactly where Phreak was; the blip glowed brightly, and it just wasn't very selective at close range. That body might be important. So she drew on her dwindling supply of energy and walked around to check those legs.

She was right. The man was in shorts, and there was blood on his head. He must have been hit hard, to knock him out or kill him, and quickly stripped. Jammed under the equipment with him was a mass of dark cloth: the businessman's suit. The poor player probably had never known what hit him.

Then the feet stirred. He wasn't dead! No—he could have been dead, but was coming back to life, in the manner of this setting. He might be a construct, in which case it wouldn't matter, but if he turned out to be a player—

The man in the captain's chair turned. He held a pistol, pointed at her face. It was Phreak, in his businessman or haunted house body, but in the spaceman uniform. She knew that if she moved or spoke, he would kill her. She could handle the death, but then Walter would be deprived of her help for at least a few minutes, and that could give Phreak a critical advantage. She had to hope that Walter would turn and see what was happening. At the moment Walter was looking into the aperture leading to another chamber; there must be other people there. Turn, Walter, turn!

Phreak got up and came toward her, the pistol unwavering. His present body was large; he had taken the opportunity to get the best the game had to offer. Inside might be a half-crazy teenager, but outside was formidable.

Maybe she should scream and make a break for it. She would get shot, and die, but maybe she could find a female body in this setting, and track Walter down again. But if she did, she might discover that right after shooting her, Phreak had shot Walter, and Walter might be all-the-way dead this time. Then the game would be truly lost, in every sense. No, she had to protect Walter, and she could do that only by distracting Phreak until Walter learned what was happening. Maybe she had made more of an impression on Phreak than she had thought, in Beirut. She had tried to soften him with feminine charm, but she lacked experience with that, and it hadn't worked. He had just gotten vituperative. But maybe that was his way of reacting to temptation. Maybe he did want her, and though her skin crawled at the prospect, she knew she would do whatever she could to protect Walter. It was only a game body, after all, she reminded herself firmly.

Then Walter turned. Phreak leaped, grabbed Baal with an arm around her neck, and put the pistol to her head. "Make my day, bunghole!" he yelled at Walter.

Walter froze. Baal realized that he didn't want to let her be harmed any more than she wanted him to be harmed. Phreak had gotten the jump on them both, using them against each other.

Phreak hauled her across the chamber to the far wall. Then he pulled them both through it, into the next set. Baal tried to catch Walter's eye, to give him some message, but she didn't succeed, and in any event she had no message. Other than despair.

seventeen

SHOWDOWN

Walter moved the moment Phreak and Baal disappeared. He cursed himself for his idiocy. Why hadn't he checked out the "captain" first thing? Why had he gotten so involved in checking the other chamber of the space station that he had allowed disaster to sneak up behind him? There were six figures there, and he had wanted to be sure that none of them was Phreak—while not checking the one he should have. Maybe he had thought Baal would warn him if there was any problem—but what was she to do with a gun pointed at her head? He knew that she would have screamed had Phreak pointed the gun at Walter, but she regarded herself as expendable, so had bided her time when threatened. And had become a hostage.

Now what should he do? Dive in after them? That might just get Baal or himself killed. But he couldn't let Phreak get away either. Without Baal, he had no way to track the kid except hot pursuit.

But his body knew the answer. He was already running to the side, into the other chamber. The crewmen there looked up at him, startled to see a Druze militiaman charging through their station. Then he dived into the wall parallel to the one Phreak had gone through. This should get him into the same set, but a bit removed, maybe another chamber. So he could come at the kid from another direction, surprising him.

He found himself in an elaborate complex of chambers, with hanging plants and multiple columns and couches. On several of the couches were beautiful young women in sheer blouses and sheer pantaloons. They screamed when they saw him, covering their faces.

This was a Harem set!

For a moment he stared. It was amazing how intriguing a healthy young woman's body could be when veiled by just the right amount of material. These creatures were twice as exciting clothed as they would have been naked. He found his eyes trying to fathom the precise curve of a breast or configuration of a crevice. The faces too were veiled, and were just as alluring. Ah, paradise!

But he had no time to be concerned about them. He ran back in the direction he judged Phreak and Baal to be. He came to a door, kicked it open, and went into a rolling dive.

Sure enough, a bullet cut through the air where he would have been if standing. He completed his roll and aimed his pistol, but Phreak was already retreating to another chamber, hauling Baal with him. Walter couldn't shoot without hitting her. That was the problem with being a good guy: he had to watch his shots.

He got up quickly and looked around. There was the body of the Sultan on the floor. Phreak had killed the man, cowed the ladies, then listened for the screams greeting Walter's arrival in the adjacent chamber.

He had to find a better way. But there seemed to be none at the moment. Because if he lost Phreak now, he might never find him again.

So this time he didn't try to circle around. He launched himself directly after Phreak, dodging as he passed the place where he had last seen him.

It was the boundary. The next set was a pretty little yard with a prettier little house. But there was something odd about it.

He had no time to be concerned about that. Phreak was standing there with Baal, but his gun was pointing at an old woman. She was small and hunched and ugly, with a huge purple wart on her nose. She seemed quite unconcerned about the pistol.

She glanced at Walter. "Oh, another little boy!" she said, delighted. "Come here, Junior."

Walter felt a powerful compulsion. This was magic! He jerked his pistol up and fired it at the woman.

Pink smoke emerged from the barrel. It writhed and formed into the word BANG! before dissolving. Then the magic overcame him, and he walked up to stand beside Phreak and Baal. He realized that all three of them had been taken captive by another player. A Witch, with witchly powers. In the Princess set, magic had worked on things rather than other people, but this was a different set which evidently had different rules of magic.

"My, what fine children you are!" the Witch cackled. "So round and sweet! So deliciously cuddly. Come into my house, dears. I'm sure you will be delightful."

She turned and hobbled into the house, and they formed a file and followed. Now Walter saw that the house was made of candy, and so was the garden; indeed, what he had taken for flowers were lollipops. The walls were cake, and the roof was thatched with pastry. The floor was paved with rock sugar crystals. This was straight out of a fairy tale, but it was no fun story.

"Get into those playrooms, children, while I heat the oven," the Witch said. Obediently they marched into the three chambers available. The doors swung closed behind them: covered with translucently fine mesh of the kind normally used in making fancy desserts.

Walter found himself free to move. He touched the mesh door, but it was tougher than it looked, and would not yield to whatever force he could bring to bear. He checked the rest of the chamber, and found that all of it was deceptively strong. The butterscotch plaster on the walls smelled delicious, and when he touched his tongue to it, it tasted delicious, but it was impervious. The crystalline candy window would not break. The prison cell was tight.

"Hey, joker, know what she's gonna do?" Phreak called.

"Bake us in her oven," Walter replied.

"Know how to get away?"

Walter considered. "No."

"Well, I know."

"Then maybe we'll watch what you do, and do likewise."

"Ain't that easy. She's on guard."

"Besides which, she's listening to us talk," Walter said dryly.

"Naw. She's deaf. I've cruised this setting before. She's got a lot of magic, and she's horny, but she can't hear."

"Horny?"

"That's why she makes the children strip for the oven. Gets her kicks outa spanking their little bottoms before she bakes 'em. Real creeps like this role."

Walter shook his head in wonder. There were weird nooks in this game. If Phreak was fazed, it had to be extreme.

Baal joined in. "Maybe we should declare a truce and cooperate, so we can escape."

Phreak hesitated. "Maybe," he agreed reluctantly. "I don't wanna get baked to death."

"So what's your notion?" Walter asked.

"Somebody's gotta distract her. Then somebody else's gotta push her in the oven from behind. 'S the only way to kill her. Then the magic lets go for a while."

"So if she dies, we all get away," Walter said.

"Right. And if she don't die, we all get baked, one by one."

"But how can anyone get out of these cells?" Baal asked.

"You're the Princess, right? You can throw your voice?"

"Yes."

"So when she's not looking, make like her voice to open a door. Then whichever man's not being baked can sneak up and push her in."

Walter saw the logic. Baal was conserving her energy, but there would be one man remaining in a cell, and he could take care of the Witch. "All right. Whichever one she decides to bake first will try to distract her. Then the other will push her. Then it's every person for himself—and we resume our chase in the next set."

"Yeah. No deal in the next set."

"Why don't you just tell us the antivenin code so we can be done with this?"

"No way, schnook!"

Well, it had been worth a try. He glanced at Baal. "You can imitate her voice?"

"If my magic works here," Baal agreed.

"It does," Phreak said. "So do the guns. She just has magic to divert 'em."

Meanwhile the Witch had gotten her oven hot. She turned and approached the cells. "Open up, gate one," she said.

Walter's gate opened. Knowing it was useless to try to resist her, he stepped out. He went to stand before the oven, whose heat bathed him in waves. The chamber was huge, readily large enough to contain him if he curled up.

She inspected him closely. "My, aren't you a big one! Take off your clothes. I don't want to spoil the meat with burned cloth."

He tried to resist, but his hands went to work. He found that he had freedom of motion as long as he was doing the ordered task. He removed his shirt, then his boots, and finally his trousers.

"Ooo!" the Witch cackled, staring at his torso. "Take off the rest. Take off the rest!"

He glanced significantly at Baal's cell. It was time for action there. Then he moved to the side just enough so that the Witch would have to gaze away from the cells while he took down his shorts.

"Open up, gate three," the Witch's voice said. The Witch, intent on Walter's striptease, did not notice when Phreak's cell door swung open behind her. Because she was deaf, she had not heard the voice.

Walter was now standing directly in front of the maw of the oven. The heat toasted his backside. He saw Phreak emerging.

"Ooo, turn around, you gorgeous hunk of meat!" the Witch exclaimed.

Walter turned, wincing as the heat blasted his frontside. The Witch reached out to pat his bottom.

"Move it!" Phreak cried.

Walter couldn't turn, because of the Witch's order, but she hadn't told him not to make other motions, so he managed to step to the side.

There was a thud. Then the Witch lurched forward, headfirst into the oven. She screamed piercingly.

Walter bent down to give her an additional boost. Together they folded her legs under and shoved her in. Then they jammed the oven door shut. It clicked into place, using the same locking mechanism that was intended to keep the "children" from getting out before being properly baked.

The screams became fainter. Then they stopped.

"Ding, dong, the witch's dead!" Phreak exclaimed jubilantly. Then he bolted for the door. Walter ran to the cells. Baal's door was now open. He went in and picked her up. "I'm sorry I lost the rifle," she said.

He had to laugh. Then he headed out, but not the way Phreak had gone. He didn't want to get shot at as he passed through the boundary. It was better to return for his van, now that he had Baal safe. They would be able to track the kid down more safely that way.

He passed through the boundary, into a dark scene. It seemed to be a marsh or damp plain. He moved on through, not caring what it was.

But Baal cared. "This is the Moor!" she whispered.

"What's wrong with that?"

"Where there's the Hound of the Baskervilles."

That gave Walter a chill. "You mean that Sherlock Holmes story?"

"That's the one. Can we hurry?"

But already there was a sound: a terrifying howl. They looked, and saw the giant canine shape on the horizon. The huge head turned as it winded them. Then it started toward them, running at a frightening speed.

Walter hastily cut to the side. In a moment he broke through another boundary, and emerged into daylight before a tremendous pyramid. A procession of ancient Egyptians was approaching.

"I don't want to be mummified and entombed," Walter muttered, and hurried on across the set.

The next boundary took them onto the heaving deck of a battleship. It was evidently making ready for an engagement. Men in uniform were scurrying to their battle stations. There was the smell of cordite.

Walter started to walk on across. An officer approached. "Who the hell are you?" he demanded.

"A naked man and a princess," Walter replied gruffly, and staggered on, hoping to get out of this set before having to step off the deck and take a plunge into the water. He was in luck.

The next boundary turned out to be the highway. The van was in sight in the distance. Walter breathed a sigh of relief and strode toward it.

Now they noticed the billboards they passed: they had just stepped out of Battleship, and next to it was Pyramid, and next to that was Hound of Baskervilles. Then Valhalla, which they had managed to miss, and Pirate Ship. And Candy House, Harem, Space Station, Boardroom, and finally Haunted House.

They reached the van, and he set her in the seat. "How are you doing, Baal?" he asked, concerned.

"I'm not hallucinating yet," she said. "Unless we *didn't* pass through Sherlock Holmes, ancient Egypt, and a battleship."

She was trying to be positive, but he wasn't reassured. He had to nail Phreak, get that code, and get it delivered out of the game, and he had to do it soon. Because it was no longer his own life in question, it was hers.

"You can still see him on your screen?" he asked as he started the motor.

"Yes. His blip is getting fainter."

He turned the van and started down the highway. "I've got to find a way to force the issue. If I thought that just killing him would do it—"

"He helped us escape the Witch," she reminded him. "It can't be because he has any compassion for us. He's trying to kill us. I tried to—to ameliorate his attitude, when he took me hostage, but he's thoroughly paranoid."

"He can't relate to women," he said. "He's a fouled-up teenager." He glanced at her. "And you're only three years older. How can there be such a difference?"

"Oh, I'm fouled up too," she said. "In fact I can sympathize with his alienation, to an extent. When you can't make it in regular human society—"

"You can make it," he said firmly. "You're a great girl."

"I'm a nothing girl. I've been trying to tell you that."

He wanted to argue, but realized that it was pointless. He was a nothing man. "If we get out of this game alive, we'll meet and talk," he said.

"I'd like that."

"Tell me when we're closest to Phreak. I may take this van into the set. It's chancy, but so is going without it."

"Because you have to carry me," she said. "I wish I could be less of a drag."

"Some drag! It gives me an excuse to hold you."

She laughed, but she was also flattered, which was what he had intended. However, it was also true. She might be in a game body that did not resemble her own, but her nuances had to be authentic. When it came to bodies, he'd had much more of a problem than she did, in real life.

He spied something beside the highway. It was a man in a Druze uniform.

Walter stared. "That's Leon!" he exclaimed.

"Who?"

"The man I worked with in the Beirut setting, hauling the explosives. What's he doing here?"

"Looking for you?"

"Let's find out." He brought the van to a halt beside the man.

Leon merely looked at him. The man was armed, but not threatening. Walter realized that Leon didn't recognize them. Because Walter was naked, and Leon had never seen Baal.

Then, suddenly, Leon's pistol was in his hand, pointed at Walter. "Get out of that vehicle," he said. "It's mine."

Oops. He had assumed that Leon would be a friend. But Leon was after his stolen van.

Walter got out. "Look, Leon," he said. "I'm Walter. We worked together in Beirut, until I got captured. This is Baal. I didn't know you would want your van in this setting."

Leon looked at Walter's naked body. "So you stole it—and a cache of guns and weapons."

"I didn't think of it as stealing. This is a different setting, and Druze were shooting at Druze. Obviously those players knew nothing of Druze honor. But as far as that goes, you're a player too. You don't own this van any more than I do, and I suspect your need for it is less than mine."

Leon glared. "So you're not even apologetic!"

Walter shrugged. "I'm afraid I'm not. I'm glad to see you, even if you're not glad to see me."

"So you're uggal."

Walter shook his head in negation. "I'm juhhal, or less. You know that."

Leon nodded. He put away his pistol. He smiled. "Just verifying. I hoped I'd find you, Walter. You proved yourself when you blew up the Hizbollah headquarters. The Druze will probably win that game, because of that, and we'll all get substantial bonuses."

"But why aren't you there? That game's still in progress."

"I got killed shortly after that. So I felt I owed you one. We do have Druze honor, and I treated you mainly as an enemy before. When that building blew, I knew how wrong I'd been, and I felt guilty. Now I'd like to treat you as a friend, making up for my prior attitude. Can I help you in any way?"

"Talk of luck!" Walter breathed. So Leon's conscience had gotten to him, after Walter gave his life for the Druze cause. He had had his own agenda too, of course, but the effect had been the same. "Yes! We need someone to take Phreak's antivenin code out of the game. We can't do it; we're both locked in. I think we could trust you to do it."

"I'll do it. Give it to me."

"We don't have it yet. We have to make Phreak give it to us. He's trapped in the game too, in this setting, but he doesn't want to let that information go. We're tracking him down now. Baal is caught too, and she's going into insulin shock, so doesn't dare expend any extra energy. We have to get that code soon, or she could die."

"I'll help you get it. Give me a lift."

"Glad to." Walter turned to Baal. "This is Leon, who I think we can trust. He came here to help. He can take the code out."

"That's nice," she said faintly. She moved over to give Leon room on the seat.

Leon spoke to her as Walter started the van. "They said there was a female hostage brought in."

"That was me," she agreed. "I managed to use the patch the game proprietors sent me, to lock Phreak into the game; he has to be in the same setting as Walter. They're trying to identify his source unit, but it takes time. Meanwhile we need to get the antivenin code from him before . . ." She faded out, her thought unfinished.

"So you got blown up too," Leon said.

"Yes. It was the only way to get out of there."

"So you contributed to the Druze cause too."

"Not really. I was just there."

"But you knew Walter was going to do it, and supported him."

"Yes, I think."

"I think that's justification for helping you as well as him. We planned for a long time to make that Druze move, and then we thought Walter had messed it up, but he helped us. Several of us are going to make Expert level when that game is done, because of the Druze victory."

"That's nice."

Walter didn't comment, but it seemed to him that Leon had
more on his mind than idle conversation. Was it possible that the
man had some other agenda? Walter was inclined to trust him,
but he made a mental note. It was just possible that Leon was not
a complete friend, though Druze honor made it unlikely that he
would betray them. Not as long as he saw Walter as a Druze.

"Here," Baal said suddenly. "We're passing it."

Walter looped around. "Which one?"

"That one." She pointed.

"Puss 'n Boots," he read, with a sinking feeling. What oddities
would they encounter there?

He turned to Leon. "I'm going to try to drive into this. If you
prefer to wait out on the highway—"

"No, I'm here to help. I'll ride shotgun." He brought up his rifle and worked it out the window.

Walter was glad. This would allow him to concentrate on his
driving, and Baal to concentrate on her screen, instead of worrying about ambushes.

He steered into the billboard. They entered a scene with
spreading farmland. One nice thing about it was that it had a
drivable road. In the distance was a castle, and along it were
spaced the hovels of peasants.

"It's right down in the direction of that castle," Baal said.

"Must be where the king lives," Walter said. "It's been some
time since I was a child. I don't remember the Puss 'n Boots
story very well, except that it has an adventurous cat."

"I remember it," Baal said. "I have read it many times to the
kids I baby-sit. There were three brothers, the sons of a miller.
When he died he left the mill and donkey to the elder two, and
his old cat to the youngest. That looked pretty bad, until the cat
spoke up and asked for a pair of boots and a sack. So the young
man gave the cat his boots, and the cat went out hunting and
caught rabbits and quail, which he gave to the king of the land,
saying they were presents from his master the marquis. Then
when the king rode by the river with his daughter, Puss had the
youth strip and jump in the water, and Puss told the king his
master was drowning after being robbed of his possessions and
clothes. So they rescued him and gave him nice clothes, and he
looked really handsome in them and got to ride with the princess." Baal grimaced. "The princess was evidently too stupid to
know the difference between a peasant and a royal person, with-

out the clue of the clothing, and was well impressed. Then Puss went to an ogre's castle and tricked the ogre into turning into a mouse. Puss pounced on the mouse and ate it, and claimed the castle for his master the marquis. Then the youth married the princess, and they lived happily ever after. It's peasant-style wish fulfillment. I always liked it, for some reason."

Which helped explain why she had chosen the part of the Princess. "With luck, we'll pass through without meeting any of them," Walter said.

"Except whoever lives in that castle," Leon said.

Then they spied a figure by the roadside. It turned out to be a cat standing on its hind legs, wearing enormous boots, with a sack slung over its shoulder. It had one paw out in a hitchhiking signal.

Walter sighed. "So do we pick up Puss?"

"That's an extremely clever cat," Leon said. "Probably best not to antagonize him."

So Walter stopped, and the cat scrambled into the van. He sat on Baal's lap. "Say, you're a Princess, aren't you?" Puss asked as she stroked his fur.

"Yes. But I'm out of my scene, and very delicate. I have to be carried."

"And you can probably feel a pea under twenty feather mattresses," Puss said. "That's the way of true Princesses. How would you like to marry my master, the marquis of Carabas?"

Walter kept his mouth shut, and so did Leon. This was one for Baal to handle in her own way.

"Why, I don't know," Baal said. "What does your master the marquis have to offer?"

"What do you want?" the cat countered.

"I want an antivenin code from someone called the Phreak."

"I don't know of any freaks here. Will an ogre do? That's his castle up ahead. I'm going there to kill him and claim the castle for my master. Never can tell when another castle will come in handy."

Baal considered. "Maybe the ogre will do, if he knows the code. Is your master handsome?"

"Extremely. He's also a charming lad, if a trifle naive. You should like him very well."

"Are you sure he doesn't have any peasant blood in him?"

"Of course he doesn't! Do you think a peasant could afford a cat like me?"

Baal hugged him. "I don't think anybody could afford a cat like you!"

Puss purred.

They drove up to the castle. It was a lot like the Princess' castle, but evidently with a different floor plan. Its drawbridge was lifted, and guards watched from the high window slits. It would be very easy to get killed here, Walter reflected glumly.

He glanced at Baal. "He's in the castle," she said. "The direction and strength are right."

Puss scrambled out the window and dropped to the ground. "Ho, guard!" he called. "Whose castle is this?"

"It's the evil ogre's castle, dunce!" the gatekeeper called back. "Now, scamper off before he decides to serve you for dinner."

"Oh, but I couldn't leave without paying my respects," Puss said. "He must be a very great ogre, to have a magnificent castle like this."

There was a discussion. Then the drawbridge came down. "Come in and pay your respects," the gatekeeper said.

Puss turned back to the van and winked. "Ogres aren't noted for their modesty or intelligence," he murmured. Then he faced that castle again. "May I bring my friend the Princess, who would like to pay her respects too?"

"Sure, he likes Princesses."

"And her bodyguard?"

"I guess so."

"And her naked servant man?"

"Sure, he likes naked people too. That's the way he eats them."

So Walter got out. He lifted Baal. Leon carried his rifle and pistol.

They entered the castle. Guards with crossbows peered down at them from upper crevices. "I think this is hostile territory," Leon muttered.

"Phreak is somewhere in back," Baal said. "But I can't be sure where."

They were conducted to the ogre, who turned out to be a big fat old man. "Oh, my, I'll bet you're the meanest creature in the territory," Puss said to him.

"I sure am, cat. Now, go down to the kitchen and jump in the pot; we'll stew you for dinner." The ogre's eyes swiveled to cover the others. "Dump the Princess naked in my bed and tie her down, sunny side up," he said to his henchmen. "Put iron collars on the men; we'll use them for toting stone blocks for a few days, until we need the meat."

"I see you're going to be unreasonable," Puss said. "We don't like that."

"Ho, ho, ho!" the ogre roared. "Who cares what you like, fatcat?"

Leon drew his pistol and shot the ogre through the head. The guards drew their weapons. Then Puss leaped up to stand on the body. "He's dead!" he cried. "The mean old fat ogre is dead! Your new master is the marquis of Carabas! While you are waiting for his arrival, treat the Princess and her men as honored guests. Got it?"

The guards hesitated. Then they decided that the story was being played out more or less according to formula. "Got it," the guard captain said.

"Is there a man in a space captain's suit here?" Baal inquired. "Who perhaps changed to a local uniform?" Then she glanced at her screen and jumped. "Oops—he's moving!"

They ran in the direction she indicated. "Thanks, Puss!" Walter called back.

"Anything for a Princess!" Puss replied. "Will she marry my master? I'm sure he'll like the look of her."

"Perhaps another day," Baal said.

Then, suddenly, they were through the boundary. They were in an elaborate pavilion with ornate rugs hanging on the walls. Across it was the fleeting figure of a castle guard.

"I might be able to get him with the rifle," Leon said.

"No. We need him alive," Walter said.

"I meant a bullet through the foot."

"Oh. Yes, if you can do that."

The figure vanished. "Too late," Leon said. "He's through to the next. This must be a narrow subset."

A bottle was sitting in an alcove. As they passed, smoke issued from it. It formed into a face. "Who trespasses in the land of the jinn?" it demanded.

"Just passing through," Walter said, and kept moving.

They crossed the boundary. Now they were on a rushing

freight train. They seemed to be on an empty boxcar. "That way," Baal said, pointing down its length.

But there was no way out at the other end. Where had Phreak gone?

"Maybe this isn't exactly what it seems," Leon said. He walked to the end and into the wall. He looked up. "Okay—there's handholds and a slide partition in the roof. He must've climbed through to the next car."

"How can a train rush through without stopping?" Walter asked. "It should run out of its subsection."

"No. The train *is* the set. Its motion is no more real than any of the rest of this."

Walter would have knocked in his own head if he'd had a hand free. Of course!

Baal sniffed. "Cabbage," she said. She was right; there was that odor here.

"Now I remember," Leon said as he slung his rifle across his shoulder and took hold of the built-in ladder. "One set's a freight train with mostly empty cars, but some have weird things in them, like dead bodies or giant spiders. The challenge is to get from one end of it to the other without freaking out. I heard the hardest one is the reptile car, because there may be a rattlesnake left in it. Course all you have to do is shoot it through the head or pin it down with a forked stick, but some folk—" He paused. "Hey—I heard somewhere that Phreak is crazy about rattlesnakes! One bit his dad, and he can't stand to be near 'em. So if that car's ahead of us, we can maybe catch him."

"That's right," Baal said faintly. "The game folk told me they think he's claustrophobic and afraid of snakes."

"He'll just step out into the next set," Walter said.

"Maybe not. This set includes the tracks and right-of-way. So he might just fall to his death. Maybe some places you can step across, like this car, and others you can't. These sets can be just as big as the game wants 'em, and there's no stepping out in the middle." He continued on up the ladder. He slid the panel aside and poked his head through. "Yep—we can cross here. I'll help you get the lady up."

Walter lifted Baal up, surprised by his strength though he knew it was merely an imperfect adjustment of the game figure. He hadn't loaded his figure with strength, but had it anyway.

Maybe strength was only relative to other game figures. Leon heaved her up through the hole with similar strength.

Walter followed. He emerged to the boxcar roof, and saw the scenery rushing by. The wind tore at his body. The landscape was of the kind that freight trains inhabited: ugly factory yards, slums, crisscrossing rails, and bridges over busy highways and polluted streams. No, he didn't want to jump off the side of this platform!

Leon jumped over the gap between cars and opened its aperture. "Farm equipment," he said, pointing to a label by the panel. Walter looked at the label by the panel they had just used, and saw that it said "Produce." That accounted for the cabbage smell.

Baal stirred. "Walter, I'm fading."

"Hang on!" he said desperately. But she did not respond. She was in insulin shock, and only some sugar for her real body, not her game body, could reverse it. She had endured as long as she could, and that was all anyone could do. She hadn't even complained. If diabetic shock brought out the underlying character traits, he liked hers.

But there would be some time—he didn't know how much—before she died. Walter intended to make the most of that time. "We have to nail that guy now," he said grimly.

"Take my pistol," Leon said, handing it over. "It only has two bullets left in it, because I ran into some trouble before we got together, but that should be enough. I'll check this car; he may still be in it."

"But then you'll be a target!"

"I'm expendable. If I get killed, I'll come back as soon as I can to help you again—maybe in the same body."

Walter nodded. It made sense for one who wasn't afraid to die. Silently he held out his hand, and Leon shook it.

Then Leon climbed down through the new aperture. There was the sound of a shot. Leon groaned and dropped.

Walter stepped across, set Baal down, and peered into the boxcar. Leon lay there, holding his stomach. Phreak had ambushed him.

Walter ran along the roof of the car until he reached the panel on the opposite end. The next link was a flatcar, loaded with wooden planks. He tried to block the panel closed, but there was no fastening. So he drew the pistol and fired the two bullets into it, at the edge. They dented it, making it impossible to slide open. Then he ran back to the other panel. Now he should have Phreak trapped inside.

But as he came to the panel and looked down, Leon stirred. "Watch!" he gasped. "Side door!"

Now Walter heard it moving. The boxcar's main doors were at the sides, for ready loading and unloading. Walter had assumed they couldn't be used while the train was in motion. But if there were handholds on the side of the car . . .

"How bad are you hit?" he called down.

"I'm done, but it'll take me an hour to die," Leon said. "I'll hang on. Go get him!"

But now Walter had no bullets left for the pistol, and if he descended to get the rifle from Leon he might lose Phreak. It was a time for desperate measures.

He picked the Princess up again. "Forgive me," he said to her unconscious form. Then he ran along the top of the car toward the flatcar beyond, carrying her.

By the time he reached the lumber car, Phreak had clambered onto it and gotten to the far end. He was about to climb up on the next boxcar, but paused.

Walter didn't hesitate. He ran to the end of his car and leaped to the top of the lumber, which was about four feet lower. His legs took the shock and held, as he had hoped they would. The game didn't take sufficient note of things like burdens; it figured that if a man could leap and land on his feet, he could do so with whatever he carried. In real life this would be hell on the legs. In fact in real life he couldn't use his legs at all, so the whole thing was glorious. He would love this game, if only he and Baal weren't locked into it.

Phreak turned back to face him, standing at the far end of the flatcar. He held a pistol. How many bullets did he have? It was impossible to be sure. But maybe it didn't matter.

"Stay back!" Phreak called, pointing the pistol. "I'll kill ya, and you know what that means!"

Walter moved forward, running as fast as he could with his burden. The gap between them closed. "Yes, it means that one of us is going to die here. It's you or me, you sorry creep. How's your nerve?" This was a bluff, because Phreak could readily kill him if he used his weapon sensibly. Walter was nervous, but he had to follow the best strategy he had. If he lost here, he lost everything, including the life of the woman he loved.

Phreak fired. The bullet missed; he hadn't taken time to aim properly. Walter kept coming. *How many bullets?*

Phreak fired again. This time the bullet hit Baal's body. That stopped it; Walter was untouched. But he felt her warm blood dripping on his bare legs. She was no empty game construct, or fantasy monster; when she was injured, she bled. If the insulin shock wasn't killing her, here in the game, the bullet wound was. But it was part of his desperate strategy. He kept moving; now he was almost upon the other man.

Phreak fired once more. Again the bullet struck the Princess. Then Walter heaved her forward. She plowed into Phreak, shoving him back so that he fell.

He fired a fourth time, into the air. "Get this thing off me!" he cried, trying to untangle himself from the body, which seemed almost to embrace him. "It's bleeding!"

Then Walter was there. He reached down and grabbed Phreak's hair. He drew the man's head up, then jerked it back against the lumber just hard enough to make his point: he could do as much damage as he chose. "Now you're mine," he said grimly. "Why didn't you flee into the next car? It might have saved your worthless freedom for a few more minutes."

"It's the reptile car!" Phreak said.

The reptile car. The one with the rattlesnake, possibly. And the kid was afraid of snakes. Walter had hoped they would encounter that one; in fact he had counted on it.

"Tell me the antivenin code," he said.

"Forget it, fughead! Whatcha going to do if I don't? Kill me? Like you killed your girlfriend?"

"No. I've changed my mind. I'm going to keep you alive."

" 'Cause you know I'll just get away if you kill me. Face it, cripple, you can't do nothing to me."

"I am going to use this lumber to make a box," Walter said evenly. "A small one, just big enough for you. Very tight, very dark, like a coffin down in a deep cold cave."

Phreak swallowed. "You can't do that! You don't have no hammer or nails!"

"I'll use the metal tape that's holding this load together; there's plenty of it. Never fear, it'll be a good solid box. Then do you know what I'm going to do?"

Phreak stared at him. There was now a tic in his left cheek. "Nothing, dork. Why don'tcha go kiss your dead girl?"

"She is only game-dead, thanks to you. Her body will recover in a few minutes, perhaps here, perhaps back at the castle in her home set. It doesn't matter. Her game body is nothing. What matters is that she will die in real life if I don't get her and myself out of the game in time to call in help for her. For that I need the code from you, and I need it now."

"Tough titty, jerk. I ain't going to let that code get out. They'll just use it to lock me out of the game forever."

"Then I am going to fetch that rattlesnake from the reptile car and put it in the box with you."

Phreak's bravado collapsed. He screamed.

"Unless, of course, you care to give me that code now," Walter said after a moment. "Then I'll merely leave you tied here, so you can't get away except by quitting the game when the code works. If it doesn't work, then I'll be stuck here too, and I'll fetch the snake. So you can try a fake code on me if you want, but I warn you, I'm apt to get nasty when I'm mad. Play it straight, and you may even get out of the game before they figure out where you're hiding in the real world and arrest you and lock you in some dank dark dungeon cell."

Phreak stared at him. Then he started speaking the code.

eighteen

WHEELS

Baal woke in the hospital. For a moment she was disoriented. She must have had another diabetic crisis. Or had she tried to kill herself? No, she had been in the Kilobyte game, with Walter, chasing after Phreak. She had tried to conserve her energy, to avoid going into insulin shock, but had finally faded out. The last thing she remembered was being on the top of a boxcar in a train rushing through the dirty belly of some anonymous city. That meant that Walter would not be able to use her to track Phreak.

So was this another game setting? If so, she had recovered a bit, and should go back to help him. Because just as long as there was any chance at all of getting that code—

She looked for her screen, but couldn't find it. That suggested reality. She relaxed.

She woke again as her mother entered the room. This couldn't be the game, because her mother wasn't in it! Which meant this really was real life, and she was out of the game. Which meant in turn that Walter had managed to get the code from Phreak, and had gotten Leon to take it out, and they had been able to quit. At last!

"Oh, Mother!" she exclaimed. "I'm so glad to see you!"

"Whatever happened?" her mother asked.

Baal was surprised. "Don't you know?"

"The police notified us that you had been taken to the hospital. I hurried right here. Your father is trying to untangle this other nonsense that came up."

"Other nonsense?"

"It seems that the bank thinks that we drew all our money out. Of course we didn't; I don't know how they came to that conclusion. It must be a computer mix-up."

"Oh. Well, I was playing the Killobyte game, and I got caught in it, and then I went into insulin shock, and I couldn't get any sugar because I couldn't get out. But if you weren't the one who found me—"

"Someone must have called."

Baal realized that Walter must have done it. "Mother, can you find out from the hospital who made that call? It's important to me."

"Why, certainly, dear. I would like to know myself." She got up and left the room.

Baal looked at the ceiling. Walter must have called the moment he got out of the game, and been persuasive enough to get an ambulance to her address. That could have saved her life. She would have to call him and thank him.

No time like the present! She dialed the number, giving her own number as the billing address—only to encounter an intercept. The billing number was not valid.

"What?" But the recording was adamant. She could not make a long-distance call. What a foul-up!

Baal hated to do it, but she was desperate to reach Walter. So she made a collect call to his number.

And it was intercepted: it was not a working number.

She stared at the phone. He wouldn't have given her a bad number! Indeed, the game proprietors had known it was valid. What had happened?

Her mother returned. "It was someone named Toland," she said. "Calling from across the country. I don't understand this at all."

"He's the one I met in the game," Baal said. "I just tried to call him. But a recording says his number is invalid—and so is ours. This is weird!"

"Something else came up," her mother said, troubled. "The hospital desk told me just now that our insurance isn't current, and that our credit is bad. They think their bill will not be covered."

Suddenly it connected. "Phreak!" Baal exclaimed.

"What?"

"He's a computer hacker, a really nasty teenager. He does things like getting into private systems and messing up folks' credit records. That's what's happening here! He must be furious about losing his virus code, and now he's getting back at me and Walter."

Her mother stared at her. "I really don't know what you're talking about, dear. Someone has a virus cold?"

"It's complicated to explain. But it accounts for everything. All our records are being messed up electronically. We have to notify the police." But it was obvious that her mother didn't understand. She predated the computer age.

Meanwhile what was happening to Walter? The same thing, probably; that was why she couldn't get through to him. But he didn't have a family; he was alone in his house. Suppose Phreak got his power cut off?

"Mother, I have to get out of this hospital," Baal said. "There's something I have to do."

"But dear, you have just had a bad episode. You must get your rest."

Baal realized that it would be pointless to argue with her mother. Or to try to explain to anyone. Who would understand just what one teenage hacker could do? That all this mischief was a lie? The average person had no idea of the intricacies of hacker crime. Baal herself had learned a lot about it only in the last few hours, the hard way.

So she made a show of relaxing. She knew that recovery from insulin shock could be quick and complete; she didn't need to stay in bed. But nobody's mother would ever believe that. "You're right, Mom. I'll get my rest. You had better go help Dad untangle that bank confusion."

But the moment her mother was gone, Baal swung into action. She disconnected the IV from her arm, got out of bed, and went to the closet. There was a hospital robe and some of the game wrappings; the medics must have been stripping them away from her body as they brought her to the hospital. Her purse was on the shelf. That was a blessing, because it contained her insulin kit and some candy as well as her money and identification. They must have seen it on the table beside her and brought it along so that she wouldn't be completely anonymous.

She donned the robe over her bra, panties, and nightshirt. She stepped into the hospital slippers and checked herself in the mirror. She adjusted her hair to cover part of her face, nerved herself for a special performance, and left the room. She acted just like a visitor, walking boldly down the hall, and no one challenged her. Attitude counted more than anything; if she had the bearing of a princess, others assumed that she was, or the equivalent. So she was making the same bluff she had tried unsuccessfully in Beirut, but with better success. Soon she was out of the hospital.

But now what? She had only a few dollars, and she couldn't go home for more, because her well-meaning folks would be appalled to find her out of the hospital. How was she going to get out of the city, let alone across the country, to rescue Walter? People in hospital robes were common in the hospital but nonexistent outside it; she would be a highly suspicious creature on the street. Walter had had the aplomb to go naked through several game sets, but she didn't want to try anything like that here.

Ah, Walter, Walter . . .

Then she thought of a possible way. It wasn't what she would have chosen, but she was a beggar now and couldn't be choosy. Maybe it would work, if she thought of herself as a really nervy and persuasive princess.

She went to a pay phone and used her small change to make a local call. She had to nerve herself anew and quell her rising pulse, hoping she didn't bungle this. This was definitely not her nature, but desperation and a certain giddiness left over from the virtual reality of the game lent her what would have to pass for courage.

She was in luck: she got Tyson Blunt, her former boyfriend. Who had gotten a car for his twentieth birthday, just about now. She started speaking the moment he answered: "Ty, this is Baal. Don't hang up on me. I need your help, a big favor."

"Baal, I wouldn't hang up on you!" he protested. "But you know I can't—you know it's over between us. I'm sorry."

"I know it, Ty, and I'm sorry too. I—I've found another man, and he's in terrible trouble, and I have to go to help him, but he's a long way away and I have no way to get there, unless—"

"You mean you want a ride?" The relief was manifest. "How far?"

"As far as Pennsylvania," she said. "Only not there."

"Where?"

"Georgia."

There was a pause. "You can't take a plane?"

"I don't think I can, Ty. It's complicated. I'm broke, for one thing. Well, I have three dollars and odd change. And people will be looking for me. I need wheels, and I need someone I can trust, and you're the only one."

"But your folks—"

"Will be the first ones to try to stop me. Because of—you know. But I have to get there in a hurry, and I don't want to hitchhike."

"Don't hitchhike!" he exclaimed, alarmed. "Look, Baal, this is awful sudden, and I don't know—where are you?"

She told him where she was. Then she hunkered down in the phone booth and waited.

In half an hour his car appeared. She exited the phone booth and went to meet it. "But what are you wearing?" he asked, surprised. "I thought you'd be ready to travel."

"I *am* ready to travel," she said. "Are you?"

"Well, I tossed some stuff in the car, told my roommate I had an emergency trip, and filled up my tank. But—"

She leaned over and kissed him on the cheek. "That's fine, Ty. Do you need help with a map?"

"No. There's five hundred miles before I have to worry about details. What I need is an explanation."

"You shall have it, with all the detail you want." Then, as he drove, she told him the story of Walter Toland, the Princess, and Phreak. He was first interested, then amazed, and then understanding.

Every time Baal saw a police car, she tightened up. Tyson finally noticed. "Nobody's after me," he said. "Nobody knows you're with me. But look—why don't we stop and you can call your folks? So they know not to worry."

Good idea! Then she reconsidered. "The number's been invalidated," she reminded him.

"Okay, I'll call my roommate and tell him to go by your house and tell your folks. It'll be a load off their minds, for sure."

"For sure," she agreed. He was a nice guy, helping her even

in this smaller way. She couldn't see that her prior judgment of him had been in error. She was on the rebound, from him, but if she had been right about Ty, chances were she was right about Walter too.

After several hours they stopped for gasoline, bathrooms, and spot supplies. Tyson made the call to his roommate. Baal went shopping at a corner grocery store, pretending that her hospital gown was the latest fashion, and no one seemed to notice. It was true: attitude spoke louder than appearance. She got a loaf of bread, margarine, cheese, jam, and a gallon jug of milk with his money. Then she made sandwiches for them as they continued.

As night approached, he began to look around. "What are you looking for?" she asked.

"Got to be a motel somewhere."

"What for?"

"What do you mean, what for! For the night, of course."

She put her hand on his arm. "Ty, understand me. A motel would be expensive and it would waste time. We need to keep driving through the night."

"But I'm going to get sleepy, and I don't want to risk—"

"I can drive, Ty. Let me take my turn."

"But—"

"It's true I'm diabetic. But I'm in control. All I need to do is check my blood sugar and take my shots, as I have been doing, and I'll be as reliable as you are."

"You took a shot? I never saw you!"

"Because you were watching the road. It's no big thing. I just bare my midriff and do it in a few seconds. I didn't bother you with it because I know you don't like to be reminded. Take my word: diabetes is not my problem on this trip. Time is."

He didn't respond. But he looked uncomfortable. So she tackled another aspect.

"Ty, you're doing me such a favor as I can never repay. If there is something you maybe want from me in a motel—"

"I didn't say that!"

"You can have it here in the car," she continued evenly. She had thought she could never act like this in real life, but having done it in the game, she knew the way. Desperation made of her a different, bolder, shameless person. "Just pull into a forest road, or behind an empty building, and I'll give it to you. Anything, anytime, any way, as often as you want. No strings attached; I'm not trying to win you back, I'm just trying to pay you. It's all I have to offer."

"Come on, Baal! I've already got a bad enough guilt trip for dumping you."

"Well, you didn't exactly dump me."

"I was going to marry you, and then I freaked out because of the needle. I feel like the world's worst heel. Don't make it worse."

"Then what do you want of me, Ty?"

"I want it to be all right between us. You happy. Me happy. No guilt. Real friends."

"You're driving me a thousand miles, at your expense, and asking nothing of me," she said. "That's about as good a definition of friendship as I can think of at the moment."

He brightened. "Yeah. Maybe so. But—"

"But what, Ty?"

"This Walter. He's on wheels, and not like mine. Paralyzed from the waist down, you said. So he can't—"

"In the game he can."

"Well, yeah. But life is not just in the game."

"And I think he can in life too, with the right woman. I mean to be the right woman. If he's not turned off by what I am."

"You said he's not like me. I mean, the needle doesn't bother him. I guess he's had plenty of needles himself, because of his accident."

"What I meant was that when he sees that I'm not any princess in real life, just a plain Jane. It may turn him off."

"Oh, Baal! You're a princess!"

"Hardly. You should know better than anyone."

"I do know, Baal! You attracted my attention because of Pennsylvania, but you held it because you're a great girl. You're beautiful."

Now she was the uncomfortable one. "Ty, you don't have to say this. I came to terms with myself long ago."

"You think beauty is just in movie stars? In the face and figure? I tried to tell you about that before. That's just a mask, a shell, and soon it falls away and the real person shows. Only a damn fool settles for nothing but that. I looked at you and I saw Pennsylvania, sure. That got my attention. Then I came to know you, and I saw character and beauty of spirit. That's when I came to love you. I still do love you. But this one thing—the needle—I know it's crazy, and I hate myself for being like this, but I just couldn't handle it. So I have to cut loose, and I know it's unfair to you, and I just want to make it right somehow if there's any way at all. And if this guy is the one you want, then I'm the first one to be happy for you. But you have to know that you don't have to settle for anyone you don't want. You've got too much going for you. Because you're a real person. The way you carried off that shopping in the store, so cool, I wanted to applaud. If only I didn't have this hang-up—" He shook his head. "Just take it from me, Baal. You're a princess. You really are. You've got this inferiority complex, and if you can just shake that—" He shook his head again. "I know you think I'm not making any sense. I mean, if I can't shake my hang-up, who am I to tell you to shake yours? But I'm telling you the truth. I've got nothing to gain by deceiving you. I wish I could make you believe."

Baal realized that he was serious. It was a revelation. She wanted to believe. But she knew better. "Thanks, Ty. But every man's different. Walter had an affair with a beautiful woman. He knows what's what."

"Then you're home free. I know that route, and I know what he's thinking now. I'll be best man at your wedding."

She laughed, but remained uncertain. She had seen enough of illusion in the game; she didn't need it in reality.

They drove through the night, stopping only for necessities. Baal took her turns driving, letting Tyson sleep. She didn't tell him that she had learned stick-shift only recently, in the game. She was thrilled to verify that now she could do it in life. It was tiring, but she kept close track of her blood and stayed in balance. They made good time in the wee hours when traffic was low.

Next day they kept moving, eating, and talking. "You know something, Baal?" he asked rhetorically. "You're good company! I'm enjoying being with you like this."

She realized with surprise that she felt the same. "I guess we did make a good match, when we matched," she said. "But I'm so grateful to you for doing this that I must be trying extra hard."

"I don't think so. It's just the way you are. Character."

She didn't argue. She just hoped she could get along with Walter as well, in real life.

Later, she realized that this was a lot like the game. She had a mission, and it was a real chore to complete, but it was exciting

too. Struggling against seemingly impossible odds, but making
steady progress, if only she didn't get killed on the way. There
were parallels between reality and the game that she was now
coming to appreciate. Life wasn't dull at all, even on a long dull
drive, when there was something important to be done and the
company was good.

At last, the afternoon of the second day, they pulled into Atlanta, Georgia. They found Walter's address.

The house was closed. The power was evidently off and the
mail seemed to have been stopped. Walter was gone.

Baal stared, trying to figure out what to do next. Her mind refused to function.

Tyson stepped into the breach. "Look, that Phreak kid's bugging him too, right? So his utilities and all have been cut off, and
he can't get it straight, so he had to go somewhere else until he
can get 'em turned on again. We just have to find out where he's
gone."

"Yes," Baal breathed, beginning to function again. "I'll ask
the neighbors."

She knocked at the door of the adjacent house. "I'm a friend
of Mr. Toland," she said brightly. "I came to see him, but he
seems to be out."

The woman was glad to fill her in. "He got arrested yesterday.
They say he held up a bank or something. That's ridiculous; he
was a policeman. But they took him away."

"Thank you," Baal said faintly. "I will check with the police."
So Phreak had struck that way too, trumping up an arrest warrant. How could the local police know it was false, if it came
over their own system? Phreak's vengeance was a frightening
thing.

But back in the car she had mixed thoughts. "I can't go to the
police. There's probably a warrant out for my arrest, or something."

"Don't be crazy!" Tyson said reassuringly. "You haven't done
anything. I should know."

"But Phreak could have trumped up a charge against me too.
This is like the game: anything can happen."

He nodded. "Maybe you're right. But Phreak doesn't know
anything about me, does he? Let me get cleaned up, and I'll go
inquire."

"Oh, would you?" She was grateful all over again. But she had to agree that he was a sight, with sweat-soaked clothing and two days' beard on his face.

They went to another gas station, where they filled the tank and did their separate chores in the rest rooms. Soon Tyson looked like a slightly rumpled college student again, and she looked like a woman in a bathrobe.

They located the jail complex. Baal waited anxiously while Tyson went in. In due course he emerged. "I have good news and bad news, and good news," he announced. "The good news is he's there and okay. The bad news is he's so tangled in paperwork they can't figure out, that he can't get out. They are suspicious that something's screwy, because they know him; he used to be one of them. But the orders on the wire don't give them any choice."

"You said there was more good news," Baal reminded him tightly.

"He's allowed visitors. I said I had a female friend who knows him, and they said it was okay."

Suddenly Baal felt weak. "Oh!" The prospect of actually physically meeting Walter frightened her.

"Come on, Princess," Tyson said. "I can't get off my guilt trip until you get together with him. Then maybe I can be jealous instead."

She let him guide her to the station and in. Then she was signing in, throwing caution to the winds, using her real name. Then she was being guided down the hall toward the cells. Tyson kept a hand on her elbow, steadying her.

Suddenly they were there, and there he was: a man in a wheelchair. She was surprised to find his face familiar: he looked like his character in the game! She realized that this was no coincidence, but still it set her back. Then they were in the cell with him. She was tongue-tied.

"Mr. Toland, this is Baal Curran," Tyson said. "Baal, this is Walter Toland."

They looked at each other, feeling mutually awkward.

The man spoke. "Needlepoint," he said.

Now she could speak. "Wheels."

He held up his hands. "This is all there is."

Suddenly she realized that Walter was as uncertain as she was. She was diabetic and plain; he was crippled. She threw what little remaining caution she had away. "I love you, Evil Sorcerer," she said, blurting out the truth.

"I love you, Princess," he responded seriously.

"Those were the words," Tyson said. "Chain's been cut. I'll just wait in the lobby." Then he was gone.

Baal walked to Walter. She took his hands in hers. She leaned down and kissed him. She had meant it to be a token, a trial effort, but it was much more than that. When it was done his hair was badly mussed, she was out of breath, and she was strewn across the armrests of his wheelchair with her robe in embarrassing disarray.

"I came to rescue you," she said. "I guess that was foolish."

"You are a beautiful angel of mercy."

She opened her mouth to make an automatic protest, but stifled it. She was tempted to believe. Walter had come to know her mind and history before he ever saw her body, and he had just seen more of that than was proper. It was possible. "The one who brought me—that's Tyson Blunt. My former—"

"He told me. He's a nice guy."

That seemed to cover that subject. "We've got to get you out of here."

A policeman came down the hall. "You're released on your own recognizance, Walter," he said.

Walter looked startled. "How did that happen? I thought you needed disinterested character witnesses."

The man rolled his eyes. "They're coming out of our ears! The phone's running off the hook, and now they're arriving in person."

"But how—?" Baal asked, getting to her feet.

"Your friend Blunt called the local gaming society. It turns out that they know all about you and Miss Curran. And about this character called Phreak. They're really filling us in on what happened. The proprietors of this game, what's it called, Kilogram, called too. It's enough for the judge. You're out, and I don't think you'll be back in."

"But it's only been a few minutes since we arrived," Baal said. "Not nearly enough time to—"

She broke off, because the man was grinning. Walter looked at his watch. "It's been an hour," he said, surprised. "It seemed like a minute to me too."

They followed him down the hall and out to the lobby. Tyson

was talking with three other men. One of them looked familiar, and she realized that she had seen his face somewhere in the game.

That man approached her while Walter was signing out and getting his things back. "Hi, Spy. I'm the Maronite officer you killed in Beirut."

Baal stared. "Oh! I'm sorry. I—"

"All part of the game. Next time we meet there, I'll klonk *you* with a crowbar! But it's truce in this setting. We have a gaming dance tonight. We'd like to have you and your friends join us, if you're not too tired."

Baal thought of all the problems they faced, getting Walter's house turned back on, getting credit restored, getting organized on every level. She wasn't ready to face any of them, and she was too wound up to rest. She suspected Walter felt the same. "We'd love to," she said. "But I have nothing to wear." She was speaking literally; she was still in the ragged and now somewhat grimy bathrobe.

"It's 'come as you are,'" he said. "We don't much care how you look in mundania."

They learned from the police that Phreak had been located, but had fled before being arrested. They hoped to catch him soon. Baal exchanged a glance with Walter: the police were probably being overly optimistic. She wasn't even sorry, really; Phreak was obnoxious, and had caused her and Walter endless trouble, but underneath he was a disturbed human being. Perhaps there was hope for him, in time. She couldn't hate him. After all, he had also caused her to get together with Walter, and that was going to change her life.

It seemed only a moment before they were at the dance. There was music, and food, and animated discussion of games and settings, some of which she recognized. The gamesfolk were evidently of every type, from board game fanatics to virtual reality addicts. Many were female, and the majority were young, right down to grade school. But some ranged right on up to retirement age. There was a certain common stamp on them; all were serious about gaming. They tended to address each other by their game identities, or the settings they preferred, and no one disparaged this. That generated an atmosphere she found she liked. She wanted to be part of this group in the future, or whatever fragment of it existed where she lived.

Then she realized with a shock that *this* might be where she
lived, after she married Walter. The physical location didn't matter very much, because they would be spending time together—
very special time—in virtual reality. Because they could do
things there with a flair that could not be managed in real life.
In fact there was a virtual reality setting phrased as a wedding.
She hoped to be the first woman married for real there, and all
the gamesfolk could attend.

She saw Tyson dancing with a pretty girl, and knew that this
two-day act of his had indeed freed him of the guilt he had suffered with respect to Baal herself. Now he was being introduced
to a realm that might change his life too. Sometimes good deeds
did have their rewards.

She turned to Walter. "Come on, Sorcerer! Let's dance."

He looked uncertain. So she took his hand and hauled him
gently onto the dance floor. Then she stepped and turned, and
tugged him so that he moved his wheelchair around in circles,
and it was working. When she whirled, her bathrobe flared out
like a skirt, showing her legs, but she didn't care. This was like
another game setting, and she felt free, here.

Two teenage males glanced her way. "The princess and the
frog," one said, laughing.

A half-familiar older man advanced toward the youths, causing them to retreat. "The princess, anyway," he said. Then he approached Walter. "May I cut in? I'm Leon, from Beirut. I just got
here."

"Good to meet you!" Walter said warmly, shaking his hand.

Leon turned to Baal, and they began to dance. Over his shoulder Baal saw a young woman approaching Walter, and in a moment the two were dancing as Walter and Baal had before.

"My daughter," Leon said, noting her glance. "She wanted to
meet the man who brought Phreak down, so I arranged it. Walter
is becoming halfway famous in our circle. But I wanted to meet
you too, in life. I'm glad I was able to help you get free of the
virus. You really are a princess, you know."

Baal was beginning to believe it.

Author's Note

Each novel is an adventure in itself, for the author as well as the reader, and this one was no exception. I had anticipated a death-at-every-turn wild adventure, but I found that I had some formidable thinking and research to do for it. I started by rereading a novel I remembered from the fifties as continuous adventure that wouldn't let go of the reader, so as to remind myself of the feel of it. This was *The Puppet Masters* by Robert Heinlein, which I bought in the restored edition as a matter of principle. Editors can be tyrants, and I'm not sure whether there is any writer who hasn't smarted under editorial arrogance. Those writers who develop sufficient reputations grow increasingly resistive to this, and also set about getting their earlier editions restored to their original states. Oh, yes, I've done it, and I continue to be militant about the matter. In fact, my text of *Killobyte* has several embedded STET messages for the copy editor, to prevent her from changing my usage to what she in her naivete thinks it should be. I've been a full-time novelist for twenty-five years, but copy editors who may have been born in the interim still tend to assume that I don't know what I'm doing. Heinlein, arguably the science fiction genre's greatest master, was squeezed through the same mill, and *The Puppet Masters* was one of the novels that suffered. So I'm not sure whether it was the fact that this time I read the restored edition, or that I was a generation older than before, that caused my impression of the novel to be revised. This time I discovered not a nearly-mindless continuous action piece, but a well-crafted adventure novel, with some intriguing implications. Had the editing reduced it from the latter state to the former? Or had my younger self simply not appreciated some of the nuances? It's hard to say. But the lesson I took from this was that I had better concentrate on the good novel values of characterization, concept, and consistency, rather than trying for continuous action. Thus right away my concept of the novel changed. The first chapter is closest to my original notion, but I felt that that was as far as that level of action should be taken. You readers will surely advise me if that decision was wrong. Twelve-year-old critics can be every bit as sure of themselves as copy editors, with similar justice.

I actually thought of this novel a decade ago, in 1981, but couldn't even interest my agent, let alone a publisher. Virtual reality wasn't known then. But my notions are for me like children; I don't forget them. When I reviewed my 1981 notes I discovered something I had forgotten: reference to an item on *20/20* TV, for 7-16-81: "Do Animals Have Rights?" which showed the appalling treatment of commercial animals. A piece titled "The Mallet" showed new-hatched chicks, one of which was black, running to join its yellow companions on a moving conveyer belt, but being swept aside by human hands. Evidently the demand was for yellow chicks. Each time the black one picked itself up and tried to get with the group, it was shoved away. Finally it fell off the end of the belt, where a huge mallet was methodically crushing the rejects. Ouch! Even ten years later, that's painful, as is the message, which I trust doesn't need clarification.

Meanwhile, in 1990, a reader had written to suggest that I have a diabetic character in a novel. Actually I did have one, a decade or two back, in *Rings of Ice,* but realized it was about time for another. For one thing, I am diabetic myself. But I must qualify this, because it may not be true. You see, I came down with a mysterious malady in 1962 whose main component was perpetual fatigue. The doctors found no cause for it, so concluded it was all in my mind. I was then excluded on an insurance policy for *all* mental diseases. I tried to tell them that this was a misdiagnosis, but the doctor replied "That's what they all say." So for a decade I was under the shadow of mental illness.

Then I saw another doctor, and was given a five-hour blood sugar test. It showed that I had a mild case of what is now called Type II diabetes: high blood sugar levels, but not nearly as serious as the deadly Type I shown in this novel. Most diabetics are Types II's, and as many as half of those may be undiagnosed, as had been the case with me. Indeed, some descriptions of mental disease read to me like diabetes. When a person can be labeled crazy because he suffers fatigue . . .

But even the mild Type II diabetes brings its problems. I don't mean physically; my prescription consists of avoiding too much sugar, staying lean, and regular exercise, which is a healthy program for anybody. I'm thinking of insurance, again. Another reader, George Cameron, M.D., told me that doctors with diabetes, as a group, live longer than other doctors. Since I am not sure whether other doctors would agree, it is mentioned only passingly in the novel. It is a point of interest to me, because I had trouble with underwriters for group insurance who made no distinction between Type I and Type II diabetes and barred me from coverage because of it, until I went over their heads and got a reversal. Then, having proved them wrong, I rejected the insurance because in the interim they had raised the rates by 50%. I once sold health insurance, and have little tolerance for ignorant or law-bending restrictions, and certain companies are so unscrupulous that they maintain lawyers to fight the lawsuits brought by policyholders when these companies renege on the payment of legitimate claims. It's cheaper to renege than to pay, you see, in the absence of punitive damages.

When I discussed diabetes with my consultant for this aspect of this novel, she advised me that the test I had taken is now considered suspect because it classifies some as diabetic who aren't. So it may be that after a decade of mental illness, and almost two more decades as a diabetic, I will move on to some other illness, such as Chronic Fatigue Syndrome, and will then find out what new inanities this brings out in my insurance. We'll see. Meanwhile, my sympathy is with those who have Type I; I stand as it were at the brink of the chasm, but they are inside it. Regardless, this is an example of how my novels affect my life.

My consultant was Christine Ternand, M.D., a pediatrician. I must say that the more I spoke with her, the more impressed I became. She seems like a fine person, with that type of caring for her patients that I wish every doctor had.

I also consulted with five Type I patients. Two of them were referred to me by Dr. Ternand, and three I found myself by keeping my eyes open. From them I made the composite case history of Baal Curran. No, not her affair with Tyson; her early illness and diagnosis, with its complications. The patients ranged, when contacted, from age twelve to full adult. Here they are, listed alphabetically by first name:

Ann Sorenson
Douglas Heuer
Jordan Crofton
Nadia Nicole Michael
Sean Kent McTavish

The game of Killobyte is invented, but the underlying concepts of computer gaming and virtual reality are not. I suspect we shall have games very like this in the next decade or so. I'm fascinated by games of all types, but I'm not a gamer, because I am a novelist: writing squeezes out everything else. So I sought the advice of gamers by setting up a program at a convention I attended, Dragon Con, in Atlanta, Georgia, the summer of 1991, while I was writing this novel. I described the general nature of the novel and asked for advice. There were some problems, not with the expertise of the gamers, but because the preceding program ran late, forcing mine to start late, but mine had to end on time. So it was squeezed. In addition, there were maybe two hundred gamers there, all of whom had input, and it was impossible to get it all in that situation. I called on as many as I could, but got only about one in ten. What a waste!

What to do? I asked those who could, to come in for another session later in the day. About twenty did, and we had a significant discussion and made many notes. But even here there was a problem: their suggestions were not simple matters of "Have a hero with red hair" but thoughtful dissections of motive and realism and computer feasibility. What made sense in what context? I enjoyed the discussion, because this is the way my mind works; I spend a lot of time on rationale. But such questions are not readily digested into spot notes. So the influence of the gamers has been felt in this novel, but in subtle rather than obvious ways. In some cases I could connect a specific notion with a given name, but I prefer not to do that, because the nonspecific notions may be as good. Sometimes I planned to use a notion, then the situation in the novel required a change, and I couldn't use it. It is evident that there are more good notions out there than I can compass. In fact, if I should ever do another novel of this type, I would review those notions and pick up on the ones I didn't use this time. This is intended as a singleton novel, but the future is as malleable as the computer game. So this section of the credits is somewhat inadequate.

But I thought of a special way to make it up to these folk: I put them in the novel proper. Oh, you won't see their actual names there, but they're all at that gamer's dance at the end, along with the few named characters from the novel, and if you were there you surely could recognize some of them. So here they are, again listed alphabetically by first name:

Adam Rixey	Gary Kim Hayes	Phil Rheinlander
Adam Szura	Gregory Callahan	Phyllis McKay
Alex Young	Jack Vanorsdale	Rembert N. Parker
Alicia Cooper	James Karwisch	Richard Morehouse
Angela Hoffman	John D. Ezell	Robert Lunsford
Anthony Francis	John E. Mailen	Roger Terrell
Bill Joynt	Josh Osborne	Ron Roberts
Bria Dunn	Kevin Rush	Sarina Mellette
Christina Evans	Laura Citzer	Shelia Sneed
Dan Davis	Lydia Murphy	Simon Astor
Dan Dietz	Marlon McAvoy	Steve Adelson
Dave Newton	Marshall Hitch	Tad Simmons
Dennis Caswell	Mike Osbahr	Wayne Osborne

A few stray credits: The rattlesnake religion was in effect suggested by Larry Miller, who sent a clipping about it. *The Baby Name Personality Survey* by Bruce Lansky and Barry Sinrod was sent by Lori Tomlinson in this period. So I started using it for characters, beginning with Lori, using the description in the book. However, what that character did with Walter has nothing to do with the real Lori, so don't get ideas. The character Phreak I adapted from descriptions in the book *Cyberpunk* by Katie Hafner and John Markoff. This gives case histories of three major hackers whose activities ranged from phone phreaking to computer viruses. Phreak is an approximate composite, just as Baal is for a diabetic. It is frightening what these hackers can do, and I think that those who are not concerned about them or computer viruses are foolish. "Safe Computing," as a parody on "Safe Sex," is no joke, and the parallel is real. Coincidentally, in this period we saw an ad in the newspaper: emergency sale of an 80486 computer system complete with printer and software for $3,000. Take my word, that's a good price for a state-of-the-art machine. So, having passed up the 386 system because the 286 does everything I need, I bought the 486, and may write my next novel on it. But I suspect the Killobyte game requires a 586 system, because full virtual reality takes hefty computing.

You may wonder why I got into Beirut. Well, I wanted a setting with real violence, and I thought it would be nice to use a real city instead of an invented one. What's the most violent city in the world? That may be it. But that meant a horrible hassle of research that would slow me down endlessly. I was already behind schedule. I had been on schedule for the prior novel, until my mother died; that interfered with my concentration, and I finished two weeks late. Thus I started this one late, and finished it two weeks late as well. There may be those who see my disciplined schedule and call me a writing machine, but the machinery is subject to emotional complications. My mother left a journal of her thoughts and memories, the last fourteen years of her life, and I read this at the rate of a few pages a day while writing this novel. It was fascinating to learn things I had never known about her, such as how she had taken "Firsts" in French and Spanish at Oxford University in England in 1931. But also depressing, not because I myself turned out to be a dunce at foreign languages, but because it reminds me that this brilliant woman who was my mother is gone from this world. It is a grief every person suffers in the normal course, the death of close family members, and I have heard from many of my readers whose lives are tragedies compared to mine. Yet it is not easy to focus on a novel at such a time. Thus, for the first time on an individual novel, I overran my deadline for delivery. Fortunately my publisher did not see fit to chop off my head.

So I handled Beirut the easy way: I had my research assistant Alan Riggs do it. He read the books and wrote summaries for me, and I drew on that digested material for my scenes. He went over it and called out errors. It still was not fast writing for me; it's easier to do straight fantasy. But in this manner I was able to have an authentic setting without destroying my writing schedule.

Thus there were three areas of research for this novel: diabetes, gaming, and Beirut. I learned things in all of them, and hope that those who know something about any of them will appreciate the work I did. I could have done the novel far more easily if I had left them out, but I feel richer for that effort. I hope you do too.

Meanwhile my life proceeded in its petty pace, not quite interacting with the novel. I had been asked to read a portion of Rupert Brooke's poem "The Soldier" at my mother's memorial service, and that poem about the thoughts of a person from England dying in a foreign land caught hold of my mind, and I finally memorized it so that I would always have it with me. "There's some corner of a foreign field that is forever England." My mother was English, and I was born in England. Perhaps it made it easier for me to orient on death, in this novel where death is a way of life. But there was also a minor positive discovery: I like to listen to music and songs, and the radio is always on while I work. Sometimes I hear a song and like it, but then can't find it again. In 1957 while I was away from my wife, in training in the U.S. Army, I heard two nice songs on popular radio. One was "Tammy" and the other was "Dark Moon." The first became famous and is still popular today, but the second sank out of sight. I seemed to be the only one who remembered it. I kept checking songs, and finally found it listed in a collection of almost two hundred in *The Best of Jukebox Rock*. I never liked rock music, and didn't listen to jukeboxes; fortunately the songs on the thirteen discs of this collection mostly aren't rock, they're conventional sweet melodies. Now I have only one song remaining to find: "The Girl in the Wood," which I heard only once, in 1956, on a Canadian station. That one influenced my first published novel, *Chthon*. So, trivial as it may seem, my heart was warmed; I had found a lost song. That may not compare to finding one's ideal life's companion, but even small satisfactions have their place.

May you also find your small satisfactions. Perhaps one of them will be the reading of this novel.

Piers Anthony,
SapTimber 1991

Later Note: My retest did render me non-diabetic, so I'm back to square one. And for a source of my books and newsletter, call 1-800 HI PIERS.

BOOK THREE OF THE MODE SERIES

CHAOS MODE

PIERS ANTHONY

Colene, the girl from Earth, Darius, the man from
another planet who won her love, and Seqiro, the
magnificent telepathic horse, reunite to face their
most dangerous adventures yet. They are joined by
an extremely unlikely companion: Burgess, a tentacled
creature from a distant universe. Together they travel
to a place called Earth, where Colene is offered a
chance to make peace with her parents.

Available in hardcover at bookstores everywhere.

G. P. Putnam's Sons
A member of The Putnam Berkley Group, Inc.